Chase stopped for a moment to admire what he was soon going to uncover. January's gaze was steady, her delicate skin already flushing, and, if he wasn't mistaken, she was already aroused. He slowly inhaled and smiled.

"What?"

There was a note of uncertainty in her voice that made him want to put his arms around her and hold her close forever.

"I'm just appreciating you."

"Then do it faster."

"Nope." He wrapped one hand around her neck and bent his head to brush his lips over hers. "I like to take my time over the important things in life—like spreadsheets, and profit projections, and making love."

She went to reply, and he angled his mouth over hers, pushing between her lips and claiming her with a long, thorough, well-thought-out kiss. But she wasn't a passive kind of woman, and he soon lost complete control as she enthusiastically kissed him back. Then he just hung on like a cowboy on a bronco, losing himself in her as he locked his mouth to hers and drew her hard against him . . .

Books by Kate Pearce

The House of Pleasure Series

SIMPLY SEXUAL

SIMPLY SINFUL

SIMPLY SHAMELESS

SIMPLY WICKED

SIMPLY INSATIABLE

SIMPLY FORBIDDEN

SIMPLY CARNAL

SIMPLY VORACIOUS

SIMPLY SCANDALOUS

SIMPLY PLEASURE (e-novella)

SIMPLY IRRESISTIBLE (e-novella)

The Sinners Club Series

THE SINNERS CLUB

TEMPTING A SINNER

MASTERING A SINNER

THE FIRST SINNERS (e-novella)

Single Titles

RAW DESIRE

THE RELUCTANT COWBOY

Anthologies

SOME LIKE IT ROUGH

LORDS OF PASSION

Published by Kensington Publishing Corporation

THE
RELUCTANT
COWBOY

KATE PEARCE

ZEBRA BOOKS
KENSINGTON PUBLISHING CORP.
http://www.kensingtonbooks.com

ZEBRA BOOKS are published by

Kensington Publishing Corp.
119 West 40th Street
New York, NY 10018

All Kensington titles, imprints and distributed lines are available at special quantity discounts for bulk purchases for sales promotion, premiums, fund-raising, educational or institutional use.

Special book excerpts or customized printings can also be created to fit specific needs. For details, write or phone the office of the Kensington Sales Manager. Attn.: Sales Department. Kensington Publishing Corp., 119 West 40th Street, New York, NY 10018. Phone: 1-800-221-2647.

Zebra and the Z logo Reg. U.S. Pat. & TM Off.

First Printing: December 2016
ISBN-13: 978-1-4201-4931-9
ISBN-10: 1-4201-4931-8

eISBN-13: 978-1-4201-4001-9
eISBN-10: 1-4201-4001-9

10 9 8 7 6 5 4 3 2

Printed in the United States of America

ACKNOWLEDGMENTS

Firstly, I'd like to thank Mike Mentink for answering my questions about police procedure back in the 1990s. I'd also like to thank Sidney Bristol for helping with all horse-related questions. Finally, I couldn't have done this without Kaily Hart and Zara Keane reading my first version and telling me that it was all going to be okay.

Chapter One

Northern California.

"You have arrived at your destination."

"I damn well have not," Chase Morgan muttered as he checked his GPS again and frowned as the narrow blue line he'd been following just blinked on a whole lot of nothing.

Pulling over onto the side of what barely passed as a road, he got out of his rental car and surveyed the landscape. Scorched golden hills, scurries of dust, the occasional thirst-defying plant, and beyond that the brooding black presence of the eastern side of the Sierra Nevada mountain range still topped with snow in March. It was a torturous, slow journey from the Bay Area and one that he chose not to make too often.

He cleaned his sunglasses on the hem of his white polo shirt and peered ahead. Had it always been this bleak? Somewhere around here was a gate that marked the driveway of Morgan Ranch. As a kid he'd known exactly where it was, so what had changed? Maybe he should've gotten a truck. The drive would've been easier and the vantage point higher.

There wasn't a lot else on the road, just the abandoned ghost town of Morgansville, which was on ranch property but still attracted those curious and stupid enough to try to get through the electric fence. Chase turned in a slow circle. He was so used to the noise of Silicon Valley that the silence hurt his head. Hearing his heart beating was downright unnerving. . . .

A turkey vulture flew overhead squawking a warning, and he instinctively ducked. He was such a city boy now. His younger self who'd practically grown up on the ranch would have been disgusted by his wussiness. He got back in the car, relishing the cold blast of the AC, and moved forward at a snail's pace.

There.

His faint smile faded. The overhead sign had fallen down, leaving just the gate, which appeared to have been propped open. Despite the relatively short distance from the Bay Area, he hadn't been to the ranch for a couple of years, preferring to meet his grandmother in the city. Reaching inside his pocket he extracted the handwritten letter he'd received two weeks ago. She hated talking on the phone.

Darling boy, your grandma Ruth needs you. Come at once.
P.S. No, I'm not dying, but come anyway.

Short and sweet, just like his grandma. Well, maybe *sweet* was stretching it a bit. For a little bitty woman she sure packed a punch. He remembered how she used to wade in and separate him and his three brothers when the fighting got out of hand. She said she'd gotten strong wrangling calves and that small boys were much easier to deal with.

His grandma was a pill. It had taken him the whole two weeks to get organized enough to leave work. He had a feeling her problems wouldn't go away, and a few days wouldn't make much difference. He pushed the gate open wide enough to let his car through and closed it behind him.

Was Ruth even running any cattle? Surely not, if she'd risked leaving the gate ajar. He winced as the rental car bounced over and dove straight into another huge pothole in the road. He should've gotten a four-wheel drive. Real men, real cowboys always drove trucks. And he should've been paying more attention to what was going on with his grandma.

He concentrated on weaving through the potholes until the drive widened out into a large circle. To his left was one of the old barns and to his right the ranch house with its wraparound porch and dainty Victorian railings. The roof was slate, imported at great cost after the original house with its shingles had gone up in flames.

Chase got out of the car and paused to stretch the kinks out of his tall frame. The door of the ranch house opened, and several dogs came out barking and yowling. He tensed as they all barreled toward him.

"Is that you, TC?" His grandma hollered over the barking dogs.

"Afternoon, Ruth." He grinned as she came toward him, smacking a few of the noisier dogs on the head as they crowded around her. "One grandson as ordered."

She reached up to cup his chin, her blue eyes in her wrinkled face as clear as the California sky. "Chase, darling. You look more and more like your daddy."

He grimaced. "Don't say that. He's a bad man."

"He certainly was a fool to throw away a fine family like this one." She patted Chase's cheek. "Come on in."

He followed her up the three steps to the porch, noticing that the house needed painting and that several of the planks on the deck were rotted right through. The screen door banged shut behind them as they entered the cool darkness of the kitchen. Inside, everything was fifty years out of date and as neat as a pin, which somehow gladdened Chase's heart. Ruth might be getting old, but she certainly wasn't losing her faculties.

Ruth took a glass pitcher out of the ancient green refrigerator, which gave a convulsive death shudder as she slammed the door shut.

"Iced tea?"

"That would be great." He was three-quarters of the way down the glass when the sugar rush hit him, and he practically tasted the fizz of enamel being stripped off his teeth. He put the glass back on the scrubbed pine table only for his grandma to instantly refill it.

She took the seat opposite and pushed a plate of cookies over to him. "Chocolate pecan. Your favorite."

He took one despite himself and raised an eyebrow. "You're scaring me now."

"By baking your favorite cookies?"

"You're trying to bribe me. It's how you used to get me to do my homework, remember?"

"You always did your homework. You were the responsible one. It was your rapscallion brothers who needed persuading."

He held her gaze and sighed. "I'm sorry I haven't been out here more often. I have a million excuses, but none of them are very good."

"It's okay. This place has bad memories for you all," Ruth said. "I had a letter forwarded from my bank a few weeks ago, and I couldn't make head nor tail of it. Do you think you could take a look at it for me?"

"Sure." Chase held out his hand, and she slapped it away.

"You don't have to do it right *now*. When did you get so impatient? Finish your cookie and your tea—unless you have to leave tonight?"

"No, I'm here for as long as you need me." He immediately qualified that. "Well, at least for a week or two."

He hadn't taken a proper vacation for almost two years. His two business partners had been making pointed comments about "burnout" and "exhaustion," and, sure, that was easy for them to say when he knew in his soul that if he wasn't there nothing got done the way he liked it. . . .

Control freak? *Him?*

And then there was all the other stuff—the stuff that was threatening to tear their friendship and their company apart.

"Good. I'm glad you can stay awhile." Ruth pushed the cookie plate right under his nose until all he could smell was chocolaty goodness. "Eat. You're too thin."

He snorted at that. "What's for dinner?"

"Pot roast made with Morgan Ranch beef."

Chase pushed the cookies away. "You *are* trying to bribe me. You know how much I love your cooking."

His grandmother's smile was smug. "I bet you don't get many home-cooked meals in San Francisco."

"I do okay." He thought about the stack of takeout menus beside his refrigerator and the fact that since Jane had left him most of the delivery guys greeted him by name.

"Hmmph."

The boards on the porch creaked a warning, and Ruth looked up as a clear voice called out.

"Mrs. Morgan? Ruth? Are you there?"

"Yes, dear, come on in."

The dogs headed out to investigate. Chase studied the

unknown woman at the kitchen door who seemed to bring the afternoon sun in with her. She wore jeans, a pink T-shirt, and sturdy brown boots. Her blond hair was tied back in a ponytail and topped with a San Francisco Giants cap that clashed with her top.

He instinctively rose to his feet as she came closer and looked down at her from his superior height. Her eyes were the dark gray of granite, and she wasn't wearing any makeup. She looked downright *wholesome*.

"January Mitchell, meet my oldest grandson, TC, or Chase as he prefers to be called these days."

The woman stuck out her hand, her warm expression immediately cooling. "It's nice to finally meet you. Ruth mentions you a lot."

"Good to meet you, too." Her handshake was firm. He glanced over at Ruth. "You didn't tell me you had visitors."

"January's not a visitor. She lives here."

Chase sat down and picked up his iced tea, his thumb rubbing away the gathering condensation on the side of the glass. "Seems an odd place to choose to live. The commute into any decent-sized town must be a killer."

"I don't commute."

He swung his gaze back to January, who had taken the seat next to Ruth and was already nibbling one of *his* cookies.

"You work as a ranch hand?"

She shrugged. "I can do that when necessary, but that's not my primary purpose here."

"Which would be what exactly?"

"I'm employed by the county to work with local landowners to preserve the history of the area." She sat forward, her eyes shining, her hands clasped together on the table. "This area is fascinating. There's the ghost town, the pioneer trail, the abandoned silver mine, and—"

"Which is all on privately owned land. *Morgan* land."

"Land that Mrs. Morgan has given me access to."

Chase raised an eyebrow and looked over at his grandmother. "Is that right?"

"Sure it is. I'm as interested in finding out about the history of this place as you are." Ruth turned to January. "When he was a kid there was nothing Chase liked more than to go out on the land and look for clues."

"That was a long time ago, Ruth. Now I'm more interested in making sure this ranch is a secure and safe place for you to live on."

"I'm not quite sure how my presence would lessen Ruth's security, Mr. Morgan."

There was a question in January's tone, which made Chase want to smile. "This is a cattle ranch. The last thing my grandma needs is herds of people wandering around admiring the historical sights. The cows don't like it."

"I'm not suggesting that should happen, and I'm hardly a herd," January said quietly. "My primary task is to make a record of these artifacts for the county and for posterity."

He leaned back in his chair until it creaked in protest and then stretched out his legs. "Does anyone care about what happened in the back of beyond a hundred years or so ago?"

"We should care." She held his gaze. "The speed at which California moves means it's easy to forget our past and destroy things we might later regret losing. It's my job to provide information about where these historical events happened so that later generations—those not so caught up in rushing into the next digital millennium—can rediscover and appreciate their past."

Chase wondered if Ruth had told January where he worked. He lived his life in a blur of intense decision making, working long hours that often stretched overnight and in an environment where his opinion might destroy a company or bring it unimaginable financial success.

"There's nothing wrong with making money and being ahead in technology."

"I didn't say there was." January fiddled with her ponytail. "My job is mainly funded by nonprofit organizations and charity foundations, and I'm grateful for that."

"I still don't see why—"

Ruth patted Chase's hand. "I've made up the bed in your old room. Why don't you take your bags upstairs and get comfortable while I visit with January?"

"You're trying to get rid of me already?" He smiled as he stood up, his gaze moving between the two women. He was glad his grandma had some company, but he wasn't sure what to make of her guest. Instinct and hard-won experience had taught him never to take anyone at face value, and Ms. January Mitchell seemed a little too good to be true.

"Get along with you." Ruth waved him on. "And change out of those clothes before you come and help me with the chores."

He paused and looked over his shoulder. "I'm back on the roster?"

She winked at him. "I never took you off. You owe me fifteen years of hard labor, darling, so you'd better get started."

January stared after Chase Morgan as he went outside to get his bags. When Ruth had said he worked in Silicon Valley, January had imagined a pale, skinny nerd, or a fast-talking snake charmer like her ex. Chase was neither of those things. For one, he was tall, broad, and, two, he had a lazy grace to him that made her think he had all the time in the world to . . .

"So what do you think?"

"Of your grandson?" January sipped at the glass of iced tea Ruth had put in front of her. "He seemed nice."

Ruth chuckled. "You don't sound very sure."

"He's not quite how I pictured him." The back door slammed, and she heard Chase whistling as he went up the stairs. "He's . . . tall."

"His daddy was a big man." Ruth sighed. "Not a good man like Chase is, though."

January took another cookie. "Are you okay with my staying here in the house while your grandson is visiting? I know he doesn't get out here much. I could move down to one of the bunkhouses and give you some privacy."

"Bed down with the ranch hands? I bet they'd love that, but I don't think you'd be having much fun with all that snoring, scratching, and farting. Stay here. I like the company."

"If you're sure."

January wasn't certain how she felt about sharing a house with a big man like Chase Morgan. She'd finally gotten used to having her own space again, and she had a sense he was going to be hard to ignore.

Eventually Ruth got up to check the pot roast cooking in the oven, and January went to change out of her good jeans into something suitable for doing the chores. Even if Chase was willing to help, there was still a lot to do. She'd thought her life in the city was busy until she'd moved to the California Gold Country. Here the work never seemed to stop year round. At least she fell into her bed exhausted every night and slept without dreaming.

Deep in thought she opened the bathroom door and was confronted by the sight of a large, half-naked man bending over the sink. She started to back up and tripped over the bath mat.

"Oh God, I'm sorry; I forgot . . ."

He turned to face her, the water dripping off his long eyelashes, and smiled. She couldn't help but notice the way water continued down his chest and over his nice tight abs.

"I guess I forgot to lock the door."

"There's no lock."

"That's right. Ruth disabled it after the twins flooded the bath twice in one week. I should have realized we were sharing when I had to fight my way through your underwear."

Her face heated as he gestured at her best bra-and-panties set, which was hanging over the shower rail.

"Pretty," he said approvingly.

She reached around his broad shoulder and grabbed the flimsy pink set. "They are handwash and air-dry, and—"

"Not a problem for me." He paused. "Unless I'd come in here at night and thought those dangling bits meant I was being attacked by a spider. I *hate* spiders."

She clutched her undies to her chest and stared up at him. "You . . . do?"

"Yeah. It's embarrassing. I'm hoping that, as we're sharing, you'll deal with all the spiders that get in here."

"And what will you do in return?"

He grabbed a towel and slowly mopped his face as he considered her. "Promise to put the seat down?"

She wanted to smile back at him, to respond to that lazy charm, but just managed to stop herself. "I'll consider it."

"I'll be finished in a minute."

"Okay." She backed away more carefully this time and only hit the door frame with her elbow on her way out. "Take your time."

She managed to find her way into the right bedroom and threw the undies onto her bed. God, she really did need to pee. If he were anything like her ex, he'd be in there for hours. There was another smaller bathroom beside the mudroom downstairs, so she might as well go and use that. Grabbing a towel from the back of a chair she went out into the hallway. Chase was still whistling and splashing around like some kind of chirpy bird, so she made her way down the stairs. The old pipes whined and groaned as the water flowed through them.

After peeing, she surveyed the small shower and realized she had no shampoo or shower gel. Stomping back up the stairs, she noticed the noises had ceased. On the landing, she found Chase, still without his shirt, at the bathroom door surveying her.

He gestured at her towel. "Most people take their clothes off when they shower and get wet."

"Ha, ha. I forgot my shampoo."

"Be my guest." He pushed the bathroom door open wide. "I'm all done."

"Thanks." She went to move past him, but he braced one hand on the door frame, cutting off her advance.

"I get the sense that you don't approve of me."

"Whyever would you think that?"

"Because you're trying really hard not to smile."

"Maybe you're just not as cute as you think you are."

"Possibly, but I think there's more to it than that."

She met his piercing blue gaze. One of her new vows was that she'd never let a man stop her from speaking the truth again.

"Why would I disapprove of a man whose grandmother adores him despite the fact that he can hardly be bothered to visit her?"

"Ouch." His smile disappeared. "That's a low blow."

"Someone has to look out for Ruth."

"And that has to be you because I'm falling down on the job?"

"Maybe."

"And why would you be willing to do that, Ms. Mitchell? What do you have to gain from hanging around with my grandma?"

"Not everyone is out to get something, *Mr.* Morgan. I like Ruth, and I do good work here."

He sighed. "Don't get her all invested in this place again, will you?"

"What do you mean?"

"She's pushing seventy-five; she can't keep the ranch running all by herself for much longer."

"You've decided that for her, have you?"

"She asked me to come and see her. I assume she needs my help to make some decisions." He hesitated. "Look, I know I'm a lousy grandson, and that I suck at visiting, but I want to do the right thing here."

"For her or for you? What's the plan? Maybe you could get her a nice condo in San Francisco where you could visit her more often."

He briefly closed his eyes. "As I said, this isn't your fight. Please don't get involved."

She gently moved him out of her way. "Too late. I already am."

Chapter Two

"You still look too fancy." Ruth's disapproving gaze ran over Chase's blue T-shirt and pressed khakis. She'd walked out with him to the barn. "Where are your jeans?"

"I didn't bring any. I don't wear them anymore." He raised an eyebrow. "Can we just get on with this? I'm dying for some pot roast."

Her expression softened as he'd hoped it would. "Sure, but don't blame me if you get covered in chicken shit."

"Oh God," he groaned. "You still have chickens? I *hate* the fuckers."

Ruth swatted his shirt. "Mind your language, young man. There are ladies present. God's name should never be taken in vain."

"I'll manage the chickens, if Chase takes care of the dogs and the horses in the barn."

He turned to see January approaching from the house. She wore a pair of jeans that were ripped to shreds, the same T-shirt, and her big brown boots, which was a wise move around horses and chicken shit. Her damp, blond hair was back in its ponytail, and she smelled of the flowery shower gel Chase had borrowed in the bathroom.

She sniffed as she approached and gave him a look. "Nice scent."

"Thanks, and right back at you. I love smelling like a bunch of flowers."

"Don't worry, you won't smell that way for long." She crossed over to stand by Ruth. "Why don't you go back inside and lay the table for dinner? We can handle this."

Ruth stared doubtfully at Chase and then at January. "Are you sure? Chase might not be strong enough to get everything done."

He grinned at her. "Thanks, darling. I'm not twelve anymore. I think I can handle it."

With a brisk nod, Ruth headed back into the house, leaving Chase with January. She turned and started toward the barn. He followed, admiring the determined way she moved and the glimpses of red panties the ripped fabric of her jeans revealed as she walked. Sure, he was on a dating hiatus, but he still had eyes, and that was one nice rounded piece of . . .

She stopped so suddenly he almost bumped into her.

"Look." She turned to face him, her gray eyes serious. "I don't want to fight with you. I just want Ruth to be happy."

"Then give me a chance to talk things through with her and see what she really wants before you assume the worst."

January took a deep breath. "Okay."

"Thank you." He wanted to tip his imaginary cowboy hat to her, but settled for shaking her hand. "I love Ruth very much, and I don't want to hurt her, but this place . . ." He turned a slow circle in the quietness of the twilight. "It sucks the life out of you."

"It's beautiful."

"You haven't been here very long, have you?"

"Almost six months." She looked up at him, her gaze clear. "It's a very special place, and I'm honored to be here."

"Living full-time on a ranch, making it profitable, keeping it together . . ." He found himself shaking his head. "These days it's almost impossible unless you diversify."

"Into what?"

"Oil?" He shrugged and started walking again, whistling to the dogs as he neared the barn. "That's the kind of money you need to keep this place going."

"I don't agree. If it were run differently, it could at least break even."

She marched alongside him until they reached the tack room and hip-checked him out of the way as she opened the door. Chase frowned as a noise in the background intensified into the recognizable shriek of hungry chickens.

"Are they still free-range?"

She was putting on a worn pair of gloves that looked far too big for her and started mixing feed into a big bucket. "The chickens? Kind of. We try to take them in at night to protect them from the coyotes. Why, are you scared of them as well?"

He grinned at her. "I'm not *scared* of spiders; I'm terrified of them. Chickens scare me—with their nasty little red eyes and sharp beaks. Ruth used to make me collect the eggs when I was a kid. I got pecked to death."

"I bet you didn't wear gloves."

"Of course not. That wouldn't have been manly."

She gave an inelegant snort and went to pick up the full bucket. He immediately did it for her, and she grabbed on to the handle as well.

"I've got this, thanks."

He tested the weight of the bucket and studied her slender form. "Are you sure?"

"Yes, Mr. Macho Muscles. Why don't you feed the dogs and start on the horses?"

She hoisted the bucket with two hands and managed to stagger out of the tack room and out of his sight. Chase located the dogs' bowls, rinsed them under the faucet, and divided up the dry kibble. There didn't seem to be any canned dog food on the shelves to mix in with it, so he put the bowls down outside and whistled.

Within seconds, a sea of waving tails surrounded him, not all of them belonging to dogs as the feral barnyard cats joined in the feeding frenzy. Making a path through the bodies involved some shoving until he reached the tack room again and took a walk down the cobbled central aisle of the barn. The structure looked in far better shape than the house, which was about normal for ranching folk.

There were four horses left in the twelve-stall barn, and he only recognized one of them. He stopped to pat his grandmother's old mare, Sugar Lump, on her graying nose and was rewarded with a gentle head-butt and a face full of slobber.

"Hey, Sugar," he whispered. "Long time no see. Do you remember me?"

She stamped her foot, the sound hollow on the concrete floor, and Chase got the message.

"Dinner's coming right up."

He walked back to the storage bins and checked the old blackboard that had always shown the feeding schedule. Behind him he heard the *clang* of an empty bucket, and January reappeared.

"You don't have to do any mucking out this evening. Just feed them."

"Good." He glanced down at his T-shirt, which was now stained with horse snot. "I've got to get myself some better clothes."

"And some decent boots."

"Is there still a general store in town?"

"Yes, and a lot of other new places, too. We even have a coffee shop." She started on the horses' feed, her movements assured and familiar, which made him feel almost unnecessary. "You can get all the basics there."

"Then I'll make sure to go after I've totally ruined everything I own mucking out stalls."

"That's the spirit."

They worked together to feed the horses, and Chase made sure all the animals had fresh water. Unused to the fresh air he was yawning by the time January collected the eggs and they turned back to the house.

"Are there other horses?" he asked as the sun sank rapidly behind the mountain range, leaving the valley bathed in a pinkish-grayish hue.

"Down by the bunkhouse. The ranch hands look after them."

"Thank God," Chase muttered. "Back in the old days, we had to help out with them all. How many hands are there left now?"

"I'm not sure. You'll have to ask Ruth."

He glanced down at her averted profile. "There's no need to poker up. I was just making conversation."

"I doubt you ever just do that."

"I love to chat."

"I'm sure you do, but I'm not going to give you information you can use against your grandmother."

"Wow, you're prickly." Chase stopped walking. "I thought we'd agreed to a truce?"

She turned to face him, and the shadows in her eyes matched the ghosts in the twilight. "The ranch is running well. Ruth is totally capable of managing it, so there really is nothing for you to worry about."

"Then why did she ask me to come and see her?"

"Because she misses you?"

"I think it was more than that. She said something about the bank."

January frowned. "What about it?"

Chase started walking again. "God, I can smell that pot roast from here. Ruth cooks like an angel."

She caught up to him, her expression worried. "What's wrong?"

"If she hasn't told you, I'm sorry I said anything. Let's go wash up and eat, shall we?"

The pot roast was sublime, and Chase ate four cookies for dessert before settling in with a mug of strong, black coffee in Ruth's best parlor. He and January had washed and dried the dishes together while Ruth explained yet again why she didn't trust the dishwasher he'd had installed for her. He and January had even shared a wry smile or two before she'd excused herself and gone to bed.

He *liked* her.

She radiated a quiet sense of competency that appealed to him at some very basic level. He'd been spinning around like an out-of-control tornado for years now. He had a strange sense that if he reached out a hand to her she might have the ability to steady his world. . . .

Snorting at his own crazy-ass thoughts, he turned his attention to the excellent coffee. The *tick* of the grandfather clock in the corner of the room hadn't changed since he was a kid. He remembered the night his life had turned upside down—the sound of the clock and the absence of his parents that grew longer and longer . . .

"More coffee?"

He jumped as Ruth came up behind him, the tin coffeepot that usually lived on the stove in her hand.

"I'm good." He patted the flowery cushion beside him. "Come and sit here and tell me what's up."

She put the pot down and reached into the pocket of her apron. "As I said, I got a letter from the bank."

This time he took it from her and started to read. When he'd finished he looked up. "This sounds like a pile of crock. What late payments?"

"That's just what I said." She sat beside him. "There's always been a small mortgage on this place for tax reasons, but I don't remember taking out any loans against the ranch."

"At that rate of interest? I should hope not." Chase frowned. "This isn't your usual bank, is it?"

"That's right. The original mortgage was with Morgan County Bank, which got taken over by one of the bigger ones in the eighties. I've never heard of this Kingsmith Financial Group. Have you?"

"Nope, but I'll find out everything I can." He hesitated. "If it makes things easier for you, I could pay them off, and—"

Ruth held up her hand. "No. I won't allow you to do that."

"But—"

"Chase, no." She glared at him. "I'm not using your money to pay off a company that says I owe money when I don't. It's just not right."

"Is it possible that someone else did this?"

"Like who?"

He shrugged. "Other family members?"

"Like your brothers?" She frowned. "Why would any of them do that and not tell me about it?"

Knowing his family, there were many answers he could give her, but he doubted she'd like any of them. Part of him wanted to ask her a million other questions, demand answers, and get everything sorted out as soon as possible. But that wasn't the best way to deal with Ruth. She'd just get more stubborn if he pushed her. He tried to be tactful.

"I wish you hadn't waited so long to tell me about this. How about I find out as much as I can about this company and we take it from there?"

She reached forward and clasped his hand. "Thank you, darling. I was getting worried. I don't want to lose this place."

He kept hold of her work-roughened fingers. "Are you sure about that? Maybe this is a sign that it's time to move on. It's a big place for one woman to run all by herself."

"I don't run it alone. I have Roy, the ranch hands, January, and other folk who are interested in preserving this place." She squeezed Chase's fingers. "I can't imagine not living here."

"I could get you a smaller spread somewhere closer to me."

"But it wouldn't be Morgan land." Her blue gaze was intent. "This place has been owned and managed by your family since the 1850s. That's a whole lot of history right there."

"Sometimes it's better to leave the past where it belongs, Ruth," Chase said. "There are too many ghosts here."

"But they are *family* ghosts. Doesn't that make it better?"

He had to smile. "I love the way you try to put a positive spin on everything."

"And I love this place. I want you boys to appreciate it and take it over when I'm gone."

"I don't think I'll ever want to do that, Ruth." Chase spoke as gently as he could. "My life and my work are on the other side of the valley."

If he didn't have a heart attack from stress and keel over at thirty-five.

"I understand that, but what about your brothers? Don't you think they should be part of this decision as well?"

Chase groaned. "We'd have to track them down and hog-tie them to get them here first."

Ruth raised her chin. "Then that's what we'll do. As it stands, I'm leaving the ranch equally to you all. That means all *four* of you will have to sit down together in person and agree to sell before I'll change a single thing in my will."

"Not another new will. How many is that now?" Chase complained. "And how the hell am I supposed to find the guys and get them here in two weeks?"

"Haven't you ever heard of Facebook?" She patted his hand in a pitying kind of way. "You are going to take two weeks to enjoy the ranch and help January with a couple of tasks."

"Like what exactly?" Chase asked cautiously.

Ruth widened her blue gaze. "You know, take her riding, show her the special places on the ranch and the secrets only members of the family know about."

"Why would I want to do that?"

She punched his arm. "Because I'm asking you to, and somewhere deep inside you I raised a gentleman who would be glad to help a lady."

"A gentleman," Chase muttered. "I don't think so. Can January ride?"

"Sure she can, but she told me she has a terrible sense of direction and is worried about getting lost on the ranch."

Chase snorted. "As soon as the sun sets, any Morgan Ranch horse worth its salt would find its own way back to the barn to be fed, and you know it. She'd be fine." He checked Ruth's expression and had to smile. "Okay, I'll take her out. I'll even promise to bring her back."

"Thank you." Ruth kissed his cheek. "You are a good boy."

"I'm thirty-two."

"And you haven't changed a bit since I first saw you being born."

Chase knew that wasn't true. His mother's desertion had changed him in more ways than he could even begin to count.

"So how did January end up here?"

"She works for the local county historical trust and is completing her thesis on disappearing California mining towns, or something like that. When she visited our ranch, she realized we had it all, and asked me if she could base her work on our land."

"And you said yes." Chase studied his grandmother carefully. "You've never let anyone do that before, and you've had dozens of requests."

"I'm getting old, and things are disappearing back into the dust. I wanted someone to see them and appreciate them before they were gone completely. January understands that. I liked her right off."

January's enthusiasm for the ranch had certainly felt genuine to Chase, although her suspicions about what *he* wanted had been sharper than he'd anticipated.

"Where did she come from?"

"Somewhere in Southern California."

She definitely had the tanned, long-legged look of a Californian girl, but not the slow-drawling accent.

"How long is she going to be here?"

Ruth gave him an exasperated look. "For as long as she wants."

"Does she pay rent?"

"No, she helps me out instead. Why all the questions? I don't think she's going to run off with the family fortune."

Ruth chuckled. "Not that we have one. She'd be better off running away with you."

Chase covered his mouth as another yawn shook through him. "I'd better go to bed. What time do you want me up in the morning?"

"Six sharp. Same as usual."

He leaned over and kissed her cheek. "I'll be there. And think about what I've said, won't you?"

"About selling the ranch?" She shook her head. "I'm not doing that, Chase. If you want to sell it after I'm gone, you'll have to discuss it with your brothers before I die."

"Or maybe this bank will decide to foreclose on your property for the outstanding loans." He walked over to the doorway, stopping to study her upright figure in the warm yellow pool of lamplight.

She had the nerve to flutter her eyelashes at him. "You won't let that happen to your dear old grandma, will you?"

He sighed. "You know I won't, just—think about what *you* want, okay? And I promise I'll think about getting in touch with my brothers."

She blew him a kiss, and he made his way up the stairs. There was no light under January's door, and the bathroom was empty except for the faint smell of mint. Outside the moon was turning everything silver in its path and was almost bright enough for him not to need to put a light on.

Chase heaved another sigh and studied his reflection in the mirror. How in the hell was he going to find his brothers? They'd ganged up on him and blamed him for their father's problems. They'd just stopped talking to him and, as Chase became more and more immersed in his work, he'd told himself he'd forgotten them as well.

Not that it was true. Damn, he'd practically brought them up after their mother's disappearance. Perhaps Ruth was right, and it was past time to sit down with his siblings and clear the air.

As if they'd ever give him the chance . . .

They hadn't forgiven him. Hadn't wanted to hear a word he'd tried to say in his defense.

But if it meant Ruth got what she wanted, trying to find them was a risk he was more than willing to take. He had two weeks to find out exactly what was going on at the ranch and how it stood financially. Taking a business apart and deciding whether it could be financially viable was his day job. Treating the ranch as just another project might help him to deal with the emotional crap the place always stirred up in him.

Sitting down with his brothers with that knowledge would strengthen his hand and prepare them all for the day when Morgan Ranch was no more. One thing he was fairly certain of was that none of his brothers would be eager to take on the ranch either. He wasn't the only one who avoided the place.

He straightened up and turned on the faucet.

And, as far as he was concerned, the day Morgan Ranch ceased to exist couldn't come soon enough.

Chapter Three

Chase padded down the stairs in his socks to the kitchen and stopped short when he saw January sitting at the kitchen table. She was surrounded by a pile of books and bits of paper and was tapping away on an old laptop.

"Sorry, I didn't mean to disturb you." He indicated the microwave. "I was going to heat up my coffee."

"Yuck." She wrinkled her nose. "I just made a fresh pot. Help yourself."

"Thanks." He moved past her and grabbed a clean mug. "Where's Ruth?"

"In town with Roy doing some shopping. She'll be back soon." January started packing up her stuff. "Sorry about the mess. I took over the table because for some reason the Wi-Fi's better down here than in my room."

Chase tipped his cold coffee down the sink and hesitated. Seeing as she'd made the coffee, he should make an effort to be sociable. "What are you working on?"

She sighed and pushed her blond hair away from her face. "I'm writing my thesis. My advisor doesn't like what I've done so far, so I'm trying to come up with a better angle."

Despite himself he took a seat at the table. He'd been

working in his room for about three days straight and had hardly spoken a word to anyone. "I left college before it got too complicated, so I doubt I can help you much."

"And I doubt you were a history major, either."

"Nope, computer science."

"You founded your company right out of college?"

"Actually, while we were at Stanford, my two friends and I wrote a piece of software that a phone company wanted really badly, so they paid us a crazy sum of money for the IP."

"What's an IP?"

"Intellectual Property. It's kind of like a patent." He shrugged. "We had to stay on retainer with them for a couple of years to make sure it worked, and to help with upgrades. After that we got paid the remainder of our money, and we were free to go."

She shook her head. "That's pretty amazing."

"We were just lucky. None of us wanted to stay in the corporate world, so we decided to use our money and tech skills for good."

"Like nerd superheroes?"

He had to smile at that. "Yeah, I suppose we were." He tried to remember the feeling of being so young and idealistic and failed miserably.

"And I'm twenty-six and still struggling to get an education." She chuckled. "I did everything the wrong way round."

"Sometimes I wish I'd stayed at college."

She held his gaze, her expression interested. "Really?"

"Yeah, academia is so much more straightforward than the real world . . . so much purer."

"Black-and-white?" She snorted. "I tell you, the drama and backstabbing and sex that goes on at those places of supposed higher learning? Amazing . . . When I get this thesis out of the way, I'm going to take a postgrad teaching course so that I can at least teach at local colleges and supplement my income."

"That's admirable."

"I wanted to do a PhD, but I can't afford it. The problem now is that with the lousy job market all the unemployed PhDs are taking all the basic academic teaching posts. That's why I ventured out of academia and into the real paying-job world."

"Good for you. No point adding more debt." Chase's stomach grumbled, and he put his hand over it. "What time is it? Hell, what day is it?"

"From the sound of your stomach, it's time to eat." She rose to her feet and stretched her arms over her head. The hem of her blue T-shirt lifted just enough to give Chase a nice view of her tanned stomach and pierced belly button. "I can make us grilled cheese."

"You don't have to feed me."

"It's only grilled cheese. I can make two as easily as one."

He stood as well. "Then let me help you."

He grated some cheese at her direction while she buttered bread and heated up the old cast-iron pan that usually hung over the stove.

"Ruth was worried that you'd died up there." She placed two pieces of bread facedown in the pan, and he inhaled the intoxicating crispy scent of frying bread. Like Ruth, January had the ability to make him feel right at home. "Are you still having to work?"

"No, I've been gathering data about the ranch and putting it into some kind of order on a spreadsheet."

"Oh." She took the cheese and sprinkled it on the bread before slapping a second slice on top of each. "How's it looking?"

"Too early to tell." That wasn't true, but he wasn't going

to share his dire predictions with January before he had it out with Ruth.

"I have some information on my laptop you might need as well." She expertly flipped the grilled cheese to reveal the browned bread and pressed down. His mouth watered. "I don't have a printer, but I can shoot you the files."

"Sure." He found two of Ruth's flowery plates and placed them next to the stove and then took the ketchup out of the refrigerator.

"Is there mustard in there?"

He got that out as well and took it over to the table where January had set the plates. She poured him a glass of iced tea, and they ate in companionable silence while the kitchen clock ticked behind them.

"This reminds me of coming home from school," Chase said and then wondered why he felt the urge to chat about the past with a woman he barely knew. Normally he kept his thoughts to himself—especially those about his child-hood. There was something about the peace of Ruth's kitchen and January that was making him relax.

That wasn't good. He needed to be at the top of his game to manage Ruth and the demise of the ranch. Reaching across the table he grabbed a pen and scrawled his e-mail address on a spare scrap of paper. He had no time to chat.

"Thanks for lunch. If you could send me those files, I'd be grateful." He stood, one-half of his sandwich still in his hand, and nodded to his companion, who was staring up at him in some astonishment.

"You're *going*?"

"I want to get that spreadsheet finished as soon as pos-sible."

"Was it something I said?"

He found his most charming smile. "Not at all. You were great company."

"Then why are you running away?" She pointed at his hand. "And FYI, there's ketchup running down your arm."

"Thanks for letting me know, and thanks for lunch."

He headed for the stairs as though the ketchup was all part of his master plan and went upstairs and into the bathroom, stuffing the rest of the grilled cheese in his mouth as he washed his hands. Wow, he was so smooth. . . .

January heard the bathroom door slam and shook her head. Why had he retreated so suddenly? She tried to recall the things they'd discussed and couldn't think of anything that stuck out. In fact, they'd been getting on really well.

She clicked on her laptop. Maybe that was it. He didn't want to get along with her because he still thought she would cause problems for him with Ruth. The fact that he was probably right didn't make his behavior any less annoying. She'd just started to like him. . . .

He was an enigma. His external charm and good looks cloaked a man who when relaxed spoke a different language that was far more "nerdish." She suspected that behind the smile lay a far harder man—to succeed in Silicon Valley you had to be tough—but that he wasn't deceitful like Kevin, her ex. Chase just liked things to be black-and-white and orderly.

January sighed as her ancient laptop finally stopped grumbling and showed her home page. She picked up Chase's note and opened up her e-mail to add his details. It took only a few moments to compile her files on the ranch and send them off to him.

If Chase *was* a black-and-white thinker, how did he intend to deal with Ruth's love of the ranch and the family history attached to it? Those things didn't show up on any spreadsheet in the world. Just for a moment, when she'd seen his more approachable side, she'd gotten hopeful, but his abrupt retreat made her worry again. She stared at her e-mail account. She needed to get Chase out of his room and onto the ranch. Only there would he, she hoped, start to remember why it was important to save his heritage.

"Thanks for giving me a ride into town," Chase said as he gripped the side of his seat while the old truck wallowed through the bottom of an almost-dry pebbled creek.

He'd been at the ranch for almost a week now and had spent the majority of his time holed up in his room compiling all the information Ruth had about the current state of the ranch into an understandable spreadsheet. He hadn't seen much of January, but, when their paths had crossed, she'd been easy company. He still couldn't work out her angle. She appeared to be as genuinely nice as Ruth had claimed.

When Ruth had finally lost patience and ordered him to leave his room, he'd taken up January's offer to go into Morgantown.

"No problem. I was going there anyway, and I don't think your rental would've managed this road," January said as she competently approached the next set of obstacles on the back road through the ranch to the small town. "It's pension day."

"Wow, you look good for your age."

She gave him a look. "Thanks, but I'll be picking up Ruth's."

"That means the whole town will be there," he said gloomily. "At least all the old folk who remember me when I was a kid."

She glanced at him briefly again before turning her attention back to the barely identifiable track. "Yup, not a lot has changed since you lived here."

"I suppose you think that's a good thing."

"In some ways." She slowed down as they approached the brow of the hill. "It's nice to see communities where everyone still knows one another."

"And sticks their noses in everyone else's business," he finished for her.

She grinned. "Better that than to die alone in your Silicon Valley apartment and have no one notice until you start to smell or you've been eaten by your dog."

"I don't own a dog."

"I wasn't talking about you specifically."

"I have a cat." Chase pondered that as they bounced down toward the small main street of the town. "Dammit. He'd definitely eat me." He sighed as they slowed down outside the general store. "Maybe I should send him a postcard. I bet he's not even missing me."

"Who's looking after him?"

"My friend Jake. He loves Jobs to bits."

January got out of the truck and waited for Chase to come around and join her. She squinted at him in the bright sunlight. "Your cat's named after Steve Jobs?"

"Naturally. He's always dressed head to toe in black, and he's definitely a vegan."

She fought a smile. "That's ridiculous."

"I know, but what can you do? I can't turn him into a killer." Chase walked up the two steps to the raised sidewalk, which had always reminded him of the sets of his favorite TV western shows. The door to the shop swung inward, and he braced himself as a woman shrieked.

"Good Lord! Is that you, TC?"

"Hey, Maureen. How have you been?" He leaned down to kiss her brown cheek. She was about his mother's age and had lived in Morgantown her whole life. She still wore her long hair parted in the middle, only the color had changed from blond to almost white. "How's the family?"

She started chatting, and, after an apologetic glance in

January's direction, he followed Maureen into the store. She kept talking, and he realized he only recognized about one in five of the names she was spouting. All he had to do was nod and agree and eventually she'd stop, and he'd face a barrage of questions. He wasn't eager to talk about himself, so he was in no hurry.

The general store hadn't changed much in twenty-five years. The lighting was better, and there was decent air-conditioning. One wall was now lined with big industrial-sized freezers and refrigerators filled with every convenience food and beverage a tourist could desire. The shelves were also well stocked with a variety of foods that had never been around or been affordable when he was a kid.

Through an archway on the left was the clothing end of the empire and beyond that every piece of equipment any rancher or rider could ever want. Some of it had sat on the same shelves since he was a boy. Maureen and her husband Stu refused to throw anything away just in case someone might need it.

"So how long are you staying with Ruth, TC?"

Maureen had finally paused for breath. "About two weeks, I think."

"That's nice. She misses you boys being around."

"I've missed her, too."

"How's that wife of yours?"

Chase smiled. "You must have me mixed up with one of my brothers. I've never been married."

"Are you sure?"

Behind him he heard January stifle a laugh.

"I came close, but the lady changed her mind two weeks before the wedding."

Maureen tutted and shook her head. "That's right. That must have been awful for you."

"Better to find out there's a problem before the marriage

rather than after," Chase said. "Now, can you show me where the jeans are? I need a couple of new pairs."

"Same place they've always been."

She walked through the archway and pointed out a wall of denim topped with faded posters of various old rodeo champions wearing any brand of jeans as long as it was a pair of Wranglers.

"Knock yourself out, dear. Holler if you need any help, and I'll get the tape measure." She gave his butt an appreciative swat as she went past him and disappeared into the main store.

"I'm sure January can help me out," Chase said, aware that she'd followed him through into the darker, hopefully quieter part of the shop.

"Hey, I'm not measuring anything."

He smiled at her. "Damn."

"In fact, I'm going to get the mail. I'll be back in a minute." Her ponytail flipped him off as she spun on her heel and disappeared.

With a sigh, he approached the almighty mother lode of denim and started looking at the labels. There didn't seem to be any system to the piles. After a while he decided to create one and started pulling stuff off the shelves and rearranging it by brand, style, and size.

He was so engrossed in his task that he didn't realize that he had an audience. It was amazing how heavy denim was to move around, but he'd started the job, and he wasn't going to stop until it was done.

"Now I can tell that you come from the valley of the nerd." He turned to see January sitting on one of the benches near the cowboy boots observing him. "ADD or OCD?"

"I just like things to be in the correct order." He wiped his hand over his brow, aware that he was sweating slightly.

"This makes much more sense. Smaller sizes at the top, bigger ones as you progress downward."

"Won't Maureen be pissed with you for doing this?" she asked.

He shrugged as he crouched down near one of the bottom cubbies and extracted a couple of pairs of jeans. "I've always done it. She used to pay me when I was a kid."

He stood and walked toward the fitting rooms, the entries to which were fashioned to look like swinging saloon doors and were fairly useless at concealing anything while you changed.

"I'm going to try these on. Can you find me a shirt? Large or around forty-two in the chest."

That should keep her looking in the other direction as he struggled into the new jeans while attempting not to fall naked-ass backward onto the floor. He stepped out of his chinos and into the first pair and immediately realized he had a problem. With a sigh, he took them off and hung them over the door.

"January?"

"Yes?"

She'd moved down the store into the racks of shirts and had her back to him.

"Stay right there, okay?"

"Why?"

He made a dash for the jeans and kneeled down to check out the sizes again. He'd put on some weight since he'd last owned a pair, and he'd need to go up a size. Thank God, he'd sorted them out beforehand.

"Where are your pants?"

She spoke from right behind him, and he jumped and clutched the jeans to his chest like an outraged spinster.

"I told you to stay there." Still holding the jeans in front of him like a protective shield, he backed up toward the fitting room. "My original pick was too small."

She grinned at him. "You did say *pick*? Because otherwise the rest of that sentence might have confused me, seeing as you grabbed a bigger size. Next time just ask me to hand you a new pair." She sauntered over and hooked two hangers containing two of the most god-awful shirts he'd ever had the misfortune to see on the door. "No one wants to see your underwear."

"You'd be surprised." He winked at her. "I fetched two thousand bucks in a bachelor auction last year."

January snorted. "You had to pay someone that much to take you on?"

She sauntered away from him again. In fact, he'd looked pretty good hunkered down in front of the jeans in his tight black boxers, his thighs strongly muscled and his ass . . .

"Aren't you going to stay and tell me how I look?"

This time she did turn around. "Seriously?"

"I'd appreciate the help."

"No one apart from me, Ruth, and the horses is going to see you in these jeans. Why do you care whether they fit or not?"

"I suppose you're right. Maybe you could check out the hats for me while you're waiting. I'll need something in this heat."

She obligingly went to look at the fine array of cowboy hats that hung over the boxes of boots in one corner.

She called back to him, her voice carrying easily in the relatively small space. "I'm not sure if they've got one big enough for your head *and* your ego."

His crack of laughter made her smile. He might be slightly overconfident, but he did have the ability to take a joke, which was unusual in the rarefied atmosphere of Silicon Valley. She'd Googled him last night, and discovered that he'd been even more successful than she'd imagined. A man who'd made his first fortune writing code while still at Stanford and had progressed from there.

"What do you think?"

It was his turn to surprise her. He'd come up behind her wearing one of the loud shirts she'd picked tucked into a pair of jeans that made his legs look endless.

She clasped her hands to her chest and blinked at him. "Every cowgirl's dream."

He raised an eyebrow. "In this shirt? More like a nightmare or a rodeo clown." He turned in a slow circle. "How do the jeans look?"

Damn fine. . . . January cleared her throat. "They look okay. Have you got enough stretch in them to sit in the saddle?"

He bent his knees and then nodded. "Feels good." Reaching past her shoulder he snagged a white straw hat from its peg. "How's this?"

"Perfect."

He held her gaze. "Careful, you almost sounded sincere there for a moment."

"I am. You look good in a Stetson. Who would've thought it?"

"Fifth generation rancher, ma'am." He tipped the brim of his hat to her, a smile lurking in his blue eyes. "Not that I intend to be a rancher for longer than two weeks."

"Why not?" January heard herself ask. "If it's in your blood, why won't you even consider it?"

He took the hat off and looked down at it, twisting the brim through his long, capable fingers. "I'm a tech nerd. There's no money in ranching. How many places like ours close down every year? Thousands, I bet. The current economy doesn't make them financially viable anymore."

"As I already mentioned, there are ways to make a significant difference to the future of the ranch." When he didn't interrupt, January took a quick breath and kept going. "If you have time to listen, I'd be more than happy to go over my ideas with you."

He studied her for a long moment. She couldn't decide whether he did it automatically to discompose the opposition or if it was just part of his regular thought process.

He shrugged. "Sure, we can do that, but first I've promised Ruth to give you an insider's tour of the ranch."

"Really?" She realized she was grinning at him. "Wow."

He stuck the hat back on his head. "Really. But only if you prove to me you're not color-blind and help me find a better shirt."

After locating some more regular designs, he turned his attention to cowboy boots, socks, and gloves. While he was trying on boots, January added a stick of Blister-eez to the pile and some big Band-Aids. She wasn't sure how long it was since Chase had ridden, but she knew from recent bitter experience that it could bring on a myriad of aches and pains in parts of the body she hadn't realized existed.

Occasionally Maureen left her daughter Nancy serving the tourists passing through the old gold trails and checked that Chase was doing okay. Otherwise they were undisturbed.

Like most men he shopped fast and with purpose. The pile of goods gradually grew until he was satisfied he'd gotten everything he needed. From reading his profile, January had to assume that paying for all the new stuff was well within his means. For a second, she allowed herself to dream about what it would feel like to have that kind of money—to be free of college debt, of divorce debt, of . . .

"Are you done?" Chase asked her.

"Yes, sorry, I was miles away." She went to help him take everything through to the front register. "Maureen's going to think it's Christmas." January hesitated with her hand on the top of the shirts. "Are you sure you need all this if you are only going to be here for another week? In the house and the bunkhouses, there are drawers full of old stuff that your father and brothers left behind."

"I'm not touching their stuff."

There was a hard edge to his voice that made her look sharply up at his face. He immediately shrugged. "I grew up sharing all my stuff. I don't have to do it anymore."

Ruth had mentioned that there had been some falling out between the brothers, but this was January's first indication that her laid-back companion had taken it hard. She wondered what else he concealed behind that easy-going exterior—probably quite a lot if he'd thrived in the shark-infested waters of Silicon Valley tech. She had to remember that.

Maureen started ringing up the pile of goods, commenting on every item, and, to January's surprise, Chase humored her, answering every question with such skill that his interrogator didn't seem to notice how little he was actually giving away. His credit card was matte black and made Maureen exclaim about its weight.

When everything was bagged up, January helped Chase carry it to the truck and load it into the backseats.

"Do you need anything else?" she asked him.

"Not at the moment." He'd already taken the tag off the Stetson and placed it on his head. It really was unfair how good he looked in it. "How about you?"

"Nope. We can go back and get ready for our ride."

He held the door of the truck open for her and then walked around to the other side. "You sound as if you are really looking forward to it."

"Of course I am. You're the only person I've met who grew up on the ranch."

She backed carefully out of the angled parking space, waving at a few familiar faces as they moved slowly down the main street.

"Ruth's been here a long time."

"True, but she came here as a bride. I want to get a sense of what it was like growing up as a fifth generation Morgan."

Chase shrugged, his attention fixed on something outside the truck. She got the sense that he wasn't particularly happy talking about his childhood or his family.

"I don't remember most of it. We just did kid stuff mostly."

"But it sounds like Ruth made you do a lot of ranch work as well."

"That's just what kids were expected to do back then. There was none of this overprotectiveness that seems to abound now. Jeez, I have friends in San Francisco who micromanage every second of their kids' lives. Ruth would kick us all out of bed at six, expect us to get our chores done, and then to go and amuse ourselves until lunch. If anyone was stupid enough to go and tell her he was bored, she'd find him something to do pretty damn quick."

The warmth in his voice when he talked about his grandmother was at odds with his lack of visiting her.

"Did you just spend the summers here, or were you around during other vacations as well?"

"We started off just coming for the summer because our parents worked, and they couldn't afford daycare for all of us. Eventually, when my dad took over the ranch work, we stayed here more and more until Ruth just up and enrolled us in the local school and that was that."

"How old were you, then?"

"About nine or ten, I think. The twins were around five,

my other brother about eight, and Rachel was born not long after."

"Rachel?"

He shifted in his seat, his expression so neutral that she immediately wished she hadn't said anything.

"My baby sister."

"Ruth mentioned there was a baby who disappeared with your mother."

"They didn't just disappear. They're presumed dead."

January bit down hard on her lip. "I'm so sorry."

"It was a long time ago," he said easily. "No problem."

January fixed her attention on the road as they neared the gate at the boundary fence of the ranch. She wanted to ask him about his mom, but she already felt like a big, insensitive jerk. He might say he wasn't bothered by his sister's vanishing and her probable death, but January had become an expert in reading body language during her brief marriage, and Chase wasn't as relaxed as he was trying to pretend.

And, anyway, it was none of her business. His immediate past had nothing to do with the history of the ranch. She was just being nosy. That had always been her problem. She always had this stupid idea that she alone had the power to make things better for people. As a result she'd spent more years than she cared to remember taking care of everyone else's needs but her own.

But not anymore. She'd finally grown a spine, and no man was ever going to turn her into a doormat again.

"What was your favorite thing to do on the ranch when you were a kid?"

"I liked to herd cattle. I was pretty good at it. My dad said I—" His emerging smile disappeared.

January desperately tried to think of another topic of conversation, but eventually settled on silence. It took all her concentration to keep the old truck on the dirt road, so she focused on that. Beside her, Chase made no effort to speak either as he hung on to the strap to counteract the swaying of the truck. He moved easily with an athlete's grace, his expression now as amiable as ever. She could only wonder how he dealt with Silicon Valley CEOs and other venture capitalists. That killer charm and calm demeanor must confuse the hell out of them.

"Are you always this relaxed?"

He glanced down at her. "When I'm being driven by someone I don't know? Nope."

So he'd decided to change the subject himself. "Is that supposed to be a compliment?"

"Well, I haven't jumped out screaming or wrested the wheel away from your control, so, yeah."

She couldn't help but grin at that. "I used to drive all the farm equipment back home." She braked hard and turned the last corner, bringing the truck to a halt with a screech of tires and a showy plume of dust. "Even the combine harvester."

He hadn't moved an inch in his seat and still looked remarkably unperturbed. She wondered what it would take to shake his composure.

"Do you ever lose your temper?" The question was out before she could stop it.

"Not really." He took off his seat belt and considered her. "I don't find it a productive thing to do."

"But you must get mad sometimes, or frustrated or—"

"Sure I do, but losing my temper doesn't help solve a problem, does it?" He got out of the truck and started to collect his bags. "I'd rather find a solution without letting things get out of hand."

"That's really . . . admirable." January grabbed two of the boxes and the mail. "What made you decide that?"

"I'm not sure what you mean." He paused to study her.

"No one's born like that. At some point in your life you

must have made a conscious decision not to lose your temper."

"Must I?" He turned toward the ranch and started walking. "Perhaps I just hated watching other people getting angry and realized I never wanted to be like that."

She followed him up the steps. "My mother was a passive-aggressive martyr. I swore I'd never be like her."

He held the screen door open for her. "I can't imagine your being passive about anything."

"I'm not." She stopped and found herself staring up into his amused blue eyes. "I do ask a lot of terribly invasive questions, though."

His smile revealed a dimple on his left cheek and his perfect teeth. "Nothing I can't handle."

She dropped her gaze and moved past him. "I'll put these things on your bed, okay?"

"Be my guest."

He followed her up the stairs, and she walked past her bedroom door to the one at the end of the hallway, which was ajar. A faded patchwork quilt covered the queen-sized bed, and the room smelled of the lavender sachets Ruth sewed and left in the drawers and closets. January put the boots down on the rag rug and turned around, bumping into Chase who was much closer than she'd anticipated.

He steadied her, his hands grasping her forearms. "Thanks for helping me out today."

"You're welcome." His hands looked big and capable as he held her. "What time do you want to go out and ride?"

"I need to check up on something at work first, and then I'll be down."

"Okay." She felt like some breathless, silly teenager as his thumb stroked the bare skin of her elbow. She had the strangest urge to lean forward, bury her face in his chest, and just inhale him. "Is there anything else in the truck to bring up?"

He stepped back. "I think I got it all."

"I'll check." She made it out of his bedroom and down the stairs in record time; her breathing uneven and choppy as she took her time making sure the truck was empty.

It was too long since she'd stood near a living, breathing man under the age of fifty. It was also obviously too long since she'd had hot and dirty sex with anyone with a pulse. For a moment she allowed herself to imagine him laying her down on that fancy flowered quilt, peeling off her jeans, and climbing on top of her . . .

"January?"

She jumped so high she almost hit her head on the truck roof.

"Yes?" she squeaked as Chase came to stand alongside her open window.

"You left your keys on the floor in my bedroom. I thought you might need them."

"Oh. Thanks."

He lingered by the door, his expression curious. "You okay?"

"Yes, I'm fine, just fine, just sitting here wondering where the heck I'd put those keys." She offered him a lame smile. "I'm glad you found them. Thanks again."

He finally went back into the house, leaving January feeling like a complete fool. She was far too old to be attracted physically to someone. She was *so* over that. What she wanted from a man now had nothing to do with looks and everything to do with his being a nice, reliable, solid kind of guy. . . .

Which apparently, according to Ruth, described Chase Morgan to a tee.

But he *couldn't* be nice. It wasn't fair for anyone to look like that, earn all that money, *and* be nice. January had learned her lessons about the masks men wore the hard way, and she wouldn't let herself be swept away again.

But she did want to touch him very badly.

Just to see . . .

With a subdued curse, she got out of the truck and headed for the barn. There was always something to do out there, and she obviously needed to do something other than think about doing Chase Morgan. Shoveling horse manure would be a great reminder of exactly what she didn't want to end up neck deep in again.

Chase wandered back to the house, grabbed a glass of cold, lemon-scented water from the pitcher in the refrigerator, and went back upstairs to change his clothes. He wasn't sure what was up with January. She went from asking him a million questions to blushing like a schoolgirl. He slowly stripped off his shirt. Had she noticed he'd held on to her for a moment too long? Had she felt that indefinable tug of attraction arch between them?

If she had, her reaction hadn't been quite what he'd been hoping for. She'd run away from him like a scared rabbit. It had been a long time since a woman had done that. Maybe he was losing his touch. His faint smile died. And maybe he was just becoming one of those conceited bastards who expected every woman he met to fall into his arms.

He should have learned his lesson about that. The faster they fell, the more likely it was that they were after something. January's running in the opposite direction was probably a good thing. And in the present circumstances probably better for both of them, seeing as they were on opposite sides of the battle for the ranch. Perhaps she'd realized that quicker than he had.

The thing was—he liked her. She was so refreshingly direct. His past girlfriends had often accused him of being insensitive or unaware of their "feelings." He had a sense that January would just flat-out tell him how she felt, which made things a lot easier. She also appealed to his more basic senses, making him wonder how she'd taste and feel and . . .

Solving the problems of the ranch once and for all had to come first. Working out the intriguing contradictions of January's personality would have to be left for another day. No one was that nice anymore, were they? Chase took his cell out of his pants and put it on the bed. Coverage was lousy on the ranch, and he barely got a signal. Even the sight of his phone made his heart rate increase. He felt adrift . . . and that frightened him. It was the first day in two years that he hadn't checked his phone every five seconds.

Realistically he knew that if problems arose, his team could handle them—damn, he'd picked every single one of them, so he knew their worth. But still . . . the urge to get on that phone and start demanding answers shook through him as if he were a drug addict facing a needle.

Which was exactly why he'd been practically forced into taking time off.

Maybe just one text . . .

He typed fast as if someone were going to come up behind him and confiscate his phone.

The reply from his partner Matt was instantaneous. **Everything's good. Fuck off. You promised.**

Chase had to grin at that. He finished dressing in his new clothes and went into the bathroom. Shock shuddered through him until he realized that he hadn't walked in on his father, but had seen his own reflection in the tall mirror over the sink. He took an unsteady breath and looked again, searching for the differences between them and finding surprisingly few.

Chase looked more like his father than his brothers, which meant he could never forget where he came from and what he had the potential to become. There was a good reason why he'd learned to keep his temper, and it was staring him right in the face. Morgan blood ran hot, and from the look of him he'd inherited every drop from his father, the murderous son of a bitch. . . .

But Chase wasn't his father, and he didn't have to be. Grabbing his hat, he went down to the kitchen and then out to the barn. The sun was shining on the metal roof, and the heat was building. There was a strange weather pattern out here. The mornings could be freezing even in the summer and the nights even colder, but during the day, heat rolled in, and the sky was a bright, cloudless blue that looked unending.

He'd forgotten that. He'd also forgotten that this place used to be his home and that he'd never wanted to leave. But farm boys couldn't survive in the tech world. He'd had to learn to adapt and erase that part of his personality. Coming back to the ranch and his memories of the happy child he'd once been was harder than he'd anticipated.

"Hey."

He squinted against the sun and saw January standing in the center of the barn.

"Where's Ruth?" he asked as he strolled into the shadows and was surrounded by the sweet scent of hay and the tang of horse manure. Above his head a couple of nesting birds tweeted at each other, sending wisps of dried grass and stray feathers dancing in spirals on the air currents.

"She left a note on the kitchen table to say she was going out with Roy to look at the herd."

"Where's it at?"

"The herd? Top northeast corner, I think. Why? Do you want to ride over there first?"

"We could do that. It's on our way."

He followed her into the tack room where she had already started to assemble bridles, reins, and saddle blankets.

There was quite a collection of stuff. Nothing was ever wasted on a ranch. A good leather saddle, if kept properly, could last for years. All the gear he and his brothers had used as kids still hung there, waiting for the next generation that if he had his way would never come to call the ranch home.

Pushing that surprisingly melancholy thought aside, Chase went to help January lug one of the saddles off its stand.

"Will this one work for you, Chase?"

He recognized the saddle as his father's. Unless Chase wanted to start in on explanations he had no intention of giving, he'd have to suck it up and use the damned thing.

"Sure. Which horse?"

"Ruth said for you to try Nolly. He's in the stall next to Sugar Lump."

"Who usually rides him?"

"Roy does when he needs a second horse, and Miguel, one of the ranch hands, takes him out and keeps him exercised." She glanced up at Chase and then looked quickly away. "I think Ruth got him in case you or your brothers ever came back and needed a ride."

And now he felt even more like a heel. Shouldering the heavy saddle and looping the reins and bridle over his arm, he put everything by the pasture fence and walked down the barn toward the stall. How long was it since he'd actually attempted to saddle and bridle a horse? Ten years? Fifteen? Hell, it couldn't be that hard, could it? He'd never thought about how to do it as a kid; he'd just done it. He didn't remember ever having a problem before.

Nolly, a good-looking brown-and-white quarter horse, eyed him as he approached the stall and took a step backward, tossing his mane as if sizing Chase up.

"Hey, Nolly." He reached in to pat the gelding and let

him nudge his nose into his hand. "You're going to be good to me, aren't you?"

His dad had always said you had to let the horse know right away who was in charge. Nolly looked like he'd already made his decision, and it hadn't gone in Chase's favor. After giving Chase the side eye as he entered the roomy stall, Nolly backed up until Chase could close the door.

"Thanks, buddy." Chase ran his hand down the horse's neck, inhaling the peppery smell of warm flesh and dust. Luckily for him Nolly had a halter on, which would make keeping hold of him while assembling the various bits of the bridle much easier.

Not relying on Nolly to stand his ground, Chase led the horse out into the sunlight and looped the halter rope around the horse's neck and tied him to the post. Chase put the saddle blanket on and then heaved the saddle up and over. He'd forgotten how heavy the damned things were.

January led out her horse and mounted up. "Be careful when you—"

"I'm good."

"Do you want me to—?"

"I've got it."

She sighed loudly enough to make a point and then started to adjust her reins, leaving him eye to eye with Nolly, who seemed to be laughing at him. He adjusted the girth and guessed at the stirrup lengths. He'd have to mount up before he could gauge them more accurately.

Chase then spent a few long moments trying to work out which piece of the bridle went where, and how to hold it so that he didn't trip himself up on the single reins or, even worse, trip the horse. He hoped to God that January was too busy sorting out her own mount to worry about what he was getting up to with his.

Grasping the brow band, he eased forward and attempted to persuade Nolly to dip his head to accept the noseband

and bit. Just as he thought he'd got it in, Nolly took a step back, and everything came off again.

He took a deep breath and moved in closer. "Come on, work with me here. I don't want the lady thinking I'm a dork."

Nolly didn't seem to care what Chase looked like. On the second attempt, Chase got the noseband on and Nolly refused to open his mouth to accept the bit, leaving Chase trying to coax him to open his jaw without getting his fingers bitten off. The third time he remembered an old trick with his thumb to get the bit in and managed to get the whole bridle on.

Nolly didn't look very impressed as Chase tightened the buckles and adjusted the straps before realizing he'd left the halter on underneath. . . .

"Damn." He started to loosen the straps to remove the halter, and Nolly almost wiggled out of the bridle again. By this time he was sweating and wondering what else could go wrong and why his fingers had turned to thumbs. Eventually the bridle was on, and he gathered the reins in his hand.

Grabbing the pommel he bounced off one foot and just managed to swing his leg over the saddle. Just as he settled in, Nolly made a disgusting farting sound from both ends, and the saddle slowly slipped sideways, depositing Chase face-first on the dusty ground.

He rolled over and lay there for a moment, looking up at Nolly, who was definitely laughing at him now. January delicately cleared her throat.

"As I was trying to tell you, that's Nolly's favorite trick: inflating his gut when you put the girth on and letting it go when you climb onboard."

"Yeah." Chase got to his feet and dusted himself down. "I got that."

He marched over to Nolly and readjusted the girth,

tightening it until Nolly must have thought he'd been stuffed into a pair of reinforced panty hose.

Mounting up again, Chase adjusted his stirrups, gathered his reins on one hand in the approved cowboy fashion, and nudged Nolly's flanks with his heels.

Nothing happened.

Nolly was obviously enjoying himself way too much. Chase kicked harder, and the horse bolted forward, almost jerking Chase out of the saddle again. For a second, Chase flailed around like a newbie, before old habits reasserted themselves and he drew on the reins, making Nolly back up and then turn in some tight circles until Chase was satisfied the horse was finally beginning to understand who was boss.

Letting out a cautious breath, Chase turned to January, who was now a few paces behind him. Her eyes were narrowed with amusement and her lips pressed tightly together as if she was trying not to laugh.

He bowed. "Ma'am? Are you ready to go?"

She walked her horse toward him, swaying easily in the saddle. "I was ready about ten minutes ago, and don't call me ma'am."

This time Nolly consented to move off, and they ambled forward together side by side.

"Ruth said you get range anxiety."

She squinted up at him. "Is that some kind of Silicon Valley joke?"

He shrugged. "Well, I thought it was funny. Electric car drivers worry about running out of power, and you apparently worry about getting lost on the ranch. It was too obvious to let go."

She laughed out loud, the sound surprising him. "Okay, I suppose it is quite funny."

"Thank you, ma'am." This time he did tip his hat to her. "That reminds me. How did you end up with a name like January? Were your parents aiming for a year's worth of kids?"

"Pretty much."

He turned to look at her. "Seriously? Do you have siblings with other calendar-month names?"

"I have two sisters called April and June, and a brother called December."

"You're kidding."

"Nope. My mom just liked the idea of naming us after our birth month. My brother was the youngest."

"Poor guy." Chase shook his head. "December. That's a bit of a mouthful. Does he get called Dec?"

"Sometimes."

"What did your dad make of all those names?"

"I'm not sure."

He glanced over at her. "He didn't stick around?"

"I grew up on a commune in Arizona. I don't think my mom was quite sure who fathered us."

Chase allowed that to sink in and tried to think what the hell to say. "Have you ever considered DNA testing?"

God, what a stupid question; he couldn't believe he'd opened his mouth.

"For what purpose?" She shrugged. To his relief she didn't seem upset. "We consider ourselves siblings regardless, seeing as it was my mom who brought us all up. I never needed a father."

"Ah, okay."

She fished in her pocket for her sunglasses. "What does the *T* stand for in your name?"

Chase sighed. He might have known they'd get on to that. "It's a stupid name."

"More stupid than January or December?"

"My dad was a big fan of TV westerns. He named me after his favorite character in *The Virginian*."

"I've never heard of that show. We didn't have TV when I was a kid."

"Good." Chase increased his pace a little until he was able to trot; he was looking outward across the floodplain of the creek toward the more wooded area to the north. Her voice carried way too clearly across to him.

"If you don't tell me I can just Google it and make a guess."

He rode Nolly in a gentle circle back toward January, who was really smiling at him now.

"It's Trampas."

Her smile widened into a grin. "Trampas Chase Morgan? That's . . ."

"Hilarious, I know."

"It's kind of sweet that your dad named you after his favorite show."

"I suppose it is." Chase looked away from her. That was the problem with being back on the ranch. Every conversation circled back around to his dad, and he wasn't sure he could handle it. "We're going to cross the creek at the shallow end and head north toward the pine trees, okay?"

She remained where she was, her gray gaze fixed on him. "You don't like talking about your father, do you?"

"No. Shall we get going? There's a lot to see before it gets dark."

Chapter Four

January let her horse fall in behind Chase's mount as he picked his way across the rocky bed of Morgan Creek. She knew from experience that the water that flowed straight down from the snow-topped mountains was icy cold and pure enough to drink. Coming from Arizona, she hadn't believed how cold it could still be in the spring and summer months on the ranch. She preferred the cold to the blistering heat. At least you could always get warm. The heat was much harder to avoid.

Chase hadn't said a thing since she'd asked him about his dad, but she didn't think he was angry with her. It was more that in typical man fashion he'd decided not to admit to feelings he couldn't deal with. He should've grown up in a commune, where as soon as you confided a problem to someone it became everyone's problem. Sometimes it had been annoying, but on other occasions it had stopped a potential issue from growing into something disruptive and had restored harmony.

She'd never forget all the adults sitting around the communal hall thrashing things out together, the kids playing around them and the older folk dozing in the sunshine . . .

"Did you say the herd was up this way?"

January rode up to Chase's side. "Yes. That's where Roy said he was taking Ruth anyway."

"Then we'll head toward the boundary with Lymond Ranch. We'll probably find them somewhere around there. Have you any idea how many head of cattle my grandmother is running these days?"

"Not that many."

"Too expensive and not enough hands to keep them under control?"

"No, she's decided to concentrate on producing a smaller quantity of high-quality organic beef."

"Whose idea was that?"

"Mine, actually. I have ranching friends who've been very successful at providing for that market. It's definitely a growing one."

He made a skeptical sound and moved on, kicking Nolly into a smooth lope as the ground evened out into grassland. January followed him, admiring his ease in the saddle—an ease she would never achieve, having learned to ride as a teenager. Despite his rocky start, Chase had clearly remembered his skill set. When he slowed down she caught up with him again.

"I suppose your dad put you on a horse before you could walk."

"Pretty much. One of my first memories is of sitting in front of him while he galloped like a madman over this very field. . . ." His smile faded. "It's hard to reconcile my early memories of him with what happened later." Even as she opened her mouth to ask what he meant, his glance flicked away from her. "I see cows and Roy's old truck. Shall we head over there?"

When they reached the truck, Roy, the ranch foreman, got out and came over to them. His smile lacked a few teeth, and his skin had the texture of a well-worn saddle.

January figured he was somewhere between seventy and ninety. He stuck out his hand.

"TC. Good to see you. How're you finding Nolly?"

January hid a smile. No asking where Chase had been or about his life, just all about the here and now and the horse. Maybe Roy had it right. Chase would probably appreciate not having to answer a million stupid questions.

"Hey, Roy." Chase dismounted and returned the firm handclasp. "He's a good horse. Likes to play his tricks, but I think I'm getting a handle on him."

As if he knew Chase was talking about him, Nolly snorted and made a spirited attempt to get out of his bridle.

"Yeah, he's a trickster, that one. He dumped Miguel on his ass the other day and left him sitting in the creek."

Chase grinned. "I'm pretty sure he's planning to do that to me on the way back. How's the herd coming along?"

The two men started talking shop, and January took the opportunity to get down and walk over to the truck where Ruth was sitting, sunning herself in the passenger seat.

"I got your pension."

"Thanks, darlin'. I see Chase got himself some new clothes. When I saw you both riding up, I thought for a minute it was his daddy there." Ruth sighed. "I bet Chase hates that."

January propped her elbow on the open window and lowered her voice. "What exactly did his father do?"

"You should ask Chase."

"He avoids the subject like the plague. He's not going to tell me anything." January took a slug of Ruth's coffee and attempted a winning smile. "I only want the basics so that I can stop putting my foot in my mouth every time I talk to him."

"Chase's daddy isn't in contact with any of his children anymore."

"Why not?"

"Because he took to drink after his wife and daughter disappeared. One day he just up and left the ranch, leaving his boys behind." Ruth shook her head. "I gave them a home and made sure they were brought up right, but losing both parents in less than a year? That was tough."

"I can imagine." January glanced over at Chase who was laughing at something Roy was telling him. Chase had tucked his gloves in the back pocket of his jeans, and his denim shirt was already sticking to his back. He might refuse to accept the label of cowboy, but he looked as if he was born to be one.

Ruth poked her arm. "You keep asking him questions. It's good for him to talk about his father and his brothers. He keeps things all bottled up inside him just like his grandpa. It's not healthy."

"I don't want him thinking I'm some kind of insensitive jerk."

"Don't worry. Chase won't be shy about telling you to back off."

"I've noticed. He just does it with such charm that you don't realize it at first. You want him to come back and live here, don't you?"

"I'd love him to do just that, but I won't force him. I've already told him that if he wants to get rid of the ranch, he'll have to discuss it with his brothers."

"The ones he doesn't speak to."

Ruth shrugged. "As I said, he needs to sort some of this stuff out. I'm just trying to help him along a bit."

January fought a smile. "Meddler."

"Guilty." Ruth positively smirked. "I want the boys to be friends again. I don't know what happened to drive them apart, but I want it fixed before I die."

"You're not planning on dying anytime soon, are you, Ruth?" Chase called out as he and Roy approached the truck. "Because it's going to be a while before I can track those boys down and persuade them to come out here."

"I'll wait."

Chase nodded at January. "Are you ready to move on? I'm planning on taking you up to the silver mine next."

"Sure." January took a last slurp of Ruth's coffee and accepted the icy water bottle Roy held out to her. "I can't wait."

Chase reined Nolly in and waited for January to catch up. She kept stopping to admire the view, which he had to agree was breathtaking, but it was all too familiar to him.

"Sorry!" she called out to him as she started coming up the slope. "I was just trying to work out the location of the original path from the boundary of the ranch to the mine."

"You'll see it much clearer from up here." He waited until she joined him and then stood in his stirrups and pointed out toward the east. "There's a line of stones that marks the edge of the old road. It wasn't that wide. A few carts came up here, but it was mostly pack mules."

She shaded her eyes. "Yeah, I can see it now."

He pointed up the hill. "And on the other side of the mine is the old railway track that led up to the stamp mill in Morgansville."

"Ah, that makes sense. I read about some kind of primitive rail system to transport the ore from the mine up to the mill."

"There's not much left of it, but you can still see the straight lines of the cut through the rock and the odd rusting nail." He hesitated. "I used to walk the line and pick up bits and pieces of metal when I was a kid. I had a whole catalog of the stuff. It's probably still at the ranch somewhere. Ruth never throws anything away."

January nodded. "I can just picture you doing that. How long did the mine operate?"

"I'm not sure. The majority of the miners left here and went on to other, bigger strikes before the end of the nineteenth century. My family and the folks from the town stayed around Morgansville for quite a while before deciding to move down to the new town. There's an old diary somewhere that my great-great-grandfather wrote about the place back then. I'll have to find it for you."

"Seriously?" She looked like he'd just given her a million bucks. "That would be awesome."

"If you like that kind of stuff." Chase didn't want to admit that he'd read every word and that, inspired by the journal, he had explored way farther underground in the mine than Ruth would ever know. "The mine isn't very stable now, so we try to keep everyone away from it."

"It certainly doesn't look like much." January eyed the boarded-up holes, rusting bits of machinery, and piles of rubble that bordered the main entrance to the mine. There were big KEEP OUT signs, which reminded her of way too many scary movies she'd watched. "When did you last have it surveyed?"

"I think my dad had someone look it over once." Chase sighed. "God, I can't seem to get a sentence out without mentioning that man. Is it any wonder I hate coming back here?"

"Why is talking about him so hard?"

"Because sometimes when I think about how he was . . . I kind of hate remembering what he became. When I was a little kid he was this"—Chase made a wide gesture with his hand—"colossus who knew everything in this world and answered every question I ever asked him. I believed in him. I wanted to *be* him." Chase forced a smile. "Stupid, eh? No one should idolize anyone like that."

"Because no one can ever live up to that," January said. "Everyone makes mistakes."

"But most of us learn from them and move on. My dad"—Chase shook his head—"just allowed himself to give up on everything and everybody."

"Ruth said he left you all here after your mom died."

"Yeah, that's right. We didn't realize he'd gone for quite a while. He'd gotten into the habit of going away on drinking binges for a few days. He always came back when his money ran out and he could bum a ride home. So it took awhile for us to notice he'd finally gone for good."

"That still must've been hard on you all."

Nolly shifted his feet, and Chase relaxed his tight grip on the reins. "To tell you the truth, it was a relief. There's nothing worse than being known as the son of the town drunk. I tried to protect my brothers from the shit, but they knew. All the kids at school made sure to tell us when they saw my dad unconscious in the street or fighting in the bar or being picked up by the sheriff's department again."

"It's weird, isn't it?" January said. "I spent my whole childhood wondering which of the men in the commune might have been my father, and building these elaborate fantasies of him being someone who had left the commune coming back to find me and taking me to live with him. I never found out who he was, and my mom still refuses to tell me. She says she doesn't remember—that it isn't important. But it was to me."

Their gazes met and held, and then Chase looked away. "I suppose the grass is always greener, right? I wish I'd never known my father, and you wish you'd had one."

"But your memories of your father aren't all bad, are they? He was good to you when you were a kid, so what changed him?"

Chase picked up his reins again and turned Nolly's head down the slope. "I'm sure Ruth already told you that."

"That he changed after your mother and sister died?" January followed him down the narrow path toward the rear of the mine. "I think anyone would struggle with that tragedy."

Chase kept his eyes forward. "Especially when he confessed to killing them."

"He did *what*?" January tried to catch up to him. "Hold on, you can't say that and then ride away."

Chase reached the flat surface where the old well and the stone foundations of the building that had once housed the mine machinery stood. He stopped and faced her, keeping his expression one of mild amusement.

"What do you want me to say?"

"Is he in prison? Is that why he never came back?"

"He avoided jail time, but he paid in other ways."

"By trying to drink himself to death." January sighed. "The poor guy. What a mess."

Chase blinked at her. "He messed up big-time and you feel *sorry* for him?"

"He lost everything, didn't he?" Her direct gaze was almost too hard to meet. "I feel sorry for all of you."

"Gee, thanks."

To his amazement she smiled at him. "You turned out okay, didn't you? So did I. Whatever our fathers did or didn't do shaped the people we became."

"I hate all this Californian psychobabble," he muttered. "Why does everyone have to look for the positives all the time?"

"Because otherwise they'll end up obsessing over a past they can't change and using it as an excuse not to be successful in their future."

"I've been damned successful."

She grinned again. "Who said I was talking about you?"

She glanced around the circular space. "Can we get down and take a closer look?"

January was surprised when he gave her a sharp nod and got down off his horse. She thought she'd blown it after their last exchange, but she'd obviously misjudged him. He might have strong views about his father and his family, but he wasn't taking out his anger on her. It was quite refreshing after dealing with a man like Kevin.

Chase took his time tying Nolly up. When he spoke he kept his back turned to her. "This place is doing a number on me. I don't usually talk about my family so much."

"Me neither." She patted Sunflower on the nose and extracted her water bottle from the saddlebag. "When I tell people where I grew up they always assume the worst— that it was some kind of weird religious group or a charismatic guru who had us all in his thrall. But it wasn't like that at all. My mother didn't want to live a conventional life, so she and a group of like-minded individuals pooled their resources and farmed and lived together off the grid."

He shrugged his broad shoulders. "Kind of like communal ranching? We didn't live like most of the other kids around here either. Not many families have an abandoned silver mine on their land and two towns and a bank named after them."

She walked toward him, shading her eyes against the glare, and decided it was her turn to change the subject. "Why do you think the settlers abandoned the original town? Despite my best research efforts, I haven't been able to work it out yet. Any family history you can remember?"

He frowned and looked over her head at the hills that concealed the old roadway to the abandoned town of Morgansville. "I think it was something to do with the water supply or the stamp mill, but don't quote me on that."

"That's a great place to start." January grinned at him. "See? You're proving useful to me already."

"I'm glad to hear it," he said dryly. "Although some might say you are remarkably easy to please."

She returned her attention to the mine, not wanting him to see that he'd made her feel all flustered again. "So are there only two entrances?"

"Officially, yes." He moved to stand beside her, the heat from his body curling around her and his size shading her from the sun. "There are several cave-ins where tunnels collapsed, and there are a few spots where enthusiastic amateurs have tried to dig down and discover the mythical lost silver hoard of the Morgan mine."

"That sounds like a great movie title. I've been to the county library and museum and read all the newspaper reports about the mine's heyday. At one point there were over a thousand people living in Morgansville, and it had twelve hotels and twenty-five saloons."

He shook his head. "I can't imagine what that must have looked like."

"Your family came all the way from Wales to the mines of California, but ended up running the stables and the general store. They were obviously smart enough to realize they could make a killing from the prospectors and the pioneers without killing themselves going down a mine."

He grinned. "Is that right? Maybe an entrepreneurial streak does run in the family after all."

"To come all the way from Great Britain for a dream?" January let out a breath. "That's amazing." She looked up at him. "Will you have time to go out to the abandoned town with me while you are here? I'd value your input."

"Sure."

She walked closer to the entrance of the mine and stared

into the unending blackness. "Can you imagine having to go down every day and stay down there for hours? I don't think I would've handled that very well."

"Me neither." His breath whispered against her neck. "They first found gold just sitting there on the riverbed of the creek. Can you believe that? My dad had a ring passed down to him by his grandfather that was made from a nugget found right here."

"Do you still have it?"

"No. I guess my dad pawned it to feed his addictions." He moved away from her. "We should be getting on. There are a couple more things I want to show you that most folks don't even know exist on this ranch."

"Wow, do tell. Do you have an alien spaceship somewhere?"

"That's it. Area 51 has nothing on us."

She hated the way he tried to pretend that his father's behavior hadn't hurt him. She had the strangest urge to grab hold of him, hug him hard, and tell him everything would be all right. She'd always been the one mothering all the kids at the commune.

But Chase wasn't a kid, and he was formidable in his own way, using that charm and arrogance to keep people away and exactly where he wanted them. She should keep away. Trying to save people was never a good idea. But she already felt comfortable with him, as if they'd bypassed all the pleasantries and were in some way connected.

"Damn it, Nolly's almost got that bridle off." Chase sprinted away toward his horse. January followed him more slowly. She took another swig of water and mounted up.

"Ready when you are," she called out to Chase, who was giving Nolly a severe talking to. Nolly looked over and rolled his eyes at January, and she had to stifle a giggle. "Do you have any more information about the mine at the ranch? Ruth said there were boxes of stuff in the attic."

"She's right." Chase was mounted and in control again as Nolly kicked up his heels and gave a little crow hop, which failed to unseat his rider. Chase was so fluid in the saddle that she found it hard to look away. "We can take a look sometime."

That didn't sound very promising, but she gave him a cheerful smile. "Cool."

He tipped back his head to observe the angle of the sun. "It's getting late. Are you okay with speeding things up a bit?"

"I'll try not to fall off, if that's what you mean." She sat up straight and gathered her reins. "Go for it."

He clicked at Nolly and took off so fast she blinked into a cloud of dust. Holy cow, he was a beautiful sight riding toward the sun and the mountains and . . .

"Damn, I'd better get after him instead of admiring his ass," January muttered as she encouraged Sunflower into a trot and then moved up through the gears to a lope. Setting her teeth January kicked once more and she was galloping, her horse following straight after Chase's. She wanted to scream for the fun of it, but had to concentrate too hard to do anything but stick in the saddle like a burr.

By the time she reached him she was puffing almost as hard as the horse, and her abs and thighs had gotten a severe workout.

"You need to sit lower in the saddle." Chase said. "Relax and go with the motion."

"Easy for you to say." She pushed the escaping strands of her hair away from her face. "I obviously wasn't born on a horse like you were."

"You did good." His smile was way too condescending for her liking. She kind of hoped he'd be sore the next morning, but knowing her luck he'd probably shake it off.

"Thanks. Now what am I supposed to be looking at?"

"It's over this hill."

They walked the horses forward, and January let out her breath. Below them lay a series of round ponds surrounded by yellowish rocks and what looked like the entrance to a cave. "I had no idea these were here. Are they marked on the ranch map?"

"I don't think so." He pointed at the closest ponds. "These two feed back into the creek and are full of fish. The ones toward the other end are supplied by an underground hot spring that emerges inside the caves."

"Bliss," January sighed. "I wondered why it smelled like a spa out here. How long have they been here?"

Chase shrugged. "I have no idea. That's your department. I'm just the guide."

She considered the terrain. "I think at some point they were adapted by man rather than nature. You see how regular the last two circles are? That's not usual. The hot springs, yeah, well, they are probably natural. Do we have time to go closer?"

He grimaced. "Not if we want to get back and do the chores. I'd hate to leave Ruth thinking she had to do everything."

"Then we'll come back another day," January agreed.

Chase considered her as he checked Nolly's bridle. "You are an interesting woman, January Mitchell."

"In what way?"

"I'd almost decided to dislike you on sight, but you keep on surprising me."

His directness no longer intimidated her. "Ditto. I thought you were going to be awful."

"I am." His smile was rueful. "I haven't taken good care of my grandmother. You're right about that. But this place reminds me of too much shit in my life, and I'm a champ at avoiding it."

"We all do that."

His grin caught her unawares and warmed her like a kiss.

"There you go again, being all nice and understanding. You asked me why I never lose my temper. How about you?"

A memory of Kevin's furious face looming over her made her shiver. "Oh, I have a temper. You just haven't seen it yet." And he never would, because getting angry with a man was just stupid when you were five foot four in your socks.

His smile died, and he held her gaze. "Seems like we both have our reasons for being the calm, reasonable people that we are." He leaned toward her, the leather saddle creaking, and she instinctively stiffened, making him pause and search her face.

"I didn't mean to scare you."

She found a smile somewhere. "You didn't. It's just that getting close to someone on a horse isn't usually a good idea."

"Especially when Nolly is involved. He's just waiting for me to mess up." Chase tipped his hat and drew back. "Next time I get close, I'll make sure we're both on our own two feet."

Her tongue seemed to have stuck somewhere in the back of her throat as she gazed at him and murmured something unintelligible.

"Let's go. We can come back tomorrow."

She nodded as he wheeled Nolly around and set off, leaving her with the dawning realization that in her quest to uncover more about him she'd actually given away rather too much about herself.

Chapter Five

Chase stood out at the back of the barn, way too close to the manure pile, where for some reason the signal was best, and pressed his phone to his ear.

"Yeah, Kingsmith Financial Group based in Orange County, California. Find out everything you can about them." He paused to listen. "I want to know if they are a legitimate organization. I'm also sending you a list of names. I want a basic security report on every one of them."

At the other end Jake groaned. "Jeez, you aren't supposed to be working. Have you forgotten already?"

"This isn't work. It's personal. It's Daizee's afternoon off, and I can't do it from here."

Chase turned and paced back the other way, watched intently by three of the feral cats sitting on the sunny side of the barn wall. "Can you get that done as soon as possible? Farm it out to Hendersons' security guys if you don't have time, and don't worry about the cost to the business. This one is on me."

"I'll have to get Hendersons on it. We're upgrading the office systems this week. I won't have time to breathe."

Chase frowned. "You're doing that while I'm *away*? Dude, are you sure—?"

"Chase, *listen*. We will be fine. Can you just trust us to do this without hovering over us like a momma bear? Matt and I are perfectly capable, dude."

"I know you are, but—"

"Stop worrying." Jake sighed. "Don't start obsessing over shit again. You can't control everything."

"I am aware of that, and I trust you guys implicitly." He paused, but Jake said nothing more to reassure him. "I've got to go and feed the horses. Later."

Chase ended the call and stared out over the horizon, focusing on the austere beauty of the mountain range. He took several deep breaths. The desire to get back in his car and return to San Francisco pulsed through him. He'd started the business with Matt and Jake and, until a year or so ago, he'd thought things were going well. But it seemed as if his partners weren't happy, and somehow he was to blame. . . .

Weird how he always seemed to get the blame for trying to be the responsible one . . .

"Are you okay?"

January came out of the barn and stopped to stare at him. There was a smudge of mud on her cheek, and her T-shirt had several feathers stuck on it.

"I'm good." He attempted a smile. "Problems at work. Sorry I had to take off like that."

"It must be hard being away. Ruth said you own your own company?"

"Yeah, in partnership with two of my college buddies."

"So why the long face?"

"Because they're doing important stuff without me." He shoved a hand through his hair and tried the deep breathing again. "Would you believe that they forced me to take time off? They said I was becoming too controlling."

"At work?"

He grimaced. "At everything. They *said* they wanted

more free time to enjoy their success—not that I was stopping them from doing anything. I never suggested they had to keep working the hours I did. I love my job, I *live* for it, but that's my choice."

"Perhaps they felt you were showing them up."

He glanced at her. "I never tried to do that. They're my best friends. But, if a business is to continue to be successful, you can't slack off when you start earning money. You have to keep building."

She sauntered over to him, her hands in her pockets, her blond hair catching the dying rays of the sun. "Building what? An even bigger pile of money?"

"There's nothing wrong with money. It makes the world go round."

"I thought that was love." She scuffed the toe of her boot in the dirt.

He gave a harsh laugh. "Try living on that."

"I did, remember? The commune was all about love and sharing."

"And you deliberately left that life behind you."

"I wanted to see the world. I didn't get very far before reality hit me squarely in the face, but I certainly learned fast." His smile was gone. "Are your friends right to be worried about you?"

He thought about that, turned it over in his mind, and eventually sighed. She always asked the hard questions. "Possibly. I was working twenty-hour days, trying to do everything myself and achieving less and less, which made me panic even more and . . ." He looped his finger around his head in an endless spiral. "I ended up in the ER. I thought I was having a heart attack, but it was just stress. That's when my buddies told me to take at least two weeks off, or they would consider getting me sidelined for good." He glanced over at her. "Don't tell Ruth, will you?"

"Of course not." January leaned against the fence

beside him, and once again he was caught by her calm acceptance of his words. "I know what it's like to want to be rich and in control. I used to dream about getting away from the commune, but I had to wait until all my siblings were in school." She shrugged. "My mom was too busy teaching other people how to become self-sufficient to be interested in raising her own children."

There was no anger in her voice about her mother's lack of care. He wished he could be so forgiving on January's behalf.

"So you went to find fame and fortune in LA?"

"Of course I did." She smiled down at her feet. "Talk about naïve. Strangely enough, no one was interested in helping me achieve those dreams, and I ended up waiting tables."

"And eventually came to Morgan Ranch."

"That was something of a long journey. I met a man in LA. I made the mistake of marrying him. After two years I divorced him and reinvented myself."

"You didn't want to go back home to Arizona?"

"I'd changed too much. I liked the modern conveniences, and I loved earning a little bit of money. There's not a lot in my field, but at least I can survive, and I get to do something that I love."

Chase shook his head.

"What?"

"Just you. You are so positive about everything."

"What's wrong with that? Negativity breeds negativity."

He grinned at her.

"*What?*"

"You can take a girl out of the commune . . ."

She punched him playfully on the arm. "Don't you start. My ex used to call me Polly Positive and not in a nice way." She met his gaze. "I'm not trying to be some do-gooder. I really believe that a positive attitude is worth more than anything."

"Which is admirable." The last remnants of stress from his phone conversation dissipated. Her smile lingered and her eyes held so much warmth that he couldn't stop himself from looking at the perfect curve of her lips. "I do have a very positive thought right at this moment."

"Which is?"

"If you stay exactly like that, with your chin tilted toward me, I can"—he bent and kissed her mouth—"do that." He raised his head. "Was that a positive experience for you?"

"Chase . . ."

"Or maybe not." He smoothed his thumb over her full lower lip, and she shivered. He immediately wanted to kiss her again. "I'm just checking here—being something of a control freak."

She covered his hand with her own. "What exactly are you checking for? It's obvious that I'm attracted to you, but that doesn't mean I have to act on that attraction."

"It doesn't?" He was surprised how disappointed he felt.

"Chase, I'm living in your grandmother's house, and I'm determined to save this ranch. Doesn't that put us on opposite sides?"

"I won't let that bother me if you won't."

She opened her eyes wide at him. "Be serious for a moment. I like you, I feel comfortable with you, and I'm scared of messing that up. It's been a long time since I've met anyone I'd like to call my friend."

"Your friend." He drew back. She obviously had no idea how serious he was being or how turned on he was. "Okay, I'm getting the message."

"Once you've talked with Ruth about what's going to happen to the ranch, you might not *want* to be around me."

She patted his arm. "You might think I influenced her decisions."

"I already know you're influencing her. You've got her running organic beef and making a profit on the herd for the first time in years. But it's not enough, January. She can't keep this place on that."

"That's not the entire plan, you know," she retorted.

"I'm sure it isn't, but—"

"You've already decided this place can't be saved, haven't you?"

He forced himself to hold her gaze. "Yeah. I've done the math as well."

"But you are *wrong*." She straightened up and looked as if she was about to stamp her foot. "It's not all about money."

Chase raised his eyebrows. "That's all you've got, commune girl?"

With a frustrated sound she leaned in, cupped his face, and kissed him hard on the mouth. For one glorious second he kissed her back before she tore herself away and retreated five steps, her arms crossed over her chest.

"We have plans for this place, Chase. Maybe if you took some time to actually *listen* to what Ruth, Roy, and I have to say, we could convince you, too." She smoothed down her hair. "That's why I don't want to kiss you."

"*That* was you not wanting? Honey, you were practically scooping out my tonsils."

She scowled at him. "If I keep kissing you, you could claim I attempted to influence your decisions by unfair means."

He shrugged. Damn, he was actually enjoying himself now. The sweet bubblegum taste of her lingered on his lips. "I've never been averse to a good bribe, darlin'; you go right ahead."

"You are so not funny, and cut out the cowboy talk."

"That's because I'm not joking. Despite all my bad press. I'm quite capable of keeping my private life and my business decisions totally separate."

At least he hoped he was. He'd never allowed himself to be attracted to a woman like January before, so he was in somewhat unknown territory.

"But how can you *do* that with the ranch? It's your family business."

"It was." He shrugged. "Times change, January. The gold rush was a hundred and sixty years ago. Everyone is flocking to Silicon Valley these days, not Sutter's Mill."

"Which is why we need a plan to adapt."

The wind picked up, bringing with it a twist of ice off the mountains. Chase moved away from the fence. "It's getting cold. Let's go inside."

She ignored his proffered hand and headed for the house, her blond head bowed. Chase followed, aware of the lights in the kitchen and Ruth's outline against the window as she looked out for them. He remembered her standing like that waiting for his dad to come back until the day he never did.

Had she been waiting like that for Chase and his ungrateful siblings? They all deserved to rot for leaving her to cope alone like this.

And now he'd hurt January's feelings. It seemed he was the only person who could separate the romance of the ranch from the cold, hard facts. He was more than willing to listen to any schemes Ruth and Roy cooked up, but he doubted they'd make any difference. When he showed them his spreadsheet, they'd admit defeat and finally sit down with him and make some sensible plans for the future.

God, it felt like he was on the opposite side of everyone he cared about these days. . . . He remembered Matt and Jake looking at him as if he'd grown two heads and now

Ruth and January. But they all had it wrong. Didn't they understand that he was trying to *save* them?

Sure, he could afford to buy the ranch, walk away from his best friends, and set up his own company, but he didn't want to do any of that. He wasn't stupid. Ruth wanted to use the ranch to engineer a reconciliation between him and his brothers and wouldn't take kindly to his buying it and selling it from under her. That was also why she really didn't want him to pay off the new debt.

Matt and Jake seemed to have decided that their company would be better off without him. Chase kicked a stone out of his path. What would happen if he weren't there to put everything together? He wasn't being conceited, but without his drive he figured the other two would practically be bankrupt within a year or so. They might disagree with his business ethics, but at least he wouldn't let them beggar themselves.

If they kicked him out now, they might decide to close the company, give up on everything they'd shared, and go on to enjoy their lives without him. Chase swallowed hard as his heart rate kicked up. And if he bought the ranch and sold it, Ruth would probably never speak to him again.

Why was doing the right thing—the *logical* thing— so hard?

January went into the kitchen, slamming the screen door practically in his face. It was funny how she felt so passionate about his old home. It was also kind of endearing. Was it because she'd never had a proper family of her own?

"Roy's coming to dinner," Ruth announced as Chase finally took in his surroundings. "He wants to talk to you."

"Sure. That will be nice." He nodded to his grandma. "I'll just go and wash up."

* * *

"I'll be done in a minute," January shouted as she splashed more water on her heated cheeks. Why the hell had she kissed him? She'd said all the right things and then given in to temptation. He'd tasted like coffee and warm male. . . . She licked her lips and then with a growl brushed her teeth with so much toothpaste that she was literally foaming at the mouth.

Chase knocked on the door again, and this time she flung it open. He took a hasty step back and pointed at her face.

"You suffering from rabies or something?"

She grabbed a towel and rubbed furiously at her mouth before attempting to push past him. He caught hold of her wrist.

"January . . ."

"I have to go and help Ruth with dinner."

His intent blue eyes searched her face. "We can sort this out. There's no need to get mad."

"I'm not mad. I just don't understand how someone as smart as you are can't see that making decisions based on a spreadsheet is both narrow-minded and, and *stupid*."

He let go of her. "You sound just like my business partners. Tell Ruth I'll be down in a minute."

January stomped down the stairs and went to lay the table, half-listening to Roy and Ruth who were having an amicable disagreement about which field the new calves should go in. It was so easy for Chase to walk in, make his decision, and walk out again. Couldn't he see the damage that would do to Ruth and to the ranch? Both of them deserved better.

"Dinner's ready, Chase!" Ruth yelled up the stairs as January and Roy took their seats at the table. The succulent smell of barbecued ribs filled the kitchen, and January realized she was starving. While Ruth put the dishes on the table and Roy handled the plates, January poured everyone a glass of sweet tea.

Chase appeared, bringing with him a waft of his newly reclaimed spicy shower gel. He also had his laptop tucked under his arm, which suggested he meant business.

Ruth took her seat, and Roy cleared his throat as he reached for January's and Chase's hands.

"Thank you, Lord, for the good food on our table. Amen."

"Amen," January murmured as Chase looked resigned.

Ruth handed out plates heaped with mashed potatoes topped with the ribs, and silence set in as they all started eating. After a while, Roy gave a discreet belch, wiped his mouth with his napkin, and patted his stomach.

"That was good food, Ruth. Thank you kindly."

"You're welcome." Ruth smiled at the foreman. "Thanks for taking me out to see those cows today." She turned to Chase. "The herd is looking good, isn't it?"

Chase put down the rib he'd been gnawing on. "So Roy tells me."

"Did he show you the preorders for next year?"

"They also look good."

Ruth sat back. "Last year January put me in touch with one of the farmers her brother worked for, and he was most helpful. Apparently all the Bay Area folk love this organically raised beef. I can run a much smaller herd and yet still make a profit."

"As long as consumers have the money to pay for expensive beef." Chase fiddled with his fork. "Just remember that prices can go up and down, and fads change even faster."

"I hardly think giving folks great-tasting beef is a fad," Ruth argued. "There are huge health benefits to breeding and selling meat from these leaner grass-fed cows."

"For those who can afford them." Chase finally looked up. "The ranch cannot depend on one product."

"Of course it can't," Ruth agreed. "That's why we've been considering a different approach entirely."

A wary look entered Chase's eye. "What exactly do you have in mind?"

"Well, firstly, we'll expand into producing more food-stuffs and cash crops. I've studied up on this, and there are things we could grow here, on the pastureland we no longer need, that would sell really well in your part of the world."

January nodded and chimed in. "We've already spoken to a couple of the big organic supermarket chains about what products they need, and they've all been very helpful."

"Do you have any cost projections or evidence to support this idea?" Chase asked.

"Yes, on my laptop." She gave him a challenging stare. "Do you want me to send you the files?"

"Sure."

"I'd like to keep pigs," Roy said.

January hid a smile as Chase blinked at the foreman. "Pigs?"

"Home-cured organic pig products are in high demand." Roy nodded. "I've always wanted to keep pigs. We can put them in that old ruined cow shed down by the low pasture. That way the smell won't reach the house."

Chase looked around the table and felt like the odd man out again. He tried to smile. "Okay, so let me see your data on all these proposals and let me calculate the costs." He hesitated. "The thing is, when you change a business model so radically, you need up-front money to make things happen. How are you going to finance this?"

Ruth smiled. "That's your job."

"But you told me you didn't want my money."

"Not to pay off those debts!" She scowled at him. "And

I don't want your money for the ranch either. I want your advice. You spend your entire life investing in companies and people, don't you?"

"Kind of." Chase eyed her warily.

"So advise *me*."

"I've already told you what I think. The only reason to invest in a project is if it is going to keep growing and thriving. We've already agreed that the ranch isn't going to stay in Morgan hands."

Out of the corner of his eye he saw January put her hand to her mouth.

"I haven't agreed to that," Ruth said. "And you can't either. I told you the only way this ranch leaves our family is after I'm dead and if you boys *unanimously* decide to sell it." She fixed him with a withering stare. "In the meantime, I would hope that you would use your expertise to work with the information we have given you and tell me whether what we propose would *work*."

Chase opened his mouth and then shut it again.

"Okay?"

He nodded. "I'll do that, Ruth." He was fairly certain it wouldn't make enough of a difference, but he had to be fair.

"Good." She nodded and got up to clear the table. "Does anyone want a slice of apple pie?"

Chase squinted at the screen and ran the numbers again. Even using the most optimistic of forecasts for the future of organic farming markets, the ranch would still fall short of being self-sustaining. He was still seated at the kitchen table, an oil lamp at his elbow, the timber frame of the house groaning and whispering around him. Everyone had gone to bed, leaving him alone.

Damn. His evening hadn't quite gone as planned. When he'd taken them through his cost projections and spreadsheet, they'd all looked at him as if he'd kicked their favorite puppy. When he reported back it was only going to get worse. . . . A stair creaked, and he turned toward the darkness where a figure stood frozen at the foot of the stairs.

"January?" he whispered.

She came into the faint circle of light thrown by the lamp. She wore a faded yellow T-shirt and pink boxers. Her hair was braided down her back, and she definitely had no bra on. She looked soft and pretty enough to eat. Chase refocused his gaze on her face. "What's up?"

"I couldn't stop thinking." She sat opposite him at the table and rested her chin on her hands.

"About what?"

"About you and why you are so determined not to allow this place to thrive."

He set his jaw. "Look, I'm fed up with being made to feel like the bad guy. The facts don't lie. You might not like the answers, but what's the point of throwing good money after bad?"

"So when you invest in a company, you always expect to get a return on your money?"

"That's not always possible. Products fail, ideas get duplicated and taken to market faster by another developer, and people implode. There are a thousand reasons why a company or an individual we invest in might not make it."

"And what do you do then?"

"We curse a lot and move on."

She sat forward, her hands clasped on the table in front of her. "So why can't you find a way to finance your own family ranch? If it fails, at least you made the effort to try to save it."

"I don't want to fricking save it."

She paused. "Wow. That's certainly direct."

He rubbed a hand over his face. "I'm tired, January. I'm

tired of being the one who has to make responsible decisions and then gets criticized for doing so."

"Who else is criticizing you?"

He sat back in his chair. "It's a long story."

"Spill. I've got nothing better to do." She got up and checked the tea kettle on the range. "I'm making hot chocolate. Do you want some?"

"Why not? It's got to be better than turning to drink like my father."

"Did he always drink?" She had her back to him as she set out two mugs and found the jar of cocoa powder.

"Not to excess," he said carefully. "He enjoyed the odd beer, but that was about it."

"Was he abusive?"

"No." He frowned at the back of her head. "What point are you trying to make?"

She finally turned around, the spoon in her hand. "I just wondered whether he might ever have turned back into the father you loved. Have you seen him?"

Mutely Chase shook his head.

"Pity."

He found his voice as she retrieved the kettle, poured the boiling water into the mugs, and added milk without consulting him.

"I have no desire to see him again." She placed one of the mugs to the side of his laptop and resumed her seat opposite him. "He doesn't deserve a second chance."

She looked at him over the rim of her cup. "You really like to compartmentalize your life, don't you?"

"Doesn't everyone?"

"I suppose so." She sipped her cocoa. "Do you want me to show you Ruth's Facebook page so that you can look up your brothers?"

"She's *friends* with them?"

"One of them. Blue, I think. Where did that name come from?"

"The High Chaparral," Chase said absently.

Blue—his next youngest brother and at one time his closest friend. They were only thirteen months apart and had shared everything, bonding even more closely when the twins had arrived. He only knew that Blue had gone into the military because Ruth had told him. He'd heard nothing directly from his brother for over ten years, which still hurt.

"Great, he hates me even more than the twins do."

January came around the table and leaned close to him as she tapped away on his laptop. The scent of her soap curled around him, and he slowly inhaled.

"You smell good."

"That's because I washed off the stink of the chickens." She straightened up, and her soft breast brushed his cheek. He wanted to turn his head and take her into his mouth and . . .

"Jeez. How come she's got so many friends?" His attention snuck back to his grandmother's page. "And how come I'm not one of them?" After sending her a friend request, that January accepted pretending to be Ruth, he scrolled through the smiling pictures until he found one that looked all too familiar.

"That's Blue all right."

He clicked on his brother's profile, but could see very little.

January nudged Chase's shoulder. "You should friend him and send him a message."

"I know." He stared at his brother's unsmiling face.

"What's the worst thing he can do about a polite message asking to reconnect?"

"You don't know my brother. He's very black-and-white about everything."

"Sounds like someone else I know," she muttered.

Curving his arm around her waist, he drew her down to sit on his lap. "Last time we spoke he told me we were done forever."

"And how long ago was that?"

"About ten years or so."

"And you don't think he might have grown up and regretted saying those words and will be thrilled to hear from you?"

"Nope."

"But you have to try. You promised Ruth."

"Maybe it would be better to wait until we *have* to face each other."

"Over Ruth's coffin?" January sighed. "You can do better than that, Chase."

"I know." He shut down the page. "I'll have to think about what to say."

"Coward."

"Yup." He reached across the table and brought her mug over to sit next to his. "Drink your cocoa."

Chapter Six

January heard a faint groan and carried on making a fresh pot of coffee. The sun was shining and, despite her worries, she was looking forward to another day of exploring the ranch with Chase.

"Morning, Chase," she called out. "Do you want to go back to the fishing holes today or out to the ghost town?"

She turned to find him clinging to the door frame and almost dropped the coffee.

"What's wrong?"

He lowered his large frame into a chair and grimaced. "I guess I'm not used to riding anymore."

"You poor thing." Even as she said the words, she kind of wanted to laugh a little. Even the man who sat on a horse as if he were born to it suffered from not being a regular rider anymore. "I know just how you feel." January hunted in the cupboard beside the stove. "Take some ibuprofen and try this liniment Roy makes. It smells bad, but it's awesome."

"I know all about Roy's wonder cure." Chase winced as he held out his hand for the glass jar and set it on the table. "It works like a dream"

She finished brewing the coffee and set an empty cup

and cream in front of him on the table. "I can make you some toast. We don't have to ride out today. I've got plenty of work to catch up on."

"Toast would be great, and I'll see how I feel in an hour or so. Sometimes sitting around just makes things worse."

She put four slices of brown bread in the toaster and poured them both some coffee.

"Where's Ruth?" Chase asked.

"Out with Roy moving calves."

"She never stops."

"I think it keeps her young. You can't really imagine her sitting in an old folks' home, can you?"

"I never suggested she should go into one. I offered to get her a piece of land to farm closer to where I work."

"I bet that went down well. She loves this land— Morgan land." January cradled her mug in her hands and leaned up against the worn countertop. "Can I ask you something?"

"You're always questioning me. Why ask for permission now?"

"I was reading up about the company you started."

"Give Me a Leg Up?"

"Yeah." She considered how to phrase her next question. "It sounded like a great idea—to use your money and investor and angel money to help individuals, small businesses, and communities."

"That was the original intention, yes."

She frowned at him. "So why did you end up in the ER thinking you were having a heart attack?"

"Because things change and grow, and the company became more than just a charity."

"I don't understand."

"I wanted to do more, to fund bigger projects and help more people. Until recently, Jake and Matt were quite happy to let me forge ahead."

There was a bitter tone to his voice that she couldn't ignore. "So you were taking on too much?"

He shrugged and immediately winced. "You could say that. For some reason they both decided we needed to rethink our investments again. They put me in an extremely difficult position with some of our newer investors."

"You own the company equally?"

"We've always gone with a two-thirds majority vote. Now it seems I'm on the wrong side of the party."

"Which is why you ended up so stressed that you thought you were having a heart attack."

"No, I ended up *stressed* because Jake and Matt let me down."

"But if they are your friends, do you think they did what they did because they realized you weren't coping?"

He glared at her. "I was coping fine. They just suddenly took offense at one of the investors not having 'green enough' credentials to be involved in one of their little projects."

"I thought your Website had a promise front and center that you wouldn't take money from big business interests?"

"This was *different*. It made total financial sense." He stopped talking and looked down at his coffee.

"It sounds like your thinking on the ranch. Money and the spreadsheet trump everything, right?"

Silence fell, and then the toast popped up, making them both jump. January assembled butter and jelly and passed the plate over to Chase. He loaded up his toast and then rose slowly to his feet.

"Thanks. I'll take it up with me."

She took a seat and nodded in his general direction, keeping her gaze fixed on her laptop screen. She stayed exactly where she was until she heard the slam of his bedroom door and let out her breath. It sounded as if Chase's inflexibility was catching up with him big-time.

Was it too late for him to see that money wasn't always the good guy? That ethics and people and history made a life worth living as well? If pissing off his best friends and ending up in the ER hadn't worked, what chance did the ranch have? She sipped her coffee. The situation with his family seemed to be making things worse.

She opened Facebook and considered Ruth's page. January wasn't friends with Blue Morgan either, but perhaps she could be. . . .

Chase put his breakfast on his old desk before walking over to look out of the window. The sun was shining, and the wetland fields beyond the back of the house were bright with tall grass that concealed the narrow channels of water and mud that could unseat an unwary rider. As he stood there, some of the ranch horses that had been let out to graze that morning came up over the brow of the hill and swept past.

He caught his breath at the beauty of the running horses, manes blowing in the breeze, heads tossing, free to run like they were meant to without humans on their backs. He leaned his forehead against the glass and groaned.

January didn't seem to understand why he'd made the decisions he'd had to make. No one did. Why couldn't they see that he was simply trying to make them all money? Jake and Matt should be grateful to him for increasing their net worth, and Ruth should understand that he wanted nothing but the best for her. Money meant security. Everything else was messy and unreliable and . . .

God. He slowly straightened up and hobbled over to the bed. Now January had made him think, and he wasn't sure he liked what she'd stirred up inside him. It was the damn ranch, turning him into that little boy again—the one who idolized his father and knew that his father would never ever let him down. That's why the ranch had to go. Chase couldn't come here and let years of painstaking effort to rebuild his life and change his personality go to waste.

He liked himself, didn't he? He pictured the disappointment on January's face as he'd justified his actions, thought of Jake and Matt. That was it. *People* made things messy. Emotions—he paused—made a man end up in the ER thinking he was dying.

"Screw it," Chase muttered, and dug his cell out of his jeans pocket as anxiety pounded through him. There were no bars. "Double screw it."

There was a knock on the door. "Are you okay in there?"

Chase took his sweet time getting to the door and opening it. "What's up?"

January bit her lip. "I wondered if you wanted any help putting that liniment on."

"Feeling guilty for psychoanalyzing me in the kitchen?"

"A little." She pushed a strand of blond hair behind her ear. "I grew up having to help everyone solve his or her problems. It's a commune thing." She met his gaze, her gray eyes clear. "But you aren't my responsibility, and I probably overstepped the mark. I even thought about contacting your brother for you."

"Please tell me you didn't."

She solemnly shook her head. "I'm not quite that dumb, although it always seems to work in the movies."

He leaned in and curved his hand around her throat. "I think I'd have to throttle you if you did that."

"Harsh," she said, but she didn't move away.

He circled his thumb over the nape of her neck, so aware of her that it felt as if they were alone in the world. "Too pretty to break."

"Too stubborn, you mean."

"Too stiff-necked? You and Ruth both." He didn't want to let her go, his body tightening and reaching for her. He moved in an inch and fought a groan. "I wish I wasn't so sore from all that riding."

"I can at least help you with that. I give great massages."

"You'd have to work a miracle to get me to where I want to be."

She smiled up at him. "We can only hope. Do you have a sheet to cover the quilt?"

He found one in a drawer and handed it to her.

"Thanks. Now go and lie down on the bed."

He paused only long enough to shed his shirt and jeans, and then he lay down on the sheet with a groan. January readjusted his pillows and then took her time admiring the broadness of his shoulders, the long curve of his spine, and finally his ass, which was covered in tight black cotton boxers. He had a swimmer's build and . . .

"I thought I was getting a massage here."

His voice was muffled, but she still jumped.

"I'm just unscrewing the lid of the jar. It's a bit tight."

He made an unconvinced noise as she scrabbled to open the jar. The pungent smell of herbs and whatever secret ingredient Roy added to his potion emerged, bringing tears to January's eyes.

Chase groaned. "What the hell does he put in there? As kids we couldn't decide if it was dead skunk or boiled squirrel."

"He won't tell me." January sat on the side of the bed and warmed her hands before dipping her fingers in the mixture. "And, as long as it works, I think I'd rather not know."

She reached out and spread her fingers over Chase's shoulders. "Your muscles are tight here."

"They are tight everywhere. My eyebrows ache. It even hurts to breathe."

"The first morning after I'd been out on a horse I literally couldn't get out of bed," January confessed. "I had to roll myself onto the floor and crawl to the bathroom. Luckily Ruth heard me moaning and sent up Roy's potion. I almost asked him to marry me, it was so effective."

Chase chuckled and groaned again as she slid her hands down his spine and started to rub away the tension and ease the tightly bunched muscles.

"That's good."

Her thumbs dug into the creases above his hips, and she leaned over him to push some weight into the motion. She was enjoying this just as much as he was—possibly more, which was bad, especially when he was in pain.

"Any better?" She continued down his legs, teasing out the knots in his thighs, enjoying his shudders of pleasure as she worked.

"Just don't stop."

She added more goop to her fingers and returned to his shoulders, running her hands down his arms. Greatly daring, she locked her bent knee into the small of his back and pressed firmly, making him sigh her name. She wondered whether he sounded this grateful when he had sex . . . not that she would ever find out, but the way his hips were rocking into the motion of her hands gave a woman ideas.

"Do you want to turn over?" she asked.

He went still. "I want to, but it's going to be awkward."

"Why's that?"

He carefully rolled over onto his back.

January couldn't help but notice he was aroused. "I thought you were in pain."

"I am." His smile was crooked, his eyes narrowed with sultry warmth. "You could fix that for me."

"I don't think so." She gave him a fake sympathetic smile. "Trust me, one touch of this mixture on your favorite parts, and you'd be screaming and not in a good way."

"Damn." He closed his eyes. "You're right. That stuff burns like the fires of hell."

"I assume you found that out as a kid."

"Not me—Blue. He always had to test things out." Chase sighed. "Let's ignore it, and maybe it will go away."

She crawled up to kneel by his waist and spread her hands on his chest. He took a sharp breath, which tightened his abs, and then slowly let it out.

"Poor baby." She rubbed the ointment into his chest and shoulders and down his arms, aware of how close he was to her, how her breasts swung against his chest as she worked.

She went still as the back of his fingers brushed against the lower curve of her breast.

"Not the only thing that's hard around here, am I?"

"And we've already discussed that our mutual physical attraction should be put on hold until the matter of the ranch is sorted out."

His fingers came back, this time capturing her nipple. "I don't remember agreeing to that. I believe I was all for exploring our physical attraction." He gently squeezed, and she nearly bit her tongue as lust slithered through her, settling low in her gut.

"Nothing's changed," she said firmly even as she leaned into his long fingers.

"Okay." He slid his spare hand up inside her T-shirt against her spine and gently brought her closer. "You go ahead with what you're doing. Just ignore me."

His teeth settled over her nipple, and she fought a gasp, her hands still braced against his now-slick muscled chest.

"This is not a good idea."

"Mmm . . ." He teased her with his tongue. She made

the mistake of looking down and . . . God, her T-shirt was now damp from his mouth and the tip of her breast was clearly visible. The hand on her back shifted lower, and suddenly he lifted her until she straddled him. She could feel the heat of him even through the thickness of her jeans—feel how hard and thick and . . .

"I'm going to kiss you now." Chase paused to search her face. "Unless you tell me no, because I'm not going to force you to do anything you don't want."

"This is stupid," she whispered.

"It's just a kiss." His smile was so hot she wanted to whimper. "I just want to thank you for helping me out here." He cupped her chin, his thumb edging close to her lower lip. She couldn't have moved away if she'd tried.

With a soft sound he drew her even closer and kissed her carefully on the mouth, his hand curving into her hair at the nape of her neck.

"Nice . . ." he whispered, and kissed her again until she responded, and the kiss turned from sweet to sinfully hot as he plundered her mouth and she forgot how to breathe . . . not that breathing seemed necessary, because damn the man could kiss like a dream.

Her thoughts stopped coming as she was consumed by the feel of his mouth on hers, of his hands gathering up her ass and pressing her against the hard, hard ridge of his shaft.

"God . . ." She choked out the word as her greedy fingers did their own exploring down his back and around his chest. She wanted to shove her hand down his boxers and feel the flex of his ass and wrap her hand around his hardness.

"Chase, are you up there?"

They both went still as Ruth's voice echoed up the stairs.

"Yeah, I'll be down in a minute, okay?" Chase shouted back, his hands still on January's hips, the throb of his erection against her needy girl parts sending tremors down January's spine.

"Have you seen January?"

He met her gaze and grinned. "Yeah."

"Then both of you come on down. I have some news."

Chase couldn't decide if he wanted to strangle Ruth or thank her for interrupting them. He didn't want to let go of January. He wanted to roll on top of her and keep her pinned to the bed in the most basic of ways, with his body and his mouth and . . .

She carefully moved off him, and he immediately missed her warmth and the scent of her arousal that counteracted even Roy's god-awful lotion. Chase was still hard, but a few minutes alone time in the bathroom would sort that out. Not that he'd get them when Ruth was expecting him downstairs within seconds.

"I'll go back to my room really quietly," she whispered. "And then go on down. I feel so *juvenile*."

He slowly sat up as she opened the door to reveal Ruth standing on the landing, her arms crossed over her chest. January gave a startled yelp, and he grabbed a pillow and held it over his lap.

"January was just helping me put on some of Roy's liniment." God, now *he* felt like a teenager again.

Ruth's nose wrinkled. "I wondered what was stinking up the house."

January edged past Ruth, muttering something about washing her hands, and disappeared into the bathroom.

Ruth continued to look at him. "You be nice to that girl, TC."

"She's not a girl."

"Really?" Ruth raised her eyebrows. "She sure looks

like one to me. She had a bad time with her ex-husband; I don't want her getting hurt again."

Chase eased his legs over the side of the bed. The massage and the heat January had raised in his body had reduced his stiffness considerably. "You can rest easy. We're both adults, and you should know me well enough to know I wouldn't mess with any woman's head."

"That's true, I suppose. You always keep your distance."

"What's that supposed to mean?" He discarded the pillow, which was no longer needed.

"You've never been good at picking the right woman."

"Thanks." He busied himself finding his shirt and pants.

"The ones I've been allowed to meet, anyway." Ruth shook her head. "That Jane was awful. Her walking out on you just before your wedding was a blessing in disguise."

"It didn't feel like it at the time, but I guess you're right."

"Why did she walk out?"

"Because I asked her to sign a prenup, and she was offended by the terms. The truth was I wasn't as rich as she'd anticipated, and she used her 'hurt feelings' over my not trusting her to get out."

"As I said, lucky escape." Ruth turned away. "Don't shower for a while. Roy says the stuff needs time to sink in and do its work."

"Great." Chase pulled on his shirt, which immediately stuck to his back. "That's all I need to make my day complete." He inhaled and immediately coughed. "There's no need for you to worry about my enticing anything feminine for the foreseeable future."

Her laughter floated up the stairs. "I've made a coffee cake."

He found his jeans. "I'll be right down."

* * *

January joined him at the table and didn't quite meet his eyes. Her cheeks were still flushed, and her gaze kept dropping to his mouth as he ate his way through a huge slice of cake. He deliberately swirled his tongue over his lips, gathering up a stray glob of frosting.

"Damn, that's good. Are you having some, January?"

"I think I already did," she murmured.

"Of course she is. I made it for her. It's her favorite." Ruth cut another huge piece and handed it to January along with a glass of milk.

"So what's your news, Ruth?" Chase asked as his grandmother produced a letter.

"We've been included on the historic ranches of Northern California tour next month."

Chase frowned. "The what?"

Opposite him January let out a whoop and high-fived Ruth. "That's awesome news! Are they bringing a guide, or do they want us to show them around?"

Ruth put on her spectacles and consulted the letter. "They'd like members of the family and any other knowledgeable persons to be present during the visit to answer questions."

"Hold up a minute," Chase said. "What's this all about?"

January turned to him, her face glowing. "It's a small tour company that specializes in trips to the California Gold Country. They'll bring folks out to the ranch and show them around. If we do okay they said they'd put us on the regular schedule. We get paid to host them."

"Enough to compensate for having a bunch of camera-clicking strangers roaming the house and looking through your underwear drawer?"

Her smile faded. "It won't be like that. I'll send you the information. It's a very professional company. Their guests are real history lovers who will respect the ranch and everything on it."

"Are they properly insured?"

"Yes." January pushed back her unfinished plate of cake. "If you'll excuse me I have to go and tell Roy. He'll need to make sure the cattle are in a secure area when they come."

She left the kitchen as quietly as she'd entered it. Chase stared at his cake and couldn't finish his piece either. He followed January out of the house and down to the barn where she was already in her truck.

"Hold up." He waved at her to stop.

She pulled up alongside him and lowered the window.

"I thought we had plans."

She looked away from him. "I just needed to get away from the house."

"What did I do?"

"You're just so negative about everything." She shook her head. "And I know what you are going to say, and I *know* that at some level you're right, but there's no need to suck the joy out of everything, you know?"

Chase stared at her for a long moment. "I was just pointing out—"

"I know what you were doing. Looking for the problems, looking for the reasons why yet another idea to save the ranch and bring in more income *has* to fail. I get it, Chase. I just don't want to have to listen to it right now."

He took an uncertain step back, and she took the opportunity to rev the engine and move on out. He watched the truck until it was a speck in the distance and then just a lingering trail of dust.

Was he really that negative, or was she just annoyed because she hadn't had answers to his totally reasonable questions? But she *had* answered him. She'd even offered to send him the files, and he knew from what he'd already read of her work that the information would be well prepared and financially sound. He turned in a slow circle and looked up at the mountain range. It always made him feel small and insignificant and realize how petty his concerns were and how short his life span.

He walked around the side of the barn and punched in a number on his cell. "Matt."

"If you've called to check up on me, go to hell." His friend's tired voice sounded remarkably like January's.

"Am I always negative about everything?" Chase asked abruptly.

"Truth?"

"Give it to me."

"Pretty much." Matt sighed. "The last year or so you've been particularly bad. You were always the careful and cautious one, and that was good for us, but when you went into hyper-obsessive micromanaging role, you lost your sense of humor and your optimism."

"Not surprising when the economy sucks and we've been struggling to find good clients," Chase snapped back.

"Yeah. Like that."

There was silence, and Chase took a deep breath. "Matt, I'm sorry, I—"

Matt still didn't speak, and after a moment Chase ended the call. Okay, so all the people he liked and trusted thought he was a miserable, joy-sucking jerk. Good to know . . .

He walked through the barn, stopping to feed Sugar Lump a carrot and to pat Nolly's head. As a kid he'd always been laughing and full of hope, but no one survived into his or her thirties without acquiring a cynical side. He'd learned the hard way that if you didn't consider everything that could go wrong, you'd end up with your whole life ruined beyond recognition.

He gazed down at his cell and pulled up the Facebook

app, clicking on his brother's page. He opened up Messenger.
What was that old saying his grandpa had loved? "Might as
well be hung for a sheep as a lamb," he murmured.

> Hey, Blue, I wanted to touch base with you
> about Ruth and the future of the ranch.
> If you get a moment, please contact me either
> through Ruth or here. Thanks, Chase.

Short and to the point like January had suggested. It
probably wouldn't do any good, but at least he'd made the
effort. He wondered where the twins were now. The last
he'd heard was that they were touring the country with the
rodeo circuit. Chase had no idea why Blue of all people
had decided to join the military at eighteen, but he'd definitely stuck with it. Chase had only known because Ruth
kept him in touch with his brothers despite himself.

He went back into the house where Ruth was cleaning
the table and loaded the dishwasher to stop her washing
everything up.

"I left Blue a message."

"Good job."

"I doubt he'll get back to me."

"I'll make sure he does." Ruth put the dishcloth away
and took off her apron. "I'm going to have a nap."

"Are you okay?" Chase paused, his hand on the chair.

"I got up early to see the new calves."

"I could've gone."

She flicked the apron at him. "I enjoy it. Stop fussing.
Why don't you take my truck and go out to the hot springs?
Roy always says that his liniment and the hot water are
the best cure for muscle stiffness ever invented."

"I might just do that." Chase needed to think, and the
hot springs might be ideal. "I'd take Nolly, but I think he'd

take advantage of my weakness and drop me off the side of a cliff."

"He's a smart horse." She gave Chase the side eye. "Maybe a blow to the head would knock some sense into you."

"Thanks for the support." He nodded at her. "I'll go and get a towel."

Chapter Seven

Peace . . .

Chase savored the quietness of the cave as he lay in one of the hollowed-out pools, his arms spread wide on the rim, the rest of his body immersed in hot, mineral-scented water. He inhaled deeply and let his breath out into the echoing silence. Above his head the light from the oil lamp caught the glitter of metallic specks buried within the yellow-white rock deposit. The more he sat there, the more obvious it became that he just needed to get a grip. He'd allowed his emotions to overwhelm him, and that was never good.

The first thing he needed to do was draw up an action list with a clear path to his desired goal. That's why he was good at what he did. He never let his attention stray from the prize at the end of the road. All he had to do was find a way to allow Ruth to live on the ranch until she was gone.

He forced himself not to think about what those words actually meant. Keeping her on the ranch hadn't been his original goal, but he wasn't stupid. If he could find a way to keep Ruth in the black and on Morgan Ranch land, he'd do it, even if he had to covertly finance the whole thing himself. If he could achieve *that,* he wouldn't have to deal with his brothers for years. Once Ruth was secure, he could go back to his job and move forward without worrying.

"Damn . . ." His quiet curse echoed off the walls, spoiling the tranquility. Part of him didn't want to go back. What about Matt and Jake? There had to be a way to sort out that mess as well. They were his oldest friends. He couldn't believe they'd really fire him. But they certainly didn't like him much at the moment, and, the more he thought about going back to work and facing their concern, the sicker his gut felt.

"Hello?"

A shadow darkened the entrance to the caves, and Chase found himself smiling. One thing he appreciated about January was that she never sulked and was always willing to take him on again.

"In here. Take your shoes off; it's slippery."

January came in holding her boots in one hand, her gaze obviously adjusting to the light. Eventually she looked down and saw him.

"Wow, this place is amazing. Can you imagine coming here on a spa vacation? I bet you could make a fortune."

"It's our family secret, remember? Not available to the hordes."

She crouched down beside the pool. "Did you come here when you were a kid?"

"All the time. My dad loved it. Best way to unwind after a hard day in the saddle."

She took off her socks and dipped one toe in the water. "It's really hot. You must be cooking in there. Did your mother ever come out on the ranch with you all?"

"Not very often until we moved here. She didn't like it much. She preferred the city." He beckoned January closer. "Take off your things and come in here with me."

She raised her eyebrows. "I'm still not happy with you."

"Doesn't mean you can't enjoy a soak." He tried to look

innocent. "And if we start arguing again, you can always push me under and shut me up for good."

"As if you'd let me." She gave him a stern glance. "I grew up with a lot of boys, remember. I know all their tricks."

Even as she spoke she was shimmying out of her jeans and T-shirt. His teasing words stuck in his throat as she revealed the opaque pink lace bra and panties he'd met on his first day, hanging over the shower rod.

"Won't they shrink?" He pointed at her bra. "You said cold wash and air-dry."

"You remember that?"

"I remember everything." He considered her. "Maybe you should take them off as well."

"*So* not happening."

"You could just wear my T-shirt?"

She gave him a pitying look. "I'll risk the lingerie. I'm not intending to stay for long, anyway."

He held out his hand, and she stepped into the pool and sat beside him on the rock shelf.

"Did one of your family members carve this seat into the rock?"

"No, I think it was here when we got here."

She closed her eyes and leaned back against his outstretched arm. "When I'm not so tired, I'm going to explore the inside of these caves and see if there is any evidence of earlier occupation."

He stroked some of the damp strands of hair away from her cheek. He wasn't a big fan of people invading his space, but she brought her own sense of calm with her that somehow managed to include him. "You mean like cave paintings?"

Her eyes flew open. "Are you *serious*?"

"Yeah, there's definitely something back there on the

end wall." He placed a restraining hand on her shoulder. "I'll show you later."

She subsided again, her chin dipping down below the water. "Okay."

He felt her start to relax, her thigh rubbing against his, her foot curved over his shin.

"Nice, eh?"

"Lovely." She sounded sleepy, and he closed his eyes as well. For a blessed moment peace stole through him. He liked her being beside him.

She fit.

"Did your fiancée really leave you at the altar?" January asked.

Chase groaned. "I suppose you heard Ruth giving away all my secrets earlier."

"It's hard not to hear everything in that old house." She nudged him with her elbow. "Is this the same woman Maureen mentioned? So she dumped you because you weren't rich enough?"

"Exactly. Can we move on, now?"

"That's a *horrible* thing to do."

He opened one eye and looked down at her indignant face. "As Ruth reminded me, it was better that it happened before the wedding rather than after it." He sighed. "I kind of knew what she expected from marrying me, but—"

"What do you mean?"

"Jane wanted to marry a wealthy man. She was very clear about that, so you can't say I didn't go in with my eyes open. She just miscalculated the extent of my wealth."

"Hold on, so you had decided to let someone marry you for your *money*?"

"Sure." He held her gaze. "What's wrong with that? At least we both knew what we wanted."

"But, did you love her?"

"I *liked* her. She was beautiful and just the sort of wife

a man needs in my position." He frowned. "What's up? You're glaring at me again."

"You don't see anything wrong in what you just told me?"

He ran the conversation back through his head. "Nope."

"You were going to marry a woman because you 'liked' her and knew she wanted your money."

"Yes."

"And you wonder why everyone who cares about you is worried that you've lost your soul?"

For some reason that hurt. "If more people married for reasons of logic and made it the commercial transaction it always used to be before our twentieth-century notions of love ruined it, I bet there would be a lot fewer divorces. If you go into a partnership when you both know the deal, nothing can surprise you."

"But marriage and love aren't *like* that."

"They should be."

"What about this inconvenient connection between us? It's not something either of us planned or agreed to, but it's still there."

"I know." He hesitated. "I can't explain it either, unless it's this place. I find it much harder to separate things out when I'm here."

"Which is why you don't visit Ruth as often as she'd like." January shook her head. "You know that's crazy black-and-white thinking, right? Without love, without passion and tears and all the emotional stuff, how can you live a full life?"

He cocked an eyebrow at her. "I manage damn well actually—well, I did until I met you."

"I disrupt your neat little boxes, do I?" She grinned at him. "Good."

"You don't just disrupt them; you trample all over them,

throw the contents in the air, and mix everything up. You mix *me* up."

"And is that a bad thing?" She held his gaze, her gray eyes serious. "I don't want to hurt you, Chase."

He gave her his best lazy smile. "Nobody hurts me."

She poked her finger in his chest, and he winced. "You are a big, fat liar. Just because you do your damnedest to keep everyone at bay with that great smile and charm and . . ." She shook her head. "You care, Chase. You care about Ruth, and, somewhere deep inside you, you care about this place. If you didn't, you wouldn't be feeling so conflicted."

He held her gaze and allowed a hint of amusement to show in his eyes. "There you go again—trying to fix me. I'm much happier without all this emotional crap, I really am, and if that's something you can't understand, I'm sorry." He leaned in and kissed her mouth.

She didn't kiss him back.

"I think I understand, Chase. You don't care, and you aren't interested in that whole messy business of emotions. Have I got that right?"

"Exactly." Chase should've felt relieved, but he was fairly certain there was a sting in the tail still to come.

"But you are interested in having . . . what with me? Sex with no strings attached?"

He went still. "I hadn't exactly—"

She grabbed his head and kissed him so hard he had to open his mouth and let her inside. And then the kiss went crazy molten hot, and he couldn't stop from shoving one hand into her hair to keep her exactly where he wanted her. At some point she climbed into his lap and straddled him, only the thin cotton of his boxers and her flimsy panties separating his hardness from her heat.

He slid his hand inside her panties over her ass and held her captive in his palm, his longest fingers circling and probing her wet heat until she was rocking against him, urging him on. God, he wanted to be inside her, wanted to fit himself to all that hotness and . . .

She pushed away from him, ducked under the water, and swam the three or four feet to the other side of the pool. He could only stare at her helplessly as she climbed out and sat on the edge. Her nipples were hard, and her skin was flushed with need.

"That didn't evoke any emotion in you at all, Chase?"

He set his jaw and waited her out with a pleasant smile that he hoped hid the turbulence of his thwarted hunger.

"You didn't feel anything?"

He shrugged. "Lust?"

She nodded and kicked her toes in the water, avoiding his gaze. "That's all?"

He opened his mouth to agree with her and couldn't spit the lie out. "Maybe—"

But it was too late; she was on her feet gathering her possessions. "See, that's the problem. I can't do just lust." She met his gaze, her chin raised. "I deserve so much more."

She left, and he stayed put, trying to analyze what had just happened and why it goddamn hurt so much to watch her walk away. What did she want? Hell, what did *he* want? He was only going to be on the ranch another week or so, and then he'd be moving on. She couldn't seriously expect him to start a relationship with her on those terms.

Could she?

With a sigh, he got out of the water and dried himself off. He should let this go, but inside him that *boy*, the one who'd loved the ranch and his father, was making him feel like a heel. He threw the towel over his shoulder and got dressed. One thing was obvious. He should never have come back. It made him vulnerable, and he hated that.

His footsteps slowed as he came out of the cave entrance and into the sunlight. He was supposed to be a problem solver and a game changer. Perhaps it was time to utilize some of his painfully acquired skill set and find a way to solve his dilemma over January Mitchell.

January heard the truck pull up and continued to muck out the stall. It was a good way to work off her sexual tension, and, if Chase came up behind her and tried to charm her out of her pants again, she'd deck him with the shovel. Trying to teach him a lesson about his need for the finer things in life—like her—had almost backfired. Once he'd started touching her so intimately, she hadn't wanted to stop at all. Her girl parts had been sulking all the way back to the ranch.

"January."

"What?"

She swung around with the shovel raised, and he took a hasty step back, hands in the air.

"Can we talk about this?"

"I thought we just did." She shoved Nolly back with her shoulder and shut the stall door. "I have nothing more to say to you. I think I proved my point." Picking up her bucket, broom, and shovel, she walked back toward the tack room.

She concentrated on washing her hands, aware that he hadn't gone away and was now leaning oh-so-casually against the door frame, blocking her exit.

"I don't want to fight with you," he said quietly.

"You don't want to fight with anyone, do you? You just smile and charm and disappear like smoke." She wiped her hands on her jeans, which kind of defeated the purpose of washing them. "It's okay; I get it."

"But I want you."

"And having grown up in a commune with no father, I don't do casual sex, okay?"

He shifted his stance. "I'm leaving the ranch in a week or so, and I probably won't be back for a while. How can any 'connection' we make not be casual?" He sighed. "And, I don't feel casual about you. I *like* you."

"I like you, too."

He met her gaze, his blue eyes serious for once. "Then can't we just be friends who have sex?"

"Friends with benefits." She blinked at him. "That's your solution to this problem?"

"It's the best I can come up with. What do you think?"

"That you are completely nuts."

His faint but definitely hopeful smile died. "Okay." He nodded and turned away. "I'll go and help Ruth with dinner."

She stared after him. He was nuts, wasn't he? Her body didn't seem to think so and was throbbing with repressed sexual tension. Could she do it? Could she have sex with a man she liked and walk away at the end of the affair with her heart and mind intact?

She'd tried marriage to get the ultimate in commitment, and her innocence and trust had been thrown back in her face. So was there a middle ground? As a new version of herself, was she mature enough to handle what Chase was offering her?

"But it's *scary*," she muttered out loud as she walked down the middle of the barn.

Nolly nudged her shoulder, and she divided up the last carrot in her pocket and shared it between him and Sugar Lump.

But it would be so damned *good* between them. . . . She knew that in her soul. Maybe being up-front about what they both wanted and expected out of the relationship would be a benefit. Oh God, she wanted to touch him so badly. . . .

She made her way back to the house still arguing with

herself, and there he was, in the kitchen setting the table and taking up all the air and space. She sat opposite him and ate and talked and nothing made sense except his steady questioning gaze and the sense that, if she didn't make a decision, she would regret it for the rest of her life.

Eventually, she followed him upstairs, and, when he turned to say good night, kept walking until she was in his bedroom. He came in after her and closed the door.

"What's up?"

She turned to face him. "If I sleep with you, you can't sleep with anyone else."

"That's a given." He leaned back against the door and folded his arms. "Go on."

"And you don't tell anyone."

"Who am I going to tell? The horses? Anything else?"

"And we both walk away and *stay friends*."

"I certainly hope so because I'll be back and forth to see Ruth, and, if you're still here, I'd like to think you'd still be pleased to see me."

"I like you."

A small smile kicked up the corner of his mouth. "So you said."

"And I want you."

He came off the door in one lithe motion and moved toward her, halting a pace away. Reaching out he cupped her chin and looked into her eyes. "I'll take care of you; I swear it. You won't regret this."

"I might." She tried to smile. "This is a new thing for me."

"Me too." He smoothed his thumb over her lips. "Let's see if we can make it work together."

Chapter Eight

Chase stopped for a moment to admire what he was soon going to uncover. January's gaze was steady, her delicate skin already flushing, and, if he wasn't mistaken, she was already aroused. He slowly inhaled and smiled.

"What?"

There was a note of uncertainty in her voice that made him want to put his arms around her and hold her close forever.

"I'm just appreciating you."

"Then do it faster."

"Nope." He wrapped one hand around her neck and bent his head to brush his lips over hers. "I like to take my time over the important things in life—like spreadsheets, and profit projections, and making love."

"What about just having sex?"

"You know this is more than that. Friends with benefits, right?"

She went to reply, and he angled his mouth over hers, pushing between her lips and claiming her with a long, thorough, well-thought-out kiss. But she wasn't a passive kind of woman, and he soon lost complete control as she enthusiastically kissed him back. Then he just hung on like a cowboy on a bronco, losing himself in her as he locked his mouth to hers and drew her hard against him.

Her hands were under his shirt, and she was making frustrated sounds because she couldn't get beneath the belt of his jeans. He managed to force a hand between them and unbuckled it, leaving her to pull it free. While she worked on his jeans, he was busy inching up her T-shirt. He didn't want to stop kissing her long enough to take it over her head, but it was worth a second's sacrifice when he already knew what she was wearing underneath.

"Mmm . . ." He nuzzled between her breasts and then brought his mouth to her lace-covered nipple. In some part of his mind he was aware that slow and steady was not happening. The rest of him didn't care. Sex had never felt this urgent or this basic before.

Her fingers tightened in his hair as he practically dragged her over to his bed and laid her on the top of the quilt. He stood beside the bed looking down at her and went for the button on her jeans. She arched her back to help him, and he wrangled the jeans off her and stripped off his shirt, dropping it on top of the steadily growing pile of discarded clothing.

She pointed at his jeans. "Take them off."

He did what she asked in record time, practically falling over in his haste to join her on the bed. And, God, climbing on top of her and feeling her skin against his was so damn fine that he almost came. She reached for him, and he sank over her like some flailing idiot, just where he wanted to be, the hard length of his cock pressed against her damp panties. Except he wanted more, wanted so much more.

He took a moment to rise up on one elbow and look down at her. "I can't do slow and sweet right now."

"I noticed." She slid her hand down inside his boxers

and patted his ass. "That's okay. You do have protection, right?"

He stared at her as a million screaming thoughts crowded through his already overwrought brain. "No."

She blinked up at him. "*Seriously?*"

He wanted to cry, he wanted to beg, and mostly he wanted to slap himself silly for being such an idiot.

"The great Trampas Chase Morgan, control-freak extraordinaire, is unprepared?"

He set his jaw and tried to ease away from her, but she hooked her foot over his ass and held him captive.

"Luckily, some of us aren't, but you'll have to go to the bathroom and look through my makeup bag."

He was off and running to the door before she'd even finished speaking. The TV in the parlor was blaring as Ruth and Roy watched a repeat of their favorite reality show, so he hoped he wouldn't be seen—half-naked and hard, running around the house like a madman. . . .

He grabbed the small box of condoms and went back into his bedroom, locking the door securely behind him, to find January smiling up at him. She hadn't moved an inch, her thighs spread wide and her arms out to the sides. He shucked his boxers and got back on the bed.

"Thank God, one of us has some sense," she commented, but he was too busy sheathing himself to comment. "I assume foreplay isn't happening either?"

"No." He practically ripped her panties off. "I'll make up for it next time, I promise."

She reached behind her back and undid her bra, and his breath caught in his throat at the loveliness she revealed. "Okay, then."

He didn't need anything else and simply thrust forward, catching his breath as she gripped him and they both groaned. He pushed forward again, rolling his hips, and eased deeper. Her fingernails dug into his shoulders as he rocked back and forth, finding an angle that suited them both and made his head want to explode with the *rightness* of it.

She moved against him, bringing her feet higher to grasp his hips, and suddenly he was in heaven, pumping into her and torn between wanting it never to end and simultaneously feeling that if it got any better he'd die of pleasure.

"Oh. God." She moaned into his mouth and came around him, making him set his jaw and hold himself still until she stopped shaking. It was so damned *good*. It was too good. He slid his hands under her ass, bringing her even higher against him, and thrust until all he could hear was his own heart thudding, and the pressure built and built until he had to come or die.

January held Chase tight as he came undone in her arms, shuddering and calling her name before slumping over her, his breathing as uneven as her own. She didn't mind his weight pushing her deep into the feather mattress and made no effort to shove him away.

She couldn't. She felt as boneless and connected to him as he did to her. She also wanted a moment to work out how Chase had given her more pleasure in five minutes than her ex had given her in two years.

"Chemistry," she mouthed against his throat, "is a very underrated thing."

He murmured something and moved away from her. When he returned, he lay on his back and drew her tightly against him. Her head fit perfectly under his chin.

"I can do a lot better than that." He bit her ear.

"I'm not sure I could take it."

He made a satisfied male sound in the back of his throat.

"Really. I forgot all about technique and good manners and just . . . took you."

He sounded quite bewildered, and January wanted to smile.

"And a very nice taking it was, too."

"I'll get some more condoms tomorrow."

"At the store? Maureen will be all ears."

He groaned. "And then everyone in Morgantown will know I'm having sex and probably with whom."

She smoothed his muscled shoulder. "I'll buy them."

"They'll still know."

"That I'm having sex? But I have so many more choices than you do—Roy, Miguel, the other ranch hands. . . . The possibilities will keep the town buzzing for days."

"I have to return the rental car. I'll get some then." Chase obviously did some rapid calculations in his head. "I'll need to go within the next two days."

"If we have sex again."

He rolled on top of her and smiled down into her eyes. "That's a given."

The sound of a cockerel woke him up. It was still dark. Reaching carefully across January, he checked the time on his cell. It was only four thirty. He tried to remember the last time he'd slept so well—especially next to another person. He studied her relaxed features in the faint gray light. Even asleep, she somehow radiated a calmness that drew him like a lodestone.

He traced the bridge of her nose with his fingertip, struggling to identify the emotions coursing through him.

"Are you okay?" January murmured sleepily. "Do you need to go back to your own bed?"

He kissed her forehead. "You're in my bed, remember?"

She groaned and snuggled her face into the curve of his

neck, which did strange things to his stomach. "It's still dark. I'll go later."

He smoothed his hand down her back, holding her close. "Fine with me."

And it was.

He couldn't believe it—but it was. That should be scary. He closed his eyes and simply relished holding her like some sappy lead actor in a romantic comedy—the kind Jane had dragged him along to see. But it didn't feel sappy. He felt more relaxed and at home than he had in years.

Of course, as soon as he thought about it, he started to tense up.

"You want me to go, don't you?" Her fingers tightened on his shoulders. "I can hear you thinking from here."

"I don't regret anything." He tried to pick his words carefully, aware that upsetting a naked woman he'd just made love to would not be wise. "It's just been awhile since I've shared a bed with anyone."

"Jane didn't sleep over?"

"She did, but in the guest room."

"You're serious, aren't you?"

"It was my choice." He sighed. "I don't sleep well. I didn't want to disturb her."

"To go by the snoring, you were sleeping just fine next to me."

He frowned. "I don't snore."

"You do when you lie on your back."

He held her gaze, saw the mingled affection and concern in her eyes, and couldn't look away.

"I don't want you to go," he offered.

Her smile was so sweet it took his breath away. "Then I'll stay for a little while." Her hand brushed over his hip. "You won't even know I'm here."

She kissed his chest and then went lower, making him suck in his abs as her tongue tickled his belly and she made little side trips to lick and nuzzle the jut of his hip bones. He tightened the muscles of his ass so that she couldn't ignore anything else down there that needed attention. She returned to her downward path, slowly sucking him into her mouth and holding him there while his hands twisted up the sheets and he breathed out a mangled plea and a prayer.

He could learn a lot from her about slow and steady as she licked and sucked and played with him until he was begging her to finish him or let him finish in her.

By the time he climaxed, one of his hands was fisted in her hair and he was sunk so deep that he couldn't escape. When she finally released him, she crawled up to smile into his face.

"Now, I'll go."

"Funny." He took hold of her shoulders and rolled her underneath him. "Not yet."

While he waited for January to emerge from the house, Chase took a moment to walk around the side of the barn and make a call on his cell. There were several chickens loitering near the fence. He kept a wary eye on them.

"Give Me a Leg Up, how can I help you?"

"Daizee?"

"I'm not supposed to talk to you, Mr. M. My other bosses won't like it."

"Screw them."

She sighed. "We all know that none of you will screw your own staff. It's a source of great disappointment to many of us."

Chase found himself smiling. Daizee was their admin, and she took no shit from anyone, including her employers.

"This isn't anything to do with the business. I need to

return that car you rented for me, and I want to buy a truck."

"Cool. What kind of truck?"

"Something big, four-wheel drive, and American." He turned and walked back toward the barn. "I need the truck there when I drop off the rental. Can you organize that?"

"Sure." Her fingers clacked on the keyboard. "What color?"

"I don't care just as long as I can have it in the next day or so."

"Got it. I'll text you the details later, okay?"

"Thanks." One thing Chase knew about Daizee was that, despite her attitude, she got things done. "How are things?"

"With me?" She snorted. "Underpaid and overworked as usual."

He mock-sighed. "Shame. As I'm not allowed to discuss the business, I can't help you with that."

She lowered her voice. "Everything else is good here, too."

"Without me?"

"Yeah, well, you were getting a bit out of hand. Half the staff would hide when they saw you coming. Especially those poor little tech nerds."

His smile disappeared. "I really was that bad?"

"You did seem to be losing your shit a little." She hesitated. "Well, a lot really, but we're all hoping you see the light and come back in a better frame of mind."

"I'll do my best."

"Gotta go. Matt's giving me the evil eye."

She disconnected, leaving Chase staring at his cell. He heard the sound of January's old truck firing up and went around the barn to meet her.

"What's up?" January glanced over at him as he got in and she released the brake. "Ruth didn't give you the third degree, did she?"

"She's already warned me off."

"That's kind of sweet of her."

He snorted. "You'd think she'd be more worried about me. Her grandson."

"She probably knows you can take care of yourself."

"So can you."

"That's what I plan on telling her when she finds out. And she will find out. That woman is sharp as a tack." January stopped the truck while he got out to open the gate and waited for him to rejoin her on the other side. "I've got to check the mail. Is there anything you need in town?"

"You know what I need. By my calculations we'll be out of protection in less than two days."

"You've done a spreadsheet for this?"

He tapped his forehead. "Nope, it's all up here." His phone beeped, and he checked his messages. "I've got to drop the rental car off in Bridgeport in a couple of days. Do you want to come with me?"

"Sure."

He turned his attention back to the road that led down to the town. This was good. They were still talking like friends. She slowed as they approached Main Street and turned into a parking space in front of the post office. Chase got out and waited outside while she went in.

The little town was definitely looking far more prosperous than when he'd last been there. The old boardwalks and steps had been restored. There were even rails to tie your horses up as if you'd just ridden into town after chasing off a few bandits. The smell of baking bread caught his attention, and he wandered two doors down from the post office to a new double-fronted store that had cupcakes in the window and was done up like a fancy French bakery.

Under the smell of bread he caught the more brazen hint of good coffee. A young woman dressed in black with a small lace apron and matching collar smiled at him as she went past with a loaded tray.

"Good morning. Are you coming inside for coffee?"

He smiled at her. "I'd rather sit out here, if that's okay."

"Sure. There's a table to the right that's free. I'll come and check on you in a moment."

"Thanks."

He went over to the table and stood by it until he saw January emerge from the post office. He waved at her, and she came toward him, a bundle of mail tucked under her arm.

"Coffee?"

"I was going to treat you." She sat down. "You've been here before?"

"Nope, I just followed my nose."

She inhaled slowly. "It's lovely, isn't it? Coffee, chocolate, and cake. The three things guaranteed to make any woman happy. Yvonne has done a great job here. She also serves lunch."

Chase looked up as the woman returned, brandishing a notepad.

"Hey, January. Is this one yours?" The woman pouted. "I was hoping he would be bribable with chocolate."

Chase winked at her. "I'm always bribable. I'll have a coffee, and the lady gets whatever she wants."

"I'll have my usual coffee and a chocolate éclair, please," January answered promptly.

The woman wrote down the order and then stuck out her hand. "I'm Yvonne."

"Chase. You're not local, are you?"

"No. I moved here around a year ago with my partner to set up this place, but he decided he didn't like it here and went back to France."

"Philistine." Chase shook his head.

"Are you working at the ranch with January?"

"You could say that."

"He's on vacation for a couple of weeks." January smiled at him. "He's got to get back to work in big, bad Silicon Valley at some point."

"Shame." Yvonne flipped to a clean page in her order pad. "It's a beautiful place. Have you been here before, or did you come specifically to see January?"

"I was born here. I came to see my grandmother and got to meet January as a bonus."

"His last name is Morgan," January said dryly. "He's a direct descendant of the man who founded this town and the ranch."

"You're a *Morgan*? Wow. How amazing to be part of something like this." Yvonne shook her head. "You must feel right at home here."

Chase went to disagree and then paused to look around at the thriving small town and the smiling faces. "Yeah . . . it's kind of cool."

Yvonne went into the shop and reappeared with their coffees and January's éclair, which looked really good. While his companion was busy sorting out the mail, Chase sneaked a hand over toward the pastry and received a slap.

"Get your own. I don't share Yvonne's éclairs with anyone."

Chase sighed and went to pay the bill. When he returned with an extra plate in his hand, January was still reading, her brow furrowed.

"Something wrong?"

She looked at him over the letter. "Not really. It's just my mom. She wants me to come home, and I just can't do it at the moment."

"What's so bad about going home?" He almost laughed at the idea of his advising anyone on that matter.

"Because nothing changes for them. Their focus is so narrow, and they are so isolated that I feel suffocated." She tried to smile. "I love to see everyone—especially the kids I grew up with—but I run out of things to say really fast because they don't have to deal with real life, or my version of it anyway."

"Did they meet your husband?"

"I took him once to meet my mother, and it didn't go well. But it was his behavior that stunk and finally made me realize I'd made a terrible mistake in marrying him in the first place."

Chase sipped his coffee, which was as good as he'd anticipated. "Why did you marry him?"

"Because I was young and stupid and desperately wanted to *belong* to someone—to do the whole commitment thing like normal folks. It didn't take me long to realize that making vows to someone didn't make him stick around or be any more faithful than any of the men in the commune."

"He cheated on you?"

"Yup." She took a bite of her éclair and a dollop of cream ended up on her nose. "He couldn't understand why I was so upset because, hey, I'd been raised on the idea of free love, so he thought I'd be okay with it."

"Idiot."

"Him or me?" She tried to lick the cream off her nose. "I saw what I wanted to see, and so did he. We were both wrong."

"He was still an ass."

"Thank you." She smiled at him. "Now I almost feel bad for not sharing my éclair with you."

"Liar." He leaned forward and flicked the blob of cream off her nose. He wanted to kiss her.

In public.

In Morgantown.

Damn, he was so screwed.

"Okay, you're right. I'm still not sharing." She finished the pastry in three more bites.

He admired her ability to analyze her marriage, take her share of responsibility, and move on. Heck, he admired a lot about her, especially her willingness to let him in.

"You're not bitter." He only realized he'd spoken aloud when she looked up at him.

"There's no point, is there? It was a stupid thing to do. I learned a lesson, and I've moved on to better things."

"Now you sound like me."

She placed a hand over her heart and fluttered her eyelashes at him. "If only I could aspire to your lofty heights of self-analysis and detachment."

He finished his coffee. The thing was, he wasn't feeling detached. The ranch and the town and the people surrounding him pulled something out of him he'd tried to forget.

Family.

He pushed back his chair and stood up. "Let's get some gas on the way back."

"Sure." She rose as well and put her cap back over her fair hair. "Ruth wanted some flour, so we can pop into Maureen's as well."

"How about you do the popping, and I take the truck to get gas? You can meet me down there."

Nodding, she tossed him her keys and set off back along the sidewalk. Chase watched her go and then went back to the truck. It took him awhile to coax the engine back to life, which wasn't surprising seeing as he estimated the piece of shit was about fifteen years old and starting to rust.

The gas station had four pumps, which was an improvement on the original two, and stood where the old town blacksmith had once operated. Chase killed the engine and hopped out of the truck.

"TC?"

He turned to see another familiar face and held out his hand. "Hey, Ted. Have you taken the place over from your dad?"

"We're currently sharing the job." Ted grinned. "He takes all the profits, and I do all the work. How're you doing? I heard you were visiting."

He'd been to school with Ted Baker, and Ted hadn't changed a bit. The same brown hair, dark eyes, and easy smile. The Bakers had been in Morgantown for almost as long as Chase's family, having once owned the blacksmith shop and converted it to a gas station when times changed.

"I'm here for a few weeks, just helping Ruth set things straight for the future."

"I imagine she's hoping one of you will come back full-time and take on the running of the place."

"She probably is, but it won't be me."

"Shame. You were always the least crazy brother." Ted winked. "How are Blue and the twins doing these days?"

"Fine. I'm trying to get them all here for a family meeting, so don't be surprised if you see a whole load of Morgans around town."

"Nate Turner's the sheriff now, and he knows your brothers pretty well. I'd better warn him what's coming."

"You do that." Chase nodded as he got ready to pump the gas. Ted turned toward the shop and then paused.

"Some of us get together on Thursday nights at the Red Dragon on the corner of Main and First. You'd be more than welcome to join us."

"That's very kind of you."

"There's not many of us old-timers left. We like to drink beer and complain about the commercialization of our town and all the money we're raking in from the tourists."

"Sounds like fun." Chase completed the gas fill-up and joined Ted as he walked back to the small shack. "If I have time I'll certainly come and buy you all a beer."

Moving into the small store, Chase picked up some gum from one of the racks, but couldn't see what he really wanted. Sighing, he returned to Ted, who was acting as cashier; Chase paid for his gas and the gum.

"Anything else you need?" Ted asked as he processed the transaction.

"Nope, I'm good."

Chapter Nine

Chase went back out to the truck and found January already sitting in the driver's seat. She smiled as he got in.

"Thanks for doing that. How much do I owe you?"

"Nothing."

She went still and turned to him. "How much, Chase?"

"You've been driving me around all week. Let me at least pay for a tank of gas."

"I don't like being beholden to anyone."

"Beholden? What century are we in? Let me pay for this for the reasons stated. I swear I won't expect extra sexual favors in return. In fact, we'll have to restrict all such activities until I get to the city."

"Too scared to ask at the gas station as well?"

To his relief she was smiling at him again.

"I know Ted Baker."

"You know everyone here."

"And I don't want them to know everything about me."

She started the truck, and they moved off, following Main Street down to the junction with Morgan Road.

"Let's take the alternate route and go up to the ghost town." He glanced over at her. "Unless you have other plans for today?"

"No, I'm good." She put her sunglasses on as they turned onto the unpaved road that led to the main gate of the ranch.

As she drove, the bleakness of the landscape continued to capture Chase's attention. It was all extremes. Bright green patches of grass, barren rocky heights, and over it all a cloudless blue sky with just a hint of frost buried within its depths. It made him take deep, slow breaths and actually appreciate the air he was inhaling. He'd been at the ranch for two weeks already, and to his surprise he was in no rush to leave.

He got out to open the gate and closed it behind them. "Ruth's not running cattle in this part of the ranch, is she?" he asked. "The electric fence doesn't seem to be working."

"There aren't any cows on this side, but I'll tell Roy. It's supposed to be on."

"I'll tell him. He wants to see me this evening to share his plan for the pigs in more detail."

She grinned at him. "Lucky you, although, it is a good idea. Everyone loves bacon."

Chase put his sunglasses back on and considered the harsh terrain. "Take a right when you reach the top of this ridge. There used to be a pile of stones there marking the town boundary."

"There still is, although it's hard to see the sides of the road." She sighed. "It's amazing how fast things go back to dust."

"Which is where you come in."

"I try to preserve what I can. Sometimes, when you see what's left, it's difficult to believe the former size of some of these old gold-rush towns." She started coughing as the road grew bumpier and the truck wheels disturbed the dried mud and dust rose high in the air. She rolled up her window. Chase did the same.

"I always forget how barren it is up here." He squinted through the dust.

"Well, the miners cut down every single tree they could find and basically deforested this whole area. Not a lot has grown back. Mainly because all the topsoil was blown away."

"The Californian dust bowl." Chase shook his head. "At one time this place was covered with trees. In his journal my great-great-grandfather even mentions there being some giant sequoias around here. I guess they got chopped down pretty fast. We humans do terrible things to this planet."

"Now you sound like my mother."

"Well, she has a point. That's one of the main things we've been investing in over the past five years. Green companies."

"That's cool."

Chase shifted in his seat. "Apart from the last couple of deals that my partners nixed. They couldn't get their heads around the idea that a big oil company would be interested in developing anything for the environment."

January didn't reply, and Chase felt compelled to continue. "But some of these corporations are so desperate to improve their images that they're willing to try anything. I don't see why a smaller green company shouldn't take their money and run with it if the outcome will be favorable to the growth of their business and the environment."

"So that's why you fell out with them?"

"Yeah," he said gloomily. "That about sums it up."

"I suppose it comes down to your core belief system, doesn't it?" She flicked a glance his way. "And whether you can live with the decisions you make. Wasn't it Machiavelli who said the ends justify the means?"

"So I'm Machiavellian, am I?" Chase stared out of the window. "He said a lot of shit. Most of it bad."

"If your conscience is clear, then I wouldn't worry about it. You just can't expect everyone to have the same reaction."

"These guys are my best friends. We all had the same vision for the company."

"And your vision has changed." She hesitated. "If it's affecting your friendship, maybe it's time to rethink your business ties with them."

"And keep everything separate?" He sighed. "I'm good at that."

"You could set up a new company with more like-minded associates who wouldn't feel compromised by your ability to make money."

"I've been asked to join other venture capital firms in the valley many times, but most of those guys are *sharks*."

"Then, you've got a lot to think about, haven't you? This break might help you come to a decision about how you want your future to be."

He turned to study her profile. "Go on, say it."

"Say what?"

"What you think I should do."

"It's not my place to tell you what to do, Chase. I'm just giving you the opportunity to share your thoughts." He snorted, and she grinned at him. "*What?* I'm serious. This is how we did it at home. We discussed everything, but the ultimate decision wasn't ours. You're a big boy. You know what you want."

"I thought I did. I was furious with those two for letting me down, and for not understanding that I was simply trying to look out for our best financial interests. I fully intended to tell them to shove it. Now, I'm not so sure."

He caught her smiling out of the corner of his eye. "Hell, you want me to eat humble pie and make nice with my buddies."

"Only if that's what you *want* to do."

"You're infuriating," he grumbled. "You make me think and then back away smiling."

"You're welcome."

He shook his head and turned to watch the view. The road had narrowed, and high banks of white chalky-looking rock surrounded them as the truck continued to throw up dirt.

"If this road wasn't so unnaturally straight, you'd never know that it was man-made," Chase marveled. "It looks like it goes nowhere."

"Which is good because Ruth says a lot of the people who come looking for it get nervous and turn around." January shivered. "I'm not surprised. It's so desolate out here."

"Even worse when the sun goes down," Chase added. "We begged my dad for the chance to spend the night out here when we were kids, and when we finally did I hated every second of it. If my dad hadn't been with us, I think I would've run all the way back to the ranch by myself."

Chase remembered being in his sleeping bag, one hand clenched into the fabric of his father's shirt just to make sure he didn't move away. Eventually, his dad had scooped them all up and made one big bed, and everyone had finally gotten to sleep.

"You stayed out here at night? I don't think I could do that. There's something about the stillness of this place that gives me the creeps."

Chase shook off the memories and peered ahead. Even in the daylight it was hard to see anything. The high rock and clay walls blocked out the sun, and the chalky surface of the road appeared endless.

"The twins came out here by themselves once, but they were always the wildest of the bunch."

"Still are, from what Ruth says."

"She's talked about them?"

"She talks about all of you." January reached over and

patted his knee. "But don't worry, you are definitely her favorite. I don't think the others regularly wine and dine her in the city like you do."

He shrugged. "I wanted to see her. I just didn't want to see her here at the ranch." He glanced at the odometer. "The old town is about a mile from here."

"Got it. I'm always bracing myself for the day when it's all gone, you know? Like if there were an earthquake or a mudslide, and it all collapsed into dust." She glanced across at him. "Did you know that the historical society is looking at ways to preserve this place?"

"What historical society?"

"The Morgantown one. They pay part of my salary."

"I didn't know there was a society. This place is on private land."

"They know that, but they're still interested in talking to you about how the community as a whole can stop Morgansville from disappearing."

"Why?"

"Because a lot of the families who still live around here have roots in this town," she said patiently. "They want their children to know where they came from."

He kept his attention on the narrow strip of road while he thought about what she'd just told him.

"I don't get it."

"That the town wants to preserve their heritage?"

"It's in the past. The fact that it was abandoned means that it failed to provide for the townsfolk. They'd be better off concentrating on making Morgantown look better."

"They do. Who do you think redid the raised walkways and hitching posts and renovated the old bank?" She slowed down to approach a dip in the road. "And why are you so against this? From what I can tell, they're just asking for your permission to come on Morgan land and assess the situation. They aren't asking you to help out or to fund the project."

"Yet," he muttered.

"Just because you live in a world where everyone is after your money, don't assume the people here are that way, too."

"Everyone wants something, January."

She didn't reply, her attention fixed on the road, which was getting bumpier by the second. The sun had disappeared behind the clouds, and the sky was now the same pallid color as the road surface, making it hard to tell what was what.

"It's probably better to come on horseback than in a truck." He looked behind them. "Stirs up less dust, and the horse can find the best path through."

"We're almost here, now."

He held on as the truck slowly came to a stop where the road widened.

January killed the engine and opened the door. Her truck was covered in white dust, obscuring the patchy green paint. "I'm not sure how much you remember about the town but this is where the livery stable and cattle were kept."

Chase got out of the other side of the truck and stood there, his head raised to the gloomy sky. He'd rolled up the sleeves of his striped shirt and left the top two buttons open. Silence enclosed them like a living, breathing thing.

Chase shivered. "It's cold. I'd forgotten that it's higher here than at the ranch."

January went to the back of her truck. "I have some fleeces. One of them should fit you."

"Thanks." He walked over to her, rolling down his sleeves and stamping his booted feet. "There aren't even any birds."

"Probably because of the lack of trees. It's the quietest place I've ever been."

"Full of ghosts, though."

She paused to stare at him. "You think this place is haunted?"

"I know it is." He pulled on the fleece, put his Stetson back on his head, and shoved his hands in his jeans pockets.

"I can't quite believe you said that. You are probably the most analytical man I've ever met."

He shrugged his broad shoulders. "I'm also a Morgan. Maybe I see things because this place once meant something to my family." He looked beyond her to the faint outlines of the buildings beyond. "I was a kid when I saw the ghosts. I've probably grown out of it by now."

She took his hand. "Do you remember much about the layout of the place or do you want me to give you a tour of what's left?"

"Go ahead and show me what's here. You probably know more about it than I do."

"I doubt it." She pointed at a ramshackle timber building. "That's all that's left of the livery stable your family founded." They walked up to the lonely structure, which had a definite lean to one side. "Can you make out the remains of the sign?" January said. "It says Morgan's L . . ."

He whistled softly. "Yeah. I never realized that was here. I'll have to take some pictures."

"I have detailed pictures of all the remaining buildings on film and digital. I'll show you when we get back. I've been trying to match up the present-day structures with the old photos. It's really fascinating."

"I bet." He walked away from her and looked up at the faded red paint of the sign. There was something in his eyes that made January stay quiet. She hadn't expected him to care about what he was seeing for probably the millionth time, but the place obviously meant *something* to him. . . . Hope stirred in her chest.

She gestured at the empty space behind the building. "There's not a lot left of the fencing and the rest of the stables, but if you look carefully, you can see the potholes where the fence posts were set. I've found a couple of horseshoes and nails buried in the dust."

"I had some of those in my collection as well," Chase said absently, his attention moving down the street. "There's not much left around this end of the town, is there?"

"I don't think there was much here anyway. The stables and the livery took up a lot of land—although, I think there was a hotel right next door called The Liberty Bell. Your family owned that, too—as well as a few of the saloons and brothels. That's how they made the money to buy the ranch."

He nodded. "The ranch was originally called The Roll of the Dice Ranch, seeing as legend had it that my great-great-grandfather won enough on the turn of a card to buy the land."

"I love that story. Although technically it should've been the turn of the card ranch, right?"

"I suppose so. Everyone calls it Morgan Ranch now, which is a lot easier."

Chase started walking slowly down what had once been the main street of the town. As they passed each boarded-up structure, January kept up a running commentary.

"Main store, barbershop, preacher's house, chapel, possibly a cemetery . . ."

"Hard to tell from the outside what's what."

"I only know because I've seen photographs of this place in its heyday. You wouldn't believe how many people lived here. There were ten hotels, around thirty saloons, and fifteen brothels."

"Sounds like Vegas."

"Probably was." January shook her head. "Can you imagine it?"

"Yeah." He turned a slow circle, his hands in his pockets. "I used to dream about this place when I was a kid, and I'd ask everyone older than me endless questions about it. I was probably a complete pain in the ass." His faint smile died. "I assume everything's boarded up for safety reasons."

"Most of it." She reached for his hand. "Come and see this."

Chase let January lead him farther down the street. The remaining buildings looked like they'd just been dropped out of the sky and landed all higgledy-piggledy in the barren dust. There were no longer any *connections*—no walkways, no gardens or trees. It offended his sense of order. He'd visited Stonehenge once in England and had gotten the same sense that what had made the place work had somehow been lost over time.

January drew him closer to the largest structure left in the row and went around to the back of it.

"Come on."

He ducked under the tape and through the gap left by two misaligned boards and stepped into a largish space lit by two large sash windows facing the front.

"This used to be the Morgan home before your family moved down permanently to the ranch." January stroked a hand over the door frame.

Chase walked farther into the room. "That's right. I've been here before. This is where my dad brought us to spend the night. He said it was still our house so we weren't trespassing." He went over to the window frame and crouched down at floor level, the old pine boards creaking under his weight. "See?"

January kneeled beside him and bent to look at his pointing finger. "TCM 1996."

He swallowed hard and touched the marks he'd carved in the wooden frame with his penknife, remembering how scared he'd been that night, and how his dad had made everything right.

"It was something of a family tradition." He pointed out some more initials. "Here's my dad and my grandfather, and my great-grandfather."

"Wow." January whipped out her phone and took pictures. "I never knew these were here."

"That was the year everything went to shit." Chase rose slowly to his feet and studied the scraps of wallpaper still clinging to the walls. "We didn't come back here after that."

January moved in close and wrapped her arms around his waist. For a long moment he simply rested his chin on the top of her head and breathed through the memories. Outside, the wind picked up and prowled down the street, making the building shudder and moan like a live thing.

With a self-conscious laugh, Chase stepped out of January's embrace. "Damn, no wonder I was scared as a kid. This place is eerie even now. Is there anything else to see?"

She looked at him, and he stepped in close again to kiss her. She went up on tiptoe to kiss him back, her hand curving around his neck to hold her steady, although he would've caught her if she'd fallen.

He'd never let her fall.

Without speaking, she led him out of the Morgan house and back into the street, taking his hand in hers as they strolled along. Sunlight broke through the cloud cover, sending slanted bright shards of yellow and white down to the ground, making the whole place look a little friendlier.

"The Catholic church was here, and this was the Morgansville bank," January said. "If you look in through the window, you can still see the original vault set in the wall at the back."

Chase squinted through the broken window. "I'm amazed that's still here. I thought the townsfolk plundered this place of almost everything to start the new town farther down the valley."

"This would probably have been too heavy to move even if they'd managed to dynamite it out. The only other building left past here is the original stamp mill."

"That was a pretty substantial building back in the day," Chase said, and they tramped up the slight rise toward it. "It was even remodeled a couple of times to process the gold and silver more efficiently. But, eventually, I suppose it got too expensive to extract the ore from the ground, and the miners moved on to easier pickings."

"That's what it looks like. What I can't understand is why everyone decided to abandon the town at the same time and rebuild it less than ten miles away." January was frowning, which made Chase want to smile. "If they thought there was no future for them all here, then why stay so close?"

A vague memory surfaced in Chase's mind. "I'm sure my great-great-grandfather says something about that in his diary. I can't remember exactly what it was. . . ."

"We're definitely going up in that attic when we get back," January said firmly. "I need to see that diary." She turned to Chase, her face lit up. "Just imagine, I could be the first person to solve the mystery of Morgansville."

He had to smile at her. "Then I'd better find a ladder."

She jumped up and kissed him on the nose. His hands closed around her waist as he slanted his mouth over her cold lips, warming her from the inside. With a sigh, she wrapped herself around him and held on as he deepened the kiss.

A door banged somewhere, reminding him that it was

going to get dark, and he reluctantly put her back on her feet.

"We'd better go."

"Sure." Her smile was warm and so sexy he began to entertain fantasies of having sex in a truck for the first time since he was a teenager—until he remembered his calculations about protection. He wasn't wasting the opportunity for a long session of lovemaking in his bed on a quick and dirty fumble in the truck. Although he'd much rather do both. . . .

"What are you thinking about?" January asked him.

"You don't want to know." He took her hand and marched back down the main street toward the truck.

"You looked like you were doing math in your head again."

"I was." He kept walking. "And the results weren't pretty."

"Are you sure? Because for a moment there you looked like you were going to let me have my way with you in the truck."

He stopped and stared down at her. "I decided it wasn't the best use of our available resources."

"Oh, so you won't be interested in what I bought at the store when Maureen was out back." She took his hand and placed it over the back pocket of her jeans where he could feel the unmistakable outline of a small box.

"Thank you, God." He breathed out the words.

"What about thanking me? I—"

"Oh, I'll thank you all right."

He stopped her from talking by picking her up and kissing her as he walked backward toward the truck. "Passenger side." He placed her carefully on her feet and got in, unzipping his fleece and unbuckling his belt with indecent haste. "Come here."

She got in and closed the door behind her, her expression amused as he manhandled her into his lap. "No foreplay?"

"I was thinking more basic than that. Minimum exposed body parts and fast."

She kissed his cold nose. "You're such a charmer. How can I resist you when you talk to me like that?"

He arched his hips, bringing the hard bulge in his jeans against her, and she gave a little whimper and a squirm that made him want to groan.

"Okay, you've convinced me." She unzipped her fly, kicked off one boot, and he helped her take off half of her jeans while they both wrestled to shove his jeans and underwear down.

He covered himself, and then she was pressing down over him, taking him inside her and sighing his name.

Yeah, it was basic all right and dirty and sexy and . . . She came hard, and he joined her, his mouth fused to hers and their bodies locked together with pleasure. He didn't want to move.

With one last kiss, she eased away from him, and then they spent a few moments untangling themselves and retrieving various bits of clothing without getting out of the truck. Eventually, they were both decent, and January was in the driver's seat again. She turned the key, and the engine coughed and died.

With a muted growl, she tried again, and this time the engine caught and she let out her breath. "One day I'm not going to be so lucky. I'll have to take up Ted's offer to have a look at the engine for me."

"Ted Baker at the gas station?"

"Yes. He's a nice guy." She reversed the truck and turned back toward the single-track road. "He said he'd charge me the local rate."

For a moment, Chase wished he could fix the thing for her, but his strengths didn't lie in getting his hands dirty.

"We could call a certified mechanic."

"You could. I can't afford it." She darted him a severe

look. "And don't offer to pay for it, okay? I don't want your money."

"Got it." Chase nodded.

Regardless of what she thought, when he finally left the ranch he was going to leave his new truck behind. If hers fell apart, he'd make damn sure she knew she was welcome to use it.

The journey back to the main road seemed just as long as the outward one and gave him plenty of time to think. The ghost town had affected him far more than he'd anticipated. Seeing the Morgan house and livery had reminded him of his roots and the sheer tenacity of his forebears.

When they reached the turnoff, his cell came to life, and he squinted down at it. Two texts and two calls from Matt. With a frown, he punched in his partner's number.

"Matt, what's up?"

"That's what I was going to ask you. Daizee says you're getting rid of your rental car. Are you coming back early?"

"No."

"Really?"

"I've decided to stay at the ranch a while longer."

Silence hissed over the network. "But you're okay?"

"I'm fine."

"Are you sure?" There was real concern in his friend's voice.

"What's the problem, Matt? I thought you'd be pleased that I've taken your advice and stayed out of your hair." Chase couldn't quite deny the satisfaction he got from saying that. "There's a lot to sort out down here. Have you or Jake heard back from Hendersons, by the way?"

"Oh, yeah, Jake said to tell you one of their guys will be contacting you shortly."

"Good. Anything else?"

There was another pause. "Aren't you going to ask about the company? There are a couple of things—"

"I'm sure you've got it all in hand. Later, Matt." Chase put his cell away in his pocket and smiled.

"You enjoyed that." January turned the wheel to avoid another lump of fallen rock in the road.

"Yeah, I kind of did. Maybe when I'm not there making all the big decisions it will make them think about how much responsibility they want for the business. It's easy for them to say they want me to slow down, but harder when they have to pick up the slack."

"Maybe they'll thrive."

He shrugged. "I'm okay with that. As you said, we have to work out whether we can still be friends *and* business partners. And this is a great opportunity for them to find out what they want without my telling them." He raised an eyebrow. "Why are you smiling like that?"

"Because I think you're working it out. And I'm proud of you."

He found himself smiling back at her. "For a woman who never offers an opinion, you sure take a lot of credit."

She winked and returned her attention to the road. Chase sat back and for the first time in a long while simply enjoyed the ride.

Chapter Ten

"I've got the ladder," Chase announced as he joined January on the upstairs landing of the ranch house. "Ruth said we can bring down anything we want and that she *thinks* my great-granddad's stuff is in the far left corner."

"Cool!" January waited as he propped the ladder against the edge of the entrance to the attic and gingerly mounted the steps to push open the door, which folded back with a loud *creak*. She handed him a large flashlight and a lantern, which he set on the upper floor.

"Are you going in?" January asked. "Ruth said there's room up there to walk around."

"She's right. There is." He was leaning into the space now, the light dancing around above him in the blackness. "It's also hot as hell up here."

She admired his long, denim-clad legs as he climbed into the attic and followed him up, accepting his helping hand to scramble in through the hatch.

"Wow, it's so well organized up here." She turned to Chase, who was fiddling around with the lantern. "Let me guess, when you were a kid you had a few spare moments and came up here to make things right."

"Actually, I had to do it as a punishment."

"You got into trouble?" She sat down, her shoulder and thigh tight against his.

"Yeah. Blue and I decided to have a fight in the house, and we broke some of Ruth's best china. She sent us both up here to work off our debt. Blue made such a hash of everything—probably deliberately—that I sent him back down and got on with it myself."

January stared out at the neatly stacked boxes and the well-regulated rows of old furniture, trunks, and various outdated bits of domesticity. "So you probably remember exactly where everything is."

"Not all of it. I haven't been up here for about twenty years. Ruth's added a whole 'nother layer of crap to the pile and moved things around."

"How dare she do that? Upsetting all your system in her own house." January pushed back the sleeves of her long T-shirt. "Where shall we start?"

He pointed at the far back corner of the space. "The oldest stuff used to be over there."

Despite the fact that the ceiling height was adequate, the construction of the house made it almost impossible for Chase to stand upright, so he had to duck between the beams. January followed him, remembering to keep her head down. She sneezed as dust floated up from the floorboards.

"Hold up." Chase went and fiddled around with a small circular window set in the outside wall. "Let's get some airflow in here."

Coming up behind him she checked the frame of the window. "This probably came from the Sears catalog. Did you know that a lot of these houses were bought in pieces like a kit and transported all the way from the East Coast?"

The window opened with a *screech*, and Chase turned to smile at her. "I know my family rebuilt this place several times when they had more money coming in. Of course sometimes they regretted it when times got tough."

"Just like Silicon Valley. Boom or bust." January flapped a hand in front of her face. "I'm just glad it survived. So many of these places burn down."

"That's why the final version used a lot of slate and stone." Chase dusted off his fingers on his handkerchief and stowed it back in his pocket. "Expensive stuff back in the day, but well worth it."

January walked past him, her gaze fixed on an old leather steamer trunk.

"You've got a good eye. I think that's one of the places Ruth said she'd stored the family stuff."

The battered leather trunk was huge and propped up on its side. It took both of them to wrestle it to the floor. The locks were obviously broken, and two straps held the sides together. January had to let Chase deal with them because her fingers just weren't strong enough.

"Here you go." He hesitated. "It looks like Ruth added a whole ton of our baby stuff on top."

January sat cross-legged on the floor and studied the pile of photograph albums, letters, and other brown envelopes adorned with Ruth's distinctive handwriting. She was dying to delve into everything, but sensed that Chase was already unsettled by what they'd found. "Let's take this layer out and see what's underneath."

She picked up a pile of the envelopes, and a couple of photos slipped out, landing on her thigh. She couldn't help but look at them. The first picture showed a man who looked remarkably like Chase sitting on a horse with a small boy set in front of him.

Chase cleared his throat and hunkered down next to her. "That's my dad and me."

"He looks a lot like you."

"Yeah."

The second picture was of a family group. Chase's father was kneeling on the ground, his arms around his four sons, and they were all grinning. A little to the right stood a tall woman with a baby in her arms. She wasn't smiling, and her gaze wasn't on her family but looking outward toward the mountains.

January handed Chase the picture. "That's your mom? She was very pretty."

He stared down at the photo without speaking, his thumb smoothing over all the faces. January kept her mouth shut as a myriad of emotions flooded his face. After a long moment he nodded.

"You can see it there, can't you? She didn't want to be at the ranch. She said it was the loneliest place in the world." He shook his head. "I didn't understand then because to me the ranch was close to being perfect. But she missed her friends, her family, and the conveniences of life in the city."

He handed the picture back to January. "I tried so hard to make her happy, but nothing seemed to work."

"You were just a kid."

"I know, and I also know I wasn't personally responsible for her happiness, but I still felt I'd let her down in some way. That nothing I ever did was good enough." He rubbed a hand over his unshaven jaw. "And when she disappeared with the baby after fighting with my dad . . ." Chase's smile was crooked. "That put her beyond my reach, and I could *never* make anything up to her again. My dad lost it big-time and insisted he'd killed her. I thought I was going to lose him as well."

January continued to sit tight as the words poured out of Chase. "But your father wasn't convicted, was he?"

Chase glanced at her. "There wasn't sufficient evidence

to convict him. The sheriff came out to the ranch. By the time he and his deputy arrived, my mom and my sister were gone, and they found my dad with blood all over his shirt, raving about killing them. They took him in and held him for seventy-two hours, but apparently under questioning his story kept changing and, as there were no bodies . . ." Chase grimaced. "They let him go and just followed up on him occasionally as they continued to search for my mother."

"Did they ever find her?"

"Not as far as I know." Chase sighed. "I always wondered whether the sheriff, who was an old friend of the family, did his job properly that night. But they didn't have tools like blood or DNA testing to help them back in the day, so there wasn't any real evidence to go on."

Chase drew one knee up close to his chest and wrapped his arm around it. "My dad went to pieces and started drinking, and our whole world was suddenly a mess. And you can imagine the shit storm the story created around here. Even back then there were media outlets whose representatives parked at the gates of the ranch, TV cameras . . ." He shook his head. "It was a fricking circus."

"I bet." January slid the two photos back into the envelope and closed the flap. She wanted to crawl over to Chase and wrap her arms around him, but she didn't know how he'd react.

"Sorry for the informational dump." Chase found one of his professional-charmer smiles somewhere, which kind of hurt her. "I haven't talked about that for years. I suppose that's why I've avoided coming here. Too many bad memories."

"I totally understand." January took out some photo albums and placed them carefully on the floor. "Let's keep going and see if we can find your great-great-grandfather's journal."

Chase nodded as January kept taking stuff out of the trunk. His hands were still shaking. Seeing his mother's face after all those years had been even worse a shock than he'd expected. Part of him remained tense, waiting for January to start up her questions again—questions he didn't want or didn't know the answers to—but she didn't say anything. All her comments were directed at the contents of the trunk beneath the photos and letters that captured his memories.

Slowly, he started to relax and help her, identifying his grandfather's army paraphernalia and the memorabilia from his precarious journey across Europe with the Allied forces after the D-Day landings. With Chase's permission, January set the letters his grandfather had written home to one side for her to read later.

She knelt by the side of the deep box, reaching farther down each time. He smelled the musty scent of the old satin lining of the box, combined with a hint of tobacco and stale perfume.

"Oh my gosh, is this it?" She reverently took out a large leather-bound book and inspected the title. "William Owen Morgan."

"The first. Yeah, that's him."

January sighed and hugged the book close to her chest. "Thank you, Chase, for your exceptional organizational skills. I can't wait to read this."

"You're welcome." He went to smile at her and then froze, his gaze fixed on something creeping over her shoulder. "Spider."

She frowned at him and put the book on the floor. "Where?"

He pointed.

She slowly turned her head and screeched, scuttling toward him on her ass, which did nothing but bring the spider closer to him.

"Get it off me!"

"No can do." Chase backed up, hands high in surrender.

January shot to her feet and started to slap herself while dancing up and down on her toes. If he hadn't been so terrified, it would almost have been funny. What wasn't funny was that when she succeeded in getting rid of the spider it flew off to land on his thigh.

His scream was louder and higher than hers as he backpedaled frantically on the floor.

"Stop! You'll fall through the hatch!"

At that moment he wouldn't have cared about a few broken bones if it had gotten him away from the spider. Out of the corner of his eye, he saw January pick something up and advance toward him. He flinched as she used an old broom to sweep the spider off his knee and far away into the blackness of the attic.

She collapsed on the floor beside him, breathing hard, and he wrapped his arms around her. He frowned as she continued to shake.

"You okay?"

She lifted her face to his, and she was laughing. "Oh my God, you really are a wuss about spiders, aren't you?"

"Yes, ma'am." He cupped her cheek. "My hero." Then he bent his head and kissed her. "I mean it."

She kissed him back and crawled into his lap, fitting herself against him as if she belonged there. After a while he relaxed into her and forgot to even look out for the return of the spider. She tucked her head under his chin, and he just held her in his arms while all around them the dust danced in the sunshine and the house creaked and shifted like an old man.

He almost closed his eyes, but the heat was building, and he wanted to get away from the memories.

"Come on." He picked January up and set her on her feet. "If you have everything you need, we can go down."

She went back to the trunk to gather up the letters and the journal and replace everything else inside before closing the lid. He closed the window and then stayed by the hatch in case she disturbed any more spiders. When she was ready he climbed halfway down the ladder and took the journal from her so that she could navigate the steps.

At the bottom of the ladder he caught hold of her by the collar. "Don't disappear on me yet."

She opened her eyes wide at him. "But I want to *read*."

"You can do that when Ruth's around. She's at the church service this morning, so we're all alone."

"And?"

He took her hand and marched her toward his bedroom. "And I have a schedule, remember?"

"What if there's another spider down my pants?"

"Then I reserve the right to run away screaming."

"Again?"

"You'll never let that go, will you?" He drew her into his room, put the letters and journal on his desk and held her pressed against the door as he locked it. "You should've seen that funny little dance you did when you thought it was in your hair." He reached behind her and released her hair from its band just in case. "I think I should search you really thoroughly."

She smiled back at him. "Be my guest."

He took her hand and led her over to his bed, drawing back the covers so that he could lay her on the cool cotton sheets. She lay quietly while he undressed her, lifting her arms at his direction and helping him, but not rushing him along. Which suited him fine. He was in the mood for a slow, thorough appreciation of her lush body.

Removing her bra, he knelt between her spread thighs and slowly kissed his way down her throat to her breasts. She sighed his name as he licked her and then nuzzled her tender flesh with his teeth.

"Nice . . ." she murmured.

Encouraged, he redoubled his efforts, using his hands and his mouth to shape and caress her rounded curves until her nipples were two hard points of need and she squirmed every time he tasted her.

He blew softly on her heated flesh and then slid his hands down her sides to encircle her waist and then lower to the swell of her hips. So different from his more angular shape, so much nicer to touch . . .

"Any spiders so far?"

"Nope." He kissed her stomach and used his teeth to tug gently on her belly ring. "But I've still got a long way to go."

"We should've showered first."

"And risked Ruth's coming back before we were finished?" He hooked his thumbs into the sides of her cotton panties and drew them down her legs. "I had to prioritize."

"You're good at that."

"I'm good at this, too."

His mouth followed his thumbs, kissing and licking at her most sensitive flesh until she arched against his mouth offering him everything. He took everything he could, sliding his fingers and then his tongue deep inside her welcoming, wet warmth and stroking her inside and out until she came for him in long, shuddering waves.

He slowly stripped off his shirt and jeans while she watched him through half-closed eyes and then shucked off his boxers.

"Can I help you with that?"

"Not this time." He covered himself, mentally reviewing his supply line. "This is all for you."

She placed one foot on the mattress, opening herself more fully to his gaze, and it almost all ended right there. He eased forward, taking his time, and watched himself join with her in a slow, sensual slide of need. He stayed still, his gaze fixed on her face as her body accepted him and settled around his hard length.

Bracing himself on one hand, he touched a finger to her lip and then trailed it down her body between her breasts, over her stomach to the juncture of her thighs. Her whole body tightened around him as he flicked his finger slowly back and forth, still holding himself still and deep.

"I can't. . . ."

"Yes, you can, darlin'."

Her head moved restlessly on the pillow, but he kept on teasing and playing with her until she came apart again, gripping his shaft so hard he had to concentrate on staying still and riding out the storm. Only when she'd finished did he allow himself the luxury of rolling his hips and pressing down even deeper as she planted her feet firmly on his ass.

Her fingers tangled in his hair and held him close as he lengthened his stroke. The pleasure grew until he had to let go and just be with her in the center of the inferno they'd created together. Finesse was gone; need was everything as he finally let go and felt her explode along with him, making the ride down twice as exhilarating.

He couldn't move.

Her hand clutched his bicep and his face was buried in the pillow beside her head. He was gasping for air.

Had to move.

With a sigh, he levered himself upright and away from her and then paused to admire her rosy skin. He bent his head to kiss her breast, and she moaned.

"No more."

He smiled against her softness. "What, ever?"

"In the next hour or so. You've worn me out."

"Good." He got out of bed and searched for his boxers. "You just stay put. I'll grab the first shower."

She opened one eye. "That's what this was all about, wasn't it? Getting into the bathroom first and using up all the hot water."

"Busted." Grinning, he turned back to the bed. When had he ever had so much fun with a lover? He scooped her up into his arms and went to the door.

She flailed at his chest. "Chase, I'm naked here."

"Which is perfect for where we're going." He set her on her feet beside the bath and wrestled with the ancient shower until it started spraying out water. "Come on. Let's do the environment a favor."

January sighed. Showering with a large, naked almost-cowboy was far nicer than showering alone. He was washing her hair now, his big hands firm on her scalp, making her purr like one of the barn cats. With his usual attention to detail, he'd soaped the rest of her body quite thoroughly as well.

Seeing as he'd given her his all in bed, the least she could do was resurrect a lifelong fantasy and get down on her knees in the shower and reciprocate. He seemed to like that idea even more than she'd expected until the water cooled off and they draped themselves in fluffy towels for the return to their respective rooms.

He picked her up again, displaying that unholy sexy grin that made her forget his opposition to the ranch and think only of what a wonderful man hid beneath the cold, analytical fact finder.

They were both still laughing when they came out of the

bathroom and ran into Ruth coming up the stairs in her Sunday-best outfit. She stopped to stare at them. Her gaze took in the lack of clothing and other things that January didn't even want to think about.

"Hmmph," Ruth said. "Make sure you don't leave those wet towels lying around. Hang them outside."

"Yes, ma'am," Chase said as she stomped past him.

January hid her face in the crook of his shoulder as he took her through to her bedroom. He set her carefully on her feet.

"What's up?"

"Ruth."

"You should be grateful she didn't see you on the way in. At least you are decently covered in a towel now."

"Thanks, that makes everything so much better."

He took a step back, his smile disappearing. "I should've checked before we left the bathroom. I didn't mean to embarrass you."

She reached for his hand. "You didn't. I loved showering with you."

"Good." He nodded, kissed her fingers, and turned to the door, his towel hanging low on his hips. "We can go and check out the ponds again this afternoon if you want."

"Sure."

January smiled as he closed the door quietly behind himself. God, he was a beautiful man—complicated, but definitely worth the effort.

She wandered over to her closet and selected some fresh clothes as the fragrant smells of Ruth's traditional Sunday roast for the whole ranch drifted up the stairs. She wasn't embarrassed about being caught in Chase's arms. Being with him felt right. She'd only known him for a couple of weeks, but that didn't seem to matter. Ruth had spent the last year telling January about her favorite grandson, so she'd felt comfortable with him immediately.

He was planning on leaving soon and didn't believe the ranch had anything to offer him. Could she handle that? Pulling on a clean T-shirt, January firmly told herself that of course she could—that she'd agreed to his terms of friends with benefits and she didn't regret it.

But what if he and his brothers eventually decided to sell the ranch?

She stopped by the door and considered that unpleasant scenario. All she could do was keep reintroducing Chase to the wonders of his family home and hope that eventually he'd admit that he cared for the place and wanted it to thrive.

After opening the door she remembered to go back and grab her wet towel. Chase had to change his mind . . . didn't he?

Chapter Eleven

Chase let out a relieved sigh as he pulled into the rental car lot in Bridgeport. "I can't wait to get rid of this pile of junk."

"It's not the greatest, is it?" January picked up her backpack and took off her seat belt.

"That's being generous." Chase put his Stetson back on and eyed the small office. "I hope there's someone there."

"Should be." January came to stand beside him. "The town might be small, but thousands of tourists come here for the fishing, and I bet they all need rentals." She glanced up at him as they walked toward the building. "What are you going to do when you've turned in the car? Have you rented something bigger or are you planning on going back to San Francisco and leaving me here?"

Chase pushed open the door, and a bell jangled above his head. "I'm not renting another one, and I'm not going back yet."

The young guy at the desk straightened up and smiled at them. "Hey, what's up?"

"I'm returning my rental. There was no one outside, so I brought the key in to you," Chase said. These days in most of the rental places you could practically drop your keys and run. Obviously not in Bridgeport.

"Cool! Do you have your paperwork?"

"It's in the car."

His smile faltered. "Cool."

Chase sighed. "Do you want me to go get it?"

"That would be super awesome of you, dude."

"I'll get it." January was out the door before he could stop her. While she was gone, Chase patiently answered questions as the employee typed everything into his computer. When January returned he'd just managed to finish everything up.

"It's all been paid for, Mr. Morgan."

"Cool," Chase said not sarcastically at all. "Do you happen to know if there's a car dealership around here?"

"Oh, yeah! You're *that* guy, aren't you? Jose told me to call him when you, like, arrived."

"Jose has my truck?"

"Yeah. I'll call him right now. He's already been around here, like, once."

Chase nodded and went with January back out into the lot. The sun was high overhead, and the asphalt was hot even through his boots. He steered January over to a shaded seating area and typed in a text to Daizee.

Where's my truck?

Should be with you right now.

He heard the rumble well before he saw what was turning in.

Hope you like it. ☺

What the hell did you get me?

F-450 Super Duty King Ranch. Seemed kind of a
match made in heaven. Enjoy.

The huge blue truck rolled to a stop, and a short, older
guy hopped out.

"Mr. Morgan? I have your vehicle."

"So I see." Chase shook Jose's hand and glanced up at
the massive truck with its double set of wheels at the back
and crew cab.

"It's loaded with every option available—reverse
camera, enhanced stereo, six-point seven-liter V8 engine,
towing capability. . . ."

Chase walked around the truck. "And it's blue."

"Blue Jeans blue. Your associate said that she thought
you'd appreciate that."

"She would," Chase murmured.

Jose frowned. "Is everything okay?"

Chase remembered his manners. "It's great. Do you
want my credit card?"

"All ready taken care of, sir. Paid in full." Jose beamed
and handed him two sets of keys. "Would you like me to
go over the specifics of the vehicle with you?"

"Nope. I think I've got it. I've driven something like this
before."

"If you're quite sure . . ." Jose looked a bit doubtful.

"I've got this." Chase tried to sound confident. "Thanks
for helping out, Jose."

"You're welcome, Mr. Morgan. Enjoy your truck." Jose
turned on his heel.

"Do you need a ride?" Chase called after him.

"I'm good."

Jose waved a hand and disappeared around the corner,

leaving Chase still contemplating the truck, which was completely blocking the entrance and exit to the lot. He turned to see January was staring at him.

"What?"

She raised her eyebrows. "You just bought a brand-new truck?"

"So?"

"Outright and sight unseen without entering into any kind of negotiation on the price."

"I needed a truck as soon as possible." He shrugged. "I asked my assistant to get one for me, and here it is."

"That's crazy. You're only going to be at the ranch for a week or two."

"So it's the best use of my time. I didn't want to waste a day haggling over something I don't particularly care about."

She shook her head. "Wow. The rich really are different."

"Why does it matter?"

"I don't suppose it does. It's just that I can't imagine being that careless about money."

"It's not a Ferrari, January. It's just a truck."

She sighed. "You just don't get it, do you?"

"I get that you don't like it. I don't really understand why." He held the passenger door open. "Are you getting in?"

She brushed past him and stepped up the considerable height into the cab. "Thanks."

He shut her door and walked slowly back to the driver's side, mentally estimating the space he had to maneuver the behemoth through without taking out half the car lot. Once inside the cab he spent a short while rearranging everything to his liking before putting on his seat belt.

"Okay. Where next?" He glanced over at January, who was still shaking her head. "Do you know any good places that do lunch and have huge parking lots?"

"There's parking at the far end of town behind the county offices and the library," January said. "I'd try there. We can get some lunch at the pizza place."

"Sounds good." He carefully turned left and followed her directions to the largely empty city parking lot. To his surprise the steering on the truck was much lighter than he'd anticipated. But Bridgeport was a small, old town, and he had no intention of sashaying down Main Street like a huge marauding bear.

"You said you wanted to go to the library, right?"

"I will do, after lunch."

"While I do some shopping. Ruth gave me a list." He patted his shirt pocket. "Is there anything I can get you?"

"I'm good."

"Are you sure? I promise I won't go and buy you a truck." He held her gaze. "You can give me the money to pay up-front for anything, if that helps."

"I suppose it's not your fault that you are disgustingly wealthy." She smiled. "It just takes some getting used to."

"It's just money, January," Chase said gently. "It makes life easier."

"In some ways." She opened the door and got out of the truck, fixing him with a challenging stare. "And, I'm buying lunch, okay?"

He held up his hands. "Sure."

January hurried into the library and nodded at the two librarians on duty, whom she'd met before. The place was almost empty, which suited her fine as she had a lot to check up on and Chase would want to get back to the ranch before the traffic got heavier.

His casual acceptance of his wealth took some getting used to. But she had to admit that he wasn't flashy about it. His reasoning for buying the truck made some kind of sense. . . . She wished she could just call up her assistant and be handed the keys to a brand-new truck.

Chuckling, she went through to the research section of the library, which had been set up in response to all the genealogy inquiries the county received about gold-rush immigrants. She wanted to check out the final set of news articles about Morgansville and see if there were any more hints about the reason for the mass abandonment. If she was honest with herself, she also wanted to read about what had happened to Chase's parents. This seemed a less intrusive way of finding out the facts when it was obviously upsetting for Chase to talk about this part of his life.

That had surprised her. Not that it was obviously painful for him, but that he'd confided in her. Sure, he'd recovered and tried to distract her with his usual charm, but at least he'd let her in a little. She sensed there was a lot more under the surface. Did she want to probe more deeply? Ruth had suggested Chase held things close to his chest and that sharing was good for him. The question was, did January deserve to know all his personal stuff, and if so, what did it mean about the supposed superficiality of their relationship?

January sighed and sank her head into her hands. She already cared about him. She would never have gotten into bed with him if she hadn't. The trouble was, she had no idea how he felt about her. Was he using sex to distract her from inquiring too deeply into his personal life? Was it just another way of keeping her at bay?

She sat up and stared at the blank computer screen. No, he liked being with her. When he was inside her, she could see into his soul. . . .

January groaned quietly, and someone shushed her. Damn it. She was so tangled up with Chase, the ranch, and its future that she might never see things the same way again. Pushing her emotions firmly to one side, she concentrated on scrolling through the newsprint. Whatever happened, her work on the ranch was important. She could at least rely on that.

Chase glanced over at January as they turned off the highway and started to make their way cross-country back to the ranch.

"You okay?"

"I'm good." She offered him a quick smile. "I'm keeping quiet so you can concentrate on driving your new truck."

"It's not that difficult. I just have to remember how long and wide it is at the back when I make a turn."

"Or take out the corner."

"Exactly." He refocused on the road, which was becoming familiar, allowing him to relax more. "Did you find what you wanted at the library?"

"Kind of." She sighed and tucked her blond hair behind her ear. "I was downloading the last of the articles about Morgansville from the newspapers. But there wasn't much there I haven't already seen."

"Hopefully the journal will give you some fresh insights."

"Yeah. I can't wait to get into it." She patted his knee. "Thanks for helping me find it."

"You're welcome." He threaded his fingers through hers and brought her fingers to his mouth to kiss—something he was pretty sure he'd never done before, especially on impulse. "Maybe you'll find that new angle you're looking for."

He released her hand, but she left it sitting on his thigh, which he liked far more than he should have. For a simple, no-strings-attached love affair, he was feeling way too much.

He let that thought sink in, waited for the rush of panic, and felt nothing but warmth and a smile tugging at his lips.

"Damn."

"What's wrong?" She looked up at him, her gray eyes filled with concern.

"Nothing. Sorry, I was just thinking about something."

"And it made you curse?"

"Just problems at work." He smiled, and she removed her hand from his knee.

"It's okay; if you don't want to answer me, you don't have to turn on the fake charm."

He had nothing to say to that, and they completed the journey in silence. By the time they pulled up in front of the ranch, it was getting dark. There was a truck parked alongside the barn that Chase didn't recognize.

"Who's that?" January asked.

"I thought you might know." Chase turned off the engine and got out and so did January. "Maybe it's one of Ruth's church things."

"She didn't mention anything to me this morning before we left." January frowned. "I hope she's okay."

Chase opened the screen door and let January go in front of him. He could hear voices in the kitchen, and, for some reason, his heart rate increased. Stepping into the light, he studied the man sitting opposite Ruth at the kitchen table, who was slowly getting to his feet.

"Well, look who turned up, Chase," Ruth said.

Chase leaned against the door and removed his hat. "BB."

"TC." Chase's brother's eyes were as blue as his and just as direct as Blue nodded an abrupt greeting.

January moved between them and held out her hand. "I'm January Mitchell. It's so nice to meet another of Ruth's grandsons."

Blue's smile was slow in coming as he assessed January and then shook her hand. "Ruth says you've been a great help around here."

Chase took a seat beside Ruth, and Blue sat back down as well.

"I've got some work to finish." January started toward the stairs. She knew all about being diplomatic. "Call me when you start the chores."

Chase watched her go and wished she hadn't. But he could hardly expect her to get involved in this particular family reunion.

"How've you been, Blue?"

"Good."

"Still in the military?"

"Just about." Blue's gaze met his. "I've just been promoted, so I won't be going off to parts unknown anymore." He wrapped his hand around his coffee mug. "That's what I was just telling Ruth. I'm going to be based at the Marine Corps mountain warfare training center just outside Bridgeport for the next year or so before I decide whether to re-up or not."

"That's . . . great."

Silence fell again as Ruth poured Chase some coffee and cut him a piece of January's favorite coffee cake that he knew he would never be able to eat.

"Do you have to live on base?"

"It depends." Blue's gaze fell on Ruth, who was smiling at him. "I'll definitely be around a lot more, so you don't have to worry about the future of the ranch."

"What's that supposed to mean?"

Blue raised an eyebrow. "According to Ruth, you've been planning on getting rid of the place."

"That's not exactly—"

Blue cut him off with a slash of his hand. "We all know

that's what you'd like to do, TC. It's not exactly a secret that you hate the ranch."

"I don't—"

"But Ruth says we all have to agree to sell the ranch. I don't agree."

"Wait a minute." Chase didn't raise his voice. He wasn't going to get into a fight here of all places. "Will you please stop making assumptions about me? You haven't seen me for ten years, haven't bothered to respond to any of my calls or e-mails or *letters*, and now you've decided how things are going to be? When was the last time you came to the ranch or contacted Ruth? You haven't exactly been here for her either."

Blue looked at him for a long moment. "You know why I didn't contact you." He slammed his hand on the table and pushed back his chair. "Nothing's changed."

Chase leaned back in his seat to look up at his brother and a wave of hopelessness engulfed him. "Great attitude, Blue. You're right that nothing's changed. You still don't want to hear a word I have to say."

"You're not getting your way about this, TC. Me and the twins won't let you throw Ruth out of her home."

Blue turned on his heel and marched up the stairs.

Chase cast an irritated look at his grandmother. "Did you have to put it to him like that? I thought we were working together to find a way to keep you here until you died."

Ruth shrugged. "I didn't say you were kicking me out *entirely*."

"Gee. Thanks," Chase muttered. "How long is he staying?"

"For as long as he wants." Ruth reached out and patted Chase's clenched fist. "You will try to be nice to him, won't you?"

"*Me?* He's the one with the problem. He barely let me speak."

"He'll listen. He's not as impetuous as he used to be."

"If he survived ten years in the Marines he's got a lot more going for him than that, and he's a lot more dangerous." Chase sighed. "I'll try to talk to him, but don't hold your breath."

Chase rose from his seat and went toward the stairs. "I'd better get on with the chores. I'll just go and change. Tell January I've got them covered. I need something to do after sitting in that truck all afternoon."

January was in the bathroom, so he took a quick shower in the small bathroom beside the mudroom and let himself out into the yard. It was quiet outside apart from the fricking chickens and the odd whine from one of the dogs gathered to escort him down to the barn.

Blue hadn't changed much. His face was harder, and his muscled body was that of a man who enjoyed working out or had to keep fit for a living. *Formidable* was the word that came to mind, but then he'd been like that as a child. Chase entered the barn and, despite the row kicked up by the chickens, started feeding the dogs and then checked the horses. Stroking Nolly and giving him a carrot and an apple Chase had filched from the kitchen helped him regain his sense of calm.

It even gave him the energy to face the evil fowl that had started sidling into the barn looking for him. He measured out their feed, cursing under his breath.

"Still hate the chickens, then?"

Chase turned to see Blue leaning against the fence rail. He'd changed into a ratty pair of jeans and a faded blue T-shirt with the word *Marines* stretched tight over his broad chest.

Chase shrugged. "Yup, still hate them. I usually leave them to January. They love her."

"I can feed them."

"It's okay. I've got it." Chase stepped around his brother and went toward the chicken coop where they attempted to collect the eggs and contain the unruly brood for the night. When he'd gotten as many as he could coerce inside the wire, he scattered more food and quickly retreated, shutting the door behind him.

When Chase returned to the barn, Blue was still there, putting away the measuring scoops and brushing down the countertop.

"Thanks." Chase took off his thick gloves.

Blue took an audible breath and stepped forward. "Look, I acted like an ass." He shook his head. "Seeing you coming into that kitchen, looking just like Dad? It just threw me for a good one."

Chase didn't say anything, but he didn't move away.

"I lost my temper," Blue continued. "When I came back downstairs, Ruth told me I'd gotten it all wrong." He shoved his hand through his military-short hair. "I know you wouldn't do anything to hurt Ruth. You love her as much as I do." He met Chase's gaze full-on. "That was unworthy of me."

Maybe Chase's hotheaded younger brother really *had* grown up.

Chase nodded. "I'm going to be here for at least a couple more weeks. I'd like to show you my calculations for the ranch's future. Will you at least let me do that?"

"My new position doesn't start for a month. I'll be here." Blue moved away to the door. "If that's okay with you."

"It's Ruth's house. It's not for me to decide."

"She said I should ask you."

"Then you're good. One more thing," Chase said, and Blue looked back over his shoulder. "Can you dispense with the TC? I won't call you BB if you try to remember to call me Chase."

"I'll try." Blue turned toward the house.

After a moment, Chase switched off the outside lights in the barn and followed Blue, aware of a knot of tension slowly easing in his gut. It might not be much, but at least they'd avoided an all-out fight. Perhaps Blue wasn't the only Morgan brother who had finally grown up.

Chapter Twelve

January glanced over at Blue as he efficiently mucked out Nolly's stall and dumped a load of soiled hay in the barrow. He was slightly shorter and broader than Chase and had more obvious muscle, which, seeing as he was a marine, made sense. His eyes were blue but far colder than his brother's and didn't make her feel very comfortable. But then she hadn't liked the way he'd looked at Chase last night, so she might already be prejudiced against him.

"Thanks for helping out," she said.

"You're welcome. I like to keep busy." Blue forked up another load of flattened hay. "Ruth said that if I want to ride I should take Messi. Do you know which horse that is?"

She pointed at the stall opposite. "He's the paint over there. Miguel's away this week, so he'll be pleased if Messi gets some exercise."

"Messi's a funny name for a horse."

January chuckled. "He's named after Lionel Messi, the soccer player. Miguel's Argentinian."

"Makes sense. I haven't ridden for a while. I used to

love it when I was a kid." Blue picked up the handles of the barrow. "I'll just dump this."

January kept him company as he walked around the barn. Chase had gone out early in his truck to see Roy and hadn't yet returned.

"Ruth said you'll be stationed near Bridgeport for a while."

"Yeah." He glanced at her as he emptied the wheelbarrow. "I'll be around a lot more, so you don't need to worry about my asshole of an older brother selling the place out from under you and Ruth."

"I don't think he's planning on doing that."

"Then you don't know him very well. When he gets the bit between his teeth, he's impossible to stop."

"Funny, he said the same thing about you."

Blue stopped walking and faced her, his expression serious. "Look, I'm on your side. I want to save this place. It's my family home. TC—I mean, Chase wants to get rid of it because it makes him feel guilty."

"Guilty about what?"

"What he did." Blue shrugged. "It's ancient history. You should ask him about it."

"I have." She picked up her bucket and took it back into the barn. "He was just a kid like you were. How come everything was his fault?"

"It's not that simple. He was the oldest—"

"He was *twelve* when your mother died or disappeared or whatever happened. He wasn't an adult, and he wasn't ultimately responsible for the decisions the adults around him made."

Blue let out his breath. "He was involved in those decisions. He made his choices, and what he did split our family apart." He shook his head. "I didn't expect you of all people to defend him."

"Why shouldn't I when no one else will?" She held Blue's gaze. "Your brother is a good man. Give him a chance."

"I've already promised that I'll listen to what he has to say. But I know how it will go. He'll try to get 'round me with logic and spreadsheets and projections until I end up agreeing with him just to make him shut up."

"He certainly likes to plan stuff out. Have you ever wondered why?"

Blue raised his eyebrows. "Nope."

"Then maybe you should." She smiled at him. "If you want to go out riding, ask Chase. We were planning on going up to see the new calves after lunch. I'm sure you'd be more than welcome to join us."

She went back up to the house and straight up the stairs to the bathroom to wash the stink of the stalls away. Despite the fact that she really should be making friends with Blue because he wanted to keep the ranch, she'd ended up defending Chase. What exactly was he supposed to have done to ruin his entire family? It wasn't as if she could just come right out and ask him. Blue might think his brother lived and died by his spreadsheets, but January had already discovered that those spreadsheets were just an attempt to impose order on his world and that underneath it Chase wasn't that tough or unemotional.

Leaving the shower, she got dressed and went back to her room to retrieve the old Morgan journal. It was hard to decipher the handwriting, and she'd had to resort to a magnifying glass at some points. Still, it was worth it. William Morgan's detailed descriptions of Morgansville town life were research gold.

Outside, she heard the rumble of Chase's truck returning and went down the stairs to the kitchen. She'd already started the coffee when he came in, removing his hat and smiling right at her.

"How's it going?" He came toward her, and she marveled at the changes two weeks on the ranch had already wrought in him. His tan was darker, the lines of stress around his mouth had almost disappeared, and his smile came from the real Chase Morgan not the fake one. He dropped a kiss on the top of her head.

"Good." She held up a mug. "Do you want some coffee?"

"Sure." He washed his hands and sat at the table. "I had breakfast with Ruth and Roy before the sun came up." He shook his head. "There's nothing quite like watching the dawn here. I'd forgotten how beautiful it can be."

She sat opposite him. "Blue helped me with the chores, so we're all clear to go out on our ride after lunch." She hesitated. "I told him he should join us."

"Why not? I always think the best way to see this place is on the back of a horse." He studied her more closely. "What's up? I can stand to be in the same space with him for a few hours, you know. He's the one who's got the problem, not me."

"So I gathered," January said.

"I'm hoping that this time he will at least give me a fair hearing." Chase sipped his coffee. "We'll never agree about the past, but maybe we can compromise on the future." He met her gaze. "I'm already trying to work out ways to make sure Ruth can at least stay here until she dies."

January reached across and took his hand. "That's a start. Knowing your grandmother, you'd better plan for at least fifty more years."

He chuckled and then looked beyond her to the kitchen door, the good humor dying, replaced by his professional face. "Hey, Blue. Thanks for doing my chores."

Blue nodded, went over to the coffeepot, and poured

himself a cup. "Ruth says we should all sit tight because she's coming in to make grilled cheese and ham on the griddle." He almost smiled at his brother. "Just like old times, eh?"

"Yeah." Chase replied easily, but January knew him well enough to sense the tension in him. "Do you want to come out and see the new calves afterward?"

"I'd like that. Ruth said the beef herd is doing good." He sat beside January. Today's T-shirt was blue with a small *Semper Fi* embroidered on it. "She also said Roy's thinking about keeping pigs."

"That's Roy's baby. I just told him to keep them away from the house." Chase spotted the journal and turned back to January. "Is it any good?"

"It's awesome." She grinned at him. "There's information in there that no one apart from your family has ever seen before. I'm going to blow my advisor away."

"I'm glad." His smile for her was genuine. "Even though I almost died a hero's death getting that thing for you."

January looked at Blue, who was watching his brother as if he'd never seen him before. "Chase fought off a spider in the attic to get me this journal."

"Impressive. He's always hated spiders." Blue poured himself a glass of lemonade. "I had to scoop them out of the bath for him. I charged him a quarter a spider."

"Apparently, that's my job now."

"Then I'd start charging a million dollars a spider." Blue winked at her.

The screen door squeaked open, and Ruth came in with several of the dogs at her heels. "Grilled cheese coming right up."

"Come on, Nolly," Chase muttered. "Don't let Messi show us up. He's behaving like an angel for Blue, so stop fricking around with me."

Blue rode ahead of Chase and January, his back straight, his hips rolling naturally into the motion of the lope. Blue had even brought his own cowboy hat and boots with him. Chase could only hope Blue would be sore tomorrow, but somehow Chase doubted the super-fit marine would suffer a single ache. Nolly was kicking up his heels and twirling as if he was auditioning for a spot in the rodeo, which was making Chase's ride way too interesting.

Below them lay the green pastureland near the bank of the meandering creek where the young calves grazed. Chase pulled up to wait for January, letting Blue gallop down the hill with a *whoop*. When she joined Chase, they proceeded at a more leisurely pace to the gate where Blue was waiting. All three of them dismounted and leaned on the fence, watching the calves.

"When's the branding going to happen?" Blue asked.

"Next week, I think," January answered him. "It will be cool for Ruth to have you two around to help."

Blue grimaced. "I'll have to practice my roping skills. I haven't brought a calf down for about twenty years."

"Me neither," Chase said. "Maybe we'd better leave that to the professionals."

"As long as I don't have to be responsible for castrating anything, I'm good." Blue shuddered, and January laughed.

"Men."

"Then you do it."

She made a face. "I'd much rather handle a vaccination syringe and do some good."

"All the wussies want that job. Is the vet coming out?"

"Yes. It'll probably be Jenna McDonald."

"Big Mac's daughter?" Blue asked.

"Niece, I think. His daughter's still at veterinary school." January leaned closer to Chase and sighed. "Poor little calves have no idea what's going to happen to them, do they?"

"It's got to be done." Chase and Blue spoke at the same time, repeating what Ruth had always said to them. Chase continued. "Better to get it all finished in one shot. Tagged, debagged, and debugged, as Roy says."

"That's funny, but disgusting at the same time." January shuddered. "I wasn't here last year, so I missed all this."

Chase put his arm around her shoulders. "You don't have to do anything if you don't want to."

"And miss such a spectacle?" She looked up at him. "Seeing how a working ranch operates helps to make sense of its history."

"Chase doesn't care about history even when it's written by the winners." Blue's laugh was short.

Letting go of January, Chase turned to his brother. "Who won, Blue? Me?"

"Dad certainly didn't."

"He chose to leave us. You can't pin that one on me."

"I suppose not—seeing as your plan was to get him locked up in prison instead."

Chase set his jaw. "I didn't want that."

"Then why did you call the fucking sheriff?"

"Because I was afraid that something bad had happened when neither of our parents came home." He forced himself to hold Blue's accusing gaze. "I was the oldest, Ruth wasn't there, and I was trying to be the responsible one."

"Yeah, responsible for sending your own father to jail."

"They didn't charge him, Blue."

"No thanks to you."

Chase let out his breath. "What do you want me to say? I did what I thought was best at the time. If I hadn't called them, Ruth would've done so when she got back. She *told* me I did the right thing, and that was good enough for me."

Blue looked out at the cattle, his mouth set in a hard line.

"I can't change what happened. I refuse to accept that

what Dad did after that night is all on my shoulders. He made his own choices."

"After his eldest son—his fucking *favorite*—turned him in to the cops." Blue shook his head. "He never got over that."

"That's not true. He never got over losing Mom and Rachel." He held Blue's stare. "Are you going to blame me for that as well?"

Blue swallowed hard and looked away before tipping his hat to January. "I'm going to do a bit of exploring on my own. Tell Ruth I'll be back in time for dinner."

Chase briefly closed his eyes as his brother mounted up and rode away. Yeah, apparently he was still at fault for every fricking thing in the Morgan universe.

January's hand slid into his, and he held on to her like she was a lifeline.

"He's still so angry." She sighed.

"That's why none of us like coming back here. We end up stuck in the past and arguing about the same old shit. And he's right. I did call the sheriff out to the ranch and started that whole damned nightmare."

"If you hadn't, Ruth would've done it."

"But she would've done it later, and maybe my dad would've found my mom rather than getting taken down to a holding cell."

She cupped his face in her hands. "Chase . . . That's a hell of a lot of maybes and could'ves. Once they knew your mom was missing, the authorities started looking for her, didn't they?"

"Of course they did, but my dad knew the ranch best, knew where she might have gone and maybe if he'd stayed around . . ."

January pressed her thumb against his mouth, stopping his words. "And he wasn't at his best, was he? Would you really have wanted him going after your mom in that state? Would she even have come home with him?"

Chase stilled and forced himself to stop the flow of words, of old hurts and promises and anguish Blue had stirred up in him. "I don't know."

"You were right in what you said to Blue, Chase. You can't change what happened, and you know what? You can't save people from themselves."

He managed a nod and exhaled. "Got it."

She went up on tiptoe and kissed his cheek. "Then let's go home."

January reined in Sunflower and counted the number of vehicles in front of the house. Along with Chase and Blue's trucks was a brand-spanking-new white Lexus with gold trim and California plates.

"More visitors?"

Chase groaned. "Maybe the twins struck it rich in Vegas and have come back to buy the ranch outright."

"We can but hope."

January dismounted and led Sunflower to the hitching post where she took off the horse's bridle and saddle. After checking Sunflower's feet and giving her a gentle rub-down, January walked her back to her stall. She could hear Chase whistling as he dealt with Nolly. There was no sign of Blue yet.

After putting the saddle away, January washed her hands and turned toward the house, Chase at her side.

"Are you going back to work on that journal?" he asked.

"Unless I get a better offer."

He reached for her hand. "I can think of one."

"With all these people in the house?"

He winked at her. "Don't you know that's what barns were invented for?"

She was still smiling when they entered the kitchen to find it empty. Ruth called from down the hallway. "Chase, darling. There's someone to see you."

He made a face. "Coming."

"Which means you won't be coming with me," January whispered, and tried to dodge past him. He kept hold of her hand and drew her inexorably along the hallway.

"Let's see who it is first, and then we can make a decision."

She was still smiling when they entered Ruth's best parlor and the man dressed in an expensive designer suit, who was sitting on the couch, rose to his feet.

"Mr. Morgan? I'm Kevin Taylor from the LA office of Hendersons." He shook Chase's hand, and then his gaze switched to January and his smile widened. "And, look who it isn't! Hey, Janny. I couldn't believe it when I saw your name on Mr. Morgan's list."

January stood frozen as he leaned in to kiss her cheek and she was engulfed in his usual cloud of expensive cologne. His fair hair had been highlighted with silver tips, and from his line-free forehead she suspected he'd been at the Botox again.

"Kevin." Chase and Ruth were both looking at her, and she tried to smile. "Why are you here? Has something happened I should know about?"

He gave his trademark hearty laugh. "Goodness, no, my dear. I came to deliver a security report to Mr. Morgan. Your being here was just an added attraction to making the trip in person."

She looked helplessly at Chase, who was frowning.

"You know January, Mr. Taylor?"

"Please—call me Kevin. Yes, I do know her rather well." He gave a charming shrug. "She's probably forgotten how she broke my heart, but that's Janny for you— always moving forward and never regretting her past."

January met Chase's suddenly interested gaze. "What

he's trying to say is that we were once married to each other. Why he's *here* is another matter entirely." She raised her eyebrows. "But, perhaps you know more about that than I do, Chase."

"He apparently works for a security firm I use."

"That's correct, Mr. Morgan. I'm one of the vice presidents of Hendersons in LA. In fact I work directly underneath Rolf Henderson himself."

"I'm still not sure why you felt it necessary to come all this way out to the ranch just to present your report," Chase said slowly.

Kevin lowered his voice. "Because there were some . . . discrepancies in the data we generated for you. If there are too many red flags, we have to step in and investigate further. That *is* what you are paying us to do for you, Mr. Morgan. And sometimes we find the best way to understand and resolve discrepancies is to interview each person concerned." He glanced from Ruth to Chase. "I apologize if you think we have overstepped the mark. The LA office is used to dealing with the super rich and famous, and we always try to be as diligent as we can."

"I'm sure you do." Chase looked across at Ruth. "Do we have somewhere for Mr. Taylor to spend the night?"

Ruth brushed down her apron. "There's the guest bedroom next to January's. I'll go and air the sheets. You're welcome to join us for dinner tonight, Mr. Taylor."

"I wouldn't miss it for the world." Kevin bowed. "Ever since January left me, I've been eating takeout or depending on the kindness of friends. A home-cooked meal sounds delightful."

January only just stifled a snort of derision. He was so full of shit. But Ruth didn't know that.

"Why don't you bring your bag upstairs and freshen up? I'm afraid you'll have to share a bathroom. . . ."

Kevin winked at January and followed Ruth out, talking

all the time. January turned to Chase, whose frowning gaze was fixed on the door.

"What security reports?"

"I always get reports on those I'm working with. It saves a lot of time and avoids many of the stupid issues that come up after someone is hired."

"What do these 'reports' include?"

He shrugged. "Employment history, finances, social media information, you know the kind of thing."

"But you don't employ anyone here."

He finally looked at her. "Ruth does. I wanted to make sure she is surrounded by good people."

January gripped the back of the couch hard. "Did Ruth ask you to do this for her?"

"No. Why would she?"

She gaped at him. "Did you get a report on her, too?"

"I might have done. There's—"

"Sometimes, I don't understand you at all."

He took a step toward her. "And I don't understand what the problem is here. In fact, I'm more interested in why your ex-husband chose to bring the information to me in person. Did you tell him you were here?"

"I've spent the last five years avoiding him." January glared at Chase. "And now—thanks to your investigating *me*—he's found me again. Thanks a lot." She turned on her heel and left, slamming the door behind her.

She stomped up the stairs, her head down, muttering uncomplimentary things about all the males in her life, and walked right into Kevin, who grabbed her elbows.

"Hey, babe."

She raised her head and looked him right in the eye. "Let go of me."

He grinned and stepped back, hands in the air. "You ran into me, Janny."

"Why are you here?"

"To deliver my report. That's my job."

"And my being here had nothing to do with that decision?"

His smile widened. "Wow, you do think a lot of yourself, don't you? But then that was always your problem." He moved past her and casually flicked her cheek. "Don't ever think you can outsmart me, little girl. I always knew exactly where you were."

He went down the stairs whistling, leaving her feeling sick and cold. She went into her bedroom and immediately locked the door. Wrapping her arms around herself she went to sit on the bed and ended up curled up on the quilt in a fetal position. Why had she hoped Kevin had forgotten her and moved on? He would never forgive her for being the one to walk away. That was *his* job.

She shivered, remembering how his eyes would go black when he was full of rage, revealing what lay beneath that charming exterior. But then she was the only person who'd ever been allowed to see that particular demon. To everyone else he was the perfect man.

Even her mother had wondered why she'd left him. No one believed Kevin had another side to him that had terrified her nineteen-year-old self. She'd given up telling anyone because she ended up looking like the crazy one. But she knew the truth of him. She'd gone to see a therapist after the divorce, and it had taken her forever to rediscover her sense of self. She would never let a man define her again.

There was a gentle knock on her door, and she went still. "January?"

It was Chase's voice. She closed her eyes. She didn't want to see him either. What kind of man ran security checks on his own *grandmother*?

He knocked again. "Dinner's almost on the table."

As if she were going to sit there with Ruth and chat

with her ex, her friend with benefits, and his brother with issues.

"January . . ." His sigh was audible as was the sound of his boots walking away from her and going downstairs.

Her stomach growled. Ignoring it, she put on her nightie and crawled under the covers. She switched on her bedside lamp and picked up the old journal. If anything could take her mind off the table of doom downstairs, it would be the amusing anecdotes of William Morgan the first.

Chase picked distractedly at his roast chicken as Kevin kept up an endless flow of conversation. He'd even managed to make Blue smile, and Ruth was glowing with his praise of her cooking. Kevin caught Chase's eye.

"I'm sorry Janny didn't choose to join us."

"She's working hard on her thesis at the moment, so she probably couldn't stop." Chase put his knife down, lining it up at a precise angle to the edge of the table.

"Thesis?" Kevin chuckled. "She's trying that again, is she? I think that's the third time she's tried to convince some institution to give her a proper qualification. Bless her heart." He leaned closer to Chase. "Did she tell you that she grew up in a cult? I think she always felt a bit self-conscious about her lack of formal education."

"As far as I understand it, the University of California doesn't let students in on their postgrad programs unless they've already gotten their first degree. I think it's safe to assume January is doing just fine."

"I'm sure she is. She's super good at getting what she wants." Kevin shook his head. "Beneath that sweetheart exterior is one hell of a tough cookie."

Chase forked up another piece of chicken and chewed determinedly. He didn't like being at odds with January. He needed to talk to her, and Kevin was not helping him concentrate on exactly what arguments he needed to make to bring her around.

"I graduated from UCLA myself." Kevin was still talking. "How about you guys?"

"Stanford," Chase said.

Blue took more chicken. "I attended the school of life."

Chase met his gaze. "And learned a hell of a lot more than I ever did."

Blue's mouth twisted. "Sure, if you want to know fifty ways to kill a man, I'm your guy."

"That skill could come in handy in Silicon Valley." Chase smiled. "You should come and work for me."

Kevin nodded. "Or me. We've always got room for ex-military folk. They make fantastic employees."

Blue raised an eyebrow at Chase, and for a moment they grinned at each other.

"So what's the plan, Kevin?" Chase asked. "Whom exactly do you need to interview in person?"

Kevin pulled out his large, flashy phone and consulted it. "Three of the ranch hands, and Janny, of course."

"Why do you need to speak to January?" Chase put down his fork.

Kevin looked apologetic. "Well, she did turn up during the time frame we're looking at and her financials . . ." He sighed and shook his head. "Let's just say that girl has never had a head for figures, and that at some point she was bound to make some financial mistakes."

"Do you have the initial reports with you?"

Kevin nodded. "I'll send you the files right now so that you can look them over. I'll include the flagged ones. There's also some information on Kingsmith Financial Group that I'd like to talk through with you tomorrow, if you have time."

"Sure." Chase nodded. "Or, we can do it after dinner."

"After all that delicious food, I don't think I'd make

much sense." Kevin patted his stomach. "If it's okay with you, I'll turn in early and be up bright and ready to play tomorrow?"

"That's fine. It gives me time to read through the rest of the information."

Ruth offered them apple crumble and ice cream, and waded through that effectively silenced conversation around the table. Eventually Blue groaned and stood up. "Thanks, Ruth, that was awesome." He nodded at Chase and Kevin. "Night, guys. I'll be up to help with the chores at six, and then I'm going for a long run. All this good food is making me sluggish."

Kevin rose as well and gave Ruth a charming smile. "Thank you. It was a real pleasure to sit down and be treated like family."

"You're very welcome, Kevin." Ruth smoothed down her apron. "And thanks for coming all this way just to help Chase."

"It was my pleasure. He and his partners are valued Hendersons clients."

"I'll show you the bathroom," Blue said, and followed Kevin up the stairs, leaving Chase to help Ruth clean up.

After a while, Ruth went into the parlor to watch TV and then went up to bed, leaving Chase alone at the table with a cup of coffee and his laptop. He opened the files Kevin had given him and scanned the contents, noting that one of the ranch hands seemed to be in the country illegally, and that a couple of the others had minor debts or obligations they hadn't fulfilled over the years. There was nothing that hinted at debt large enough to necessitate their stealing money from the ranch or taking out loans against it.

But then he hadn't really expected there to be. He was fairly certain that, if money was being spent, it had something to do with his immediate family. A floorboard creaked on the upstairs landing, and Chase went still. It was now past midnight. He recognized the light tread on the stairs. Keeping his back to the door, he pushed the plate of food to the side of the table.

"Your dinner's here. Two minutes in the microwave should do it."

January came into the kitchen. He waited until she walked into view and frowned.

"I made you *cry*?"

She moved past him, her arms tight around herself, and then picked up the covered plate. She wore a long robe belted tightly at the waist, and her hair was loose around her face, shielding her expression.

"January . . ."

"I'm fine. I'm just hungry, okay?"

One thing he'd learned was that when a woman said "fine," things rarely were. He rose to his feet and took the plate out of her hands. "Sit down, and I'll fix your dinner."

The wary look in her gray eyes made him want to slap somebody—probably himself for putting it there.

"Sit." He heated the plate of food and put it in front of her with silverware, a napkin, and a glass of iced tea. "Eat."

Rather than hover over her, he retreated to his seat and kept his gaze firmly on his screen as she slowly ate her way through the chicken dinner. At one point, he got up to refill her glass and brew a fresh pot of coffee. He wasn't planning on sleeping until he got things sorted out with January.

"Were you waiting for me to come down?" January asked.

He poured them both some coffee. "I was working, but I knew you like to wander around late at night, so I hoped you'd put in an appearance." He risked a covert glance at her face. "I also know you like to eat."

"And that hunger would drive me into your trap?"

He looked at her. "I'd never try to trap you, January."

"That's right. We're just friends with benefits. Friends who get secret reports on each other. Oh, no—that's just you, isn't it?"

"I asked for the report *before* we became friends with benefits." He grimaced. "I never expected someone to turn up here in person and blab about it. I *certainly* didn't expect it to be your ex-husband."

"But you still asked for those reports."

"I had no choice."

"Because you don't trust anyone."

"It's not that simple. We've had some bad experiences at work dealing with fraudulent individuals. We find it simpler to run a basic clearance report on everyone we deal with. Can you blame me for being careful?"

She didn't look convinced. "What exactly do you think we're doing out here? Rustling cattle and stealing from the defunct silver mine?"

He reached across the table and gently uncurled her fingers from their fist. "Of course not." She allowed him to hold her hand. "Have you really been avoiding Kevin for years?"

"Yes."

"Has he threatened you?"

"Oh, no, he'd never do that." Her mouth twisted. "He has a reputation to maintain."

"He didn't seem . . . hostile to you. In fact he sounded as if he missed you quite a bit."

She tried to ease out of his grip. "I doubt it."

He held on. "So, what am I missing here?"

"Nothing. I just don't like being around him anymore. He reminds me of how young and stupid I was." She hesitated. "He's not staying long, is he?"

"I think he'll be done by tomorrow."

"Good." This time she did move away from him. She

picked up her plate and cup and put them in the sink. "Thanks for saving me dinner."

"There's apple crumble still warming in the oven."

"Oh God, I love Ruth's crumble. I'll take some up with me."

As she turned toward the door, Chase cleared his throat. He had a sense that if he didn't sort things out with her, he wouldn't feel right. "I don't suppose you want me to join you tonight—what with your ex-husband sleeping right next door."

She went still, put the tray down to the side, and swung around to face him again. "Did you really just say that out loud?"

He winced. "My reasons for getting the reports had nothing to do with you personally." He didn't normally share his private life with anyone these days, but he wanted to make things clear between them, and he'd already messed things up, so he might as well keep going. "Ruth asked me to come out here to check over some financial issues. I decided to ask for the reports because of that—not because I imagined some enterprising silver-mine scavenger would be after me."

"Okay."

"So we're good?"

Her smile wasn't reassuring. "But there *is* a report on me?"

"There really is one on Ruth, too, if that makes you feel any better."

January opened her mouth and then closed it again, slowly shaking her head.

"Have you read mine?"

"Not yet."

She leaned back against the countertop and folded her arms. "I can save you the trouble. My credit rating is in the toilet, I'm still paying back massive student loans and other debts from my divorce, and I was caught shoplifting a lipstick when I was about twelve. Anything else you want to know?"

This time he meekly shook his head.

"Good. Did you get reports on all your fiancées, too?"

"I only had one, and yes, of course I did."

"Of course."

"Just for the record," he offered, "you're nothing like Jane or the other women who were attracted to me for my money."

She raised an eyebrow. "Who said I was attracted to you?"

He rose slowly from his chair and advanced toward her. She straightened, but made no attempt to flee. He stopped and placed both his hands on the countertop on either side of her, caging her in.

"You *are* attracted to me." He leaned forward and buried his face in the crook of her neck. "You're shivering."

"It's cold in here."

"Liar," he whispered against her throat. "I'm sorry I investigated your past, but I did it before I really knew you." He kissed the taut line of her jaw. "And I totally understand that having your ex-husband sleeping next door to you might cramp your style."

She slowly raised her head, and he glimpsed a whole series of emotions warring within her gray eyes.

"What's wrong, January?"

She pushed hard on his chest. "Move."

She took off so fast that he almost backed into his chair and knocked it over. To his surprise, she went out of the kitchen door. It took him less than a second to disentangle himself from the chair and follow her out. The moon was full, and the yard was bathed in harsh white light.

She was heading for the barn. Chase turned back into the house and went to the mudroom, where he snagged a couple of old quilts, and then followed her. By the time he reached her she stood in the center of the barn, murmuring sweet nothings to Sunflower. He noticed her fluffy bunny slippers for the first time and that she wore a nightie with pink hearts on it under her robe.

She looked almost fragile, and he took a step toward her, and then another, and simply wrapped her in his arms.

She reached up to touch his face, and her voice was fierce. "I can't let him define me anymore, Chase. I refuse to let him stop me from getting what I want."

"What do you want?"

"You." She kissed him. "In this barn. Right now."

Still keeping one arm around her, he bent to retrieve the quilts. "Yes, ma'am."

He took her up the ladder to the hayloft where there were bales arranged in tidy rows he could only approve of. The doors of the loft were open to the night sky, and the moonlight gilded everything with silver.

He threw both of the quilts over a couple of the hay bales so he and January could avoid the prickles and then gave his attention fully to January. He backed her up against the side of the hay until her knees buckled and he was able to lower her down. Her hands landed squarely on his chest, and he hesitated.

"No. *You* lie down."

Chase did as he was told and stretched out, one arm behind his head, the other at his side on the quilt. January climbed up next to him and slowly undid the buttons of his denim shirt, pushing the fabric wide so that she could kiss and nip at his chest. Chase did nothing to stop her as his body stirred to life beneath her hands.

She took off his belt and started on the straining top button of his fly, sliding her hand inside as she brought the zipper slowly down over his eager shaft. He rolled his hips, pushing himself into her fingers, and groaned her name.

Her hair brushed his stomach, and he inhaled sharply as her thumb circled the wetness gathering on his cotton boxers.

With a soft sound, she bent her head and sucked him into her mouth, cotton and all. His hips jerked upward, and he threaded his hand through her hair, holding her exactly where he wanted her.

"That's . . . good," he managed to murmur. "Take more."

She raised her head to look at him. "Oh, I'm taking it all tonight. You owe me."

"And I'm more than willing to pay up."

He eased one booted foot up onto the hay bale to steady himself against the rhythmic tug of her mouth. If she kept this up, he wouldn't last long.

He almost shouted with gratitude when she used her teeth to peel back his now-soaking boxers and then settled back down to teasing him with her mouth and tongue. His fingers tightened in her hair as she finally took him deep and schooled him properly. When she released him, he almost cried out, and then she was shimmying out of her panties and covering him and—

He wasn't a man who thought about sex in terms of fireworks and explosions and ecstasy. But then he wasn't thinking much as she mounted him and rode him straight to heaven. He was just experiencing, holding on to her hips as she bucked and mastered him, making him feel things that made words irrelevant and meaningless. Making love with January meant he'd never think about sex in the same way again.

The sight of her over him, her back arched, her head thrown back like a rodeo rider conquering a bucking steer, would stay with him forever. He wanted to bow down at her feet, lick her toes, and beg her to take him like that again. This wasn't safe. This was messy and life changing, and addictive.

Slamming his heel down into the hay, he offered her more, and she took it, using him until he was nothing more than her willing slave. Reaching up he untied her robe and fought with the buttons of her top until her breasts were bared to him. Shifting his weight so that he was half sitting up, he brought his mouth to her breasts, making her writhe down on him, sending them off into another spasm of need that brought him closer to completion.

She cried out as another orgasm ripped through her and bent to kiss his mouth, pushing him back onto the hay. The shock of impact had them coming together so hard that for a long moment he forgot to breathe, how to see, and who he was.

January collapsed over his chest, and he held her steady as he tried to gather his scattered thoughts. This wasn't how sex was supposed to be. So what was it? He wanted to keep her pressed against him, her body limp and satisfied, and then he wanted to do it all again to make sure Kevin knew what he'd lost, what he hadn't valued.

Chase opened his eyes and stared up at the roof of the barn.

He was in very deep shit.

Chapter Thirteen

The sound of banging brought January out of the kitchen onto the wraparound porch, where she found Blue on his knees repairing a piece of flooring. She watched him for a moment because—well—he was a gorgeous, muscled man with a tool belt doing something manly.

He looked over his shoulder and gave her a guarded smile.

"Hey."

She pointed at his empty mug. "Would you like some more coffee?"

He wiped a hand over his forehead. "Sure. I'm surprised someone hasn't fixed these loose boards already. They're dangerous."

"I had it on my to-do list," January admitted. "Along with painting the place."

"I'm surprised Chase hasn't ordered a team of contractors in to do it."

"Give him time." She grinned at Blue, and he reluctantly smiled back.

"You seem to get on well with my brother."

January thought about how she'd behaved the previous

night with his brother and felt her cheeks heat. "Yeah. I quite like him."

"Better than your ex, I guess?"

"Duh. He's my ex for a reason."

Blue stood up and handed her his cup. His T-shirt was stuck to his skin with sweat, and his tool belt weighed down his jeans until they barely skimmed his hips. "Kevin seems like a nice guy."

"Yeah." She turned to go. "Shall I bring you some water as well?"

"That would be awesome."

She went back into the kitchen, where Ruth was rolling out pastry.

"Who put that look on your face?" Ruth sprinkled flour on the wooden board. "You and Chase arguing already? Although, goodness knows that man needs to be told the truth sometimes."

"It's not Chase." January took a cold water bottle out of the old refrigerator and rinsed out Blue's mug.

"Then it's Kevin?" Ruth dusted the flour off her hands. "He told me he really regrets losing you, my dear."

January forced a smile. It was business as usual. Everyone always felt so *sorry* for Kevin, which must mean she was the problem.

"I'm just going to take these out to Blue." She held up the water bottle.

"It's okay; there's no need. I'm right behind you." She turned to see Blue coming into the kitchen. "I'll need to go into town and get some supplies to finish fixing the porch." He took his tool belt off and hung it over the back of a chair. "Does the general store still have absolutely everything?"

"If Maureen doesn't have it, there's a small lumberyard and hardware store just beside the gas station now. The

Baker family runs it." January handed him the bottle. "They definitely have wood."

"Then I'll try there." He drank the water down in one gulp, tipping his head back, and chased it with the coffee. "I need a shower first. Are Chase and our guest out of the bathroom now?"

"They're sitting in the parlor having their meeting," Ruth said as she rolled out the pastry.

"About what?" Blue asked.

Ruth shrugged. "Something to do with his business, I expect."

January looked down at the table and concentrated on watching Ruth's expertise with the rolling pin.

"He never stops, does he?"

There was a mixture of admiration and puzzlement in Blue's voice that January was starting to know well.

"And he's done well for himself because of that."

"He won't use any of those millions to help you though, will he?"

Ruth cut Blue a sharp glance. "I wouldn't want him to. Don't think he hasn't offered. I turned him down." She slapped the metal dish on top of the rolled-out pastry and cut around the edge. "I also told him that the decision about what to do with the ranch after I'm gone is up to the four of you, and has to be unanimous. It's in my will. If you can't agree, the ranch doesn't get sold."

Blue groaned. "He's going to attempt to buy us out, and God knows what the twins will do about that. They are always short of money. *I'm* going to be the only one holding out."

"If you can't agree, I'm considering leaving the whole place to the Morgantown Historical Society."

January's head shot up. "*What?*"

Ruth smiled at her. "It seems like the obvious solution to me. If the boys can't come to an agreement within two

years of my death, the place will be gifted in its entirety
to the society."

"Um, have you mentioned this to Chase yet?" Blue
asked.

"Not yet. It only just occurred to me." Ruth lowered the
pastry into the pie dish and added the contents of a pan
from the stovetop. "I'll go and see my lawyer when I'm
next in town and make sure he puts the right language in
there."

"Poor old Henry must be sick of seeing you in his
office." Blue put his coffee mug in the sink. "But you go
right ahead, Ruth. And please make sure I'm around when
you tell Chase. I can't wait to see the look on his face."

"But he doesn't need the money from the sale of the
ranch," January said slowly. "The only people who will be
worse off will be you and your brothers. You'll get nothing."

Blue's gaze was cool. "This isn't about money. It's about
this place surviving. Even if it no longer belonged to my
family, I could still come and visit and remember what my
ancestors created out of nothing. Hell"—he smiled—"I
might even be able to get a job as a guide here."

January nodded. It was almost funny. She should be
Blue's friend with benefits, not Chase's. Blue was saying
everything she'd ever wanted to hear from his older
brother. "I understand that, Blue. I agree that saving the
ranch is the most important goal here."

"Then maybe we should keep this conversation between
ourselves." Blue looked at them both. "If Chase doesn't
know that the ranch will be gifted to the society in two
years? Maybe that's how it should be allowed to play out.
The twins will never agree with him about anything on
principle."

"I'm not lying to him." Ruth cut out another circle of
pastry and laid it over the top of the dish.

"I'm not asking you to. But if he doesn't mention it, you

don't have to tell him, do you? Hell, you change your mind about that will of yours at least six times a year anyway, so it probably won't even happen."

"I don't want to lie to him either," January admitted. "I feel bad even talking about him behind his back."

"He'll survive." Blue picked up his tool belt. "I'm going to take a shower. Do you want to come into town with me now, Ruth?"

"I can't while my pie is cooking."

"I can watch it if you want to go," January offered. "I've got some work to do on my laptop, and I can sit right here."

"That's very kind of you, dear." Ruth glazed the pie with beaten egg, added a few fancy leaves to the top, and put it in the oven. "It'll take about an hour. I'll just go and wash my hands and get my purse."

"Take your time," Blue called over his shoulder as he headed out the door and then spoke again. "Hey, Kevin, do you need the bathroom? There's another one behind the mudroom, which is closer."

January heard Kevin say something to Blue as they passed on the stairs and then his footsteps went back toward the parlor. She waited for Ruth to set the old-fashioned timer and helped her put the kitchen to rights. When Blue came down he and Ruth set off for town, leaving January in possession of the kitchen table and with the onerous responsibility of not burning the pie. She opened her laptop and sighed.

She wished she hadn't heard Blue and Ruth's conversation. Part of her wanted to run and tell Chase. The other part of her that wanted the ranch to go on forever was totally onboard with Ruth's idea. Creating a nonprofit to run Morgan Ranch and keep it intact would be a dream come true for any conservationist or historian.

Would Chase prefer his brothers to come out with nothing from the ranch? She had a sneaking suspicion that he'd feel better if he could buy them out, because for him money solved a lot of issues he didn't want to deal with. It also meant he'd end up in control of the ranch. What would he do then? Would *he* consider leaving it in the hands of the historical society? Maybe she could at least ask him that.

Chase nodded as Kevin went through the last of the ranch-hand files. He was a good speaker and presented the information in a knowledgeable and precise way that Chase approved of.

"You read through the flagged files, Chase?" Kevin asked.

"Yup. The only one that might be a problem is the illegal immigrant. I'll talk to Roy and Miguel about him when Miguel gets back from Argentina next week."

"Sure, it's always wise to double-check these things. We do our best, but sometimes things slip through the cracks." Kevin paused for breath. "You read through Janny's file as well?"

"Yup," Chase said. "Now tell me about Kingsmith Financial."

"Despite my personal connection with Janny, I wouldn't consider myself a professional unless I noted that she is in serious debt."

"I saw that. Can we move on?"

"Of course." Kevin opened his briefcase and took out another folder. "She did attempt to consolidate some of her loans a couple of years ago, making the monthly payments smaller, but for a longer term. That was certainly prudent of her."

Chase said nothing and waited for Kevin to get a clue and move forward.

"So Kingsmith Financial bought up a number of smaller loans and policies from various provincial banks over the past ten years." Kevin shrugged. "You know how that goes." He drew out a sheaf of papers. "From what I can tell, the original paperwork was done in 1991 with the Morgan County Bank just before it closed its doors."

"1991?" Chase frowned. "By whom?"

"I believe it was in the name of William Morgan."

"My grandfather, William Morgan? So why is Ruth adamant that she didn't take out the policy?"

"Is it possible that William arranged it without consulting her?"

"It's possible. He was a bit old-school about a woman's place." Chase took the copies Kevin handed him. "But why has it suddenly resurfaced now?"

"From what I can see, it was a term life insurance policy associated with a second mortgage that resulted in a payoff being due in twenty-five years if the named person didn't die beforehand. That imminent payoff probably triggered Kingsmith's systems, and when they investigated they seem to have decided that there were some missed payments recently."

"Recently?" Chase asked. "Which means that someone has been paying it off since 1991. Do you have any information as to exactly who that is?"

"They wouldn't talk to me over the phone. Said they would only discuss the matter with the payee." Kevin cleared his throat. "I did get them to accidentally slip up and admit the last name of the current payee was also Morgan."

"Which narrows it down somewhat. It doesn't make any sense."

"I agree." Kevin handed him the folder. "I've made copies of everything I could find about the loan and about Kingsmith, who are a legitimate concern. I've included a report on their financial stability as well."

Chase looked up from the paperwork. "One more thing.

Who was supposed to be the beneficiary of this insurance payout?"

"I believe that would have been your mother, Anne."

"But she's dead."

Kevin grimaced. "So I understand. You'll have to talk directly to Kingsmith to find out the implications of that. I'm sorry I can't be more helpful. When these policies get rolled over so many times and end up somewhere completely different, it's hard to keep track of all the information."

"I know. One of my partners lost his mortgage for a while."

Kevin nodded sympathetically. "The financial system certainly got messed up for a few years, didn't it?"

"Still is."

"But your company is doing okay?"

"Yeah, but we are conservative with our investments, compared to most businesses, and very hands-on." Chase gathered the paperwork together and put it on the couch beside him. "I've arranged for you to talk to the three ranch hands this morning. I'll take you down to the bunkhouse right now."

"And Janny?"

Chase stood up. "Is it really necessary to interview her as well?"

"I'd like to make sure I did a thorough job after coming out all this way, Chase."

"Sure." Chase opened the door and headed for the kitchen. The fragrant smell of something baking in the oven tantalized his senses. January was sitting at the kitchen table, typing on her laptop.

"You might as well talk to January before we head down to the bunkhouse." Chase looked over his shoulder at Kevin. "Take a seat while I make some fresh coffee."

Kevin halted behind him. "Janny, are you okay with Mr. Morgan's being here while I talk to you?"

"Talk to me about what?"

Kevin sat down. "Mr. Morgan asked Hendersons to do some preliminary checks about ranch personnel. Obviously, your name was on the list. I just wanted to ask you a few questions."

"I would've thought you knew everything about me, Kevin." January wore a pink T-shirt and her usual jeans. Her hair was twisted up on the top of her head, skewered with a pen. Chase wondered how she did that.

"You walked out on me five years ago, Jan. I hardly spent a lot of time following up on you. I was too upset and too worried to do much more than call you and beg you to come home." Kevin pulled out a file from his briefcase and studied it. "You've accrued a lot of debt since you left me. It must have been difficult to get used to not having me around to pay for everything."

"Not really. I grew up without a dime, so I'm used to managing on very little."

"The extent of your debt is extremely high compared to your current income."

"I have a ton of student loans."

"So I see." Kevin ran his finger down a long column of numbers. "Do you think that was a wise decision to make for someone with your lack of experience in dealing with money and your financial history?"

"If I wanted to get an education, yes." January folded her arms and leaned back in her chair. "I'm not sure what this has to do with Morgan Ranch."

"Nothing as far as I'm concerned," Chase said as he measured out the coffee.

"You *have* missed a couple of payments," Kevin said.

"I'm aware of that."

"But it hasn't encouraged you to get a proper job?"

"I work, Kevin. I get paid by the historical society and the county to do good work here on Morgan Ranch. I'm also funding my PhD with a full scholarship. I restructured my loans a couple of years ago, and I haven't missed a payment since. Have you finished?"

"That's up to Mr. Morgan. I just provide the information. He's the one who has to decide whether you are trustworthy enough to live in his family home and befriend his grandmother."

"Well, thank goodness for that." She shut the lid of her laptop and pivoted to face Chase. "Are we done here?"

Chase handed her a cup of coffee. "Fine by me." He turned to Kevin. "Would you like some?"

Kevin was looking between him and January. "That would be great."

"What's cooking?" Chase asked as he sipped his coffee.

"Ruth made a chicken pie with the leftovers from yesterday's dinner."

"It smells good."

"She's gone into town with Blue, so I'm watching the pie." January smiled at Chase as he refilled her cup, and he briefly touched her shoulder. "She'll kill me if it burns."

"I know. At least she won't whoop your ass like she used to do to me." They shared a grin as Kevin shuffled his papers and finished his coffee. He spent a few minutes checking his phone and lamenting the lack of Internet service and then stood up.

"If I'm to get on the road today, we should go and meet with the ranch hands, Chase." Kevin smoothed down the collar of his golf shirt. "In case I have any follow-up questions for you, Janny, babe, I'll need your phone number and e-mail."

January's smile faded.

"I have that information," Chase said. "I'll send it on to you if you need it, Kevin."

"Perfect." Kevin gave them both a broad smile. "Do we need to drive down to the bunkhouse?"

Chase glanced down at Kevin's fancy leather shoes. "I'd recommend we drive. We can go in my truck. I'll just get my boots on and meet you outside."

January remained sitting at the table as Kevin fussed around with his briefcase and put his sports jacket on.

"I see you've got quite a good thing going for yourself here, Janny."

She didn't bother to look up.

"Mr. Morgan seems pretty damn keen to protect your sweet little ass. How long did it take you to wrap him around your finger?"

January let out her breath and thought about good things like the morning sun on the Sierras, Chase's letting her take him down to the barn and make love to him . . .

"How long, Jan?"

There was an edge to Kevin's voice that made something inside her tighten. She finally looked up at him, noticing his amiable expression had long gone. But she was no longer a frightened teenager without a lick of sense.

"You'd better get going. I can hear Chase's truck out front."

"You're fucking him, aren't you?"

She held Kevin's gaze. "That's none of your business."

"You're disgusting, you know? You jumped on me five minutes after we met and clung on like a parasite until I had nothing left that you wanted, and now you're on to someone richer." Kevin shook his head. "You're a piece of work, honey. How many guys have you done this to? What the hell is *wrong* with you?"

"I'm good, thanks."

"No, you are not. You need to get some serious help with your issues, Janny, before someone wises up to you and you don't get to run away first."

"I've done plenty of therapy. I know exactly who I am. How about you?"

"Still in denial then? I feel sorry for you and for anyone stupid enough to let himself fall in love with you."

Kevin waited by the door, but she had nothing else to say to him. Getting sucked back in to one of his endless arguments would solve nothing and potentially eat away at her self-esteem. She wouldn't allow him to define her again. She refused to believe she was nothing.

"You should go."

Kevin turned on his heel and stomped out, leaving her shaking. He couldn't bear the fact that she'd dumped him, and he'd never forgive her for it. He'd counted on her teenage infatuation with him to last forever. She hated that he now knew where she lived and could, thanks to his job, keep tabs on her. And he would, because he was that kind of man.

January took a deep breath and turned back to her laptop. Kevin was leaving the ranch today. That was a blessing. She couldn't change the fact that he'd found her again, but at least she didn't have to see him every day. She wondered what he was saying to Chase about her, and whether Chase would start looking at her funny when he returned. Kevin had gradually turned all her friends against her or, if they'd refused to accept his version of events, he'd gradually cut them out of January's life.

Surely Chase would see through Kevin? But Chase had already mentioned that Kevin seemed to regret her loss. She couldn't control that. Either Chase believed in her or he didn't.

* * *

Chase glanced over at Kevin, who was staring out of the window at the green fields.

"You're going to stay for lunch?"

Kevin sighed heavily. "If that's all right."

"Sure. Ruth would never allow you to leave this place hungry. I assume you're not planning on driving all the way down to LA today?"

"I've got to visit some other clients in San Francisco and San Jose tomorrow. I'll probably go home from there."

"I appreciate your coming all the way out here." Chase maneuvered the truck over another bump and drove into the yard beside the barn. He turned the engine off. Kevin still sat there.

"I suppose you've guessed that I really wanted to see Janny." Kevin grimaced. "She just walked away from *everything*, and it was really hard for me to deal with." He forced a smile. "I just wanted to make sure she was all right."

Chase didn't say anything, and Kevin continued.

"I've never met anyone like her, and I bet I'll never find her equal. I wish I could turn back time and understand what I did *wrong*. I loved her so much." He managed to laugh. "Hey, I'm sorry to dump on you. It's just that I feel . . . so upset."

"She's a good person."

"Yeah, she is." Kevin heaved another sigh. "I just wish she had the ability to stick around when things don't go her way. But she was very young." He took off his seat belt. "But, hey, enough about my problems. I'm sure looking forward to my last taste of Ruth's home cooking. That woman is a national treasure."

He got out of the truck, and Chase followed suit. It was interesting hearing Kevin talk about January. He seemed really cut up about what he'd lost. Chase could understand that. It was rapidly becoming clear to him that January was not the sort of woman you got over easily. What was even more interesting was that January's brief explanation about why she'd left the marriage seemed to bear no relation to how Kevin still felt about her.

Chase let Kevin go through into the house in front of him and spotted Blue kneeling on the floor of the wooden porch.

"You coming in for lunch?"

"In a minute." Blue banged another nail in.

Chase leaned against the spindles and wooden railing, which creaked alarmingly under his weight. "I was going to hire someone to fix all that."

"I'm happy to do it. I like to have something to do with my hands."

"Then don't forget to use the ranch accounts at the hardware store and Maureen's to pay for the supplies so you aren't out of pocket."

"It's only a few bits of wood and some nails, Chase. I can afford it. Not a lot of places to spend my pay when I'm overseas." Blue tucked his hammer away in his tool belt and stood up. "Is Kevin staying another day?"

"Nope, he's off after lunch."

"He seems like a nice guy."

"He's certainly good at his job."

Blue grinned. "January's pissed with you because he turned up, isn't she?"

"She's been avoiding him for five years, and I gift-wrapped her and handed her over."

Blue halted in front of the kitchen door. "By doing what?"

"I had reports done on all the ranch personnel by the security firm Kevin works for, and January's name came up."

"Security reports? Why the hell did you do that?"

"Don't you start." Chase glared at his brother. "Ruth's had some financial issues. I was just making sure that no one who worked here had any major reason to be syphoning off ranch funds."

"What financial issues?"

"BB." Chase held his brother's suspicious gaze. "Can we talk about this after Kevin has gone? I'm pretty damn sure January doesn't want to be sitting at that table all by herself right now making small talk with her ex."

"Okay, but I'm holding you to that." Blue pushed open the screen door, and Chase followed him inside.

"Of course you are," Chase muttered.

Perhaps it was time to gently introduce the subject of Kingsmith Financial to Blue and see how he reacted. Chase didn't think Blue was secretly paying off their grandparents' debt. He would be far more likely to bring the problem to Chase's attention, wave it in his face, and keep at it until the matter was resolved to his satisfaction.

As the fragrant scent of chicken pie reached him, Chase smiled. If Ruth's cooking didn't turn Blue up sweet and receptive to Chase's questions, nothing would. Now all he had to do was sit beside January and stop her from getting too much attention from her ex. He owed her that.

Chapter Fourteen

January stared out from the porch of the ranch house at the trucks, horse trailers, and people who had answered the call to help with the spring branding. There was a huge crowd of folks, and the place was humming as horses were unloaded and gear was stacked and sorted. The sun still hadn't fully risen, and it was cold enough to condense her breath. She stuck her hands in the pockets of her jeans and hopped from foot to foot, wishing she had put her thick ski jacket on.

Behind her the screen door creaked open.

"Hey."

She half-turned toward Chase, who had just emerged from the kitchen with his coffee in hand.

"Wow. I didn't even know there were that many cowboys left around here. Did you, Chase?"

"It's a tradition that everyone helps one another out. We'll be returning the favor many times this spring."

He moved closer, and she caught a hint of leather, coffee, and his shower gel. He'd put on his Stetson and a thick jacket and looked ready for anything.

"Where's Blue?" January asked.

"He's coming. Do you want to drive down to the field

in my truck and take Ruth?" He nudged her. "It's got heated seats."

"You tempt me greatly."

He wrapped his arm around her shoulders. "It would be a big help. Ruth's loaded the truck bed up with food and drink, so you could give her a hand dispensing that to everyone."

"I'd be glad to. What's your designated role in all this?"

His smile flashed out. "Whatever I'm told to do. Roy's the boss."

"You're not going to ride dear old Nolly into the fray?"

"Not if I can help it. I'll leave the tricks to Blue. Have you ever seen calves being branded before?"

January shook her head and stole a sip from his coffee mug.

He handed over the cup. "It's pretty messy and danger-ous work. If everyone works together with this small a herd, we'll get it done in a day."

She looked up at him. "You almost sound like you're looking forward to it."

"I am." His smile was wry. "I'd forgotten what an occa-sion it was. Almost like a cowboy wedding, except you see everyone you've ever known in one muddy field covered in cow shit."

Behind them the screen door squeaked again, and Blue emerged dressed for the cooler weather and with a deter-mined expression on his face.

"You coming, Chase?"

Chase bent to kiss January on the lips. "I am now. If Nolly doesn't kill me on the ride down, I'll see you and Ruth at the lower pasture."

The look Blue gave her before he turned away should've made her feel like the traitor she was, but she didn't care what he thought of her. He was wrong about Chase, and she didn't need to defend herself. She knew in her bones that Chase was coming around to keeping the ranch. Today would only help cement those relationships with his neighbors that he'd previously chosen to ignore. He wouldn't be able to turn his back on his family home and history for much longer.

She let out a breath. When had she stopped thinking about the ranch as an academic project and started loving it and the people who worked there instead? It wasn't about money like Kevin thought. It was that sense of place and history that growing up in a commune, even with all her siblings, hadn't offered her.

Was her interest in Chase just because he belonged and she didn't? She shook her head. Kevin was wrong about that, too. Chase was the frosting that made sense of the cake. But the cake was still good. She started grinning as her stomach rumbled.

"January?" Ruth called from the kitchen, and January turned to go back into the house. There was certainly plenty to do, but first she'd go upstairs and add a few layers to her clothing.

January handed out hot coffee and cups of soup and met more people than she'd realized existed near the small town. What was funny was that almost all of them knew something about her from Ruth or Maureen at the store, or were members of the historical society. January chatted and smiled so much that she almost lost her voice.

Eventually, she wandered over to the fence to watch what was going on in the field. Chase joined her, his big body radiating heat along her side. She sniffed the air.

"You smell like hamburger. Eew."

"I was manning the branding iron for a while." He wiped a smudge of what she hoped was dirt off his cheek. "It's weird. You kind of feel sorry for the calves until you get kicked one too many times, and then you start smelling that beef and dreaming."

January elbowed him in the side. "You're a horrible man."

He grinned at her. "You want to have a try? I know the boss; I can get you in on the action, if you want."

"I think I'd rather watch this year and let you explain it all to me."

Chase eased her in front of him, allowing the sides of his sheepskin-lined denim jacket to close around her. "Okay, you see the four guys on the horses?"

"Yeah."

"They are roping the calves by the heels and bringing them down to the ground. It's a lot harder than it looks. When we were kids, Blue and I used to practice by lassoing an old bucket, but even that's not the same. There's a rhythm and a motion to it that even the best get wrong sometimes."

They watched the cowboys for a while as they attempted to catch the calves, who were more than happy to run all day.

"Here we go," Chase said. "Roy's got one."

The calf was instantly surrounded by a crowd.

"A couple of poor fools have to kneel on them to hold them down. One practically sits on the head. The calves might be small, but they can still kick out and break something." Chase absently rubbed his nose.

"I can see that."

"While the calf is immobilized, they'll vaccinate him and treat him for parasites." Chase pointed at the crowd of people converging on the mewling calf and working fast. "See Jenna with the two syringes? Someone else will tag the ear with the E.I.D."

"Which means?"

"Electronic Identification Device. And the last guy does the castrating and removes their horns."

"No wonder they bellow." January muttered as she leaned back against Chase's broad chest. "I bet you wouldn't like it much either."

"I wouldn't. Apparently, doing it all at one time is less stressful for the animal overall."

"Like we've asked them. It's enough to turn a girl vegetarian."

"Jenna is. She told me earlier when I was commenting on the acrid smell of scalded cowhide."

Even as he spoke a cloud of steam billowed from the field, carrying with it the scent of burned hair and beef. January abruptly closed her mouth.

"Jenna the veterinarian?"

"Yeah, she's a nice lady."

"I know. I met her when she came out to see the chickens last month."

"Shame she didn't take them away with her. I'm pretty sure they've turned feral."

"You like their eggs, and you certainly ate your share of that chicken pie yesterday.

"That's because I have no conscience." Chase hesitated. "Are you still mad about Kevin's turning up?"

She sighed and kept her gaze on the field. "Coincidences happen. In a way it was good to see him again. It confirmed my decision to walk away from him."

Chase didn't say anything, but he kept his arm around her, which had to mean something. The latest calf was released and ran straight back to the herd, shaking its head and bawling. Within seconds another was laid in its place, and the whole series of interactions began again.

"We're about half done. Ruth told me to call everyone for lunch." Chase cupped his hands around his mouth and bellowed to the workers.

"Lunch, everyone. Come and get it!"

He took January's hand and started back up toward the circle of trucks. She squeezed his gloved fingers.

"You okay about everyone seeing us holding hands?"

He looked down at her. "I was hoping they'd all be thinking I was being kind and helping some old lady up the slope."

January stopped walking to grin at him. "And Blue thinks you have no sense of humor."

He winked. "I don't. Come on."

When they reached Chase's big blue truck, he picked her up around the waist and hoisted her up to sit on the tailgate. Blue was already there drinking coffee and chatting to Roy. Around them the other families were putting out tables and erecting canopies for shade. Various bowls of food were placed on the central tables near where Ruth was standing, directing operations.

"Looks like a feast," January commented.

"Folks get hungry." Ruth came over to pick up a pile of paper plates and cups. "Do we have napkins?"

Blue grabbed them and the plastic forks from a box on the backseat of the truck. "We've got everything. Where do you want me to put these?"

January went to slide off the flatbed, and Chase patted her knee. "You can stay put, if you like. I'll get you a plate."

"That's sweet of you." She smiled at him. In her current position she was level with his rather lovely blue eyes. "But I'd rather get my own."

"If you're sure."

"You don't know what I like."

"Which means if I pick all my favorites there are bound to be more leftovers for me." He lifted her down and kept his hands on her waist. "I always have a backup plan, you know."

"I never doubted it."

He angled his head and kissed her, his warm mouth lingering. "I like this friends-with-benefits thing."

"You do?"

He drew back a scant inch. "You don't?"

She searched his gaze and found only warmth and genuine interest in his eyes. "It's pretty cool."

"It's damn cool."

"Hey, you two." Blue's voice intruded over January's shoulder. "Stop grinning at each other and get some food."

Still chuckling to herself, January headed toward the back of the line, and Chase followed behind her. His cell rang, and he took it out of the pocket of his jeans.

"Hey."

January tried not to listen as his carefree expression disappeared and his mouth tightened.

"I'm busy, Matt, and I don't have access to my laptop." He pressed the phone harder to his ear. "No, I can't go and get the figures for you. I'm out on the ranch, I'm covered in cow shit, and I'm just about to have lunch."

A crease appeared between his brows. "I'm not fricking avoiding anything." He suddenly thrust his phone at January. "Take a picture of me."

"What?"

"Take a photo of me and give me the phone back."

"Um, okay." She turned and took the picture. "Here you go."

He texted something before bringing the cell up to his ear. "Satisfied? Yeah, covered in cow shit. I'll call you tonight."

He stuffed the phone back in his pocket and grabbed a paper plate.

January cleared her throat. "Something up at work?"

"Just the usual."

"They still expect you to have all the answers, right?"

He let out his breath. "I usually do. But I'm not running

back to the house to get the information right now." He picked up three dinner rolls and dumped them on his plate. "Two weeks ago I would've done it, you know? Rushed off to get that shit for Matt. But I can't walk away from all these people who've come to support the ranch."

January said nothing as she followed Chase along the packed tables, loading her plate with good food. She might not have done any branding, but she sure was hungry after the early start and the briskness of the cold air. She kept her attention on the food because she didn't want Chase to see that she was smiling.

"Over here." Ruth beckoned to them. "I saved you both a seat."

January walked over to the spot beside Ruth and sat down. Blue, Roy, Miguel, and Jenna were already eating. Chase took the seat on January's left.

Blue was making some kind of point to Jenna, his finger stabbing the air. "Yeah, I get what you're saying, but are you sure your practice is up-to-date on that issue?"

Jenna raised her eyebrows. "I didn't realize you were a veterinarian, Blue. Where did you study?"

January winced at the sweetness of Jenna's tone, but Blue just carried on, digging himself deeper. "I'm hardly that. I've just picked up some information over the years. I thought the general opinion about how animals felt pain had shifted."

Jenna blew him a kiss. "Well, bless your heart, you'll have to come by and explain your theories to me one day. I'd *love* to hear them. No one would guess that I'd spent endless years at college learning stuff that apparently has no validity at all and could be picked up on the Internet for free."

She fluttered her long eyelashes at Blue, who finally shut up and returned his attention to his food.

January caught Jenna's amused gaze. "He means well."

"I'm sure he does. I just get a little tired of all the menfolk around here telling little old me how to do my job." Jenna stood up and gathered her used dishes. She wasn't very tall, but January already knew she was a lot stronger than she looked. "I'd better go and check if my stock of vaccines will hold out."

"Do you need any help?"

"No, I'm good." Jenna grinned at January. "Thanks for lunch."

"Thank Ruth. I'm just helping out."

Jenna went off toward her truck, and January turned to see that Blue was looking after her. He caught January's eye.

"I messed up, didn't I?"

"With Jenna?"

"I didn't mean to offend her."

Beside her Chase snorted. "Blue, I'm famous for my lack of sensitivity. If even I noticed you putting your big feet in it, you messed up."

"Maybe I should go and apologize." Blue tapped his fork against his plate. "I was trying to be friendly and put her at ease."

"By telling her she didn't know jack shit about her own profession?" Chase shook his head. "Yeah, that'll work every time."

"Shut it, bro."

Chase raised his chin. "I'm tempted to say make me, but I think we're a bit old to start fighting, and Ruth would get all pissy."

January smiled sympathetically at Blue. "An apology probably wouldn't hurt. She is new in town, so she needs some friends."

Blue gave her a sharp nod and started eating again.

* * *

Chase looked up at his brother and decided to be merciful and change the subject. "Roy says we're more than halfway through. Is that right, Ruth?"

"Yes. Thank goodness for this smaller herd. It used to take three days back when we had the whole ranch tied down to beef." She nodded at Chase. "Go on, then."

"On what?" He lowered his piece of chicken.

"Stand up and thank everyone for coming."

"That's your job."

"And, I'm asking you to do it." She scowled at him and then coughed a couple of times. "My throat is sore."

He threw her a skeptical look and then checked with Roy and Blue, who both shrugged.

"Go ahead, son." Roy said.

Chase turned toward the packed tables, noticing faces he knew, younger versions of the same faces, and the new-comers who were all staring up at him expectantly. He banged on the edge of the table until everyone went quiet.

"I'd like to thank you all for coming to Morgan Ranch to help us out today."

There was a chorus of shouts and cheers and raised plastic cups.

"Enjoy your lunch, and, remember, we'll be there to return the favor when you need us."

"Yay!" Maureen's youngest daughter, who had her mother's white-blond hair, jumped up and down and gave a piercing whistle. "We're just glad the Morgan boys are finally back!"

There was a chorus of feminine agreement that made Chase look around for Blue, who was grinning like a Cheshire cat and waving his hat at the ladies. January was smiling too, and Chase couldn't help but grin. Ruth came to stand beside him.

"There's lot's more to eat, so please help yourselves."

Chase leaned down to her. "Weird. Your throat sounds fine now. Loud as a bullhorn."

"It comes and goes." She hugged him. "Thanks for being here. I appreciate it more than I can say."

"It's been . . ." He tried to think of the right word. "Okay."

"*Okay?*" Ruth jabbed him in the ribs, and he winced. "That's all you've got?"

"I've enjoyed it."

She patted his cheek. "That's better. Now, January and I are going to start cleaning up, and you'd better get back to work."

He watched her disappear into the crowd, talking to everyone, making sure to personally thank every family who had turned up to help them. The odd thing was that despite his absence he could recall all of the families and they all remembered him. How long had they been coming to Morgan Ranch?

He walked over to where January was stacking paper plates and sliding them into a black trash bag.

"Does great-great-grandfather William have anything to say about cattle branding in his journal?"

She paused to look up at him. "I think so. Why?"

He gestured at the groups around them. "I was wondering whether any of these families had been coming out here since William's time."

"Wouldn't that be awesome?" Her gray eyes gleamed. "We can check when we get back. It might make an interesting article for the historical society newsletter."

Chase handed her another pile of plates. "I've got to get back out there and help. Do you want to join me?"

"I promised Ruth I'd do this." She smoothed her hair behind her ear. She wore a pink knitted cat-type hat thing with fluffy ears. "But if you're still working when I'm done, I'll come and find you."

He tipped his Stetson to her. "It's a deal."

"It sure is, cowboy." She went on tiptoe and kissed his mouth. "Go and be all manly. It suits you."

He walked away from her with a smile lingering on his lips, wishing he had a gun belt on and a swagger to match his gunslinging ancestor Mad Black Morgan. Had she come across the long-dead bounty hunter yet? Chase had secretly wanted to be him for years. Chase paused at the fence as the ropers remounted and took up their stations. Some version of this scene had been played out on this ranch for over one hundred and fifty years. Did it mean something?

Should it?

"Chase? Come on," Blue called out to him. "I'm going to try roping, so you're needed to man the tags."

Chase went through the gate and closed it behind him.

"I left a casserole simmering in the oven all day and baked potatoes, so when you've all cleaned up, come down and help yourselves," Ruth said as they all trailed wearily into the house. They'd already waved good-bye to everyone, tended to the horses, and cleared out the trucks. It wasn't that late, but the sun was dropping behind the mountain range, and the temperature was plummeting.

Chase stood back to let January go by him. "You can use the bathroom first."

She grinned up at him. "Thanks. Do I smell that bad?"

"Well, you did face-plant that cowpat at the end there. . . ."

He'd eventually persuaded her to try her hand at holding down the calves, and she was now as covered in mud and crap as he and Blue were.

"And now I smell just like you." She headed up the stairs with a wink. "I'll try not to use all the hot water."

"I'll shower down here." Blue went past him as well. "God, I'm tired."

"You did good," Chase said. To his surprise Blue paused and turned back toward him.

"Considering I haven't roped a calf for fifteen years? Yeah, I'm quite proud of myself."

"Did you make it up with the vet?"

"I tried." His smile was rueful. "She's a sharp one. I don't think I'll ever get the chance to put things right with her completely."

"Women," Chase said.

"Yeah." Blue moved off down the hallway and into the small shower next to the mudroom where they'd all left their boots.

Chase heard the water turn on and then made his way back into the warm kitchen, which was empty and smelled of chicken. He didn't think he'd be able to look a hamburger in the eye for weeks, let alone eat one. It was nice to share a moment of conversation with Blue without any animosity. He'd missed his brother's acerbic sense of humor. Chase's cell buzzed, and he held it to his ear.

"Yeah?"

"You're not playing at being a cowboy, are you?" Jake said. "You really are getting down and dirty."

Chase subsided into a chair and stretched out his aching feet toward the stove. "Spring branding. What can I do for you?"

"Moleculo were after some information today."

"And you couldn't help them?"

"That's one of your deals, Chase. You know how Matt and I feel about working with those environmental pirates."

"Oh yeah, that's right. Dirty money." Chase paused. "Do you know how many of your ecological projects will get off the ground because of that money, Jake? Fifty. Fifty brand-new start-ups."

"That many?"

"Yeah. Please listen to me very carefully. If you and Matt don't want the Moleculo money, tell me right now, and I'll tell them the deal is off."

"That sounds like a threat."

Chase sighed and shoved a hand through his hat-flattened hair. "It's not meant to be one. If you can come up with another way to offer all those emerging companies a start, then *tell* me. You just can't have it both ways. You can't leave me with having to go out and seek investors and then turn your noses up at the kind of companies I bring in. We started this together, so how come I'm the one taking all the risks and then being shot down for taking them?"

"Because you changed. You wanted more."

"I wanted more for all of us." Chase let out his breath. "Listen, when I come back, let's talk this out once and for all. I value your friendship too much to want things to end like this."

"You do?"

Chase winced at the note of uncertainty in his best friend's voice. "Yeah."

"When *will* you be back?"

"I'm not sure."

"We miss you."

"Yeah, you miss my telling you what to do and managing everything, right?"

"No, I miss *you*." Jake hesitated. "You sound much more relaxed at the moment."

"It's this place. It makes you think."

"Jobs is missing you as well."

"I bet he isn't. I bet you're giving him canned cat food every night rather than kibble."

"Canned? I'm *cooking* him fricking fish and chicken. That's what you *told* me to do."

"Yeah, but I never thought you'd do it." Chase found himself grinning. "That cat must think he's died and gone to heaven."

Jake was laughing now as well. "Come back soon, okay? We can sort this out; I know we can."

Chase's phone buzzed with a text message, and he clicked on a picture of a very fat-looking black cat eating some delicacy out of a fancy china bowl.

"Dude, he's going to weigh twenty pounds soon."

Jake snorted. "At least. By the way, you make a very convincing cowboy. I barely recognized you under all that dirt when Matt showed me the picture."

"It's in my blood. My family has owned this property for over a hundred years."

"Wow. I'd like to see it one day." Jake paused. "How come you've never taken us there?"

"It's a long story. I have to stick around and help my grandmother out for a while longer, and then I'll be back. Give Moleculo my direct line, talk to Matt, and make a decision about what you want to do about them, okay? We haven't signed anything yet, so we can break off negotiations at any time."

Chase heard the water turn off above his head. "I have to go. The shower is calling my name."

"Okay," Jake said. "I'll talk to Matt. Later."

Chase groaned as he stood up and stretched his arms over his head. Despite everything, he felt good. His time at the ranch had definitely helped him unravel some of the kinks in his system and given him a better perspective on his issues at work. He didn't want to lose any more friends, which meant he was going to have to compromise or walk away from the business.

He waited for his gut to tighten and for his heart to pound, and nothing happened. Maybe that meant he was finally making the right decisions after all.

Chapter Fifteen

"My advisor likes the William Morgan angle!"

January sat down and placed her laptop on the table beside Chase's.

"Really?" He looked up at her, his smile warm. He'd rolled up the sleeves of his shirt and left the top two buttons undone. He'd started to look underdressed without his cowboy hat on his head. "That's great, right?"

"It means I can reframe all the research I've already done around the view of Morgansville your ancestor's journal has given me. No one else has had access to this primary source material before. Thank you *so* much."

"Don't thank me; thank Ruth."

"You'll all get a mention in my acknowledgments. I just can't believe I'm actually going to get this thing done."

"Yeah, Kevin said you had difficulty finishing things."

January looked over at Chase, who had already returned his attention to his screen. "Did he?"

Chase looked up. "I didn't mean to suggest that—"

She offered him a tight smile. "It's okay. Kevin likes to talk about my failures."

"Actually he sounded quite concerned about you."

"Yeah. That's why he went over my head, pulled my funding, and canceled my classes when I tried to attend college."

"He did what?"

January opened her laptop and busied herself starting it up. "It's nothing."

"It obviously is something. Why the hell did he do that?"

"It was his money. He decided we needed it for something else. It wasn't a problem once he explained it to me. There's nothing for you to worry about."

"I'm not worried," he said slowly. "He made it sound as if . . ."

"I'd flaked out. Yeah, I know. When I asked him about that at the time, he said it was easier to blame me than to admit to having any financial problems to his business colleagues. He was sure I'd understand." She managed another smile. "Can we talk about something else? I'm going to be in the Bay Area in a month or so for a meeting with my advisor. Maybe we can have lunch."

"That would be awesome. You can stay with me."

"I'd like that." She smiled, meeting his eyes.

"Maybe we can make this work."

"What work?"

"This." He reached for her hand. "Us."

"There's an *us* now?" she teased, but inside she felt a slow blossoming of warmth. "I thought we were going to part as friends."

"I'm still here, and so are you. I'm not planning on us parting ways just yet."

"Despite Kevin's saying I'm a flaky loser?"

His slow smile died, and she kicked herself for saying the *K* word. Leaning in, she kissed Chase's mouth and then sat back in her chair.

"Trying to distract me?" he murmured.

"Maybe. Is it working?"

"Maybe. You might have to try it again to *really* convince me."

There was a loud throat-clearing sound from the door, and January jumped as Blue came in. He headed straight for the coffee.

"You two should get a room."

"I would if I didn't think Ruth would haul me straight out of it," Chase said.

"She's in town." Blue kept his back toward the table. "And I'm going out to fix some fencing around the barn. I'll be gone for at least an hour or so."

"Good to know," Chase said. "What are your plans, January?"

"I'm writing out my presentation for the historical tour tomorrow."

Chase groaned. "Damn, I'd forgotten those guys were coming."

January fixed him with a hopeful stare. "You and Blue are both going to hang around so that the guests can get an authentic family-run ranch experience, aren't you?"

Blue also groaned. "Do we get paid?"

"No, you're going to do it for Ruth and the future of the ranch."

"Hell, I'm up for that." Blue cast Chase a challenging glance. "How about you, bro?"

"I'll stick around to make sure none of your precious guests make off with any of *my* authentic family ranch."

"That's the spirit," January said. "Ruth's cooking them a big lunch, and they'll be gone by four."

"Shame, because if they'd stayed a bit later, they could've helped out with the chores," Chase muttered. "Maybe we could move those up?"

"I'm sure they'd love to feed the chickens and the horses.

What a *great* idea," January said, enthusiastically pretending to ignore the identical horrified expressions that passed over the brothers' faces. At least she was offering them the opportunity to bond over something. "I'll give you both a schedule for the day so you can follow along."

"Hold up," Blue said. "Schedule?"

January rose to her feet and headed for the door. "Can't stop. I have to go up and get the journal from my room. Thanks for the awesome input, guys."

She ran up the stairs and just about avoided laughing out loud before she shut her bedroom door behind her and threw herself facedown on her bed.

"You thought that was funny, eh?"

She shrieked as Chase followed her down, rolled her over and captured her hands over her head.

"Not at all."

He grinned at her. "Yeah, I can see that." He traced the corner of her mouth with his thumb. "I love seeing you laugh." His expression intensified. "I love seeing you come even more."

January was suddenly aware of the silence of the house settling around them and the sound of Blue's whistling fading away down toward the barn. Chase had her trapped beneath him on her bed, and she didn't want to be anywhere else in the world. He very slowly bent his head and kissed her, his mouth gentle and searching.

She let him, closing her eyes to further appreciate the sensation of his tongue flicking against hers and the rasp of his stubble against her cheek.

"Mmm . . ."

"You like that?" Chase murmured.

He kissed her again, his hand locked around her wrists that were stretched over her head. He eased his knee between hers until his lower body was cradled between her thighs.

Even through his jeans she could feel the rock-hard length of him pressing against her.

A curious sense of lassitude washed over her, and she sighed as he edged up her T-shirt, placing one large hand on her stomach.

"Don't stop."

"I wasn't intending to." He spread his fingers wide, nudging both the underside of her bra and the elastic of her panties. "But which way to go first?"

"You probably need a spreadsheet to work out all the possibilities."

"I already have one." He kissed her belly ring. "It's fairly complex. It could take me hours to explore all the possible ramifications."

"Wow, talk dirty nerd to me some more."

"I'd much rather show you." He used his tongue to toy with her metal piercing as his fingers began a slow glide upward to caress the underside of her breasts. He half-allowed her to sit up as he stripped her out of her T-shirt and undid her bra, leaving her half-naked and him still fully clothed. Not that she minded because when he lowered himself over her again the cotton of his shirt brushed against her skin, making her shiver.

He kissed his way down her throat and lingered there, nuzzling her neck, making her arch up to him in an instinctive appeal. His attention to detail made him a very thorough lover who remembered all the little places that made her squirm.

"Thorough," she breathed.

"Mmm?" He raised his head, his blue gaze questioning.

"You are."

He dealt with the snap of her jeans and eased down the zipper. "It's important to get these things right."

"I'm not arguing with you about that."

"For instance"—he bit gently on the curve of her shoulder,

and she barely restrained a whimper—"if I bite you here, you just go to pieces, don't you?"

"Yeah, all gooey like maple syrup."

"I knew it." He trailed his mouth down to her breast. "You like this, too, don't you?" She clutched at his hair as he licked her nipple. "Yeah, you do."

"What else do I like?"

His smile was full of promises as he eased her out of her jeans and panties in one smooth motion. "Hold on. I'll let you know."

"Please," January whispered.

Chase raised his head and wiped languorously at his mouth. "More?"

"I want all of you."

He glanced down at her needy flesh. "Are you sure? Because I'm fairly certain I've missed a few spots."

"You can catch up with them next time." She hooked her foot around his hip and jammed her heel into his ass as if she was spurring him on. "Take me, cowboy."

He knelt over her and very slowly unbuttoned his shirt, removed his belt, and shucked his jeans.

"Better?"

She mock-scowled as his beautiful body emerged from his clothing. "One day I'm going to tie you up in the barn, strip you naked, and lick you for days like a salt block."

"Is that a threat or a promise?"

He covered himself and came down over her.

"Whatever works." She sighed, as he pressed deep and held still. "Once I've gotten you tied up, I'll decide how it's going to go down."

He rolled his hips. "As long as something goes down in some way, I'm up for it."

She rolled her eyes at him. "Will you stop trying to be funny and concentrate?"

"Yes, ma'am. I will."

And then she forgot how to speak as he started to thrust, and then she forgot how to form actual words and could only make pitiful, encouraging noises, which seemed to excite him as much as her.

"Oh God." She breathed into his shoulder as she climaxed and clung to him with all her might. "That's . . ."

He slid his hands under her ass, bringing her higher and tighter into his short, jabbing thrusts, and the tension started to build again until she was simply fused with him from mouth to toes and coming with him. She didn't want to let him go as he collapsed over her, panting for breath, so she just held him close, enjoying the weight of him and his particular scent. She wondered if he felt as at home as she did in that old-fashioned brass bed in his family's home. The sounds of the ranch reemerged around them . . . the banging of Blue's hammer, the sound of a truck arriving in front of the house.

"Chase."

"Mmm?"

"I think Ruth and Roy are back."

"Mmm."

She patted his back, and he lazily surged his hips against her, making her catch her breath.

"We should move."

"No, we damn well should not."

She smiled against the muscled curve of his shoulder. "Ruth might be looking for us."

"Let her look. The woman will run away fast enough if she peeks in here and gets a view of my naked ass."

January allowed her fingers to play with the now-damp ends of Chase's dark hair and imagined what it would be like to wake up with him every morning and share each day.

She stared up at the ceiling. Oh God, this was bad. Chase was supposed to be her friend with benefits, not her forever man. They'd made a very clear bargain, and she knew he liked things to be clear. But she wanted the sweetness and the *rightness* of it so much it almost hurt.

Chase groaned and kissed the side of her face before easing out of her. "I mean it, January. I could roll over, tuck you under my arm, and sleep for hours right now."

Even though she knew it was weak, she allowed herself to relax into his arms and closed her eyes. She might be imagining a forever-after that would never happen, but she could at least enjoy the dream for another hour or two.

Ruth looked up from her newspaper as January came down the stairs.

"Roy was looking for you."

"Did he want to talk about tomorrow?" January self-consciously pushed her hair away from her face and sorted through the pile of paperwork she'd left on the table. "I have a schedule for him here. If he's home I could take it down to him?"

"You can do that in a minute. Sit down."

January sat and resisted the urge to fiddle with her papers. "Sorry about the mess. I got distracted."

"A man will do that to a woman."

January sighed. "Is this about Chase?"

Ruth held out her hand, palm up. "Good job."

"What do you mean?"

"Good job with my grandson. I've never seen him look so happy."

"Really?" January smiled. "I thought you were going to get mad at me for overstepping my professional boundaries or something."

"Your what?"

"Exactly." January kept hold of Ruth's hand. "But I

want you to know he's quite safe with me. I'm not going to hurt him. He'll be able to go back to work with his heart and mind intact."

Ruth looked puzzled. "I don't want him going back there and being exactly the same. I want him coming back here and settling down."

"Which is not something I can control or would ever try to influence."

"If there is something here he wants, he'll be back." Ruth patted January's hand. "I've seen the way he looks at you."

"What way?" She felt like a teenager, but she had to ask.

"As if he can't wait to get you into bed." Ruth chuckled. "I should take up matchmaking full-time."

"This was all your cunning plan, Ruth?"

January jumped as Chase's quiet voice came from over her shoulder. She turned to him and got quite a shock. He didn't look like he got the joke.

Ruth shook her head. "As I said, if I'd realized you two would click, I would've made you come out here months ago."

"Right." Chase turned on his heel and left the house, banging the door behind him.

"Good Lord. Now he's in a snit," Ruth said. "Some men can't bear to be pushed, and Chase is definitely one of them."

January was already half out of her chair, anxiety knotting her gut. "I'll go talk to him."

She headed down to the barn and found Chase leading Nolly out of his stall. He barely glanced her way as he tied the horse up and started checking his feet.

"You're mad at me," January said.

"I don't get mad."

"Then what? It was just a joke."

"I know." He slowly stood up, ignoring Nolly's playful

attempt to head-butt him. "It is kind of amusing. Get Chase into bed and bring him over to the dark side?"

January studied him carefully. "You're okay about this?"

"Why wouldn't I be?"

"Because most men wouldn't be. My ex—"

"I'm not your ex, and I don't get mad." He held her gaze. "Are we clear on that?"

She lowered her eyes and stared at his checkered shirt, counting the buttons up and down, up and down. "If you truly believe I would do that to you, or to *anyone,* then we have nothing more to say to each other."

He didn't reply for a long moment, and she unconsciously braced herself for any fallout. One of the barn cats rubbed itself against her legs and then coiled its tail around Chase's boot, linking them together.

"Are you sure this is really about me and not about your ex?"

She blinked at him. "What?"

"I'm not going to take some silly joke and make it into something we have to fight about."

She let out a very long breath. "I'm sorry."

"For what?"

"For jumping to the wrong conclusion." She grimaced. "I kind of . . . panicked."

"But we're friends, aren't we? I thought that was the whole point of our relationship. Friends don't do things like that to each other."

She almost sagged with relief. "Ruth did tell me a lot about you, but she never, ever suggested we should get together."

"For the record there *was* a moment there when I didn't like hearing two people I care about discussing me as if I were some kind of project to be won over, but I know what Ruth's like. She's always trying something."

January brought her hand up to cup his cheek. "I would *never* do that to you."

"Okay. Then let's agree that no one likes the thought of being used."

"That's it?"

"What else is there to say?" He kissed her nose.

He was *so* not like her ex-husband. She would've been paying for that little joke for days.

Chase kissed her again. "What if I promise to stick around all day tomorrow and help out with the historical groupies?"

"That would certainly make me very happy."

She kissed him back, and his slow smile emerged. One thing she loved about him was his ability to let things go and move on. Kevin would've made her suffer. Once or twice he'd even slapped her. She shouldn't have assumed Chase would be the same.

Nolly neighed and stamped his feet as if reminding Chase that he was still waiting.

"I've got to go and see Roy," January said.

"Take Sunflower, and we can ride over together." Chase started brushing Nolly down. "It's a lovely afternoon."

Chapter Sixteen

"And this is the barn. It's actually original and predates the current house by about fifty years. It was constructed around 1855 by the original William Morgan and his wife." January stepped aside to allow the dozen tour guests to wander into the open space. "The cement floor and drainage was added more recently, and the whole structure was retrofitted for earthquake issues."

January winked at Margie Frost, the organizer of the tour, as all the cameras came out again. Margie sidled up close.

"This is going really well. Thanks so much for all the prep you put into the tour."

"You're welcome. I'm researching the ranch for my thesis, so it wasn't hard to pull out some interesting information. I've also compiled a pdf document so your guests can have something to reference after they've left."

The door of the feed room opened, and Chase came out, his gaze roving over the tourists and settling on January.

"Oh, *my*," Margie breathed. "Is that a real, live fifth-generation Morgan cowboy?"

"Yup."

"I think I need my smelling salts."

January heard a familiar whistle from the other end of

the barn. "Well, don't get too excited, but there's another one approaching from the west."

Chase strolled over and tipped his hat to her. A collective sigh ran through all the women on the tour.

"January? Do you want to introduce me to these folks so I can answer any questions?"

"That would be very kind of you, Chase."

January stood back and let him field the comments and inquiries, which he did with good grace and humor. She wasn't surprised by how much he knew about the ranch anymore. He'd just hidden it well at first.

Within minutes he had them all trailing after him to feed the chickens and meet the horses. To her surprise, Blue was leading Nolly and Messi out from their stalls.

She paused to watch him tie them up at the rail. "What are you going to do with the horses?"

"We thought we'd demonstrate how to put a saddle and a bridle on a Western horse and maybe do a bit of riding."

Impulsively, January kissed Blue's cheek. "That would be awesome!"

"As I've mentioned, I want this place to succeed. I'm more surprised that it was Chase who suggested it."

"He's trying to get back into my good graces."

Blue's grin widened. "Cool. Keep it up." He looked over her shoulder. "He's coming back. Get them all to gather around here, would you?"

January leaned back against the corner of the barn and watched the two brothers take the visitors through a comprehensive guide to saddling a ranch horse.

They worked well together. Most of the women and the recently married gay couple who were on their honeymoon couldn't take their eyes off Chase and Blue. Even the men were interested in the technicalities, and everyone asked lots of questions.

Eventually Blue looked at his brother. "Now we've gotten

them ready to go, maybe we should take them out into the field and show you a few tricks of the trade."

"Tricks?" January muttered, and checked her itinerary. "That's not on my agenda."

No one was listening to her, and the guests obediently moved away from the barn to the fenced-in field and hung over the railings. She followed and opened the gate as Blue and Chase mounted up and flowed past her into the pasture.

"Damn." Beside her, Margie sighed. "They sure are a beautiful sight. We could sell a thousand tours a day if everyone got to come and see these two guys."

"They aren't always here." Even though January really wanted the historical tour guide to put them on the regular schedule, she thought it was only fair to set Margie's expectations low. "They both have other careers."

"But they *might* be here," Margie said as she surreptitiously took another photo with her phone. "That's still a selling point."

January smiled as she closed the gate, checked the time, and went to stand by the fence like everyone else.

Chase rode over to Blue. "What's the plan?"

"I thought you had one. This was your idea."

"Let's take them through the basics and then talk about some of the more specialized skills a rancher needs to run cattle." He gave Blue an encouraging grin. "Good thing you remembered how to rope a calf. You can demonstrate that."

"No calves in this field."

"Then you'll have to improvise."

Blue raised an eyebrow. "You could run around, and I could hog-tie you."

"Only if you can get me off my horse." Chase saw the

competitive flash in Blue's eyes and turned back to the fence. "Let's go."

January was standing by the gate, her chin propped up on her forearm, watching him intently. He winked as he rode by, and she frowned and tapped her schedule, which was kind of amusing.

He sat back in the saddle and drew Nolly to a stop.

"Okay, here we go."

Blue returned to his side after demonstrating how to form a loop with his rope and lasso a fence post, and Chase nodded at him.

"Nice job." He shot a glance at January and the tour guide, who were the only people not staring at him and Blue. "Are we done?"

Blue coiled his rope back up and placed it over the saddle horn. "Not quite. How about we finish on a high note?"

"What exactly were you thinking of trying?" Chase asked warily.

"That trick we used to do."

"Which one?"

"The Roman charioteer one."

"You're kidding. We haven't tried that for twenty years."

"Wuss."

"What if we mess it up?"

"Double wuss."

Chase sighed and led Nolly to the fence. "You're crazy, you know?" He unbuckled the heavy saddle and removed the blanket underneath, balancing them on the fence. Blue did the same thing, and then they both mounted bareback by vaulting onto the horses.

January stopped talking and came right up to the fence again. "What—?"

"Let's go," Blue said.

Luckily Messi and Nolly were of a similar size and had stride patterns that worked well together. Chase and Blue rode around the perimeter of the field at a lope so closely together that their knees and the pointed tips of their cowboy boots almost touched.

"Go." Blue ordered.

"*You* go. You're the marine."

"Okay, wuss."

Blue swung one leg over the side of Messi, grabbed Nolly's mane, bounced down onto the ground and immediately bounced back up to sit behind Chase. He still held Messi's reins in his hand, and the horse continued to pace alongside Nolly. There were a few yelps and cheers from the spectators.

They completed another circuit, and, as they approached the onlookers again, Blue passed Chase the second set of reins.

"We've got this. You're going to have to stand up first."

Chase sighed as he measured the gap between Nolly and Messi. "God help me."

He shifted his weight, came up into a crouch, and planted one foot on Messi's broad back.

"Yeah!" Blue boosted him from behind and, within another second, Chase was standing, one foot on each horse, the reins held high in his hands. He felt about as secure as a mouse at a cat convention. Blue stood, too, his arm around Chase's waist bracing him, and they continued around again to the applause of their audience.

"If that doesn't make January forgive you, nothing will," Blue yelled way too close to Chase's ear. "She's grinning like a loon."

Blue had the nerve to remove his cowboy hat and wave it while he hollered like a Vegas showgirl. Chase kept his attention firmly on the horses.

"Okay, now here comes the tricky part." Blue's grip tightened on Chase's shoulder. "You stay put, and I'll transfer over to Messi."

Chase held on grimly while Blue moved behind him until he was astride Messi again.

"Hand over the reins and step back across."

Chase complied and sank back down onto Nolly's back. His legs were trembling like Jell-O, but as far as he could tell, he and Blue were both in one piece.

They stopped back at the gate to rapturous applause. Chase dismounted and found his brother grinning at him. For a moment their eyes met and held, and they shared nothing but the excitement of the present. All it did was remind Chase of what he'd lost. Blue turned away to talk to the crowd around him, and Chase stepped back.

January came dashing over to him, her eyes shining.

"That was *awesome*! Thank you so much!"

"You can thank Blue. He made me do it."

"It was amazing." She kissed Chase's cheek. "I never knew you could do tricks."

"Neither did I." She picked up the saddle, and he started back to the barn with Nolly. "I haven't done anything so stupid since I knew better and valued my future existence."

"You did good," Blue said from behind him. "I thought you'd refuse."

Chase turned to his brother. "And risk your calling me a wuss forever after?" He cleared his throat. "It was kind of fun."

"Yeah." Blue nodded. "I'd say we should do it more often, but I don't think I'm quite up to it either."

They shared a crack of laughter, and then Blue moved away to tend to Messi. January returned from putting the saddle away, and the historical tour guests got a light-hearted lesson in putting a horse to bed.

By the time they left, January's schedule had been

torn up and thrown away, and a dozen people were busy declaring that their visit to Morgan Ranch had been the highlight of the tour by far. Margie had thanked them all several times and promised to be in touch. Ruth had provided the guests with a sumptuous tea and had wrapped up several cakes and sandwiches to see them on their way.

All in all Chase thought January should forgive him his transgressions for the next six months. He went into the kitchen to find Blue and January sitting at the table, passing out plates and silverware and chatting about the day. He took a seat and just listened in, nodding occasionally.

Ruth came in with a pile of mail and placed it on the table. "Roy picked this up in town this morning. Sort it out, will you, Chase?"

There was a pile of junk mail, a handwritten letter addressed to January from Arizona, and a couple of bills for Ruth. Chase stilled as he recognized the Kingsmith Financial stationery.

"Do you want me to open this?" he asked Ruth, showing her the letter as she stirred something on the stove.

"It'll just be another threat."

"Threat?" Blue said, all the good humor draining from his face.

Chase held his gaze. "I told you about this company the other night. They're chasing Ruth for repayment of a loan that was taken out twenty-five years ago."

Blue subsided into his chair. "I thought you said you had that sorted."

"I'm working on it. That's one of the reasons Kevin was here."

"With all your money and contacts, you still can't fix it?"

"That's enough, Blue," Ruth intervened. "Chase is doing his best."

"I'm more than willing to pay off the loan," Chase

said evenly. "Ruth doesn't want me to because she doesn't believe it's her responsibility."

"Then whose is it?"

"Someone called Morgan. That's all I know." Chase shrugged. "You said it wasn't you."

"But you suspect it might be the twins?"

"I doubt it, seeing as they were only toddlers when the loan was taken out. Something's not right, though."

Blue sat back. "No, it isn't. Of course, if you hadn't meddled all those years ago, we might have parents sitting down with us at this table who might know the answer."

Chase schooled himself not to show the ragged hurt Blue's comment stirred in him. "I thought we'd been through all that. I called the sheriff, Blue; that's all I did."

"That's not quite true, is it?"

Chase sat perfectly still as Blue continued talking.

"You forget I was there. I heard you tell the sheriff that you'd seen Dad attack Mom with the kitchen knife."

"Yeah, I did."

"Why the fuck didn't you keep your mouth shut?"

"Blue, that's enough, and mind your language!" Ruth snapped.

Chase said nothing and kept his gaze fixed firmly on the table. He hadn't realized Blue had heard that part of the nightmarish evening. It sure put a whole new perspective on his brother's dislike of him.

"Chase . . ." Ruth sat opposite him and covered his hand with her own. "Did you really tell the sheriff that?"

Great. She sounded even more shocked than Blue. Chase drew a slow breath. "I can't change what happened, Ruth. I still don't think every damned thing that transpired after that can be laid at my door."

"Of course it can't," January said quietly. "If your father was covered in blood, then the sheriff would have taken him in regardless of what Chase said or didn't say. This is really unfair of you, Blue."

"With all due respect, January, I think you should keep out of this one." Blue held up his hand.

Chase fixed his brother with a glare. "If you insist on bringing shit up over the dinner table, then anyone sitting around it has a right to his or her opinion."

Blue grimaced. "I'm sorry, January." He shook his head. "I just don't get it, Chase. That man loved you."

"Yeah." Chase stood up, his chair screeching on the floorboards. "And, hey, guess what? I loved him right back." He headed for the door, ignoring Ruth's pleas for him to stay, and walked blindly out into the night.

He kept going until he reached the barn and let himself into Nolly's stall, burying his face against the horse's neck and just breathing him in.

Twenty years . . .

He'd never regretted something so much, and he doubted he ever would.

January glared at Blue, who was cursing quietly to himself as Ruth turned back to the stove.

"*Nice*," she said.

"He didn't deny what he did, January."

"He was *twelve*. Why do I have to keep saying that? Your parents were adults. They made their own choices."

"I know that. It's just that, when Chase starts in on someone in the family, I feel like a little kid again, watching helplessly as my whole goddamn life falls apart."

"Chase's life fell apart as well, and he had to put up with you and your brothers treating him like a pariah."

Blue met her indignant gaze. "He should've lied, January. Even if he did call the sheriff for all the right reasons, he should have protected our father."

"One thing I do know about Chase is that he is as straight as they come." January looked over at Ruth. "*Could* he have lied, Ruth? Would it even have occurred to him?"

"Only if his daddy told him to, and, even though Billy made some mistakes, I don't think he would've asked Chase to do that."

"Then maybe Chase just told the truth." January looked at Blue. "And maybe you just don't want to believe it because it's easier to idolize your father and make Chase the scapegoat." She stood up. "I'm going to see if I can find him. Thanks for all your help today, Blue. I really appreciated it."

"Sure," Blue nodded. "I . . . hope Chase is okay."

January went out of the kitchen and walked down to the barn. It was so dark you could almost taste the velvety blackness on your tongue. She stopped by the entrance of the barn and inhaled the smell of sun-warmed hay and horse.

One of the horses chuffed out a breath, and she moved quietly down the row of stalls counting heads until she realized Nolly was missing. She went back to the tack room and grabbed her old jacket and made her way out toward the field behind the barn where the brothers had performed their tricks. She wasn't surprised to see a horse and rider moving competently around the space.

She climbed over the fence and watched the man and horse work together in perfect harmony as the moon appeared from behind the clouds, illuminating the space. There was almost no wind, and she could hear Chase's soft commands as Nolly obediently changed speed or direction or some other horse thing January didn't quite understand. All she knew was that she was watching perfection.

After a while he came toward her and drew to a halt, reaching down his hand.

"Come on up."

She put her foot on his boot and was hoisted upward to sit in front of him, her ass snug against the front of his jeans and his left arm wrapped tightly around her waist. He clicked at Nolly, and they were moving toward the gate, which Chase bent to open, and then they were flying across the water meadows toward the eerie stillness of the mountains.

She leaned back against the roll of his hips as he effortlessly controlled the horse. He'd tried to explain to her that riding wasn't about sawing on the reins or kicking the horse, but all about core strength. Sitting in front of him she finally got a true sense of what he was saying. His hands and feet were almost relaxed. All the motion came from his thighs, hips, and abs.

No wonder he looked so good naked. . . .

He dropped Nolly down into a walk and headed toward the banks of the creek.

"Are you cold?" he murmured in her ear.

"No, I'm good." He was warm enough for both of them, and she did have her jacket on. "Are you okay?"

He sighed, the sound stirring the ends of her hair. "Not really."

"Do you want to talk about it?"

He nipped her ear. "That's a remarkably generic question, January. Have you been practicing your tact?"

"I might have been."

"There's no need. Blue's right. I did tell the sheriff that my dad had attacked my mom with the knife."

She shrugged, the motion bringing her back against his broad chest. "I doubt the sheriff would have missed seeing the blood for himself."

"Yeah, but I could've lied. I could've said my dad had cut himself carving the turkey or something."

"When your mom was missing and your dad was acting out of character?"

"I should have tried."

"I don't think lying comes naturally to you somehow."

There was a long pause. "No, it doesn't," he said softly. "It sucks, it—" He stopped talking and let Nolly walk on. "We should be getting back."

She turned her head to look up at him and caught the hint of shadows in his eyes. "Whatever happened, Chase, I don't think Blue is right. I think at his core he knows that, too."

Chase snorted. "Then he has a funny way of showing it."

"Yes, it's time he grew up. I told him so."

"You did?"

She touched Chase's cheek. "Sure I did. It's about time someone defended you."

He blinked and moved his lips until they brushed her palm. "I don't think anyone has ever stood up for me about this before. Thank you."

He sounded almost surprised, which made her want to slap Blue Morgan and the other brothers silly. "You're welcome."

He bent his head and kissed her very sweetly until Nolly spoiled the moment by giving a little bunny hop sideways. Chase's arm tightened around January's waist, holding her steady, and then relaxed again.

"Let's go home."

She turned to face the front and stared out between Nolly's ears as the horse walked back to the ranch. She still had a sense that something wasn't quite right, but she was damned if she knew what it was. Either Chase was a better liar than she could possibly imagine or there was something she didn't yet know.

She was pretty sure it was the latter.

"We're almost there. I'll take care of Nolly. You go on up to bed," Chase murmured in her ear.

"If you're sure." She was so tired she was yawning hard

enough to dislocate her jaw. It had been a busy day, but a deeply satisfying one. Margie had pretty much guaranteed them a spot on future tours if they wanted it. She just had to make it official and generate some paperwork. Ruth was going to be thrilled.

Chase stopped Nolly at the foot of the steps leading up to the porch and helped January down.

"Are you sure you're okay?" January looked up at Chase.

"I'm good. Thank you for . . . coming to find me and, hell, for believing in me even though you don't know everything."

"You could tell me everything," she invited.

His smile was wry. "I wish. I keep my promises though." He tipped his hat to her. "Night, January. Sweet dreams."

She started up the steps, pausing at the screen door to open it carefully before remembering that Blue had fixed it earlier that day and that it no longer squeaked.

"At least he's useful for something." she whispered to herself as she crept up the stairs.

There was no light under Blue's door, and the bathroom was empty. January washed and put on her long-sleeved T-shirt. From the window, she could just make out the barn and the single light showing where Chase was tending to Nolly. She got into bed and was just about to close her eyes when something occurred to her.

"What promises?"

Chase gave Nolly one last pat and turned toward the house. He'd decided to keep Nolly for his personal use when he returned to the ranch and get another horse for Miguel and Roy. If Blue was intending on coming out more regularly or even living with Ruth, he would probably be happy to exercise Nolly.

Or maybe he wouldn't.

There was still a light on in the kitchen, and Chase slowed his step as he came into the room. Blue sat at the table, nursing a bottle of beer.

"Hey."

Chase nodded at him.

"This is probably getting boring for you, but I'm apologizing again." Blue grimaced. "I'm reacting to you like a kid, and January's right. It's not fair."

Chase took the seat opposite his brother. "She bawled you out, did she?"

"Yeah. She reminds me a lot of Ruth. That's a compliment, by the way."

"She certainly makes me think about shit I don't want to think about," Chase confessed. "I don't want to fight with you, Blue. I don't want to feel like every time I come back here we're going to have to go through all this again. What can I do to make things right between us?"

Blue sighed. "I think that's my problem, not yours. As soon as I get back on ranch property, the past kind of comes back to life. I was so fucking *happy* here, and then it all fell apart."

"I know the feeling."

"But January made me think. You were just a kid and such a Dudley Do-Right. You probably felt you had no choice but to answer the sheriff's questions."

"Something like that." Chase held Blue's gaze. "If I could go back and change what happened that night? I'd do it in a heartbeat. But I can't, and we have to find a way to move on from there. It's been twenty years, Blue."

"It's just that things have remained so . . . unfinished. They never found Mom and Rachel's bodies, so we never got real closure, you know?"

Chase nodded. "Yeah, I know. I've spent quite a bit of money on private detectives over the years, trying to find new evidence, but there's nothing."

"Did you ever ask Dad about it afterward?"

"When I felt guilty as hell and he was slowly drowning himself in alcohol? No, I can't say I had the nerve to bring it up."

Blue took a slug of his beer and slowly wiped his mouth. "Me neither. I couldn't bear to look at him, let alone talk about shit. And that's part of my problem. I feel guilty as hell about letting him down when he needed me, and it was easier to take it out on you."

"You were only eleven. I was the oldest. I was supposed to be the responsible one."

"And you were, weren't you? I've tried to convince myself otherwise, but you damn well brought us up after that." Blue buried his face in his hands. "God, I'm sorry, Chase. You don't deserve all this crap. I've had my head up my ass for way too long about this."

Chase reached out and tentatively patted Blue's shoulder. "It's okay. I just want us to get along and make good decisions for Ruth and the future of this place. If you're going to be around for the next few years, I'll feel a lot happier about leaving the ranch in your capable hands."

Blue straightened up. "Considering what a shit I've been to you, that's really nice to hear."

"We're still family. I didn't exactly make much effort to sort stuff out with you guys, did I? I just buried myself in school and then work and left everything festering. I regret that now."

"At least you had the balls to contact me."

Chase grinned. "Actually, that was January's doing. She goaded me into it."

"She's a keeper, Chase."

"Yeah." He let that notion sink into him and waited for the usual panic to set in. Nothing happened, except he suspected from the way Blue was looking at him that he had a stupid goofy smile on his face.

"You are so screwed," Blue teased, confirming Chase's suspicions.

"Yeah, well." Chase stood up. "I'm going to bed."

Blue looked up at him. "Night, TC."

"Night, BB." Chase went up the stairs and into the bathroom, where he washed and stripped down to his boxers before dropping his clothing in the laundry basket at the top of the stairs. Blue had sounded like he meant what he'd said. Chase sure hoped so.

He went into his room and crossed over to the window to draw the drapes against the shine of the moon. It was so quiet out there that he could hear the horses down in the barn and some stupid cockerel that had decided it was morning already.

"Damn birds," he muttered as he turned toward the bed.

"Hmm?"

His breath stuttered in his throat as his hand connected with a warm, naked body.

"January?"

"Who else?"

"What's up?" He walked around to the other side of the bed and got in, rolling onto his side to face her. "I thought you'd be asleep by now."

She cupped his chin. "What did you mean when you said you'd kept your promises?"

"About what?" He knew exactly what she was referring to, but he pretended not to.

"Don't try the innocent act. We both know you remember every single thing that's ever happened. What promises did you make that night and to whom?"

"I didn't mean it quite like that," he prevaricated.

"Chase . . ."

He met her stare. "I can't tell you, okay? That's what a promise is."

"So there is something to tell?"

"Even if there was, I wouldn't tell you. There's no point. It's over and done with." He kissed her nose. "And I have much better things to do with a naked woman in my bed than argue about the past."

"But—"

"January, I'm not willing to break any promises I made to anyone that night, so can we just let it go?"

She studied him intently, her face so close that he could make out each individual shard of silver and gray in her eyes.

"If I work it out, will you tell me if I'm right?"

"No."

He moved on top of her, and she squeaked before he managed to cover her mouth with his own and kissed her for all he was worth. After a few moments she grumbled low in her throat and kissed him back. He knew he'd only won a temporary reprieve, but he was more than willing to exploit it for all it was worth.

Tomorrow was another day and with Blue now willing to forgive and forget, the subject was unlikely to be aired again. At least Chase hoped it wouldn't be. But for now, he'd enthusiastically apply himself to making sure the only thing January Mitchell was capable of thinking about was his lovemaking.

Chapter Seventeen

"So how much longer is he staying here?" Yvonne asked.

"Chase? I'm not sure. Another week maybe?"

January stacked the final chair on the last coffee shop table and watched as Yvonne locked the door and turned the sign to CLOSED. It was six in the evening. The café was now their private domain for a few hours before Yvonne went to bed at nine, in order to be ready for her four a.m. start. January didn't know how Yvonne did it, but her friend insisted that baking the bread and pastries fresh every morning was worth the early nights and that she had no life anyway.

"I saw Chase at Maureen's with his younger brother," Yvonne purred. "Blue, isn't it?"

"Yeah, they're quite a pair, aren't they?"

"I've heard they both look even better on a horse."

"True." January grinned. "Every woman's cowboy fantasy come to life."

"I envy your living out there sometimes." Yvonne brought a pot of coffee over and a plate of leftover doughnuts and cream puffs.

"And I envy your having access to all this sugar," January said as she pondered what to choose.

"I'd rather have a real man in my bed. You're sleeping with Chase, aren't you? That special smile only comes from being well satisfied in bed."

"I can't complain in that department." January took a sugared doughnut and bit into it, almost moaning when she discovered it was full of jelly. "Mmm . . ."

"Is it serious?" Yvonne propped her elbow on the table and handed January a napkin to wipe the jelly off her chin.

"Well, I like him a lot, but we kind of agreed not to get too heavy, and to have a kind of no-strings-attached thing."

"Okay."

"Chase likes to know where he stands with women."

"So, he's a commitment-phobe then?"

"We agreed to keep it light and fun." January chewed determinedly on her doughnut and then sighed. "And I want to settle down on the ranch and have his babies."

Yvonne started to laugh. "Seriously?"

"Yup. I'm an idiot."

"Have you told him about this slight change of plan?"

"Of *course* I haven't. He'd probably run away screaming."

Yvonne nodded wisely. "Commitment-phobe."

"No, it's more that he stated up-front what he wanted, and I agreed with him." January made a face. "I didn't want the one-night-stand thing, and I tried the married-for-life thing, and neither of them worked for me. So I thought I'd try the friends-with-benefits route."

"You do know that none of these options work if it's not the right man?" Yvonne asked.

"I just thought that if we were both honest about what we wanted right from the start things would work out. Now he's going to think I'm like all the other women who chase after him and want to marry him so they can gain access to his money."

"He's rich?"

"Millionaire," January said glumly. "Hence, the women throwing themselves at him. Apparently it gets old."

"Well, duh." Yvonne shook her head. "It must be *so hard* for him being great-looking *and* wealthy. I don't know how he manages to drag himself out of bed every morning."

January shot her grinning friend a look. "Work with me on this, okay?"

"So, maybe you should tell him how you really feel."

"But what if I do that and he runs away in terror, and never comes back to the ranch to see Ruth again?"

"You really think that will happen?"

"God, I don't know." January groaned. "Really, I should tell him and then leave myself, but I've got to finish my thesis, and I need to be at the ranch."

"You could stay with me in town and go out to the property when you needed to."

"If Ruth would let me."

"She doesn't approve?"

"She wants Chase to stay on the ranch and settle down. If I'm the reason he stays, she would be ecstatic. If I mess this up and send him running for the Sierras again, she'll be pissed with me."

"It's certainly a dilemma." Yvonne ate the chocolate topping off an éclair. "Has he ever mentioned wanting to make things more permanent?"

"He told me that he thinks the friends-with-benefits thing is working really well. And he offered to put me up if I have to visit the Bay Area."

"Well, that's positive." Yvonne said brightly. "Perhaps you could wait until you go and see him in San Francisco before you tell him the awful truth."

"That's certainly an idea. I could make a quick getaway if everything went south. I suppose there's always the possibility that I might not like him as much without his

Stetson on." January finished her doughnut. "And I've only known him for a month or so. It's really too fast to be making any major relationship decisions." She groaned. "Oh God, I'm such a liar. I just feel so certain that he's the one."

"If he is 'the one,' he'll stick around and work it out for himself."

"You're so wonderfully practical."

Yvonne winked at her. "It's all that time I spent studying in France. The French are such a strange mix of the pragmatic and the passionate." She patted January's hand. "Just hang in there, okay?"

"As long as I don't go blurting out the *L* word, I'll be fine. And there's always duct tape." January turned her attention back to the plate of cakes. "Now, if you don't mind, I have some serious eating to do."

Chase finally located his cell under a pile of Ruth's magazines in the best parlor and held it to his ear. "Yeah?"

"It's Kevin, Mr. Morgan. How are you doing today?"

"I'm good, how can I help you?"

"I have some more information for you about King-smith. I was just about to make my return trip to LA, and I thought I could come by and share the data with you in person."

Chase frowned. "You can't just tell me over the phone?"

"I'd rather not. A man in your position should never discuss personal matters over the airwaves. It really is no trouble to pop by."

Chase sighed. Like anyone "popped" into Morgantown. It was beyond the back of beyond. "Sure. When do you think you'll get here?"

"I'm actually just passing through Bridgeport, so I'm not far away. Would you prefer to meet me in Morgantown at the hotel or at the local bar? I have a reservation at the hotel for the night."

"That's a great idea and will save you fifteen minutes or so of driving out here. What time do you want me?"

"Around seven?"

"Cool. I'll meet you in the bar of the hotel."

After he ended the call he checked the time. It was just past six. January had gone out to see Yvonne at the coffee shop, and Blue was working in the barn. Chase left the parlor and went into the kitchen where Ruth was busy peeling a pan full of potatoes.

"I'll be out for an hour or so. Will dinner keep?"

"For you?" She smiled at him. "Sure. I'll put you up a plate."

He bent to kiss her head. "You smell like ginger."

"That's because I made some banana bread earlier."

He groaned. "You're trying to fatten me up, aren't you?"

She patted his flat stomach. "Can't cook fast enough to do that. You've never had a problem keeping the weight off, just like your daddy."

Chase hesitated. "Do you think Blue was right? That if I'd lied to the sheriff things would've turned out differently?"

She met his gaze steadily. "No, I don't. Your mom and dad had their own paths to lead, and they were already set on them."

He kissed her on the nose. "Thanks for that."

"No thanks necessary. You've always been a good boy, Chase, and you were put in an impossible situation that night."

He went still. "What do you mean?"

"Your mom wasn't happy here, and your dad just couldn't understand why. I told him not to push her too hard after the baby was born, but he didn't want to listen to me and insisted on dragging you all out here before she was ready to leave her friends and family."

"I don't want to talk about her."

Ruth sighed. "I know you don't, and I know why. I understand why you did what you did." She patted his cheek and turned back to the stove. "Now you get along and let me finish making dinner."

Chase stared at her back for a long moment. Part of him wanted to ask more questions about what exactly she thought she knew, but the rest of him wanted to lay the matter down and run. He picked up his hat and his jacket.

"See you later, then." He wandered down to the barn, where Blue was still repairing the wooden siding. He waited until his brother stopped hammering and handed him another nail.

"Hey, I'm going into town. Can you do the chores?"

"Sure." Blue wiped his forehead on his sleeve. "You going to get January?"

"Nope, she's busy with Yvonne."

"Yvonne runs the coffee shop, correct? Speaks with a hint of a foreign accent and is tall, dark, and an excellent pastry chef?"

"That's the one." Chase gave his brother an amused look. "You should get January to introduce you."

"I intend to." Blue's answering nod was full of promises.

Chase was smiling as he got into the cab of his monstrous blue truck and started the engine. Blue was definitely planning on settling in and making a few friends in his childhood town. What would it be like to live on the ranch full-time and become immersed in the local community? A month ago Chase would've been horrified at the thought of it, but now it didn't seem so bad. Having people who cared about you and knew your family history suddenly seemed like a blessing.

He got out to open the ranch gate at the back end of the property, drove through, and closed it behind him and the truck. If January were at the ranch all the time, he'd definitely be coming back a whole lot more. . . . But could he ask that of her? Could he expect her to hang around and wait for him to breeze in from the city and then leave again? She deserved better, and she'd only wanted a casual relationship.

But then so had he.

When had that changed? He noticed he was sitting still as a stone and hadn't moved off. When had he realized he wanted more? She'd reached inside him and made a place for herself without his even noticing. And, for the first time in his life, he wasn't scared. Was it because he'd met her at the ranch and she'd seen the real him, the cowboy inside the businessman that he couldn't ever completely erase?

She seemed to like him just the way he was.

Chase moved off, remembering to turn on his lights as the dusk deepened and the shadows lengthened and he bumped along the uneven track. He had no idea how a man went about convincing a woman to take him on more permanently; he'd always been the one hunted down. Perhaps it was time for him to find out.

Hayes Historic Hotel was an old wooden-fronted building that had been put up in the 1920s and looked even older. These days the lobby was decked out like an old-fashioned saloon with mirrors running along the back wall and a long antique walnut bar stretching almost the length of the room. Chase always expected to hear the tinkling of a piano in the background and the sounds of a bar fight or a gun battle to emerge from the bar.

The Hayes family, who ran the hotel, had been there since the 1930s. Mrs. Hayes was the housekeeper, and her various offspring got pressed into service depending on the hotel's staffing needs and their need for money.

"Hey, Wade." Chase grinned at the youngest of the four brothers, who staggered by with a set of luggage.

"Hey, Mr. M."

Chase obligingly stuck his boot in the door of the elevator to stop the doors from closing, and Wade puffed past him.

"Thanks, dude."

"You're welcome."

Chase made his way through into the main bar, nodded at Tom Hayes, who was shaking a cocktail behind the bar, and spotted Kevin in one of the booths, staring at his laptop screen.

"You want a beer, Chase?" Tom called over to him.

"Yes, please." Chase halted by Kevin. "Can I get you something to drink?"

"I'm good." Kevin's smile didn't reach his eyes. "Thanks for coming to see me."

Chase slid into the seat opposite Kevin. "What's up?"

Kevin shut the laptop. "I spoke to a friend of mine who knows someone who worked for Kingsmith. She managed to get me some more information about that insurance policy."

"Okay."

Kevin consulted his paperwork. "Apparently, the loan was being paid off by a Mr. W. Morgan. The payments stopped six months ago, just before the annuity attached to the loan was due to be paid out. Your grandmother's address was the only one on the file, so I think the company assumed the William in question must have been your grandfather."

"Who couldn't have been paying anything since he's been dead for about twenty years." Chase took a moment to let that sink in.

"I did some more checking and found another William Morgan who is still alive."

"Do you have an address for this man?"

"Yes." Kevin passed over a piece of paper. "That's his last known address anyway. Apparently, he likes to move around."

"Yeah, he would."

"Do you know this individual?"

"I think I do." Chase put the paper in his pocket. He wasn't actually surprised at all. In fact this made everything make sense in a weird kind of way. "Too many Williams in my family tree. It's easy to make a mistake. Is there anything else?"

"Do you wish me to follow up on this information or would you prefer to deal with it yourself? We have the necessary manpower in that area to make personal contact if you'd like us to do so."

"I think I'll handle this myself." Chase nodded. "Thanks for your help."

"You are most welcome. I couldn't bear to leave the investigation half-finished."

Chase managed a smile and sipped at his beer. "Do you think this contact of yours in Kingsmith would talk directly to me?"

"I'm not sure. I can ask if you like."

"I'd appreciate that."

Kevin refilled his coffee cup from the pot at his elbow. "It's been a long day."

"It sure has," Chase agreed. "Are you driving back to LA?"

"No, I'm flying out of the Mammoth Yosemite Airport. They have a direct flight."

"Really? Out of that tiny place? That's good to know."

"Are you planning on moving out here permanently then, Chase?"

"I haven't made any major decisions yet, but I do intend to spend more time on the ranch. Having easy flight connections to some of the cities I do business with would make life a lot easier."

As Kevin added cream and sugar to his coffee, Chase wondered how soon he could make his excuses and leave.

"I got the impression from Janny that you were intent on getting rid of the ranch pretty soon."

"Not while Ruth's around."

Kevin looked confused. "Really? That's not what I understood from Janny. She told me that, if you couldn't reach an agreement with your brothers soon, Ruth was gifting the place to the Morgantown Historical Society."

"That sounds just like Ruth."

Kevin smiled. "Blue did mention something to that effect, but he still took her into town to see her lawyer about changing her will again."

"Poor Henry. He probably hides when he sees my grandmother coming." Chase picked up his hat and slid to the end of the seat. "I have to be getting back for dinner. Thanks for all your hard work. I'll give Ruth your best."

"You do that, and say hi to Janny for me if she's still there."

"She's there."

"I suppose she would be, seeing as she'll benefit if the ranch really does end up belonging to the historical society. Ruth said Janny offered to run it." Kevin frowned. "Maybe you'd better warn her that Ruth changes her mind a lot so Janny won't get her hopes up and hang around for nothing. She won't like that."

Chase jammed his Stetson on his head. "I'll certainly mention it to her. Thanks again for all your hard work."

He left ten bucks on the table and walked out of the bar, nodding to Tom and winking at Mrs. Hayes, who was manning the front desk. He didn't stop to chat; he needed all his resources just to keep moving and not go back in the bar, pick Kevin up, and shake him until his teeth rattled.

Chase reached his truck and got inside. The superior height of the cab allowed him an excellent view down the sweep of Main Street. The lights were muted in Yvonne's café and bakery. Only Maureen's store was brightly lit and the Red Dragon bar's flashing neon Bud sign.

If Chase had understood the subtext of Kevin's speech correctly, he was meant to believe that Ruth, Blue, and January were working together with the soul aim of taking the decision making about the ranch away from him and giving it to the historical society. Chase tried to view the idea of the society's taking ownership of the place dispassionately. The ranch would be in safe hands. Ruth would probably be able to live there for the rest of her life without any more worrying. Most important, he wouldn't have to convince his brothers to sell the place or pay them off.

It wasn't a bad solution.

His brothers wouldn't make any money, but maybe that wasn't important to them. It certainly hadn't been about money for Blue.

Sure, Kevin had an agenda, which included making January look bad. But Chase couldn't deny that the job of managing Morgan Ranch for the historical society would fit January perfectly.

Which left him exactly where?

"On the outside looking in, as usual," he muttered as he started the truck. Dammit, it hurt that the three people he was closest to on the ranch had started making decisions that didn't include him. And telling fricking Kevin before him? That sucked.

Chase turned the engine off again and got out of the truck. He wasn't in the right frame of mind to go meekly back to the ranch and have dinner. He needed time to come up with a way to approach Ruth about her "decision-making" process.

The blinking pink and red lights of the Red Dragon bar,

named for the Welsh-born Robert Williams who had arrived in California with the Morgans in the 1800s called out to Chase. He made his way along the street, studiously ignoring the coffee shop, and went in through the door. He was greeted with the blast of several TVs, the sweet smell of beer, and Maureen's eldest daughter Nancy serving at the bar. In one corner a darts match was going on, and on the other side of the room the two pool tables were busy and Jay Williams, the current owner, was keeping score.

Chase took a seat at the bar and glanced up at the blackboard, which had information about all the beer and food specials. Thank God, Saint Paddy's Day had come and gone, or else everything would've been green or boiled.

"Hey, Chase." Nancy wiped the counter in front of him and smiled. "What'll it be?"

"Beer, please."

"Which kind?" She took a deep breath. "We have—"

Chase held up his hand. "How about you pick something for me to try?"

"Sure!" She leaned on the bar, giving him a close-up view of her spectacular rack. "Anything else I can do for you?"

"No, I'm good, thanks. Is Henry in tonight?"

"Yeah, I think he's playing darts."

"Then I'll find him."

It wouldn't hurt to check out whether any of what Kevin had told him was true. In fact it was the only logical way to proceed. Chase drank the beer Nancy set in front of him without tasting it and asked for another. By the time he'd polished off that one, he spied Henry Parker returning to his seat in one of the corner booths.

"Excuse me, Nancy."

She waved at him as he put a twenty under his empty glass, slid off the stool, and went over to Henry.

"Evening, Henry."

"TC, how nice to see you, my boy! Sit down. I saw your grandmother only a few days ago."

"Was she bugging you about her will again?"

Henry chuckled. "She's gotten a bee in her bonnet about giving the place to the historical society. I told her it wasn't that simple, but she didn't want to listen." He rolled his eyes. "But what's new?"

Chase nodded and spent a few minutes catching up with Henry and hearing about all his grandkids and his plans to retire somewhere warm. Chase didn't have to say much, just nod in the right places and go with the flow. One thing he'd noticed about Morgantown was that folks didn't make small or busy talk like they did in the Bay Area. They didn't tell you about their possessions or what they wanted you to do for them. They just talked and expected you to listen.

Sometimes they talked a lot.

The door opened. Chase looked up to see January, Yvonne, Avery Hayes, and an unknown older woman coming in. It was strange seeing January when she hadn't yet seen him. She was wearing her best jeans and one of the new T-shirts she'd picked up on a trip to town with him. Her fair hair was around her shoulders, and she was grinning at something Yvonne had just said to her.

She looked beautiful and so damn wholesome it made him doubt himself again. As if she were affected by the intensity of his stare, her gaze swung around the bar and fixed on him. She smiled, and the warmth of it flowed over him as he got to his feet.

"Hey, you." She walked over to him. "I wasn't expecting to see you in town tonight." She went on tiptoe to kiss his cheek. "Hey, Henry. How are your grandkids?"

Henry started talking again. After he'd finally stopped,

January touched Chase's arm and drew the woman who'd arrived with her forward.

"I'm glad you're here, Chase. I've wanted to introduce you two to each other for weeks. This is Bridget O'Hara. She's the new chairperson of the Morgantown Historical Society."

"Nice to meet you, ma'am." Chase touched the brim of his hat.

"It's a pleasure to meet you, too. January's told me so much about you." Bridget smiled at him. "This is hardly the place for a discussion, but one day I'd really like to sit down and talk to you about the future of the ranch, and about the restoration of Morgansville."

"So I hear."

She visibly relaxed. "So Ruth did tell you about her possible plans for the place?"

"I'm certainly aware of them now." He glanced over at January and discovered one heck of a guilty look on her face. His stomach tightened. What the hell had been happening behind his back? "I'd be happy to talk about the future of the ranch with you. Give Ruth a call and set it up, okay?"

Chase patted Henry's arm, nodded at Bridget, and turned toward the exit.

"Chase?"

January followed him out onto the sidewalk. He very reluctantly stopped walking and turned to face her.

"Yeah?"

She regarded him carefully. "Are you okay? Do you really think Ruth's idea is a good one?"

"Don't you?"

"It certainly is one way of sorting out the problem,"

she said cautiously. "Are you sure you're not mad about something?"

He raised an eyebrow. "I never get mad; you know that."

She sighed. "Look, I told Ruth and Blue it was a bad idea not to keep you in the loop about this possibility."

"About your taking over as ranch manager for the historical society and saving the ranch from my evil clutches? You'd be damn good at managing the place, wouldn't you?"

She blinked at him. "*What?*"

"Ranch manager. You. Who better?"

"Who told you that?"

"Does it matter?"

"I think it does."

"Kevin told me."

"*Kevin.*" She sighed. "Of course. How the hell did he know anything about anything?"

"Because you fricking told him."

January stared at Chase's hostile face. It felt as if she were being pulled back into the crazy hall of mirrors living with Kevin had become. Once she started down this black hole, defending herself, pleading to be believed, she'd no longer be the person she'd fought to become.

Chase carried on talking as if nothing momentous had happened—as if his decision to even *listen* to Kevin made perfect sense.

"I'm not a fool. I didn't just rely on Kevin's evidence. I checked with Henry. Ruth did change her will."

She heard the hurt behind Chase's words as he tried to be fair, even while he condemned her.

"It's okay." He shrugged. "I totally understand why you chose to put the ranch first."

"You do?"

His mouth twisted. "Yeah. It's important to you to preserve the place. Hell, I even admire you for doing it.

You told me right from the start that you intended to save the ranch and that nothing would get in your way."

"And you think I'd do anything to achieve that aim?"

"I—" He looked away from her down the street. "I'm just looking at the facts."

"So despite us being *friends*, you think I slept with you, lied to you, talked about you with my ex, and you find all that *completely understandable* due to my obsession with saving your family home and taking over as the boss?"

"That's not what I'm saying. I'm *saying* that I wish you'd told me and not shut me out. I'm sick and tired of being on the wrong side of every fricking decision the people I care about make." He took a deep, shuddering breath and looked past her down the street. "I am *not* going to fight with you, January."

"That's a shame because I'd like to see you lose your temper, Chase. It might mean you had stopped analyzing and started feeling." She met his reluctant gaze. "You want some facts? I didn't tell Kevin a damn thing, and I had no idea that anyone was considering me for the mythical job of ranch manager in the far-distant future."

She forced a smile through the shards of her breaking heart. "I'm also sorry that your grandmother has a habit of changing her will on a whim." She took a much-needed breath. "I'm not really involved in this. Surely you know deep down in your heart that Ruth would *never* leave me in charge of a single blade of grass as long as you and your brothers existed?"

He frowned, an arrested look in his eyes. "I—"

"If anyone is on the outside, it's me, Chase."

She walked back into the noisy, cheerful roar of the bar. Chase thought he was being kept out of things? She'd stupidly fallen in love with a man and a place where she would always be the interloper. He had a home and a family who loved him, and he'd almost thrown them all away. Damn right she would fight to keep those things. How come she saw that better than he did? She kept going until she reached the relative safety of the ladies' bathroom, and only then did she allow herself to cry.

Chapter Eighteen

Chase saddled up Nolly and led him out of the barn to tie him up by the fence. There was no sign of January's truck. He didn't think she'd come home the night before. A sick feeling stirred in his gut. He hated it when people didn't turn up when they were supposed to.

He heard Blue whistling before he saw him arrive at the barn, toolbox in hand, a bottle of water shoved into the ragged back pocket of his jeans.

"Hey. Did January come back last night?" Chase asked.

Blue halted and looked at him. "She called Ruth to tell her she was staying with Yvonne. Why? What did you do?"

Chase returned to tightening Nolly's girth. "Nothing." He eased a knee into Nolly's gut, and the horse finally cooperated and released the air. "So what's the plan about giving the ranch to the historical society?"

"Oh, hell," Blue groaned. "January told you about that?"

"Nope. Kevin did."

"How did he know? He wasn't there." Blue grinned. "Unless he was listening at the door. I wouldn't put that past him."

Chase looked at Blue. "Maybe January told *him*?"

"I doubt it. She wasn't happy about keeping the plan from you. I was kind of okay with it." Blue set down his toolbox. "I take it you don't approve."

"Of the Morgantown Historical Society running this place?" Chase shrugged. "The idea certainly has its merits."

"So you're just pissed that no one told you."

"Wouldn't you be?"

"Look, Ruth comes up with these new ideas for her will all the time. They never happen. All she said was that if we couldn't come to a decision between the four of us on how to deal with the ranch by two years after her death, she'd leave the place to the historical society."

Chase blinked at him. "Hold up. Two years after? Not like in the immediate future?"

"See, that's the trouble with people who eavesdrop. They never get their facts right. Kevin obviously didn't hear the whole conversation. Ruth wants the four of us to inherit the place. That's her bottom line. And come on, you would never let us argue for two years over anything; you're way too bossy."

Chase lengthened his stirrups. "You do realize that if we don't sell the place you don't get any money?"

"Yeah."

"And that doesn't bother you?"

"No." Blue held his gaze. "It isn't always about money, Chase. This is our family *home*."

Chase mounted up and looked down at Blue from Nolly's back. "I'm off to check the new calves. Tell Ruth I'll be back for lunch."

"Will do." Blue picked up his toolbox. "I'm finishing up the repairs on the exterior of the barn today, and then I'm going to start on the roof."

"I really appreciate all the work you're doing around

here, Blue." Chase nodded at his brother. "It makes a big difference."

"I enjoy it." Blue shrugged.

Nolly crab-walked sideways, and Chase brought him back to a stop. "I might have a lead on that loan thing Ruth's being harassed about."

"Good. Sort the fuckers out."

Chase forced a smile, clicked to Nolly, and headed for the far pasture. He knew where January was, which was good. He couldn't forget the look of confusion on her face when he'd confronted her about her plans for the ranch. When he'd mentioned Kevin, her bewilderment had changed into something else—a weary acceptance that there was no point in even defending herself anymore.

But Blue had insisted that the conversation hadn't even included Kevin and that nothing would happen until Ruth was dead. Had Kevin overheard part of the discussion when he'd been at the ranch and made up the rest of it to discredit his ex-wife?

Chase snorted. Of course Kevin had, and, worse, Chase had fallen for it like a complete dope. It was hardly surprising that January had turned and walked away from him last night. He was a complete ass. He'd allowed his hurt feelings to cloud his judgment even while protesting that he was just being logical. He coaxed Nolly into a lope and went to find Roy. Chase had a couple of things to sort out with the ranch manager, and then he would get back and find January. He'd messed up again, but this time he was determined to make things right.

January stuffed her backpack full of essentials and went back down to the kitchen, where Ruth was sitting at the table having a cup of coffee and reading the local newspaper.

"How long are you intending to avoid Chase, then?" Ruth inquired.

"I'm not avoiding him, I'm just . . ." January waved her hand in the air. "Okay, I am avoiding him. He thinks I'm some Machiavellian witch who used my evil powers to wrest control of the ranch away from him."

Ruth looked at her over her glasses. "He does? Fancy."

"This isn't funny. He thinks I sucked up to you to become the manager of the ranch."

"You'd make a damn fine manager." Ruth nodded. "I'll tell him if he asks me."

"Don't tell him that!" January flapped her hands and practically jumped up and down on the spot. "He's already feeling like we all conspired against him."

"Which we kind of did."

January kept talking. "Only because Blue and I both knew you'll never go through with it. Why doesn't Chase know that too?"

"Because for once I suspect he's not thinking with his head, but with his heart."

January sank into a chair. "Don't say that. I told him the complete opposite." She groaned. "I don't want to hurt him."

"Of course you don't; you love him."

January slowly raised her head to stare at Ruth. "You noticed?"

"It's pretty damn obvious." Ruth reached over and patted January's hand. "You're a good girl, January. He could do a lot worse."

"Than what?"

January almost leapt out of the chair as she heard Chase's low voice behind her. She mimed zipping up her mouth at Ruth, who winked at her.

"Hey, Chase, I'm just"—she gestured at her backpack—"picking up a couple of things."

His faint smile died. "Where are you going?"

"Yvonne needs me." She grabbed her belongings. "I promised to help her out for the next couple of days."

At least he got out of her way when she dashed past him. She'd made it down the steps and was almost at her truck before she heard his voice behind her.

"January . . . you don't have to go. I'm—"

She fumbled for the door and flung it open before turning back. He wore his jeans, work boots, and a checkered shirt with the sleeves rolled up to his elbows. Six foot two of gorgeous cowboy nerd. It hurt to look at him.

"It's okay. I'm not leaving for good—if that's all right with Ruth. I just think I need to be away from you, I mean away from this place for a few days so that I can get my thesis written up in peace and quiet and . . ." Now she was babbling like an idiot.

He waited her out, his blue eyes concerned and so focused on her that she wanted to cry.

"What I'm trying to say, January, is that you don't have to leave."

She held her breath and nodded for him to go on.

He shoved a hand through his dark hair. "I'm flying back to the Bay Area today, but I'd really like to talk to you before I head out. I—"

Something inside her curled up and died, but she managed to nod as she pivoted toward her truck. "Cool. Have a great trip. Maybe I'll see you when you come back next time."

"*Shit*," he breathed. "I did it again, didn't I? Don't go right now!"

She got into the truck, her knees trembling. He came after her and put his hand on the lowered window.

"January, give me a chance here."

"Like you gave me last night?" She met his gaze. "You'd already decided I was after your ranch. You believed that slimeball Kevin, who wasn't even *present* at that conversation, instead of me."

"A conversation that deliberately excluded me," Chase cut in.

"Not deliberately! It was just Ruth being Ruth. Don't you know your own *grandmother*? She'd never give the ranch away to anyone who doesn't have Morgan blood in his or her veins."

He opened his mouth, and she spoke over him. "What's the *point* of explaining anything to you, Chase? You don't want me to be a good, trustworthy person because then you might have to *like* me."

"I do like you. When I thought things through, and after I talked to Blue, I realized I'd made an error—"

"See, that's my problem right there. You shouldn't have to fact-check everything I say." She thumped her chest with her fist so hard it hurt. "You should believe me *in here,* like I believe in you."

He let his outstretched hand fall to his side. "I'm not good at this emotional stuff; you know that."

She leaned out of the window and stuck her finger right in his face. "Then damn well get good at it!"

She raised the window and started the truck, leaving him standing in the dust, her whole body trembling with a horrible combination of rage and unshed tears. A half mile out of the ranch she had to pull over and have a good cry.

"Idiot," she muttered to herself. "No man is worth your tears." Blowing her nose, she took a deep breath. The thing was, she'd really begun to believe that this one was.

"Wow, smooth, Trampas."

Chase turned around to see Ruth and Blue watching him

from the porch of the ranch house. January had shouted loud enough for the whole ranch to hear. Blue was even giving him the slow handclap.

"Way to make a lady feel special. Tell her you're leaving."

Chase stormed back up the steps. "Shove it, Blue."

"How could you believe Kevin over January?"

"Because I'm a complete fricking idiot!" Chase yelled. "*Okay?*"

He never yelled.

"Language," Ruth tutted.

"And you." Chase turned on his diminutive grandmother. "Stirring up the pot with your stupid will. I could strangle you right now."

Blue put a protective arm around Ruth's shoulders. "You leave her alone. Don't blame her for your own thoughtless shit."

"Well, I did mess with his head a bit, Blue, but he sure did deserve it," Ruth said. "What are you going to do about January?"

Chase glared at Ruth as he sought the ragged ends of the temper that he never lost. "I'm going to fly back to San Francisco and sort out that loan matter for you. Then I'll come back and see if January is willing to talk to me."

"Good luck," Blue muttered.

"Thanks for nothing, Blue Boy." Chase stomped into the house to pick up the bag he'd packed earlier and came back out to find his audience still there. "Right, I'm off."

"Where exactly are you going?" Ruth asked.

"To see William Morgan the fourth." Chase kept moving and got into his truck.

"What?" Ruth and Blue yelled in unison.

He ignored them, drowning out any further questions by gunning the engine and driving away with an airy wave. He had a suspicion that if he didn't locate his father at the address he'd been given real fast, the man would disappear again. And this time, Chase was determined to get the answers he required.

On the way to the airport, he took a call from Margie Frost, confirming that the historical tour group wanted to put Morgan Ranch on their permanent schedule. He also spoke to the head of the Morgantown Historical Society about her plans to save the ghost town. By the time he boarded the plane, his head was buzzing with new opportunities and solutions. It took all his experience to push them to the back of his head and focus on the interview to come.

As soon as he'd realized that a different William was paying off the loan, his heart had sunk into his boots. His father had always been called Billy, so it wasn't as obvious as anyone might have thought. But why had Billy decided to keep paying, and what had made him stop? It made no sense. Untangling the mess and making sure that the fall-out didn't affect Ruth was Chase's number one priority. If it meant seeing his father for the first time in years, well, that was a sacrifice Chase was willing to make for his grandmother and the ranch.

The weeks he'd spent at the ranch had made him think hard about the night his mother and sister had disappeared. January had helped him and Blue realize that they couldn't let that night define them and their ongoing relationship forever. It followed that Chase had to learn to forgive his father. He couldn't say he was quite there yet, but seeing his father and maybe talking things through man-to-man would be a big step forward.

At the San Francisco airport Chase decided to take a cab to the unknown address rather than go home first. His sense of urgency had increased with every mile. The city street was narrow and on such a slope that, when he got out of the cab, his knee touched the sidewalk. He gazed up at the purple and green–painted row house and then leaned in to talk to the driver.

"Can you wait for a few minutes while I check to see if this guy's home?"

"Sure, cowboy. I'll leave the meter running."

"Good of you," Chase murmured, realizing that in his mad dash for the airport he'd forgotten to change into city clothes and looked a mite out of place on the streets of San Francisco in his Stetson.

He checked the number of the apartment and went in the front door, which was held open by a piece of hemp rope. In the narrow stairwell the smell of incense and pot engulfed him. He climbed up two flights of stairs and knocked on the door numbered 12C. Eventually it opened, and a young woman with long, brown hair and a ring through her nose smiled at him and then clapped her hand to her mouth.

"Oh my God," she screeched. "You look just like Billy!"

"I'm his son. Is he here?"

"No, he said he had someplace he had to go."

"Locally?"

The woman's eyes focused on a point somewhere over Chase's shoulder as she wrinkled her nose. "No. Far away. He pawned all his stuff to buy a bus ticket." She shrugged. "That's so sad that you missed him. He'll come back eventually; he always does."

"If he does, can you give him my card and ask him to call me?" Chase handed over his business card, and the woman read the words slowly, her lips moving, and then looked back up at him. "I've heard of you guys. You've been on TV. You're rich, right?"

"Not really." Chase tipped his hat. "Thanks for your help, ma'am. I must be going; I've got a taxi meter running."

She blew him a kiss. "You're so cute with that hat and those boots."

Chase went back down the stairs. Somehow he'd known in his gut that he wouldn't find his father today, but at least he'd made the attempt. Next time he might even be able to face him. In the meantime, he had to swallow his disappointment and get back to the ranch to talk to January.

In the cab, his cell rang, and he picked up. "Hey, Matt."

"Your grandma said you're in the city?"

"Yeah."

"For how long?"

Chase thought wistfully about the ranch. "I was planning on leaving tonight."

"Can you come into work first? *Please?* Jake and I would really like to talk to you."

Chase considered. How many days did a righteously angry woman need to calm down? He didn't have a spreadsheet for that. No man did.

"Matt? I'll stay another day."

The offices of Give Me a Leg Up looked as clean and welcoming as ever, and Chase smiled as he came through the door. They'd done the place up themselves in clean, simple lines, using as many recycled products as possible. The low cubicle walls were built from old water bottles wrapped in chicken wire, and the flooring tiles were made from recycled tires. Some of the local schools provided the art, which was changed out on a regular basis.

"Mr. M!"

Daizee came around her desk and gave him a big hug. She wore her usual black, and this week her long hair was dyed purple and braided down her back.

"Hey." Chase returned the hug. "What's up?"

"Nothing much." She took a step back and looked him up

and down. "But look at you! Smiling, tanned, and dressed like a real cowboy." She grinned. "It suits you."

"Thanks."

She walked back with him toward the main office, which was pretty empty. "Matt and Jake are hanging out in the conference room. I'll bring you some coffee."

Chase went on through without knocking on the door and found his two partners eating pizza and arguing about a Giants game. Some things never changed. Some of his tension eased as he took a seat, helped himself to a dripping slice of everything pizza, and joined in the discussion.

Eventually, even the pizza had gone, and they'd moved on from baseball, through basketball, and were now speculating about the football season. Beer had replaced the coffee, and the rest of the staff had gone home. Matt glanced at Jake, and they both turned to Chase.

"So, can we talk?"

"Sure." Chase sat back and nodded. "Shoot."

"We missed you," Matt said, and Jake nodded. "We didn't realize how much of the workload you were carrying by yourself until we had to deal with it."

Chase inclined his head. "Most of that was my fault. I always think I do everything best, and I took on too much." He grimaced. "I'm trying not to be that person anymore. I'm *trying* to remember why we founded this company and how I've managed to suck all the joy out of it."

Jake raised his eyebrows. "You admit that the company has gone in a different direction than we originally planned?"

"When you end up in the ER at thirty-two, thinking you're dying from stress, you kind of have to question what you are doing," Chase said wryly. "You two making me walk away for a few weeks was the best thing that ever happened to me."

"And the worst thing that happened to us," Matt said.

"We've become complacent partners. And that sucks, Chase. That wasn't fair to you either."

"I just wanted to make our lives as financially secure as I could," Chase said. "I've realized lately that money isn't everything and that friends and family should come first." He winced. "Now I sound like some sappy movie, but I damn well mean it."

"Yeah, we get that. We're more than willing to pull our weight if the mission of the company can remain the same. We've got more money than we'll ever need already."

Chase nodded to disguise his emotions. "So we need to regroup, right?" He hesitated. "That is, if you still want to be partners?"

Matt grinned at him. "Hell, yeah."

As he studied his two oldest friends a deep sense of well-being flooded through Chase. He almost wanted to get up and hug them. Probably best not to scare them too much with the new, improved version of him.

"Then let's work out a new road map for our future success." Chase got out his laptop, and the other two groaned. "I have just the appropriate spreadsheet right here."

Chapter Nineteen

"So where is she?" Chase asked Yvonne. He was standing in the coffee shop, getting in everyone's way as he tried to talk to the suddenly very elusive owner.

"Who?"

Chase raised a sardonic eyebrow.

Yvonne finally stopped moving long enough to face him. "January's out somewhere."

"Where exactly?"

"I don't know. Probably at your damned ranch. Have you checked?"

"I just got in from the airport. I wanted to see if January was still staying with you before I went on home."

"She is still staying with me." Yvonne shook her head. "You really are a dork, you know?"

"Yeah." Chase had to agree with her. "But I'm not going to be able to redeem myself if I can't find January, am I?"

"Okay, she definitely went out to the ranch." Yvonne gave him a hard stare. "Now, please don't mess up again because I can't have my friend being unhappy. She eats way too much of my profit."

Chase grinned at her. "Thanks, Yvonne."

She went back into the kitchen and came out with a box, which she put in Chase's hands.

"Doughnuts and éclairs. She'll be putty in your hands."

He was about to leave when he recognized Bridget O'Hara, the historical society chairperson, sitting at one of the outside tables.

"Miss O'Hara?"

She looked up. "Mr. Morgan! And do call me Bridget. I was just reading through the e-mail you sent me and considering my reply." She patted the seat next to her. "Do you have a few minutes? It would be much easier just to talk to you, rather than doing all that typing."

Chase sat down and placed the box of pastries on the table. He knew where January was now, and he doubted she'd be going anywhere for a while. He gave Bridget his best smile.

"Please, call me Chase, and tell me what you think about my ideas."

January stubbed her toe again and muttered another curse that echoed through the cave. She'd finally gotten around to exploring the area behind the hot springs on the ranch. The problem was that she kept remembering how luscious Chase had looked, stretched out half-naked in the pool, and missing her step.

Darn it, she kept thinking about him all the time. Everywhere she turned on the ranch she had a fresh memory, most of them good. She tried to remind herself that he'd chosen to leave, but that didn't make her feel any better. By the terms of their relationship, he'd owed her nothing, and she shouldn't be feeling like this. He didn't know she'd had a change of heart, so she couldn't blame him for riding blithely off into the sunset.

"Ouch!" She bumped her head. Yes, she could blame

him. He was a complete idiot, but at least she'd shared *that* with him before he'd gone. Which probably meant he was unlikely to come back . . .

"Oh, wow . . ." Her flashlight illuminated the stick figures etched into the back wall of the cave, and she sank down to her knees, fumbling for her camera. Forgetting everything except documenting the ancient cave paintings, she made sure to examine every angle and crevice within the passageway.

Eventually, her knees protested the hard floor. She rose to her feet and packed away her gear before turning toward the main cave where the hot springs were located. Crystalline rock caught the beam of her flashlight, making the place glimmer like a fairy cavern. Glancing down she saw a rip in her jeans and a smear of blood. She sat beside one of the pools and soaked her handkerchief in the mineral-laden water before applying it to her throbbing knee.

There was no one around, and she wasn't in a rush to get back to Yvonne's and eat more cake, so she took off her jeans and attended to the wound properly. Another longing glance at the warm water made her strip down to her bra and panties and lower herself into the pool. The heat made her gasp and then groan as her tired and stressed limbs responded to the warmth surrounding them.

She closed her eyes and leaned back against the side. She hadn't slept well the last two nights. Her mind kept going over that last scene with Chase when she'd basically told him to change his very nature. Yeah . . . like he'd be willing to do that for her. Or was even capable of doing it.

She tried to shut off the familiar litany. It didn't matter. She'd said her piece, and it was up to him now. She hadn't quite managed to get to the "I say this because I love you" part. Would that have made a difference? It was possible she would never know.

Surely, he wouldn't come back from the city and just expect her to jump into bed with him. . . . She opened one eye. He wouldn't, would he? Even he wasn't that dumb? She could just picture him riding up on Nolly, tipping his hat to her, and . . . God, she'd go to bed with him in a heartbeat.

She groaned, the sound echoing around the cavern, and heard the unmistakable sound of approaching footsteps.

"I thought I might find you in here."

A shadow came across the bright sunlight slanting in through the cave opening, and January sank down as low as she could in the water.

Chase approached the pool and stood looking down at her, his expression grave. He was the most beautiful sight she had ever seen. He placed one of Yvonne's pink cake boxes on the ground in front of him like an offering.

"Are you still mad at me?"

"I don't get mad." January mimicked his voice.

"You sure looked mad. You almost poked my eye out." He took off his Stetson and started on the buttons of his shirt.

"What are you doing?" January squeaked.

"Stripping. I can't apologize properly when I'm towering over you up here."

"I'm not sure we have anything to say to each other." Wow, she sounded super snippy.

"Well, I have a whole damn lot to say to you." He unbuckled his jeans and shucked them and his boots and his socks in one easy motion. "You can just listen. In fact, that would be awesome."

January snorted inelegantly as he slid into the pool opposite her, wearing just his tight, white cotton boxers. He looked muscled, fit, and totally lickable.

He sighed and ducked his head under the water. "It's good to be home."

"I thought your home was in San Francisco."

He slicked his wet hair out of his face and gave her the eye. "My, you are a little testy today."

"I've given up being nice. Especially to men. It's just not worth it."

He yawned and leaned back against the side of the pool, his muscled arms curving around the edge. "God, I'm tired. I couldn't get used to the noise in the city. And Jobs wasn't very nice to me either. He spent the whole evening sulking with his back turned to me."

"Smart cat," January muttered.

"I'm still not sure what to do with him. Do you think he'd like it here? Or should I leave him in the city with Jake?" He looked at her and then away. "I'm planning on being here about half the year, so—"

"You? Here?"

"Yeah, that's one of the reasons I went back to San Francisco, to sort out all that shit with my partners."

"So you've decided to break up the company?"

"No. We worked things out. I'm opening a satellite office at Morgan Ranch."

January paused to digest that startling piece of news. "Ruth will be delighted."

"I hope so." He paused. "How about you?"

She shrugged and flicked her toes in the water. "It's really nothing to do with me. When I've finished writing my thesis, I'm out of here."

There was silence until she had to look up at him. He rubbed his unshaven jaw. "That friends-with-benefits gig not working for you anymore?"

She shook her head.

"Me neither." He held her gaze. "I'd like an upgrade."

"To what?" January whispered.

"A real, one-hundred-percent relationship with feelings and commitment and all that stuff."

"You would?"

"Yeah." He nodded slowly. "That's what I want. You in my bed and in my life."

January just stared at him as speech proved impossible.

"Is that a yes?" Chase asked cautiously.

She fought the urge to leap across the pool and throw her arms around his neck. "It's an 'I'll think about it.'"

He sighed. "I know I've been behaving like a real dick, but I've never been in this situation. I've never wanted anything to be so right before, and it terrifies me."

"Okay." She took a deep breath. "I've got to get back to Yvonne's now." She slowly exited the pool, feeling his gaze on her as she forced her still-wet legs into her jeans and put on her T-shirt.

"You could stay and have dinner with us at the ranch," Chase suggested, and tapped the pink box. "Yvonne sent pastries. She knows you're here."

It was tempting. . . .

So tempting.

"I've got a couple more things to do, and then I'll see whether I can make it or not."

"Cool."

She picked up all her gear and exited the cave, taking deep gulps of the warm air. He wanted to have a relationship with her. A committed one. Could she believe him, and was it what she wanted? She drove down to the field full of calves, parked, and got out to lean over the fence. It was a calm and peaceful scene; the sky looked limitless, the mountains ominous, and the calves moved serenely through the tall grass, grazing on its sweetness.

She loved this place.

Okay, so could she trust him? She'd thought Kevin had destroyed her ability to believe that any man could be good and true. But Chase was honest, quick to admit a fault, and tried to make things right when he messed up.

She liked that a lot. She tried to imagine leaving and never seeing him again and caught her breath.

She didn't want to leave the ranch or the man. But if she had to make a choice, she'd follow the man anywhere. The ranch might represent the home she'd never had, but Chase was in her heart. They were bound to disagree a lot because he sure could be exasperating. She might even tempt him into losing his temper occasionally just to show him that they could still make things right between them. But was she willing to risk her heart again? That was the million-dollar question.

January stared at the calves and then nodded before turning around and getting back into her truck.

Chase parked, went into the barn, and found Blue and Ruth about to start feeding the animals.

"Hey."

Ruth turned around and studied him, hands on her lean hips. "You're back, are you?"

"Yes, ma'am."

"Hmmph." She looked at Blue. "Are we talking to him?"

"After that bombshell he dropped? I don't think so."

Chase took the feed bucket out of Ruth's hands. "I'll explain over dinner."

"You think I'm feeding you after that?"

He bent to kiss her forehead and narrowly avoided the elbow she angled at his ribs. "I promise I'll tell you everything I know."

"You'd better." Ruth finally cracked a smile. "Now you two get on with the chores, and I'll worry about dinner."

She walked out of the barn, a tiny figure in her jeans and checkered shirt that she still bought in the kids' department. Chase watched until she was safely inside the house.

Blue measured out chicken feed and added water. "She was worried about you. That's why she's mad."

"I got that."

"January's just mad at you, period." Blue picked up the water bucket. "But I did get to go and see her at Yvonne's, so that was a bonus."

"Sure, take advantage of the cracks in my love life, why don't you?" Chase grumbled. "January might be coming to dinner. I should have told Ruth."

Blue slapped him on the shoulder. "Quick work, bro."

Chase turned toward the horses. "I suspect she's going to make me work a lot harder than that."

"Good for her."

Eventually, Chase walked back to the main house and went upstairs to change. The quietness of the place spread over him and through him, and he took a slow, deep breath. Tragedy could happen anywhere and to anyone, changing lives in seconds, but he didn't have to let it dictate his future. Life went on, the ranch remained, and nothing could change that unless he forced the issue.

Down in the kitchen, Ruth was setting out plates and stirring something that smelled like Bolognese sauce on the stove. There was no sign of January, but Chase added a place just in case.

They were already sitting down and had just said grace when January came in the door. Her hair was still damp from the hot springs, and she wore the same rumpled clothes. Chase stood and pulled out the chair next to his.

"Evening, January," Blue said around a mouthful of garlic bread.

"Evening, all." She glanced at Ruth. "I hope you're okay with my joining you?"

"Of course I am, darlin'." Ruth gave Chase a look. "This is still your home."

"Thanks." She dove into the garlic bread, and Ruth piled

spaghetti and sauce on her plate with a lavish hand. Chase figured January got twice more than he had, which wasn't surprising.

They ate mainly in silence because the food was so good and because fresh air just made a man hungry. After a pecan pie for dessert and Yvonne's pastries, Ruth passed around the coffee, and Chase cleared his throat.

"You both okay with January's hearing all this?"

Blue looked from him to January. "You've told her?"

"Most of it," Chase said apologetically.

"Not a problem. Unlike you, we don't get mad because we're not included in every conversation in the entire world." Blue waved him on, and Ruth nodded. "So why were you after Dad?"

"Kevin found out that the original loan and life insurance policy wasn't taken out by Grandfather William Morgan, but by another William, our father." Chase glanced over at January to explain. "No one ever called him William. He was always Bill or Billy. When the Morgantown Bank set up the paperwork, they probably thought it was obvious which Morgan it was. But as the policy was sold elsewhere, the information got lost."

"Well, at least Kevin was useful for something," January muttered. "He's always been very conscientious."

"I think he wanted an excuse to stick the knife into you actually, January, so he tried extra hard on this one so he could see me one more time."

"Oh, you worked that out, did you?" January said.

Chase met her gaze, saw the vulnerability under the sass. "I've worked with a few narcissistic CEOs in the valley. It took me awhile to realize that Kevin was right up there with them."

"Bingo." Her eyes filled with tears, and she blinked hard, bringing a lump to his throat. He wanted to drag her out of her chair, sit her on his lap, and hold her close while he apologized for doubting her for a second.

"So what happened then?" Blue prompted.

Chase refocused his attention. "Kevin managed to get an address for our father in San Francisco. I've tried to keep tabs on him over the years, but he's moved around a lot."

"Hold up—*you've* been keeping an eye on him?" Blue said.

"Yeah. I . . . wanted to be able to help if things went badly wrong."

Silence filled the kitchen, and Ruth groped for his hand and held it tight. "You're a good boy, Chase Morgan."

"I decided to fly back, take a chance, and look him up." He sighed. "He wasn't there, but he'd definitely been there, because the woman I met in the apartment told me I was the spitting image of her Billy."

"Did she say where he'd gone?"

"She said he'd bought a bus ticket, but she didn't know where he was going. She thought he'd be back eventually. I gave her my card and asked her to call me if he did return."

"Damn." Blue dabbed his napkin over his mouth. "I don't get why he would be paying that loan, especially when it sounds like he lives such an nomadic lifestyle."

"I don't know why either," Chase confessed. "And why did he stop paying six months ago after all those years?"

January frowned. "What kind of loan are we talking about here?"

Chase turned to her. "Twenty-five years ago someone from the ranch took out a second mortgage attached to a term life insurance policy, which would pay out in the event of the beneficiary's death or with a lump sum after twenty-five years." He flicked a glance at Ruth. "I only found out about it when my beloved grandmother told me that she was being hounded for payment, and that it might affect the financial stability of the ranch."

Ruth shrugged. "Well, I might have exaggerated *just* a little bit to get you to come back."

"A *little*?"

"How much exactly *is* the loan payment?" Blue asked.

"Thirty-two dollars and nineteen cents a month." Ruth replied.

"Is that *all*?" Chase shook his head. "I thought we were in this for thousands of dollars."

Ruth sniffed. "It might not be a lot to you, Chase Morgan, but it is for some people."

Chase raised his eyebrows. "So really, the loan payoff is so small that it won't affect the ranch at all."

"But it got your attention." Ruth's smile was definitely unrepentant. "And I do want to know what's going on. Those unpaid bills were sent to me. They could affect my credit rating."

January looked at Ruth. "So the loan was actually taken out by your son William?"

"Exactly." Ruth patted Chase's hand and let it go. "I've changed my mind about something. If you want to pay off those last few months, Chase, you go ahead. I want to see what happens next."

"*Now* you want me to pay it off?" Chase grumbled. "I'm not even sure if I can."

"Then give me the money, and I'll do it. I still have all the paperwork and payment slips from Kingsmith Financial."

"That could work," Blue said cautiously. "If they aren't paying close attention to which Morgan should be paying what."

"They haven't done so for twenty-five years, so I'll take the risk." Ruth nodded. "I want to see if there is any payoff, don't you?"

"Kevin said the beneficiary of the policy was Mom,"

Chase said carefully. "What I'd like to know is who gets the money if she's dead?"

"And why Dad would continue paying something for someone who no longer exists," Blue added.

"Wouldn't the insurance company have been informed of your mother's death and paid off the policy then?" January asked.

"I'm not sure if she was ever legally declared dead," Chase admitted. "Do you know, Ruth?"

"I can't remember. I suppose Billy might have done it. We were so busy dealing with you boys and then your father that I'm sure some things got forgotten. Even if it was all legalized, I doubt anyone had time to notify an insurance company." She got up from the table and returned with her purse. "I'll write that check for the rest of the payments and hope they'll take it." She held out her hand. "Chase?"

He groaned, but pushed back his chair. "I'll get my checkbook."

January stacked the last plate in the dishwasher and turned it on.

"You're all set, Ruth."

"Thank you, my dear." Ruth was on her way into the front parlor, her knitting bag under her arm and a copy of the latest *TV Guide* in her hand. "Chase? Walk January to her car."

"Yes, ma'am."

Chase came up beside January and opened the kitchen door with a flourish. "After you."

She'd parked by the barn, and they walked side by side down the slope in the darkness. It wasn't that late, but everything was still, and the stars and moon were bright and distinct in the blueberry-tinted sky.

"Hey," he said softly as they reached her old truck. "Thanks for coming to dinner. I really appreciated it."

She leaned back against the truck and looked up at him. "You're welcome."

Their gazes caught and held as he braced his hand on the roof of the truck and slowly bent his head, giving her every opportunity to escape what she knew was coming. She didn't close her eyes as he came ever closer and brushed his mouth against hers.

"I've missed you."

January stayed still as he kissed her with closed mouth again.

"I've really missed you. I'm so goddamn sorry, January." He looked down at her. "When I was away, all I could think about was the ranch and you and how badly I'd messed everything up. You might not want to share my life in the city, but I'd wither and die if I stayed there and didn't have you to come home to." He kissed her again, his tongue tracing the seam of her lips. "It occurred to me that in order to function there, I need something inside me to keep me honest.

"In case you haven't worked it out yet"—he framed her face with his hands—"that's you."

This time when he bent his head, she let him deepen the kiss until it became her everything. Her hand crept up around his neck and held him close as she kissed him back.

Eventually he drew back, his expression serious. "I don't want to lose you, January. I know I mess up and say the wrong thing, but my heart is in the right place." He took her hand and thumped it against his chest. "Right here. With you."

She just stared at him, hoping she didn't look too bemused as he started speaking again.

"I made myself believe that Kevin's version of things was correct because I was so damned *hurt*, and I don't *allow* myself to get hurt or angry." He swallowed hard. "My dad . . . had a temper. I'd seen what loving someone too much could do to a man. I've never wanted to feel like that about another human being. And then I met you, and you made me face the real me. A man who gets emotional when he cares."

January nodded, her gaze fixed on Chase's face.

"Damn." He slowly exhaled and took a step back. "You'd better leave now or I won't be able to let you go."

She gathered her shattered thoughts. "You think I'm capable of moving after that incredibly romantic speech?"

He shoved a hand through his hair. "It was okay?"

"Did you practice it?"

"No, it just seemed to flow out of me. From the heart. Just like you wanted. I kind of surprised myself."

She started to smile, and his mouth kicked up at the corner.

"Haven't you got something to say to me?" Chase asked.

"About wanting to wake up in that big old bed with you every morning and have your babies?"

His smile disappeared. "You want babies?"

January clapped a hand over her mouth. "Did I say 'babies' out loud? Okay, pretend I didn't, and let me re-phrase. Chase Morgan, I would very much like to be in a one-hundred-percent-committed relationship with you."

He took a step toward her. "And have my babies?"

"That's a discussion for another day."

He took her in his arms. "What if I like the sound of that?"

"Then you're obviously besotted with me, and I can't stop that, can I?"

"No, you can't." He kissed her. "I love you, January Mitchell."

"And I love you, too." She squeaked as he swept her off her feet and into his arms. "What are you doing now?"

"Taking you to my bed so you can wake up with me in the morning." He mock-frowned at her. "Although we're not starting on the babies just yet."

She sighed and rubbed her cheek against his shoulder. "Okay. I can wait."

Chapter Twenty

Chapter Twenty

"Someone's happy today." Blue gave Chase the side eye as he sat down at the table with his coffee.

"Yup." Chase grinned at his brother.

"January was smiling like a loon as well, so I take it you two have made up?"

"Yup."

"And you're going to stick around?" Blue held up his hand. "Don't say yup again."

"I'm going to run part of my business from here. We can coordinate our schedules so that Ruth's not on her own."

"Sounds good to me. I've got to check in at the base in two weeks for orientation. I'll probably get my orders then."

"Cool." Chase's cell vibrated, and he picked it up. "Yeah, Roy?"

"There's someone walking up the main drive to the ranch house."

"And?"

"You might want to go pick him up."

Chase frowned at his cell as Roy ended the call.

"What's up?" Blue asked.

"Roy's being mysterious." Chase checked that he had his keys in his pocket. "I'll be back in a minute."

He reversed his truck, turned in a circle, and drove slowly away from the house. It wasn't long before he spotted the solitary figure approaching him. He slowed to a stop and just waited for the man to reach the truck. He stepped down from the high cab and braced himself. "Hey."

"TC?"

"Yeah." He walked around to the passenger side of the truck and opened the door, his heart thumping fit to burst. "Why don't you hop in, Dad?"

Chase couldn't speak on the short return journey, too aware of the living, breathing replica of himself beside him. In the seconds their gazes had met, he'd been so aware of his father's blue eyes brimming with such fear . . .

Chase turned off the engine and stared at the steering wheel. "I came to find you in San Francisco."

"So I heard. Amy said you looked just like me."

"What made you decide to come out here after all this time?" Chase asked.

"Because there are things I need to say."

"After twenty years of silence?" Chase opened the truck door, but his father didn't move.

"Do you want me to leave?"

Chase finally looked up at him. "No. We've come this far. Why don't you come in, and let's settle this once and for all."

He didn't wait for his father, but went on into the kitchen, where Blue still sat at the table, with January now beside him.

"Is Ruth around?" Chase asked.

"She's upstairs changing sheets." January put down her mug. "Why, what's up?"

Chase patted her shoulder. "Ask her to come down, will you, please?"

January nodded and went up the stairs, leaving Blue

staring over Chase's shoulder, his eyes widening as he took in the new arrival at the door.

"*Holy shit.*" He breathed. "Dad?"

"BB. How are you doing?"

Chase pulled out a chair. "Come and sit down. Would you like some coffee?"

"That would be great." Billy looked briefly up at Chase. "Thanks for being so welcoming."

"It's your ranch," Chase said. "Ruth will be down in a minute."

"*Billy?*" Ruth came in. "Good Lord above!" She wrapped her arms around her son's shoulders and held him tight. He reciprocated, burying his face in her shoulder and almost lifting her off her feet.

"Mama."

"Thank God, you came back." Ruth patted his face, her eyes full of tears. "I knew you would one day."

Chase had to look away. Blue had an equally skeptical expression on his face. It was hard for Chase to even look at his father; he kept sneaking little glances and then looking down before he was caught showing any interest. He jumped when January took his hand and squeezed it hard.

"It's going to be okay, Chase," she murmured. "I'm sure of it."

He didn't share her quiet confidence, but her support steadied him. He sat silently while Ruth fussed over Billy, offering him water and food and a slice of coconut cake fresh from the oven. She touched him constantly, little pats and caresses as if she couldn't bear to let him go.

Finally, Ruth settled down, and they were all facing one another over the kitchen table.

"So what finally brought you here?" Ruth asked.

Billy scrubbed a hand over his neat gray beard. "Chase asked me the same thing. It all started about six months ago when some guy came nosing around, asking questions about me. I was living in Arizona." He looked right at Chase. "I know you've been keeping an eye on me over the years, but this guy was more . . . persistent."

"We hired a new firm of investigators about a year ago," Chase confirmed. "Hendersons."

"This guy started asking me questions about all kinds of stuff, so I left town."

"I didn't authorize that level of interference in your life. I'm sorry it happened. He was supposed to make sure you were alive and not in need of anything."

"It's no big deal." Billy clasped his scarred hands in front of him on the table. "The thing was, he got me nervous. It took me a few weeks to locate Amy again and find work in San Francisco."

"You work?" Blue asked.

"Yeah, after I got out of rehab I started washing dishes in a restaurant and eventually went to catering college to become a certified chef." He shrugged. "It's one of those professions where you can always find work. People have to eat."

Chase studied the deep grooves bracketing his father's face. "You stopped drinking?"

"Ten years sober. Still miss it though."

"That's . . . awesome."

Billy flicked him a smile. "Nearly didn't make it. Took three tries and the intervention of the state penitentiary to make it stick."

Chase sat back. "That's still a great achievement."

"It would've been better if I hadn't started drinking at all." Billy met Chase's gaze fully for the first time. "I damn well near ruined this family."

Chase wanted to tell him that wasn't true, but he couldn't seem to form the words. Billy was watching his face.

"It's okay. You don't need to lie. Part of accepting that you are an alcoholic means admitting what you've done and apologizing to those you've hurt without expecting anything in return." Billy shook his head. "I'm so goddamn sorry about what happened to you boys; I just couldn't bring myself to face you."

"You're here now," Ruth said fiercely. "We understand."

"You might, Mama, but they won't. What kind of father walks out on his own children? A useless, drunken one."

"You were grieving, Dad. We understood that at least." Chase heard his own voice and couldn't believe he'd found the ability to speak up.

"But I did wrong by you, Chase. I made you lie for me."

Chase went still. "You don't have to go into that now. It was a long time ago; I understood why you asked me to do it."

"To lie to the sheriff?" Billy winced. "You were just a kid, and I involved you in the mess of my marriage because I was too scared to face up to what might happen if the truth came out."

"What did happen that last night?" Ruth asked. "I always assumed it was Annie who attacked you."

"Yeah. She hadn't been well since Rachel's birth. That particular evening we had a row and she threatened to kill herself and the baby. I attempted to get the knife off her." He sank his head into his hands. "I tried so damned hard not to hurt her, but it was impossible. She was slashing at my chest, and I grabbed her wrist to turn the knife away and caught her shoulder with the tip of the blade. She screamed like a banshee, shoved me hard against the wall, and I . . . slipped and went down and hit my head so hard I was seeing stars. When I eventually got to my feet, she was gone, and Chase was at the bottom of the stairs, staring at me. Just staring at all the blood . . ."

January's hand slipped into Chase's under the table.

"I told him to call nine-one-one, and I went after Annie. Her truck was still there, so I knew she hadn't gone far, but

I couldn't find her." He grimaced. "I just couldn't find her anywhere. That's when the sheriff found me wandering around like a madman, covered in blood. He brought me back to the ranch and called for backup. While he was doing that I got hold of Chase and made him promise to tell the sheriff that everything was my fault—that I'd attacked Annie, and she'd run from me."

"Why?" Blue demanded. "Why implicate yourself like that?"

"Because I wanted to give her time to get away from me."

Chase held his breath as Billy shook his head. "I reckoned that with the sheriff occupied with me, she'd have a chance to escape."

"But she was not functioning properly. She tried to kill you," Blue said.

"She was depressed. She didn't want to be on the ranch, and I'd made her come out here. I didn't listen. . . . I didn't let myself believe she needed help. I even took out that stupid loan to buy her a new truck I was so desperate to keep her happy." Billy groaned. "You told me she was hurting, Mama, and I ignored your advice until it was too late."

"So, we still don't know what happened to her?" Ruth sighed. "The poor girl."

"I don't know about that. . . . I always thought—" Billy hesitated. "But that's not important now. What's important is—"

Chase held up his hand. "I'd like to hear what you've got to say." He glanced over at Blue, who nodded. "I think we have the right to know, don't you?"

Billy nodded and took a deep breath. "Okay. She was hanging around with one of the ranch hands quite a lot. A guy named Mike."

"Hell," Blue said softly. "I remember that guy. I remember seeing them together in the barn a couple of times. Mom was laughing. That's why it stuck in my memory."

"Yeah, well, I thought maybe he could give her what she needed."

Chase looked up. "That's why you kept paying the loan and term life insurance policy, because you didn't think she was dead. And that's why you refused to formally have her declared dead."

"Yeah. That's about it." Billy nodded.

"So why did you suddenly stop paying?"

"Because, as I said, that guy came nosing around. I began to think that maybe he wasn't one of your guys, TC, but from the insurance company trying to verify that your mother was still alive. And then I had to leave my job, and money got tight. By the time I found work in San Francisco, I was way behind on the payments. And I didn't hear anything, which made me even more suspicious."

"That's because the reminders were turning up here." Ruth dumped her purse on the table and pulled out her checkbook. "They had the ranch address and the wrong William Morgan." She showed Billy the check stub. "We just agreed to pay them off. Roy mailed the payment this morning when he went to town."

"You didn't have to do that," Billy protested. "I'll reimburse you as soon as I can."

"Chase paid the bill," Ruth said. "You can sort it out with him."

"I wanted the money from the policy to give to you boys," Billy said. "I figured it might make up for—"

Blue suddenly stood up. "For fucking walking out on us for twenty years? For letting a depressed woman take our baby sister and fucking *disappear*?"

"I didn't *know* she had gone and gotten Rachel while I was out for the count." Billy scrubbed a hand over his face. "I only found that out at the sheriff's office when it was too late." He searched Blue's hard face, his blue eyes pleading.

"You've got to believe me. I never would've let her go if I'd known she'd taken the baby."

"You shouldn't have let either of them go! And you should've stuck around."

Blue pushed past Chase, who had also gotten to his feet, and stormed out, slamming the kitchen door behind him. Chase turned to his father.

"For what it's worth? I kind of agree with him."

He followed Blue out and found his brother leaning against the railings on the side of the house, looking out over the mountains. He joined him and considered what to say.

"I shouldn't have let him rile me up like that." Blue smacked his palm against the wood.

"Why not? He needed to hear how you felt. How *we* felt."

"He let you deal with all our shit and all because he made you lie for him." Blue glanced at him. "Why didn't you *say* something?"

"Because I promised him I wouldn't. For all these years it felt like the only way I could keep faith with him," Chase confessed.

"You're an idiot." Blue exhaled. "So what do you think happened to Mom and Rachel? Did she leave with Big Mike or what?"

"I don't know, but it's definitely a new lead and maybe something to build on."

"I've always thought she was dead."

"Me too." Chase stared out at the mountain range. "Otherwise, why didn't she ever come back to see us?"

"Fuck." Blue rubbed the corner of his eye. "Now I feel like bawling."

Chase patted his shoulder. "It's all good. Let it out, little bro."

That earned him a scathing look and all suggestion of tears disappeared, which was exactly what Chase had hoped for. If big, tough marine Blue started crying, Chase would be joining him.

"Boys?" Ruth appeared at the screen door. "Come back in now. It's getting cold."

Chase glanced at his brother. "You okay?"

"Yeah. I can do this." Blue jerked his head in the direction of the kitchen. "Question is, what are we going to do about him?"

Chapter Twenty-One

"So what's going on?" January asked for the hundredth time as Ruth took yet another cake out of the oven.

"I told you. I'm having a little party."

"For what?"

"Mind your own beeswax." Ruth gestured at the table. "Collect those plates and cups, find a box to put them in, and then load them in the back of Blue's truck."

"Where's Chase?"

"How should I know?" Ruth carried on working.

"You know everything," January said darkly. "And something's going on." She filled the box and took it out to the yard where Blue's truck was pulled up right by the steps. There was no sign of Blue, but she'd seen him walking down to the barn with Billy earlier, so she suspected they were still there.

Things hadn't been easy.

January sighed as she dumped the box and returned to the kitchen. Twenty years of hurt—even when both sides were trying their best to make amends—was a lot of ground to cover in five days. Billy was doing his best to accept responsibility for his behavior and to allow his sons to approach him on their own terms and in their own way. She had to admire him for that, but it was hard to watch.

Chase was still more reserved than Blue, who tended to ask the questions and demand the hard answers. She'd heard that the elusive twins had been contacted, but had declined to come and meet their father at the ranch, which had caused yet another row.

But these were good things because uncovering all those old hurts and grievances could only make things better in the future. Chase was lighter in himself, no longer holding on to his promise to his father and more willing to try again with his brothers.

"January? Come and get these cakes and then go and find Blue," Ruth yelled.

With an elaborate sigh, January did as she was told and then headed down to the barn. Blue and his father were just walking out of the tack room, heads together, talking. Looking at Billy, January could see what Chase would look like in twenty-five years. It was quite disconcerting.

Blue saw her first. "Hey, is everything ready to go?"

"Apparently." January sniffed. "Not that I know anything about it."

"Which is just how it should be." Blue winked at her. "Come on, I'm driving you, Ruth, and Dad to the party." He eyed her old jeans and faded T-shirt. "You're going like that?"

"She looks fine to me," Billy said.

January smiled at him. "Thanks. I don't see why I should get all dressed up when no one will tell me what's going on."

"Have it your way then, but don't blame me later." Blue opened the door of his truck and stepped out of her way.

January hesitated as he boosted her into the seat. "Wait—"

"Too late." Blue shut the door on her.

Ruth was getting in the truck, and no one was paying any attention to January anymore as they moved off down the road. The truck turned off onto the rougher surface, and they bounced over the creek and across to the water meadows and the copse of pine trees that shaded the west bank.

There were tables and chairs and awnings and was that music playing? Beyond the campsite there were several parked vehicles, including, in the distance, what appeared to be a small plane.

"What the heck is going on?" January asked.

"You'll find out." Blue grinned lazily at her as he stopped the truck. "Let's get this stuff unloaded first."

Determined not to ask any questions at all, January threw herself into helping Ruth set up the food tent. The occasional burst of laughter or conversation drifted over to her, but she ignored everything.

"Hey."

A light touch on her arm had her spinning around to confront Chase. He wore a crisp new blue shirt that matched his eyes, his white Stetson, and clean jeans and boots. He bent to brush a kiss on her cheek, and he smelled like he'd just showered and shaved, making her suddenly conscious of her less-than-immaculate appearance.

She narrowed her eyes at him. "What's going on?"

His smile was way too innocent. "Come and meet a few people with me, okay?"

"Why?"

He grinned at her. "Because I'm asking you to?"

"Okay." She took his hand, and he tucked it into the crook of his arm and led her toward the tables.

"You know most of these guys from town." Chase made an airy gesture that included Maureen's family, the Hayes family from the hotel, and the Bakers.

"Is that Yvonne hiding over there?"

"Yeah. I asked her not to tell you she'd be here, so don't be mad." Chase led January toward another group. "I'd like you to meet Matt and Jake, my two best friends and business partners."

Jake was fair, and Matt was dark, and they both looked like typical Silicon Valley millionaire nerds, but she'd forgive them because they were Chase's best friends.

"It's a pleasure to meet you, January." Matt shook her hand, and then Jake gave her a hug. "Chase won't shut up about how awesome you are."

"Really?" January felt her cheeks heat. "He's very fond of you guys, too."

"Come on." Chase tugged at her hand. "We're on a schedule here."

"We are?" January let him lead her away and then her steps slowed. "Oh, of course we are if you organized everything. Hang on. Is that my *mom*?"

"Yeah. She's very sweet, isn't she?" Chase said. "Hey, Mona, here's January."

He stepped back as Mona gave January a big hug. "Darling, Chase is a very nice man. A big improvement on Kevin, I must say. We had the best discussion on reusable plastics, and he's planning on introducing me to his business partners so I can offer advice to their up-and-coming ecological and environmentally sound companies."

"That's . . . great," January said, her gaze darting to Chase, who was nodding his agreement. "I'm glad you two get along."

Chase bent to kiss her mom's cheek. "If you'll excuse us?"

He took January's hand again and led her toward the table that sat facing the others. "Time to begin."

"Chase . . ."

He pulled out a chair right at the front for her and clapped his hands. "If everyone will take their seats."

His laptop was on the table and behind them was a big

white screen. When all went quiet, he typed a few quick commands on his keyboard and stood up.

"Welcome, everyone, to the first meeting of what I hope will be many of the Morgan Ranch Restoration and Guest Resort Project."

Chase glanced at January, but she was staring open-mouthed at the first slide he'd just put up.

"After consulting with my family, the current staff, and other interested parties including the Morgantown Historical Society and Frost's Historical Tours, it occurred to me that there was a perfect solution to keeping the ranch not only financially viable but historically relevant."

Chase paused for breath and to scan the interested faces. He'd chosen to invite the locals because any decision about the ranch would impact their businesses. He hoped they liked the idea as much as he did.

"As January has pointed out to me on numerous occasions, Morgan Ranch is a very special place. Not many families grow up with a ghost town, a silver mine, hot springs, *and* a pioneer trail in their backyard. But a lot of families would sure like to experience what it feels like to live there, even for a few days. With help from the historical society and the local tourism board, and with backing from some environmentally aware investors in the Bay Area, I believe January is right. We can keep Morgan Ranch as a working cattle ranch *and* open it up to select groups of guests."

There was a murmur of interest and lots of chatting broke out.

He held up his hand. "Now, this isn't a done deal. What we're doing now is getting a sense for how we could make this work for all of our benefits without destroying what we have now. January and I will be coming and talking to you regularly to make sure we're all on the same page."

Maureen waved her hand. "So does this mean you boys will be sticking around?"

"Yes. Blue and I will be working together so that one of us is always here on the ranch with Ruth and January."

There were a few whoops and catcalls, and Chase felt himself relax a little. He finally turned to look at January.

"We should all thank January for coming up with such an amazing idea."

Everyone clapped as she stood up and came toward him. Her smile warmed him from the inside. "*My* idea?"

"Yes. It was all in your files. I just worked out how to make it happen." He drew her into his arms. "You were right. This place *is* amazing. If we do it this way, the ranch is preserved, other people get to appreciate it, and the Morgan family remains in control." He paused. "I'm kind of hoping you're going to help run the place."

She grinned at him. "As if you could keep me away."

"Cool." He held on to her hand and turned back to the assembled guests and gave a piercing whistle. Now came the really scary part. "There's one more thing."

When he had everyone's attention, he went down on one knee and looked up at January. "January Mitchell, will you marry me?"

Blue gave a whoop, but all Chase's attention was on January's stunned face.

After way too long for his nerves, she nodded. "Yes. Mr. Trampas Chase Morgan, I will."

He picked her up and spun her around in a circle as everyone cheered and clapped. When he set her down, he kissed her with everything that he was and everything he intended to be.

"You won't regret it, January," he whispered. "I'll make you the best damned husband in the world."

"I know you will." She kissed him gently on the lips. "Welcome home, Chase."

His gaze swept the smiling faces of his family, friends, and neighbors, and he kissed her back. "Welcome home to both of us."

Ruth's Chocolate Chunk Pecan Cookies
(Chase's favorite.)

Ingredients

- 1 cup unsalted butter
- ¾ cup brown sugar
- ¾ cup granulated sugar
- 1 teaspoon salt
- 2 teaspoons vanilla extract
- 2 large eggs
- 2¼ cups all-purpose flour
- ½ teaspoon baking soda
- ½ teaspoon baking powder
- 2 cups semi-sweet chocolate chunks or chips
- 2 cups coarsely chopped pecans, toasted

Instructions

Soften butter until melted.

Add both sugars to melted butter and stir until combined. Add salt, vanilla, and eggs, stirring until smooth. Stir in flour, baking soda, and baking powder until just combined and a soft dough forms. Fold in chocolate and pecans.

Scoop dough in desired cookie size onto lined baking sheets. Refrigerate until firm, about 30-45 minutes, depending on the size of the cookies. Leave room between cookies for some spreading.

Preheat oven to 350°. Bake cookies until golden around the edges but a little soft in the center. Baking time will vary depending on the size of the cookies. Smaller cookies (2-inch diameter) bake for 13-15 minutes. Larger cookies may require up to 18 minutes.

Cool on baking sheets on wire racks for a few minutes. Then, transfer from baking sheets to wire racks to cool completely.

More recipes at http://www.themorgansranch.com

Ruth's Chocolate Chunk Cookies
(Makes twelve)

Ingredients

1 cup mashed butter
1 cup brown sugar
½ cup granulated sugar
1 teaspoon salt
2 teaspoons vanilla extract
2 large eggs
2¾ cups all-purpose flour
1 teaspoon baking soda
½ teaspoon baking powder
2 cups semi-sweet chocolate chunks or chips
2 cups semi-sweet chopped pecans (optional)

Instructions

Soften butter until melted.

Add both sugars to melted butter and stir until each mixture incorporates, vanilla, and sugar, stirring until blended. Sift in flour, baking soda, and baking powder and fold in chocolate and stir into a thick mixture. Fold in the chips and pecans.

Spoon doughs in desired dollops onto a fine lined baking sheet. Bake better until firm, about 10 – 12 minutes, depending on the size of the cookies. For best results recommend not overbaking.

Preheat oven to 375°. Bake cookies until golden along the edges but the inside will still be soft; the baking time will vary depending on the size of the cookies. Smaller cookies (2 inch diameter) bake for 11-14 minutes. Larger cookies may require up to 18 minutes.

Cool on baking sheets on wire rack for a few minutes. Then transfer from wire sheets to wire cooling rack completely.

More recipes at http://www.themorganfamily.com.

The heartbreak of their childhood drove the Morgan brothers far from their family's California ranch—and one another. But as they face the wounds of the past, each feels the land calling him home . . .

Blue Morgan never thought he'd crave long days on horseback, working the cattle ranch where he grew up. But after a decade of getting shouted at and shot at in the Marines, fresh air and hard work are just what he needs to settle his restless energy.
Except no matter how hard he tries to focus, his mind wanders to the pretty, prickly new veterinarian instead.

There's no denying the spark between Jenna McDonald and Blue. But with her job at risk and her own family's expectations to wrangle, Jenna isn't looking for another sparring partner. Blue needs her expertise on horses. And if she can help solve the mystery of his mother's disappearance, she's willing to pitch in. But she'll leave his ideas about how love should be scheduled to him. Jenna is tired of being told what she can't have—and ready to reach for what she wants . . .

Please turn the page for an exciting sneak peek of Kate Pearce's next Morgan Ranch novel,

THE MAVERICK COWBOY,

coming in February 2017
wherever print and eBooks are sold!

Humboldt-Toiyabe National Forest. California.
Marine Corps Mountain Warfare Training Center.

"Holy shit!"

The sight of a one-hundred-and-thirty-pound marine flailing around like a chicken—a marine Blue Morgan was tethered to on the side of a sheer cliff face—was not good. With a yell, the idiot lost his grip, and his booted feet scrabbled for purchase, narrowly missing Blue's head. The only thing keeping them from plummeting to the bottom of the canyon was the steel pin driven into the rock. It still meant Fielding swung out on his rope like a pendulum, jerking his unfortunate instructor up to meet him.

Blue barely had time to brace himself before he smashed into the other man. His head did a weird flick-flack and then mercifully everything went black.

"Gunny? You okay?"

Blue opened one eye and saw two versions of Mel, his fellow instructor, dancing against the bright Californian sky. He winced and retreated back into the darkness.

"Gunnery Sergeant Morgan?"

"Yeah." He managed to croak. "Is Fielding okay?"

"He's fine. Blubbing like a baby, but nothing broken. You took the hit for him."

"Tell me about it." Blue attempted to roll onto his side and broke out into a sweat as nausea engulfed him.

"Take it easy. The corpsman's coming." Mel patted Blue's shoulder. "I got you down. You two were unconscious for a while and swinging back and forth like a brace of pheasant."

"Funny," Blue muttered. "It wasn't Fielding's fault. He startled some kind of bird."

"He still panicked though."

"Which is why this is called basic cliff-assault training, so he'll learn not to do it somewhere important."

A shadow came over his other side, and someone touched his shoulder. The smell of antiseptic swept over Blue, making him shudder.

"It's Ives. Do you know where you are?"

"Still in the Marines?"

Ives chuckled. "Specifically at this moment."

"Flat on my back with the headache from hell."

"What's your name and rank?"

"Gunnery Sergeant Morgan."

"What day is it?"

"Tuesday."

"Good. I'm going to check you over and take you back to the hospital, okay?"

Hospital.

Blue had seen quite enough of them to last a lifetime. He only had three months left in the military. He'd hoped to see it out peacefully in his home state. This was his last training course. He'd managed to complete his final deployment in the sandbox without a scratch, and now this.

Sometimes life sucked.

Ives placed a collar around his neck, and Blue was gently lifted onto a board. He assumed the other six guys who had been climbing with their group had already been taken back to base. He was loaded into a vehicle, and Ives got in behind him. Two others followed, and the doors were shut.

Blue tried to relax, but the pain behind his eyes kept growing.

"Sorry, Gunny."

That was definitely Fielding, the little shit. Blue didn't have the ability to reply as his head started to pound and he literally saw stars. He set his jaw, aware that it would be bad if he puked because he was strapped to a board and couldn't even turn his head. He'd been in far worse situations than this. There was nothing left to do but hang on and hang in there.

"Concussion, whiplash, two broken ribs, and a black eye." The doc shook his head. "The newbie boot got a little graze on his widdle nose when he collided with your helmet."

"Figures," Blue muttered. "When can I leave?"

"You'll need to stay overnight so we can check on that concussion. You've had a couple in the last few years, so we've got to be extra careful. We'll see how you're feeling in the morning, okay?"

The doc was way too cheerful and loud for Blue's liking, but that might be Blue's headache talking. Pretty much everything was too much at this point.

"Can I sit up?"

"In an hour or so we'll raise the head of the bed."

"Do I have to keep the collar on?"

"For a couple of weeks minimum. We called your grandmother."

"God, no," Blue groaned.

"She says to give you her love, and she'll see you soon. Command are working on a security pass for her."

"Great."

The thought of Ruth descending on him was half-comforting and half-terrifying. She'd never been one to let her grandkids sleep in and was highly suspicious of any attempt to get out of chores. On the other hand, if you were really hurt, she would coddle you like a newborn calf. . . .

Blue drifted off to sleep again only to be woken up by a nurse because—concussion. He'd been there before and wasn't looking forward to a night filled with fitful sleep and wake-up calls. He longed for the peace and quiet of his bed at the ranch, where the only sounds came from the livestock, his grandma's TV, and his brother and January getting too loud in their bedroom.

He could have done without the last one. But Chase only grinned when Blue reminded him to keep it down and suggested Blue was jealous. Blue thought about that. Was he jealous that Chase had found the right woman?

Nah.

He liked his life just as it was. He was in control, and no one was ever going to take that away from him. Twelve years in the Marines had made him a man to be reckoned with. It hadn't been easy. When he'd enlisted he'd been something of a hothead and had soon learned that didn't work in the Corps. They'd knocked him into shape and taught him everything he needed to know about how to survive.

But he had a new purpose now—to save Morgan Ranch and make it profitable again. Ruth and Chase were relying on him, and he was looking forward to the challenge.

"Blue, darling?"

The smell of apples and cinnamon drifted over him, and

he opened his eyes to see his grandmother sitting beside his bed. The lights were still too bright, and it was now dusk outside.

"Ruth. You smell like pie."

"That's because I was making them when the call came through."

The nurse raised his bed so he could see his grandma's worried face. She had the same blue eyes as him and Chase, and her lined skin had been baked brown by the harsh sun. She barely topped five feet, but she was still formidable.

"You look terrible, BB."

"Thanks."

She patted his hand. "What were you doing dangling off a cliff? Didn't I teach you not to do stupid stuff? I would've thought the military would have drummed that into you by now."

Jardin, his nurse, gave a snort of laughter and winked at him as she arranged his pillows.

"It's my job, Ruth. I was trying to teach some idiot how to climb."

"Well, stop doing it."

Blue raised an eyebrow, and even that hurt. "I can't just stop when I feel like it—although I'm pretty much done here anyway."

"Why?" Her sharp gaze moved over him. "Is there something they didn't tell me?"

"Nope, I'm good. It was my last training exercise."

A voice came from the bottom of the bed. "Mrs. Morgan? I'm Blue's physician. He's going to be just fine, but he will be on light duty. Best guess, his command will probably just put him behind a desk until he separates."

"Might as well shoot me now," Blue groaned.

"Can I take him home?" Ruth asked.

"Not yet. We have to keep him here because of the

concussion, but I'm sure he'll be able to come visit you soon. It's nice that you're so close."

Ruth sighed. "Well, that's a pity. I brought Chase's big truck so I could put him in the back."

Blue tensed. "Wait a minute. You didn't drive that monster all the way up here, did you?"

She fixed him with a quelling look. "I'm quite capable of driving anything I want, young man. I brought January with me. She's waiting in the truck."

"Okay, then." Blue subsided back onto the pillow, which suddenly seemed very welcoming. Holding his head up was hard work. "I don't suppose you brought some of that pie?"

"There's a hamper beside your bed with three different kinds of pie in it. I knew you'd be asking." She stood up and gently kissed his forehead. "Now you take care of yourself, BB, and no more getting into trouble, you hear me?"

"Yes, Grandma," Blue murmured as she smoothed a hand through his short hair as if he were five again. "Tell January to drive carefully."

She kissed him one last time and then went off, chatting to his doctor. He closed his eyes and heard a scraping noise, which brought him instantly alert.

"What are you doing with my pies, Jardin?"

The nurse patted his knee. "I'm just going to put them in a safe place until you are allowed to eat solid food."

"Like the staff refrigerator?" He snorted. "They're fine right there."

"Sorry, the cooler's a fire hazard sticking out like that. Don't worry; I'll save you a piece."

He already knew that Ruth would've brought enough pie to feed fifty, so he didn't really mind the hijack.

"Peach," he murmured as he started to fall asleep again. "That's my favorite."

"You've got it." Jardin's voice faded, and Blue let himself fall into the blackness.

"Well, this isn't good."

Blue rubbed his aching temple and studied his desk, which in his five-day absence had acquired about ten two-foot-high stacks of paper. He'd been released from the hospital, his ribs were taped up, and it hurt when he breathed too hard. His black eye was determined to capture every color of the rainbow, and he had at least another week in the neck brace. He was going to ditch that sucker as soon as no one was around to see him do it.

Carly Hughes, his liaison from admin, smiled sympathetically. "The separation process for leaving the service is paved with more paperwork than a very messy celebrity divorce." She moved one stack closer to another. "And while you're doing all that, you'll be attending classes to prepare you for reentry into civilian life and to help to find you a new career."

"I already know what I'm doing next."

She glanced at him. "Really?"

"Yeah. My family owns a cattle ranch near here."

"So you're a *cowboy*?"

He shrugged. "More of a rancher, but I can ride a horse."

"And you rope cattle and all that kind of dirty, messy, manly stuff?"

She sounded all kinds of *breathy*. Was she one of those women who thought cowboys were romantic? Blue put more space between them. "I do what needs to be done."

She sat down on the corner of his desk and studied him carefully. "That's good to know."

He picked up the nearest folder and looked inside. There were about ten forms in there alone. He hastily put it back on the stack.

"As I can't climb, and I'm on my way out, I've also got to help the other instructors with scheduling and lesson plans." Which was about as exciting as it sounded. The other guys had been delighted to pass all the shit jobs over to him.

"Then you're going to be a busy man." She stood up and brushed down her skirt. "Let me know if you need any extra help."

"Will do."

She waited a second longer than necessary, but he slid into his chair and started firing up his laptop. Carly was a great-looking woman, but he'd already set his sights on the next phase of his life, and getting involved with someone still in the service wasn't going to work out. Getting involved with someone, *period*, was going to have to wait a few years until he'd established himself at the ranch.

He had a plan, and nothing was going to stop him from making Morgan Ranch the best historical dude ranch in the state of California, if not the world. He was a marine. When he set his mind to something, he never failed.

Taking a deep breath, Blue took another file, scanned the contents, got a pen, and started to fill in the blanks.

"Mom . . ." Jenna McDonald sighed and held the phone farther from her ear as her mother started in on an all-too familiar theme. "Let's not do this right now, okay? I just called to wish you happy birthday."

She closed her eyes. "Yeah, I wish I was with you, too. No, I don't want you to look for a safer job for me where you live. I'm really happy here with Uncle Ron and Aunt Amy. Yeah. I also know that when Faith gets back I might be out of work."

Her mom kept talking, and eventually Jenna just let it

flow over her. It was almost three, and afternoon surgery was due to start, which meant she needed to move things along. Adopting her most cheerful, nonaggressive, super-validating tone—the one she'd learned in family therapy—she cut across what her mom was saying.

"I know you worry because you care, Mom. I understand your position *perfectly*, and I will think about every single thing you have said to me today. Now why don't you go and have a nice dinner with Dad? Call me tomorrow and tell me all about it, okay?"

She barely waited for her mom to make some kind of agreeing noise before she said an airy good-bye and put the phone down. She loved her mom, but sometimes it was like trying to stop a river during a flood. Not that her dad was any better, but at least he tried to listen to Jenna occasionally and had been instrumental in finding her the job with his brother at the most northern end of California, far from her mother and hyper-successful sisters.

"Jenna?" Meg, one of the veterinary techs, put her head around the door. She was an older woman who'd been with the practice for years and had saved Jenna's ass on several occasions already. "You okay to start seeing folks? You're the only one here."

"Sure." Jenna grabbed her white coat and slid her reading glasses on top of her head. "Do we have many waiting?"

Unlike doctors in most modern veterinary practices, her uncle preferred to let the afternoon office hours remain a free-for-all, which meant sometimes there were twenty people crammed into the small waiting room and other days it was crickets. Jenna didn't mind. It was all new to her, and every appointment helped her gain valuable knowledge. Most large-animal veterinary practices didn't deal with the smaller pet stuff, but they were the only surgery for forty miles, so they happily coped with everything.

"Only three so far. I've put Monica Flaherty in exam room one. So you can start there. Files on the outside of the door."

"Got it."

Jenna went into the exam room, closing the door quickly behind her because she never knew exactly what she'd be facing. There were many desperate would-be escapees who didn't want to be there—and that was just the humans.

Ha.

"Hey, Monica. What's up?"

The teenager frowned. "Where's Dave?"

"He's out on a call." Inwardly Jenna sighed. Her cousin was thirty-one and single and the cause of intense local feminine interest. "Do you want to go back to the front desk and make an appointment to see him specifically?"

Monica's sigh was almost loud enough to rattle the window glass. "No. It's okay. I found this by the side of the highway last night." She pointed at a box on the metal exam table.

Jenna cautiously opened the lid and peered inside. There was a towel covering the bottom of the box, and coiled within it was a large white and brown–patterned snake.

"Did you find this guy in the actual box or on the road?"

"On the road. I put him on the damp towel and sat him on top of the water heater last night."

"Great idea. He was probably way too cold out there to survive." Jenna checked over what she could see of the snake's lean coils.

Monica came to look over her shoulder. "What kind is it?"

"It's a California king snake, I think. He's not poisonous

or anything, but he is a powerful constrictor." Jenna glanced at Monica. "You probably know that, seeing as you picked him up."

"I made Finn do it. He thought it was a rattlesnake."

"They sometimes rattle their tails to scare predators into thinking they *are* rattlesnakes." Jenna closed the lid of the box. "I assume you don't want to keep him?"

"I'd like to, but my mom said no." Monica pouted. "Can you find him a good home?"

"I can certainly ask around, but he could survive in the wild if he was tucked up somewhere warm He's native to California, and he's not called the king for nothing."

Monica fiddled with the box. "Dave knows a lot about snakes, doesn't he?"

Which was probably why Monica had made her boyfriend pick the snake up in the first place. The poor guy. "He sure does. I'll check in with him when he comes back. Do you want me to call and let you know what happens?"

"When you talk to Dave?" Monica perked up. "Maybe he could call me himself?"

"Someone will definitely call you when we've made a decision." Jenna hid a smile as she washed her hands. "Thanks for bringing the big guy in."

"Okay."

Jenna patted the teen's shoulder as she left the exam room and belatedly picked up the chart Meg had left in a slot by the door. Jenna wrote a quick summary of the visit. It was weird going back to writing notes with a real pen after using tablets at her last job. Attempting to decipher her colleagues' handwriting was another head-numbing task altogether.

Meg came out of the second exam room, and Jenna handed her the file. "Monica found a California king snake by the side of the road yesterday night. I don't know enough about them to tell if it's injured or not. Can we put it out back in the heated terrarium until Dave comes in?"

"Sure." Meg nodded. "I'll take it right out and then come back to assist you. Pet rabbit in two."

"Got it." This time Jenna remembered to pick up the clipboard and then went into the room. She found one of the Hayes family that ran the local hotel clutching a large black-and-white rabbit to his chest. "Hey, Wade, who's this?"

The boy cuddled the rabbit even closer. He was the youngest boy in the big Hayes family, and Jenna reckoned he was around twelve. "Duke."

"That's a great name." Jenna perched on the edge of the table and gently stroked Duke's nose. "So what's up with him?"

"He's been, like, acting really strange."

"In what way?"

"Getting cranky with me, trying to dig his way out of the cage, and like moving stuff around the place into big piles in the corners."

"Weird," Jenna said. "Can I take a good look at him?"

"He's like real grumpy at the moment."

"I'll be careful," Jenna promised as she set the rabbit on the exam table. She kept petting him with one hand as she palpated his abdomen with the other. "Do you have any other rabbits?"

"Yeah, one more called Stan, short for Stanford."

"Do they share a cage?"

"Yeah, why?"

Jenna looked at Wade over Duke's head. "Is your mom here with you?"

To her dismay, the boy's eyes teared up. "Duke's going to die, isn't he? You can tell me. I don't need my mom here. I'm almost twelve."

"He's not going to die." Jenna held his gaze. "Duke's going to be a mother."

"What?"

"He's female, and he's pregnant."

A dull red color rose from Wade's neck to cover his face. "He's a . . . *girl*? Do you mean, like, that he and Stan . . . ?"

Jenna nodded. "Yeah, I think they did, and judging from the size of Duke's belly, she's going to give birth fairly soon."

Almost before the words left her mouth, Wade was running for the door. Jenna waited for a minute, and then started to smile. Meg came in and raised her eyebrows.

"What did you say to Wade? He ran past me like he was being chased by something with teeth. Is there something wrong with Duke?"

"Duke's a girl, and she's pregnant," Jenna said, patting the rabbit. "Wade was horrified by every single word in that sentence." She grinned at Meg, and they both burst out laughing.

"The poor kid." Jenna eventually collected herself. "Can you see if Mrs. Hayes is out there so I can talk to her?"

"Will do," Meg said.

While Jenna waited for Mrs. Hayes, her thoughts flew back to her parents. They would probably never understand how a day like today could make her love her job even more. They thrived on order, and the life Jenna had chosen wasn't like that at all. To say that she loved a challenge was an understatement. After years of knowing exactly what was expected and obeying every demand made of her, surely she was entitled to enjoy a little bit of chaos?

* * *

Much later she was sitting in the back office writing notes about the cases she'd seen when the back door banged and opened to admit her cousin Dave. He stomped in looking tired and rumpled. The veterinary offices were housed in the original McDonald homestead, and the family had moved up the hill into a larger, more convenient house. It made the commute to work fairly straightforward, although they spent most of their time on the road, visiting the various ranches around Morgantown.

Uncle Ron kept saying he was going to rebuild the surgery, but he'd never gotten around to it, and Jenna doubted he ever would. Which meant that they all put up with the inconvenient old ranch house and made the best of the space available.

Jenna wrinkled her nose. "What did you fall into?"

"Pig shit. I did shower."

"Still eew."

"I was on a call near Morgan Ranch, so I went to check out the new arrivals." Dave dumped his bag on the table and turned to take off his coat and wash his hands. He'd already removed his boots in the mudroom and wore mismatched socks. "The darling little piggies tripped me, and the mama pig sat on me when I was down."

"I don't suppose Roy got that on camera?"

"I hope not. I think he was laughing too hard." With a groan, Dave sat down at the table and shoved his hands through his spiky black hair. "Sometimes I wonder why I do this job."

Jenna patted his shoulder. "Because you love it?"

"There is that."

"I didn't know Ruth was thinking of keeping pigs," Jenna said as she got up to make some more coffee.

"She wasn't. It's all Roy's idea. Apparently, he's always

wanted to keep pigs, and Ruth decided it would add authenticity to the idea of a self-sufficient historical ranch."

Jenna tended to the old coffee percolator, which needed a firm hand, and got out two clean mugs. "Do you think the Morgans are going to make that idea work?"

"The historical dude ranch and guest house thing?"

"Yes."

"I don't see why not. With Chase Morgan's financial connections and Ruth and Roy's experience, it could work out really well."

Jenna put one of the mugs in front of Dave, who added three spoonfuls of sugar. "And don't forget January and the Morgantown Historical Society."

"How could I when my parents are on the board?" Dave groaned. "Next thing you know I'll be dressed up like a cowboy and expected to fake being an old-fashioned veterinarian or some such crap."

"Ruth would probably love that." Jenna took a sip of her coffee. "Was January back or was she still in San Francisco with Chase?"

"She's back, but she and Ruth had to dash off to the marine place near Bridgeport. Apparently, BB was in an accident."

"Blue Morgan? Oh, wow, what happened?" Jenna hadn't taken to the arrogant marine when she'd met him at spring branding, but she still hoped he was okay.

"BB was in the base hospital with concussion after a fall from a cliff or something. Ruth was going to go by herself, but January offered to drive her."

"Why do you call him BB rather than Blue?"

"It's his name."

Jenna raised her eyebrows. "His actual name?"

"His initials are BB. His full name is Blue Boy."

"You're kidding me, right?" Jenna started to grin. "The big tough marine is little boy blue?"

Dave shuddered. "We stopped saying that around second grade after he'd beaten the crap out of us a few times. His dad named him after a TV cowboy show I think. You'll have to ask him which one. I'm not doing it."

The marine did have very blue eyes. She remembered that. She also remembered his Internet-derived assumptions about her profession. She hated being talked down to. But he had at least tried to apologize before she'd brushed him off. She'd appreciated the gesture, which had taken her by surprise.

"Monica Flaherty brought in a snake for you."

Dave perked up. "What kind?"

"California king, I think. I'm not sure if there's something wrong with it, or if Monica just saw the darn thing and wanted an excuse to come in and see you."

"Where's the snake?"

"In the terrarium next to the vaccine refrigerator. Where else would it be?"

Dave was already moving, his mug gripped in his hand. Jenna sensed he got tired of dealing with horses, cattle, and various large animals sometimes. She followed him into the other room and waited as he took his first gander at the snake.

"Looks in pretty good shape to me," Dave commented.

"I couldn't see any obvious injuries, but I don't know a lot about snakes," Jenna confessed. "She did find him out at night, so he might have gotten cold too quickly and been unable to get back to his burrow."

"True." Dave opened the terrarium and ran his fingertip over the coils of the snake. "We can keep an eye on him for a day or two. If he's capable of eating live food, we can probably release him back into the wild." Dave replaced the terrarium lid and washed his hands.

"Do you want to call Monica and tell her?" Jenna asked.

"No thanks." Dave mock-frowned at her. "There's no need to encourage her."

Jenna snorted. "From what I've seen, you don't need to do anything to encourage them. They all just fall in love with you at first sight."

Dave refilled his coffee mug. "God knows why. Vets aren't exactly a catch. We're usually covered in shit, are unavailable on the weekends, and are always in debt."

"They should go after the Morgans." Jenna said. "Local gossip says the Morgans have all the money."

"Well, Chase does. But, he's engaged to January, BB's in the military, and the twins haven't been back for years and are pretty wild." Dave lingered by the door. "Are you coming up to the main house?"

Jenna looked at her pile of paper. "I'm just about done, so I should go and eat. Amy said something about a nut casserole."

"Then you've got to come right now. Ma makes a really good one." Dave held open the door. "And I want to talk to you about Morgan Ranch."

"You want me to do what?" Jenna asked.

Dave sat back in his chair and let out a loud and very indiscreet belch. They'd eaten dinner together in the large pine kitchen and then taken themselves into the den. There was no sign of Amy or Ron, who tended to go to bed early and watch TV until they fell asleep. If Dave's groupies could see him in his natural habitat, smelly socks and all, Jenna doubted they'd be quite so infatuated with him.

"Horses are your area of expertise, right?"

"They're supposed to be, but—"

"Then you are the perfect person to help the Morgans out. First, they need to assemble a stable of rideable horses for the guests, and then they need to keep them healthy. You can start by helping them select good stock."

"I suppose I could," Jenna said doubtfully. "But won't it take up a lot of my time?"

"Look, I know Dad's stepping back, but—" Dave sat up, dislodging his huge feet from the coffee table. "If you want to stay, and Faith decides she wants to practice here when she graduates, we're going to need all the work we can get to justify employing three vets. Don't get me wrong, we *want* you to stay; we love you. But if it comes down to it and we don't have enough clients, Dad's going to pick his own daughter over you."

Jenna nodded. One thing she really liked about Dave was his honesty. "Do you think Morgan Ranch could end up being a really lucrative client?"

"Yeah, with the grass-fed cattle and the dude ranch? Definitely."

"Then I'd be happy to do whatever needs doing."

Dave winked at her. "Good girl. I'm not kidding, it could become a full-time job if the ranch does well."

Jenna clinked her mug against his. "As long as the younger Morgan brothers keep away, I think I'll do just fine."